Mr H

ALSO BY THOM BRAUN

Fiction
Hungerford Stairs: An Untold Tale of Charles Dickens
Holy Orders
Free Spirits
kingdom.com

Non-Fiction
Disraeli the Novelist
The Philosophy of Branding

As Editor
Benjamin Disraeli, *Coningsby, or the New Generation*
(Penguin English Classics edition)
Benjamin Disraeli, *Sybil, or the Two Nations*
(Penguin English Classics edition)

Mr Hogarth's Morning

THOM BRAUN

Copyright © 2024 Thom Braun

The moral right of the author has been asserted.

Apart from any fair dealing for the purposes of research or private study, or criticism or review, as permitted under the Copyright, Designs and Patents Act 1988, this publication may only be reproduced, stored or transmitted, in any form or by any means, with the prior permission in writing of the publishers, or in the case of reprographic reproduction in accordance with the terms of licences issued by the Copyright Licensing Agency. Enquiries concerning reproduction outside those terms should be sent to the publishers.

This is a work of fiction. Names, characters, businesses, places, events and incidents are either the products of the author's imagination or used in a fictitious manner. Any resemblance to actual persons, living or dead, or actual events is purely coincidental.

The cover design is based on the engraving of William Hogarth's 'Morning', (second state of two: 25 March 1738).

Image courtesy of The Metropolitan Museum of Art, New York: Gift of Sarah Lucas, 1891.

www.metmuseum.org

Troubador Publishing Ltd
Unit E2 Airfield Business Park,
Harrison Road, Market Harborough,
Leicestershire LE16 7UL
Tel: 0116 279 2299
Email: books@troubador.co.uk
Web: www.troubador.co.uk

ISBN 978 1836280 767

British Library Cataloguing in Publication Data.
A catalogue record for this book is available from the British Library.

Printed and bound by CPI Group (UK) Ltd, Croydon, CR0 4YY
Typeset in 11pt Minion Pro by Troubador Publishing Ltd, Leicester, UK

For Sally

The town of London is a kind of large Forest of Wild Beasts, where most of us range about at a venture, and are equally savage and mutually destructive one of another.

Anon., *A Trip through the Town containing Observations on the Customs and Manners of the Age* (1729)

And when the Omnipotent, with dread Command,
Banish'd our Parents from bless'd *Eden's* Land,
Another Garden, says he, I will give,
In which with Pleasure ye may happy live,
Second to Eden only but in Fame,
For Bliss and constant Spring exact the same,
To th' happy Spot let *Covent* be the Name.

Anon., *Tom King's: or The Paphian Grove with the Humours of Covent Garden, The Theatre, Gaming Table, etc. A Mock Heroick Poem. In three cantos* (1741)

Contents

A Note on the Picture	viii
Dramatis Personae	ix
Plan of Covent Garden Piazza	xi
Prologue: The Fall	xiii
Act I The Painted Lady	1
Act II The Missing Portrait	137
Act III The Fraudulent Copy	279
Epilogue: Not the Last Word	433
Historical Note	435

A Note on the Picture

Mr Hogarth's Morning revolves largely around an image.

William Hogarth created 'Morning' in 1736 as the first canvas in a quartet of paintings known collectively as *The Four Times of the Day*. The painting of 'Morning' now hangs in Upton House, a National Trust property in Warwickshire, and can be viewed online via the Art UK website.

Two years later Hogarth produced an engraving of the same scene. The print includes more visual detail and reverses the overall composition. It can be viewed via a number of online collections (e.g. those of the British Museum and the Metropolitan Museum of Art).

The Historical Note at the end of this book provides more information on the images.

Dramatis Personae

Jeremiah Potts	An artist's runner
Kitty Smith	A Covent Garden Lady (deceased)
Mr and Mrs Flint	Tenants of the house in Tavistock Row
Felipe ('Al') Alcazar	An artist
Mrs Alcazar	His wife
Mr Pargeter	A print shop proprietor
Catherine Pargeter	His daughter
Prudence Hyssop	A resident of Covent Garden Piazza
Master Fleabane	Miss Hyssop's young ward
Abigail	Miss Hyssop's maid
Tom & Moll King	Proprietors of Tom King's coffee-house
Black Betty	Assistant to Moll King
Dr Richard Rock	A purveyor of patent remedies
Jonathan Smallow	An artist
Sir Marmaduke Ransome	A baronet
Lady Belinda Ransome	His wife
William Hogarth	An artist
Jane Hogarth	His wife
Louisa Crust	A friend of Prudence Hyssop
Francis Hayman	An artist
Samuel Scott	An artist
Sarah Bell	A young woman
Mr Samson	A one-legged man

Plan of Covent Garden Piazza in 1736

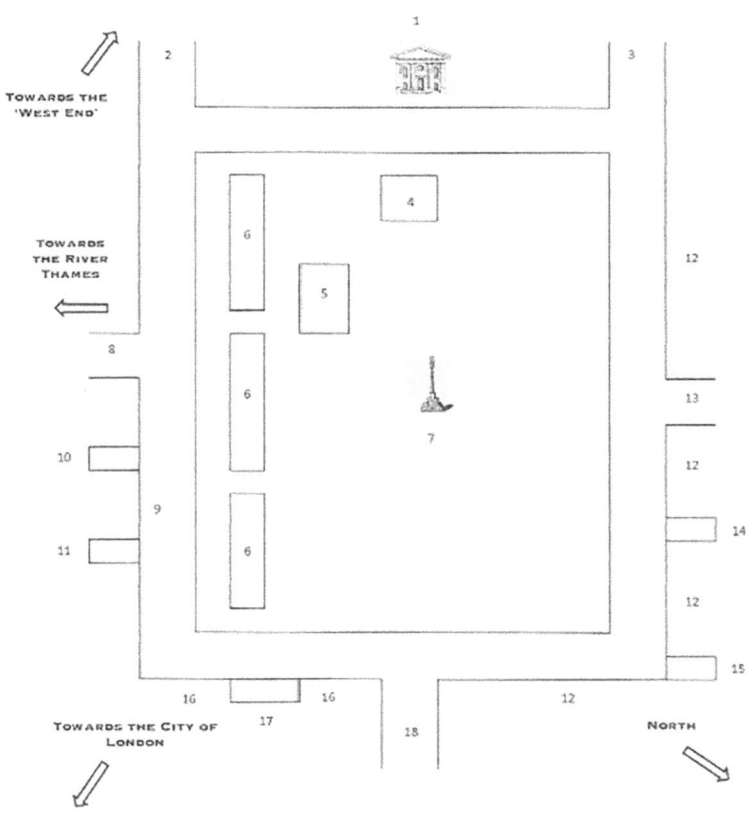

1. St Paul's Church
2. Henrietta Street
3. King Street
4. Tom King's in the painting
5. Actual location of Tom King's
6. Main market buildings
7. Sundial column
8. Southampton Street
9. Tavistock Row
10. The Bedford Arms Tavern
11. The house where Jeremiah lives
12. 'The Great Piazza'
13. James Street
14. Prudence's house
15. Covent Garden Theatre entrance
16. 'The Little Piazza'
17. The Hummums bagnio
18. Russell Street

PROLOGUE
The Fall

*Tavistock Row, Covent Garden Piazza,
Christmas Eve 1735.*

It was a tall, thin house, nowhere near as grand as those directly opposite.

Situated towards the east end of Tavistock Row on the south side of the Piazza, it had four floors. Each floor had one room.

At the top was the attic where Jeremiah Potts lived. Narrow stairs, boxed in against the wall, led down to a small landing and Kitty's room.

From there a flight of ramshackle, shadowy steps descended to the floor below, where old Mr and Mrs Flint kept themselves to themselves.

The staircase was more substantial from there to the ground floor, where the artist, Mr Alcazar, lived with his wife and as many of their children as managed to stay alive.

Death was a frequent visitor to the house.

As were the gentlemen.

It was impossible not to be aware of Kitty's visitors.

Mr Flint was grateful that his wife's deafness spared her the noise. The cries and creaks from the room above. He had grown used to it – and to the gruff curses of those stumbling up and down the rickety stairs. It was only a matter of time before someone fell, he said to anyone prepared to listen. Which was usually Jeremiah.

So there were voices and footsteps – both before and after the crash.

But it was the ensuing silence that drew Mr Flint's attention. It was so unusual and complete. Then the soft sound of someone sobbing. Enough to make him leave his chair.

When he opened the door it was Jeremiah he saw first. He was on his knees, hunched and shaking. Then Mr Flint saw the mess that lay below. He held the tallow candle higher, over the head of the crouching man.

Kitty's eyes were wide and staring, giving her a look of startled indignation. As if death had been the last thing on her mind. Her neck and one leg were twisted. Perhaps this was what upset Jeremiah most, as his body heaved and shook.

Only a matter of time, Mr Flint said again as he backed into his room. Someone was bound to fall.

Jeremiah stood up and felt his way below in the dark.

He knocked on Mr Alcazar's door, though it was now almost midnight. Together they carried Kitty down to the hallway and covered her with a paint-splashed sheet.

From outside in the Piazza came shouts and whoops and screams of laughter. For many the night was just beginning.

For Kitty it was over.

Any progress now at an end.

In the days that followed, the unfortunate demise of a Covent Garden Lady drew little comment. An accident said some. So easy to lose one's footing.

A judgement said a few. So easy to lose one's bearings.

One way or another it was soon forgotten. Except by Jeremiah.

He had barely known Kitty. They were close neighbours but hardly friends. Yet his nightmares lasted for weeks.

Months.

He wanted to speak to someone about it. But how could he?

Kitty had once mentioned a sister. In the country. But where? And what could he say to her?

Perhaps he could talk to Catherine.

But that was unthinkable.

No.

He would have to keep it to himself. Along with everything else. And hope that some of it would go away.

ACT I

The Painted Lady

Prudence Hyssop was a long-term resident of The Great Piazza.

Born at the very end of the old century she had lived all her thirty-six years in the same house. It was halfway along the grand arcaded walkway that adorned the north side of the square between James Street and the entrance to the Covent Garden Theatre. Impossible for her to imagine living anywhere else. Even though her own nature and that of the Piazza were so different.

The constant, noisy presence of the fruit, flower and vegetable sellers in the middle of the square had always encouraged activities that were quite literally 'round-the-clock'. Taverns, bagnios, gaming rooms or houses of ill repute all gave expression to the tide of humanity that flowed through the place. It was sometimes dispiriting but never less than compelling. Prudence had learned to appreciate the challenges in ways that provided particular opportunities for her sense of Christian charity.

This meant that she rarely felt compromised by the space, no matter how difficult it might occasionally be. Indeed, she regarded her situation as exceptionally fortunate, and Covent Garden as a location worthy of admiration and note. No more so than on a bright Spring morning teeming with life.

And certainly no more so than today. The twenty-fifth day of March.

The first day of the New Year.

1736.

It seemed fitting that the New Year should begin on such a day. So much more appropriate than the first, cold day of January, which was when some would have it start. But a New Year was surely better launched on a Spring tide. It was a thought to make her smile as she walked the very short way home from church.

One of her many blessings was to have such an elegant place of worship so conveniently positioned. St Paul's Church, on the west side of the Piazza, was no more than a hundred yards from her door. By the time Morning Prayer had ended, just after half-past seven, the market was in full swing. The square was crowded with customers and carts, vegetables and flowers, busy-ness and bustle. It was one of her daily delights to prolong the short walk home so as to enjoy a leisurely meander through the throng. Hardly ever did she make a purchase, for that would have imposed upon the duties and pleasures of Abigail and Master Fleabane. But it was an opportunity to observe the diversity of both people and produce. It also provided the chance to exchange a few words with neighbours and acquaintances.

Today, however, she was determined to make her circuit of the marketplace shorter than usual. For her New Year's resolve meant that she had another purpose brimming her mind. To change the nature of her journal.

She had kept a written record of some kind since the

age of thirteen. It had once been her most confidential companion. Within its pages she had written of life and love, of growing up and the adventures of youth. In more recent years, however, she had committed little to paper that was not commonplace. She knew why, of course. She understood only too well that she had become wary of opening her heart and her journal to the things she had lost. Her written recollections were poorer as a result. But they were at least possible. And relatively painless. There was, after all, something to be said for routine.

On returning to the house, she went to the small closet adjoining her bedroom and took the journal from her escritoire. The last ten or twelve pages were mainly accounts of what she had bought and eaten. These were interspersed with notes about people she had met, and visits made. There were comments on conversations: 'Louisa: trenchant views on women who solicit the lewd at noon.' And summaries of discussions at the Green Group, a small gathering of friends. 'Much animated feeling around whether or not the church of St Paul's could truly be described as a Tuscan Temple.'

It was all diverting and brought a smile to her face. But she knew it might be so much more. As it once had been. An account both eloquent and honest in its revelation. But that was then. In those days before the loss of the two things that broke her heart and tore her soul. First, Sam. And then innocence itself.

Although perhaps, even now, something of that could be recovered. Perhaps the journal might once again be the companion, the confidante she so desperately desired. A repository of confession and compassion. This *new* New Year was surely a prompt. A prompt to begin anew.

It would, of course, require a fuller expression of her life and experiences. It would need to be more about *her*. Not just what she had done, but who she was. And ultimately it would have to face up to what happened. Back then.

She turned the thought over in her mind. In some respects, it seemed an indulgence. She should be concerned more with the world outside her door. Less with her own private dilemmas. On the other hand, the journal might become what it had been in her youth. Before the narrowing down that defined the last fifteen years of her life. The journal might return to being something – almost some*one* – in whose company she could unburden herself. With no husband and no dependents – if one did not include Master Fleabane as such – the journal might be her most constant support. She needed to trust it. And she needed to trust herself.

The journal might still include notes of the suppers she most enjoyed. It could continue to record a miscellany of interesting remarks and unusual incidents. But she should at least strive to recapture some of the boldness that lit up her youthful jottings. The curiosity, wonder, questions, honesty, and, yes, love. In several respects, it would mean starting over again. Filling in the gaps. Laying down enough of the past to make sense of it, rather than hiding away.

She took a deep breath and spoke aloud the thought that had been running in her head since the moment she had woken.

'A New Year. If not now, then when?'

Turning the page, she stared at a clean, blank sheet. Then, taking up her newly-inked quill, she wrote in a fair hand: 'Prudence Hyssop: Her Story'.

She gazed at the words and allowed herself a knowing smile at the preposterous nature of the ambition. When she was thirteen it seemed the most natural thing to do. Was she not then just beginning the story of her life? But now? Aged thirty-six? A woman entrenched in middle age. Even to suggest that such an unremarkable life might constitute a *story* was absurd.

Well …

She would at least try. After all, it would be for her eyes only. An exercise in thinking – and remembering – as much as writing. In that respect, person and journal would be well matched. Equally private. Equally anonymous. Equally unnoticed by the folk who thronged the public spaces just yards from her door.

Those reflections might, however, have taken a different turn had she been aware of the extent to which – for all her assumed insignificance – she had so recently been the subject of close, detailed and covert observation. Surveillance, indeed. And by someone who had been following her movements with his own particular purpose in mind.

§

Tom King's coffee-house was a major attraction in the middle of the Piazza.

More shed than house, the wooden structure had been a familiar feature of the marketplace since 1720. Run by Tom King and his wife, Moll, it had grown in popularity as Covent Garden's nocturnal activities flourished. Whilst it was open for much of the day, it was only after midnight that it came into its own. By that time various would-be rakes were emerging from theatres, gaming rooms, and brothels. They were hot with desire for yet more drink, scandalous behaviour, and acts of alcohol-fuelled bravado. Tom King's provided the perfect arena for this mix of manly pursuits, and Tom and Moll were model hosts. Their hospitality was supplemented by a complicit bevy of sirens. Together they ensured the so-called gentlemen parted with whatever money they still possessed during the hours that followed.

Around four or five o'clock in the morning – later in the depths of winter – the market activities would begin. Carts stacked with produce rolled into the Piazza as market sellers set up their shops and stalls. By seven o'clock the wholesale selling had been done and independent shoppers were starting to arrive. Throughout these transitional hours, as night dissolved into day, Tom King's remained a key focal point. It provided refreshment to those stumbling away from cock-pits, card games, or the clutches of an accommodating bawd. No matter how the night had started, there was always the expectation that it would end at Tom King's.

Dr Richard Rock, supplier of patent remedies – some might say 'quack' – was well acquainted with the place. The years when he would spend the whole night there were, however, in the past. Maturity had encouraged a more temperate existence. His preference now was to enjoy a last drink or two around midnight and then retire before the company became too rowdy. He sat in a corner with his head propped against the wall and a look of quiet inebriation on his florid face. He was a corpulent man and his fleshy hands clasped one another across a wide, well-tailored waistcoat. A large periwig sat awry on his bulbous head.

Rock's companion presented a less relaxed figure.

Jonathan Smallow was about forty, short and squat with an air that was unmistakably bumptious. He too was well dressed, although his appearance indicated more obvious signs of fastidious preparation. Certainly, his round face had a pink, smooth shininess about it that suggested a severe regime of soaping and shaving. He called to one of the girls for more arrack. Then he continued to question the doctor who had been extolling the virtues of his patent cure for the pox.

Why, Smallow wanted to know, should one not imbibe such a cure on a regular – even a daily – basis? Why not do that, rather than wait for the affliction to raise its fiery head? Would it not be better to forestall the onset of the malady?

Rock made a mildly explosive sound, expressing derision tempered by regret.

'If only that were possible, my dear fellow,' he said. 'I should be delighted to suggest that a man might quaff my Very Special Cathartic Antivenereal Electuary each and every day. Such consumption would certainly ensure a rather more stable income than the poor pittance on which I survive.'

Smallow scowled as he stared at the expensive lace showing beneath Rock's coat cuffs.

'Unfortunately, however,' the doctor went on, 'I fear that the promotion of a daily dose would be unwise.'

'You mean it would lose its effectiveness,' said Smallow.

'I mean, dear sir, that it might well prove fatal,' said Rock. 'The bodily organs, you see. They are not equipped to deal with the purging qualities of the Very Special Cathartic Antivenereal Electuary in excess. I always advise my clients to use it sparingly, lest its potency lead to dissipation. Or worse.'

He slumped lower on his seat as if to provide an illustration of dissipation. It meant that he did not notice the increased attention in his companion's bloodshot eyes.

'It is a poison, you mean?' said Smallow.

'Poison is an ugly word,' said the doctor. 'Certainly, for one in my profession. I should prefer to stress the remedy's efficacy. After all, one might argue that *anything* taken in excess may constitute a poison. I once heard of a man who died of a surfeit of cucumbers.'

Smallow laughed.

'If you poison us, do we not die?' he muttered. 'By whatever means.'

Rock did not know what Smallow meant to imply by this. He was simply pleased that *something* had finally amused his sour-faced friend.

But the man with the shiny cheeks had not been entertained by the notion of a death by cucumbers. He was laughing at the idea that a treatment for the pox might be the means for murdering a man.

Even so, when Rock hauled himself to his feet to take his leave, Smallow was relieved to be rid of him. There was only so much of the pompous old quack he could take. He looked about him for more adventurous company. Where was Ransome?

§

Lady Belinda Ransome – who until recently had been Miss Belinda Parrish – did not see much of her husband.

It was, she had soon discovered, an arrangement not without its benefits. It had, however, become a subject of comment amongst those who knew. Especially as the marriage had taken place only five weeks before.

In the absence of any meaningful married life, Belinda focused her energies on the new Ransome residence. This was a grand 'West End' establishment in St James's Square. She decided it should be not only a statement of fashion and good taste but also an expression of her own exuberant personality. With her voice being as full as her physique, both house and hostess should create a harmonious impression of abundance.

It was an aspect of this abundance that had appealed so strongly to Sir Marmaduke Ransome. Having found himself in increasingly impecunious waters, he was grateful to be thrown a lifeline by the financial settlement that Belinda's father conferred upon their union. No matter that Mr Parrish was a professional man with no family history or estate to speak of. His liquid assets spoke volumes. They were, Sir Marmaduke had decided, no more than a reasonable reward for his having granted the lady a share in the radiant Ransome name.

Belinda had therefore moved out of her father's house in Bow Street – just around the corner from the home of her very good friend, Prudence Hyssop – and into a place befitting a woman of substance. She was sorry to leave the circle of friends and neighbours with whom she had spent many happy times. But those connections would be extended by the new acquaintances who would beat a path to her door. She would stay in touch with a few representatives of the old company, like Prudence. But Belinda's sights were now set on a whole new social sphere.

To enable that, however, the house would require a good deal of attention. It was already beginning to fill up with too much of the old-fashioned furniture and accessories that Sir Marmaduke was having sent up from his dour and dingy country residence. Belinda could see that the paintings in particular would not pass muster in the precinct of St James's. There were too many pictures of dead pheasants and badly executed views of dull fields. The only portraits of note dated from the first half of the last century, and even they exuded a bleak anonymity. Were they notable Ransomes or just forgotten Herefordshire worthies? All in all, it was a depressing collection. And so Sir Marmaduke had reluctantly agreed that a new selection of paintings be commissioned to grace the walls of the St James's Square residence.

The baronet expressed no great enthusiasm for

the project, but he was prepared to be pragmatic. He calculated that the expense should not be so great as to threaten the more enterprising ways in which he planned to spend Lady Ransome's fortune. It would, he reasoned, be acceptable for his wife to oversee the scheme, so long as a clear financial framework was established. The proposal he put to his wife was therefore that he should commission one artist to create all the various works. This would, he assured Belinda, not only provide continuity of style across a range of executions. It would also ensure that the works, and their attendant costs, could be managed in the most efficient way.

Belinda had no basis for making a counter proposal, so she waited to be informed who the chosen artist was to be. Perhaps it might be the husband of another old friend and near neighbour, Jane Hogarth. She had not seen Jane for some years, during which time Mr Hogarth had become the most celebrated painter and engraver in London. That would indeed be something of a coup. It would also be a guarantee that people would flock to her house to view both herself and her paintings.

She had told herself, of course, that such an outcome was distinctly improbable. Mr Hogarth's elevated stature made it unlikely he would wish to take on such a wide-ranging and domestic commission. He was concentrating on generating hugely successful print series, like *A Harlot's Progress*. Indeed, Sir Marmaduke and Lady Ransome had been presented with copies of the recently available *Rake's Progress* on the occasion of their wedding. At the time Belinda had not appreciated quite how ironic a gift it was.

So, yes, for one reason or another, the artist would almost certainly not be Mr Hogarth.

What Belinda did not expect, however, was that the person chosen would be someone of whom she had not even heard. Someone who was, so far as she could ascertain, simply an occasional drinking companion of her husband.

But it was not only that she had never heard of the man before. What troubled her more was the look on Sir Marmaduke's face when he told her. It was smug. The look of someone who felt he had come up with a particularly smart response to an unpropitious set of challenges.

And so, for a reason Belinda could not quite put her finger on, the name of Mr Jonathan Smallow gave her only a sense of impending doom.

§

Shortly before eight o'clock in the morning the baronet arrived at Tom King's.

By then the place was nearly empty. Moll King was clearing up behind the bar. Black Betty was sweeping the floor.

'Where's Rock?' demanded Ransome.

A sneer of disdain contorted the flat features of his face. It gave him the air of someone who perpetually had a bad smell under his nose. His wig was clean, but his clothes were stained with food and other matters. He looked as if he had not slept for some time.

'Long gone,' said Moll.

She made no attempt to mollify him. Sir Marmaduke was not one of her more affable customers. She only stopped herself from being rude by thinking of the money he regularly spent there. Hearing the baronet's strident voice, the bulky presence of Moll's husband appeared from a small alcove behind a curtain.

'No doubt he'll be out and about again soon,' Tom said. 'You'll be able to catch him in his chaise while he's getting ready to sell his wares around the Piazza.'

Ransome's sneer became a contemptuous smile.

'And you honestly think I'm about to discuss my personal requirements across an open space and in front of an audience?' he said.

He concluded his remark by projecting a jet of phlegm into a spittoon.

Tom bit his tongue. He too would have liked to tell Sir Marmaduke where he could stick his personal requirements but feared it might not be good for business. For all that Ransome was not a pleasant man, he had a wide circle of acquaintances. Several of those numbered amongst the Kings' more accommodating customers.

'I could ask him to call at your residence, Sir Marmaduke,' said Tom.

He was trying to be helpful but knew the suggestion would meet with derision. Ransome cast an even more withering look in his direction and spoke through tight lips.

'Or I could simply take out an advertisement in the *Penny Gazette* announcing that I have a particularly irritating bout of the clap, I suppose.'

Moll stuffed her pinafore into her mouth to stop herself from laughing. Black Betty looked the other way and pretended to cough.

'When you see him,' Ransome continued, pausing to inspect the shape of the dark-skinned girl, 'make sure you tell him to be here tonight. And *after* midnight.'

Tom said he would certainly do that.

'In the meantime, Sir Marmaduke,' he said, 'is there anything I can get you?'

Ransome considered the question. Once more he cast a leering glance in Black Betty's direction. Thinking better of it, however – or perhaps remembering another engagement – he turned and strode towards the door.

'Just remember,' he said over his shoulder. 'Tonight.'

Once out in the hubbub of the marketplace he could not hear the murmur of curses and giggles that followed close on his exit.

§

Jane Hogarth could not believe her eyes.

She stared at the unfinished canvas, mouth agape. What on earth was he was playing at? Yes, her husband had always displayed a streak of unpredictability. It went with his stubbornness. But this!

Why? Why choose *her*?

It was baffling.

She had come into his studio to ask whether he would be at home for dinner. But he was not there. That was when she saw the canvas for the first time. So far the central figure had been no more than lightly painted in, but there was still no mistaking the similarity. Surely it could not be a coincidence. Perhaps he was not aware of who it was. Although that was not like him. His portrayal of persons was always so precise.

So why choose *her*?

She would have to talk to him about it. And sooner rather than later.

But where *was* he? He usually let her know if he was going out. And it was not like him to leave the studio unattended.

It was four years before that Mr and Mrs Hogarth had moved the half-mile from Covent Garden Piazza to Leicester Fields. The property, in the south-east corner of what was starting to be considered a 'square', was known across the London art world as Mr Hogarth's place. The success of *A Harlot's Progress* as a series of prints had provided the financial means for making the move. It was an ideal address for an artist. Only a few minutes' walk from Covent Garden but closer to the growing 'West End'. The artist had set up over the doorway a gilded bust of his hero, Sir Anthony van Dyck. The substantial building with its four floors and basement, plus the sign of van Dyck's golden head, reflected Mr Hogarth's sense of status.

It was not, however, the most prestigious address in Leicester Fields. That honour belonged to Leicester House which took up most of the north side of the square. It had been the London home of the current king, George II, when he was Prince of Wales. At his accession to the throne, it had been bequeathed to his own eldest son, Frederick, the current Prince of Wales.

Jane was about to leave the studio and return upstairs when there suddenly appeared a loose-limbed man in his early thirties. He was agitated and decidedly pink about the gills.

'Mrs H!' was all he could say.

'Jeremiah,' said Jane.

'Mrs H,' repeated Jeremiah.

His flexible face made it clear that he was thinking as quickly as he could.

'You won't tell Mr H, will you, Mrs H?'

'Won't tell him *what*, Jeremiah?'

'That I'd slipped out for a moment,' he said. 'To say something. To a friend. Who was passing. It took no more than a few seconds. But I'm supposed to be minding the shop. Keeping an eye on things.'

He was more flustered than she had seen him before, and Jane raised an eyebrow. She had known Jeremiah for several years and judged him to be a reliable aid to her husband. He was primarily a courier, running errands between artists and suppliers. It was not a well-paid job. But it meant that, one way or another, he had his finger on the pulse of the artistic community. It also gave him the chance to drop into conversation the names of local luminaries for whom he worked. They included eminent figures like George Bickham and William Hogarth as well as more modestly appointed painters like Felipe (or 'Al') Alcazar. He also did jobs for less recognised artists, including that odious little man whose name Jane knew could never be mentioned in William's presence. Mr Smallow.

'And where exactly *is* Mr Hogarth?' said Jane.

It was more important to ascertain the whereabouts of her husband than pursue the matter of Jeremiah's slipping out.

'He's across the way,' he said, waving his arm in the air. 'Over at Leicester House.'

Jane frowned.

'He'd heard a rumour,' continued Jeremiah. 'Someone said the Prince of Wales was due to arrive. And Mr H wanted to get a glimpse. Wanted to see how he looked, he said. I was a bit surprised. I'd not had Mr H down as a royalist.'

He stopped suddenly and looked embarrassed again. Perhaps he had overstepped the mark by commenting on his employer's loyalties.

'Mr Hogarth is interested in everything,' said Jane. 'And everybody.'

Her words confirmed that it was indeed not for Jeremiah to remark on such things.

'I shall go and see for myself,' she said. 'And I shall leave *you* to "keep an eye on things",' she added caustically.

She liked Jeremiah but wanted to be clear that his 'slipping out' constituted a dereliction of duty. Moreover a lapse that might have proved catastrophic. What if a thief had come into the studio while it was empty and stolen something? A sketch or an engraved copper plate. What if someone had stolen a *painting* for heaven's sake? What if it had been the painting she was looking at only moments before? It did not bear thinking about.

But no such thing had occurred. The painting was there. The studio appeared undisturbed. And Jeremiah was back at his post. No harm done.

It was therefore in a positive frame of mind that Jane made her way out into the fresh air of Leicester Fields. It was cold enough to warrant a shawl or her cape, but she could not be bothered to go back for either. After all, she would not be out for long. And if *he* could not be seen, then no matter.

She was not thinking of William. He would turn up in due course. He always did. But, like her husband, she wanted to know if the Prince of Wales looked anything like the prints she had seen. If he was intending to use Leicester House as his main London home, it would be useful to know more about her new neighbour. Including how he dressed and conducted himself. The same thought, she decided, must have occurred to William.

She had gone no more than a few steps when she saw him. William, that is. He looked to be on his way back from Leicester House. She could see, past his shoulder on the far side of the square, a small crowd dispersing. If the Prince had indeed been there, it would seem that the event was now over. She crossed the intervening ground and met William half-way. He had a strange look on his face that she thought she recognised. It was a look that combined an air of total distraction with intense concentration. It was the face her husband wore when he had had an idea.

As he caught sight of her, however, this expression was replaced by a more puzzled gaze.

'Ah, Jenny,' he said, scratching at the stubble on his

chin. He had noticed that his wife was not dressed for a chilly morning walk. 'Going somewhere?'

'Apparently not,' she replied tartly.

He stared at her, not pretending to understand the meaning of such an answer. Women could be remarkably oblique in their use of language, he reflected.

'Well?' she said when it was clear he was not going to volunteer any information.

'Well?' he repeated as they began to head back towards the sign of the golden head.

'Did you see him?' said Jane, her voice taking on a more distinct edge.

'Who's that then, dear?'

She managed not to slap him.

'The Prince of Wales,' she said tightly and with what she considered to be remarkable restraint.

'The Prince of Wales?' he repeated. And then he began to chuckle in a sly and conspiratorial way.

Oh, for goodness' sake, thought Jane! Sometimes it's like talking to a sponge. I'll ask him again later. When I speak to him about the other thing.

§

In beginning my journal anew, I should provide some relation of my early life.

My first memories are of being four or five years old. They must therefore date from the Year of Our Lord 1704 or 1705. Queen Anne had been on the throne for three years or more, and I had become used to hearing my great aunt talk about her as 'the poor Queen'. I did then think it a great pity the Queen should be poor and found it a source of bewilderment that the People of this land could not do something to help. Perhaps by giving her some money so that she should not be poor.

Those earliest memories are shrouded in mist and shadows. Faces are blurred, places are dark, illusions arise fleetingly in my mind, only to fade away or change into strange shapes and phantasms that have no sense. Even now I have the apprehension that nothing stayed still. Yet I know that much of my early life must have been measured by the absence of movement.

When first I began to grow into a womanly state, I had been prompted to reassemble what I understood of my origins. I was reliant on what my great aunt was content to tell me but, as I grew older and bolder, I began to ask questions. My great aunt was not always pleased to answer but I was patient and did choose the most propitious times.

My great aunt. I must say something of her.

Mrs Mary Fullbright is a name that was not the most fit for a lady for whom both fullness and brightness were never natural characteristics. Mrs Fullbright (née Hammersley, a more suitable designation) had been born during the last months of the Commonwealth and seemed to carry with her the severity of that Puritan era.

In her later years, and throughout the time I shared her home, she was certainly of a saturnine disposition, inclined to bouts of melancholy and ardent prayerfulness. Perhaps she had been of a different mind as a young woman. The man she married, a Mr Augustus Fullbright, was by all accounts an indomitably cheerful character. But alas a late flowering of the plague in 1679 carried him away and my great aunt never threw off her mourning. Her only sister and husband followed Mr Fullbright to the grave shortly thereafter, leaving an infant daughter as my great aunt's only niece and living relation. It was soon after then that she moved into Covent Garden Piazza, the beneficiary of a last will and testament that granted her tenure of one of the arcaded houses in perpetuity. More recent endeavours through the Court of Chancery have succeeded in throwing no light on the bequest, and legal opinion is inclined to regard it as an instance of eccentricity so convoluted that it would serve little purpose to enquire into its history.

Assuredly my great aunt seemed always to regard the house as a favour from God and gave thanks for His munificence throughout her life. It is a prayer of humble gratitude I have been blessed to repeat every day since. And it is most certain that the gift of the house, together with a capital sum the late Mr Fullbright had inherited from his corn-chandler father, did mean that his widow was able to provide a home for the infant baby girl, Constance, who was to be my mother.

Constance was a pale and delicate young lady who escaped her aunt's house by marrying an unavailingly optimistic young curate, name of Henry Hyssop. When Constance expired giving birth to her own pale and fragile baby girl, Mrs Fullbright found herself once more cast in the role of sole support, as the Reverend Hyssop quickly succumbed to a combination of anxiety and typhus shortly after the demise of his wife.

My great aunt told me on a great many occasions that she was able to countenance this new duty with an even greater fortitude than she had demonstrated through the raising of my mother. It was a clear endorsement of God's judgement that she – childless herself – should be chosen to provide for one frail young person after another. And thus it was that she set hard her stony face and adopted a largely humourless demeanour in carrying forward her Christian service as the guardian of another poor unfortunate.

And so I, Prudence Charity Hyssop, was conveyed to Covent Garden in the presence of the wet-nurse appointed on the day of my birth.

As I began to grow, however, my great aunt could see that I possessed a stronger constitution than had Constance. My mother and I may have shared some physical characteristics, but our temperaments were at variance. Whereas my mother had been mostly docile and acquiescent, I evinced a quickness and adaptability that made it easier to thrive within the constrained limits of my circumstances. It was not immediately apparent whence these attributes derived, as neither of my parents had been noted for their spirit. My great aunt, perhaps understandably, chose to regard my temperament as a tribute to her own character, and a confirmation that the bringing up of children by hand in the Christian tradition was the root of all goodness in what was otherwise a manifestly wicked world.

It was not a school of nurture that offered a deal of formal or unaffected stimulation. But it was a childhood that, by virtue of its location, provided a range of inspirations.

§

Mr Hogarth appeared more than usually good humoured.

Focusing his attention on a picture always channelled his energies in a positive way. It assuaged almost any sense of grievance. More than that, it reminded him that he was a figure of renown. Some people might say he had a chip on his shoulder, but they were wrong. He commanded respect – and not just because he had married the daughter of Sir James Thornhill. Five years had now passed since *A Harlot's Progress* made his name. Five years! The success of that series of prints had clearly not been a flash in the pan. Just last year there had been his follow-up triumph, *A Rake's Progress*. He was unstoppable. The most talked about and sought after artist in London. And that was not just good luck. It was down to genius. *He*, at least, was sure of that.

He was even smiling when Jane walked into the studio. She had come to interrogate him about the picture. However, he pre-empted her as he pointed towards the canvas on the easel.

'Well, what do you think?' he said. 'What do you think of *her*?'

Jane stared at the canvas with a thoughtful look on her face. There was no shock this time. He did not know that she had already seen it. He assumed her frown was simply a sign of serious intent. For she always took his work seriously. And the more satirical its purpose, the more seriously she took it.

Her husband's fame had been built on his engravings.

But several of those prints – most notably the *Harlot* and *Rake* series – originated as paintings. He would first create the images in lush and colourful oils and exhibit the paintings to advertise his intention of turning them into prints. A set of completely new images would then be engraved on copper plates using a sharp tool called a burin. These plates followed the overall composition of the paintings but included a great deal more detail. Each copper plate was inked and pressed onto a sheet of paper. This meant that the final print was a reverse image of the original. Not that prospective buyers would necessarily know that – not unless they had seen the paintings as well. Most people only saw the images as engravings. The prints were therefore more famous than the painted versions. They were also, of course, far more accessible. *A Rake's Progress* – eight fine prints in all – sold for two guineas. The copper plates could then be adapted to create a relatively limitless supply of cheaper copies that sold for as little as sixpence a sheet. It was a more innovative way of making money than relying only on the sale of the paintings. And no one managed the end-to-end process more efficiently than William Hogarth.

There remained the risk of piracy. In the interval between exhibiting the paintings and issuing the prints, unscrupulous print-makers could publish their own 'copies'. The previous year's Copyright Act had – in theory at least – provided a degree of protection. But the pirates had adapted, of course. They changed just enough of an image to claim the work as their own. Nevertheless, the Act was better than nothing. And the benefit of showing the paintings first – with the publicity that created – made the risk worthwhile.

Jane knew all about his plans for the new series. Not a *Progress* this time but four views of London showing aspects of the city's diverse culture. There would be four oil paintings, under the over-arching title of *The Four Times of the Day*. Then, as with the *Harlot* and the *Rake*, those paintings would be adapted as prints.

That was all fine. A good plan. But now, faced with the first of the paintings, what could she possibly say?

She knew he was expecting her usual frank view, but she was struggling to overcome her earlier shock. It was not the theme or setting that was the problem. William had created many images with a more obviously provocative subject.

It was the woman. The woman whose figure was the main focus of the picture. It was the woman that caused Jane to gasp when first she saw it earlier that day.

The painting showed the west end of Covent Garden Piazza – the end where the church stood. The church of St Paul's. There it was, looming in the background. The sky was dark. Snow on the ground. The church clock showing seven o'clock. Early morning. Although the presence of two rakish men fondling a couple of market girls suggested the end of a long and lecherous night. But the building there in front of the church …

Tom King's? Really? The Piazza's infamous 'coffee-house' right in front of the church?

At least it gave her something to say that was not about the woman. A way to open the conversation.

'You've moved Tom King's,' she said.

The large shed of Tom King's was located on the south side of the Piazza's open space, close to the market buildings. However, William's painting showed it repositioned in front of the church's august portico. Jane knew that her husband never did anything without a clear purpose. His satire was often based on visual juxtapositions that forced you to look again. To see things afresh.

He stared at her from under his heavy brow. It was a face that said, 'Yes. *And* …?'

'That's clever,' she added quickly.

His grim expression curled into a smile. It was smug rather than cheery. But he still enjoyed being appreciated by his wife. If *she* said it was good, it was an early confirmation of his instincts. If Jane liked it, so would the others.

'Moving Tom King's. And setting it against the church,' she went on. 'Yes. That's clever. Sharp. A neat contrast.'

'I thought so too,' he said, with his usual modesty. 'So where do you get *your* spiritual salvation, my good man – or woman?' he added, adopting a more theatrical voice. 'From a bible? Or a bottle?'

Yes, he was obviously very pleased with the visual contrast. And with himself too. He might be famous for his pictures, but he could also turn a phrase.

Jane nodded slowly. Her husband was never anything less than smart. *Too* smart, some might say. But then there had always been people who were jealous of him.

So, yes, it was a very good setting. A cold, dark morning. The church. The market getting underway.

The night-time frolics at Tom King's just coming to an end. A fire with some beggars trying to keep warm. A typical Covent Garden view. Mixed. Cutting. Provocative. Compelling.

But what about the woman?

The main focus of the painting was a woman walking across the square, from right to left. On her way to church presumably. Or Tom King's? No, surely not. The church was a more likely destination. And her dress. It was yellow and glowed brightly. A real highlight in the otherwise dark composition.

Her face, however, ...

Jane kept coming back to her face. There was no getting away from it.

'But,' she began. She did not want to rile William. Yet she had to know.

'*Yeees*?' The word oozed from him, seeping with suspicion.

Did his wife want to change the nature of the conversation? To something more critical perhaps. What had he missed? What was wrong with the painting?

And, of course, she sensed his irritation, surfacing in that one word. *Yeees*? For someone so obviously successful, he could be incredibly prickly.

'The woman,' she said.

'*Yeees*?' he said again.

'She's ... well done,' said Jane. 'Another fine contrast. But why *her*?'

'What do you mean?' he said. His eyes narrowed as he came and stood alongside her, staring at the canvas.

'Why did you paint *her*?' she said.

He appeared puzzled. Or at least confused.

'*Who*?' he said.

Jane exhaled deeply. Was he playing games? Or did he really not know?

'Miss Hyssop,' she said.

§

Master Fleabane – Miss Hyssop's ward – had a talent for noticing things.

As a young man of thirteen years, it might have been assumed that his knowledge of life was limited. But what he lacked in experience he made up for with an insatiable curiosity and a fecund imagination. Both qualities had been encouraged by his learning to read, for which he was indebted to Miss Hyssop. He was not well-versed in the standard texts considered recommended reading for a young man of his age. His personal taste veered more towards newspapers, particularly those accounts relating to violent and criminal acts. It was an interest that shaped much of his recreational life, and he considered no metropolitan spectacle quite so enlightening as a good hanging. It was probably the most significant aspect of London life on which his views diverged from those of Miss Hyssop.

On this particular damp morning Master Fleabane was busy about the Piazza as usual. He had bought some provisions for his mistress's kitchen and delivered letters to a few of Miss Hyssop's friends. But these jobs still left him with time to watch the world go by. And to notice things.

He noticed Dr Rock, who had arrived as usual with his horse and chaise, quickly attracting a small crowd of onlookers. The horse was exceedingly placid, and Dr Rock was able to stand up in the chaise without fear that the nag would bolt. From that elevated position he addressed the assembled company on the benefits of his famous Tincture for the Teeth and other proprietary medicines.

Master Fleabane noticed Tom King's coffee-house, which so often provided some kind of diversion. He passed it every morning as he accompanied Miss Hyssop to church. Even at such an hour there would still be signs of the previous night's raucous activities. Half-drunken gentlemen stumbling out into the open air and making free with the market girls.

There was always so much to see wherever you looked.

Within just a few yards of Miss Hyssop's house were the Covent Garden Theatre, the Shakespeare Head Tavern, and the Bedford coffee-house, each one the scene of some regular rumpus. There was the market itself, throbbing and heaving with life through most of the day and part of the night. And there were the many other buildings that bordered the busy Piazza. Some were private residences like Miss Hyssop's house. But many were guest houses, bagnios, shops, brothels, gaming dens, and artists' studios.

One building Master Fleabane tended to notice more than others. This was partly because it was on the south side of the square, directly opposite his own small bedroom window. Local legend suggested it had once been a guest house run by a fearsome old bawd called Sally Sparker. On her death it had been divided into smaller dwellings.

At the top of the building lived Mr Potts – Jeremiah to those who knew him. He was a familiar face around the Piazza and a casual acquaintance of Miss Hyssop. Master Fleabane had formed the impression that he had once been an actor, dancer, or tumbler. In time spent at the Drury Lane Theatre, Jeremiah had presumably tumbled and danced through a great many plays – *Hamlick*, *MacDeath*, and *A Fellow*, to name but three that Master Fleabane had heard of. More recently, however, Jeremiah had adapted himself to a less strenuous occupation as a conveyor of artists' materials.

The room below Jeremiah, Master Fleabane had learned, was now occupied by a lady who ventured out only after dark. The room had been difficult to let, due to the previous tenant having fallen on the stairway and broken her neck. Putting these two facts together, Master Fleabane came to the not unreasonable conclusion that the new lady was probably a Vampyre. This would explain her lack of fear about the stairs – given that she was already dead – and also her nocturnal activity. It also corresponded with a newspaper account he had recently read on the subject of Vampyres.

Below the Vampyre lived an old couple. They could be seen wandering round the Piazza together, the old gentleman shouting into his wife's ear. It was generally accepted, by those who knew no better, that the man was a tailor, name of Flint. But Master Fleabane had never seen anything that gave credence to such a suggestion. He was more inclined to believe that the old fellow was in reality a former highwayman. There was admittedly scant evidence for this, other than the way he shouted at his wife. But Master Fleabane felt that such behaviour betrayed a high-handed and highwayman-like nature.

In the room directly below the old highwayman and his mistress lived Mr Alcazar and his family. Master Fleabane knew his rather odd name because Miss Hyssop was inclined to pay the painter and his wife an occasional visit. She had also sent them more than one note of condolence over the last year.

Master Fleabane also noticed people who visited the building. Sometimes he saw them because he was loitering in the Piazza. Other times he observed them from his high vantage point in Miss Hyssop's house. There were, in truth, not so many visitors to be seen. Master Fleabane assumed they were calling on Mr Alcazar or Jeremiah. It seemed unlikely that either the highwayman or the Vampyre would encourage callers. Two men in particular had been seen visiting the house in the weeks before Christmas. They were easy to notice because they were both so well dressed. One was tall and one was short. But that had been months ago. Before the lady fell to her death. And before the Vampyre moved in.

Indeed, Master Fleabane might have forgotten the two men altogether. Except for the fact that he saw one of them as he was returning along Tavistock Row on that same damp morning. It was the short man. He was knocking at the house's front door but getting no response. Master Fleabane knew the door was sometimes left unlocked during the day, so he stopped and stared.

At that moment the short man turned round with an air of irritation. His mood was not improved by seeing himself stared at.

'You, there!' he said, pointing an accusing finger in Master Fleabane's direction. 'Do you know Potts, the artists' runner?'

Master Fleabane said that he did.

'Then give him this,' said the man. He handed over a small printed card. 'And tell him to call on me before tonight with the brushes I'm promised.'

The man then turned on his heel and walked away in the direction of Russell Street. Master Fleabane looked at the card and read aloud to himself the following words:

Jonathan Smallow, Esquire
Gentleman Artist

Then he repeated the last two words and laughed slyly to himself.

Gentleman Artist indeed!

For Master Fleabane had decided that Jonathan Smallow Esquire was nothing of the sort, but rather a bloodthirsty desperado of the worst kind.

§

William pulled a face.

'Who's Miss Hyssop?' he said. Rather unconvincingly, Jane thought.

'You know exactly who Miss Hyssop is,' she said. 'The

lady who lives on the north side of the Piazza. Who has lived there for as long as I can remember. Just a few doors from where my parents lived!'

William nodded. Then he shrugged.

'I didn't know her name was Hislop,' he said. 'Or, if I did, I'd forgot.'

'Not Hislop,' Jane said. '*Hyssop*. Like the flower.'

He smirked.

'Well, I've painted her like a flower,' he said.

'Hyssop is not yellow,' said his wife.

He pulled another face.

'I was joking,' he growled. 'And, anyway, she's not exactly blooming, *is* she?'

Jane ignored the remark.

'But why paint her at all?' she continued. 'Why choose Miss Hyssop of all people?'

'It's not meant to be *her*,' he said. 'Not specifically.'

'But it *is* specifically her,' Jane insisted. 'It is very specifically the image of a person who used to be a neighbour of ours!'

'We've had a great many neighbours, my dear,' he said. 'Everyone in London is my neighbour. Am I not to paint *any* of them?'

He was impossible. He knew exactly what she meant. And she was not going to allow herself to be drawn into a debate about whom he should and should not paint.

'But Miss Hyssop!'

William shook his head. His wife was a good deal easier to deal with – and to understand – than most women. He loved her dearly. And sometimes she made him quake. But, even so. She still tried his patience. It was, he supposed, the price he paid for having selected such an independently minded partner.

'She's never done you any harm,' continued Jane.

'Harm!' he said. 'And I've done *her* no harm.'

He paused, looked at the painting, and then back at his wife.

'It's a *picture*!' he went on. 'There's no harm in a picture, my dear.'

'Hah!' she exclaimed. 'Now I *know* you're making fun! Your pictures are *always* harmful!'

Was this a sweeping judgement or a compliment? He was not sure. But it made him smile. He enjoyed the sparring. It suited his pugnacious spirit – and their relationship. For her part, Jane could see that she had won him round – as she usually did. So she built on it.

'That's a big part of your talent,' she said.

'Genius,' he corrected her, with a grin. 'I think you mean "genius".'

'Genius,' she repeated. It was a familiar routine. 'So why Miss Hyssop? Why make a sweet lady like that look so … so …?'

'So *what*?'

She glowered at him.

'So … indelicate!' she said.

He chuckled. Jane's lips tightened. Once again she wanted to slap him. Or hit him with something heavy.

'I like "indelicate",' he said.

'But Miss Hyssop won't,' said Jane. 'She'll be mortified. And she won't understand why you've done it.'

He was not entirely insensitive and could tell that his wife was upset and bewildered. He needed to be more accommodating. He valued her robustly positive spirit too much to risk losing it.

'I didn't realise she was your friend,' he said.

'She's not my friend,' Jane said. 'I haven't spoken to her for … years. And I hardly said more than a few words to her even then. But she's a very respectable person.' There was a pause. 'Despite what *some* people may say.'

He cleared his throat. Respectability was not his thing.

'But more than that,' Jane went on, 'Miss Hyssop is still almost a neighbour. Even if we no longer live in Covent Garden, we're still part of it. That place never leaves you. *You* know that more than most.'

She paused to let her words sink in before continuing.

'And Miss Hyssop has lived in the Piazza for much longer than *we* ever did. Probably longer than my parents did. *Everyone* knows her. Or at least everyone knows who she is. And, yes, I understand that you're not thinking of the neighbours. I know you're thinking of your audience. The people out there.' She made a sweeping gesture with her hand. 'People who don't know the individuals portrayed. People for whom your characters are universal. The Harlot. The Rake. Representative figures. Your commentary on human nature. And you do it so well, of course. So why make *this* so obviously one particular person – and a very harmless person at that?'

They both stood there, staring at the woman depicted crossing the Piazza in the chill of early morning. Jane could feel the restless energy emanating from William's body. She knew he was struggling to keep it under control – that he wanted simply to say 'Hrrumph', or something worse.

'It's well done, though. Don't you think?' he said, focusing attention back on the artistic rather than the moral merits of the image.

'It's *very* well done,' Jane said. 'As always. You've captured her perfectly.' There was another small pause. 'Although I'm sure she covers herself up more when it's cold.'

'Ah,' he said, scratching his bristly chin. 'But that's the point.'

She turned towards him and smiled. Quite how she continued to find this short, uncouth, difficult man attractive, she did not know. She reached out a hand and scratched away some white paint from the side of his nose. He grabbed the hand and kissed it.

'The way she's dressed suggests ulterior motives,' he said. 'She's on her way to church – but flaunting herself at the same time.'

'But that's also *my* point, my sweet,' said Jane. 'Miss Hyssop most certainly goes to church – probably too often. But, whatever else she does, she does *not* flaunt.'

He pulled a face, as if he had been found out.

'But as you expressed it yourself,' he said, 'my figures are universal. I take the particular and I make it general. I hold a mirror up to the world. It's not a picture of Miss Hyssop. It's a picture of a woman. A certain kind of woman.'

Jane smiled again. He was incorrigible. No point in trying to turn back the tide.

'But Miss Hyssop!' she said again.

He made a noise down his nose. Was it some kind of admission?

'It's too good to change,' he said.

Jane knew the limits.

'Of course,' she said.

Although the more she looked at it, the more she could not help thinking that just a touch would transform Miss Hyssop's face into someone else entirely.

'Well, perhaps,' she began slowly. 'Perhaps you could show it to her.'

'Show her?' he said. 'The painting?'

He was not sure if he was shocked or just completely at a loss as to what might be gained by doing such a thing.

'At least then it wouldn't come as a surprise,' Jane went on. 'You could suggest that she had ...' She was searching for the right word. 'That she had ... inspired you. To include her. In a painting of the Piazza.'

She kept her eyes focused on the canvas as she continued.

'It would demonstrate your great understanding. And sensitivity.'

Again the flattery. Plus a flagrant untruth.

'Not to mention your neighbourliness,' she threw in as an afterthought.

'My neighbourliness!' He almost choked.

'You could invite her in,' Jane went on. 'Show her the studio. Make her feel special.'

The idea did not land as badly as she feared. It would, after all, give him another chance to show off. Jane could arrange to be there herself. It would give her a chance to get to know Miss Hyssop. She was not obviously the type of woman Jane would select as an acquaintance. Her prim exterior suggested a conservative personality. But perhaps there were hidden depths.

'You could even invite Flea,' she said, sensing that he was beginning to see her logic.

'Flea!' he said, eyes wide. 'Who the hell is Flea?'

§

Sir Marmaduke did not have to wait until midnight.

As he approached the Hummums bagnio at the east end of the Piazza he spied Dr Rock shuffling through the arcade on his way to collect his horse and chaise from the Bow Street stables.

'Rock!'

Ransome was not happy – the consequence of too little brandy and even less luck at cards.

Rock reeled back against one of the arcade pillars as if he had been shot. The movement upset his wig and he had to resettle it again before he could see clearly.

'Ah! Sir Marmaduke,' he managed to utter as the baronet's sweaty glare fixed him to the spot. 'What an unexpected pleasure.'

Rock's startled face expressed the unexpected far more than the pleasure. He had not been inside Tom King's since the previous night and had therefore received no forewarning of Ransome's desire to meet.

As he backed away into the shadowy depths of the

covered walk, Rock could not see the threatening curl of the other man's lip. But he flinched from the stench of tobacco and alcohol that hung about the baronet's body like a miasma.

'I need your damned potion again,' snarled Ransome. 'But stronger this time.' He nodded towards Tavistock Row. 'The dose of clap I got from that cheap whore over there has come back again. And with a vengeance this time. It is not a pretty sight I can tell you!'

He laughed in a demonic way that made the doctor's eyes dilate with fear. There seemed little doubt that Sir Marmaduke was not in his right mind – whatever that might be. Rock did not wish to provoke him further but felt the need to defend his product.

'But, Sir Marmaduke,' he said. 'That ... incident ... it was a good two or three months ago, if not more. Might not your present condition be due to some more recent ... dalliance?'

'Hah!' spat Ransome. 'Dalliance, indeed! You brew your words like you brew your compounds! And, yes, I daresay I've had quite some ... *dalliances* since then. But they've all been cloaked in armour – now that I'm a married man. Shrouded in a fucking sheath and tied up tight with a pretty pink bow! Which is why, good doctor, I know it must be that dead cow who's to blame!'

Despite what he already knew of Ransome's cruel nature, Rock was shocked by the other man's callous language.

'The poor girl paid a heavy price for her ... misdemeanours,' he ventured with a quivering voice.

'Poor girl! A pox on her, in faith!' Ransome roared. 'She's lucky she fell when she did. Lucky to be dead. For if her neck were not already broken, I would break it for her now! Just like that!'

He snapped his fingers in Rock's face.

The doctor's eyes widened still further. Such a murderous reference was unsettling, to say the least. He wanted to get the conversation back onto a more business-like footing.

'But, yes – the Very Special Cathartic Venereal Electuary, Sir Marmaduke,' he said. 'That will most certainly work its … magic.'

He paused briefly, before adding: '*This* time it will, I'm sure.'

As he said it, he began to feel a new surge of anxiety coursing through his body. For what if it did *not* work? He certainly did not believe what Ransome had said about using a sheath. That was not the sort of devil he was. Almost certainly this latest eruption of the disease had been caused by a more recent escapade. But then it did not matter what Rock believed. All that mattered was what Ransome had convinced himself was true.

The reference to the Very Special Cathartic Venereal Electuary was, however, enough to turn the baronet's mind from murderous thoughts and back to the matter in hand.

'Magic! Hah!' he said, sneering at the doctor whose large body was now trembling visibly. Rock could feel himself shaking and wanted to say something by way of explanation.

'It is a v-veritably c-cold n-night, Sir Marmaduke,' he stammered. 'C-cold enough to make m-mortal flesh p-p-palpitate.'

Ransome looked at him with contempt. But he also knew the price of redemption – or at least the worth of a potential remedy. He pressed a coin into the doctor's palm. Even in the gloom of the arcade he could see Rock's eyes light up.

'I shall send Smallow to you tomorrow,' Ransome said.

'Smallow?' said the doctor. 'Mr Smallow the painter?'

'He owes me a favour or two,' said Ransome. 'Especially with regard to *this*. For I am indebted to Mr Smallow for introducing me to the poxy slut.'

Rock winced again. Ransome gazed across the Piazza with a look of disgust on his face.

'Are you still on Ludgate Hill?' he said.

Rock confirmed that he could certainly be found at that address on most afternoons, Monday to Friday. Mornings, he declared, were largely dedicated to his mission of taking cures to the people.

'Damn your mission,' said Ransome. 'Smallow shall visit you tomorrow. Make sure you're there. And make sure the potion is strong enough this time. Strong enough to last.'

Sir Marmaduke had moved to within a few inches of the doctor's face and his pungent breath was almost enough to make the other man retch.

'Do not fail me, Rock. Or I shall take more from you than you can afford to lose.'

And with that, he gave the doctor's nether parts an

encouraging squeeze before continuing on his way into the bagnio.

§

William had the feeling that things were missing.

It was not easy to tell, of course. His studio was stuffed with so many materials of one sort or another. It was impossible to keep track of exactly what was there. Canvases, stretchers, oils, pigments in powder form, brushes of every shape and size. Crayons, pencils, palette knives, charcoal, paper of different thicknesses. Easels, pots and pans, cloths, bottles of this and that, mahlsticks, and miscellaneous pieces of wood. In some respects it was a total mess. But it was a mess he was familiar with. A mess through which he could navigate his way.

The studio was always half-filled with finished and part-finished works, as well as canvases, boards, drawings and copper plates in various stages of completion. In that sense, the place was an expression of the great process of creativity to which he had dedicated his life. Some of the images were little more than sketches, hinting at what they might become. Others were evolving through states of adaptation and revision. Only a few stood proud as complete works, awaiting their final touches before being released into an expectant art world.

The things that seemed to have gone missing were of much less value than these examples of his genius. They were base materials – blank canvases, brushes, paints. The things he had most of. Which made it difficult to know whether they were missing at all. Had there not been more of those small canvases when he last checked? He did not count his brushes – there were too many. But what had he done with those large ones? It was more difficult to have even an inkling of which paints and oils might have disappeared. But surely his stock of that new Prussian Blue had not been so low last week.

It prompted him to check his engraving tools and materials. But they were all in order. Whatever it was that was spiriting away the paints and canvases seemed uninterested in his copper plates and burins. The leather pad, on which the plates were placed while they were being engraved, was safe on his work-bench. So what was going on? Was he simply losing touch with the number of items he was having delivered? One thing was clear. He should keep a better track of his store.

Perhaps it was one of the boys who played outside the house. They were a suspicious lot. Boys! You only had to think of all those quick, sly fingers whipping apples off the stalls in Covent Garden. On the other hand, getting into his studio was not easy. And, anyway, he would have surely noticed a boy with a canvas under his arm!

But it made him that much keener not to have boys anywhere near the place. And that included – what was his name? – the one Jane mentioned. When they were talking about Miss Hyssop.

'His name's Flea,' said Jane. 'I thought you might know him. Miss Hyssop's young ward. He's a familiar figure around the Piazza. I remember him from when he was a child. A scrawny boy, if truth be told. He used to sit and watch the stallholders for hours. "That's Miss Hyssop's Flea," they'd say. "He's a remarkably curious young lad." I'm sure you must have seen him. Thin face, lank hair.'

William thought one troublesome boy looked much like another.

'Flea!' he said, almost spitting out the word. 'What sort of name is *that*?'

If he needed any additional proof of the ne'er-do-wellness of boys in general, then such a name most certainly did the job. Fleas were small, dirty parasites – as everyone, including his wife, must know.

'It's a shortening of Fleabane,' said Jane. 'A flower. When you think of it, Fleabane's rather a fitting name for someone living in Covent Garden. To be named after a plant, I mean. Fleabane. Hyssop. All so … appropriate.'

She smiled. It had not occurred to her before, but now the notion had entered her head she was quite taken with it. She tried to think if she knew anyone else in the Piazza whose name was like a plant. There was Jeremiah Potts, of course. But that was stretching a point.

'Quite a few have more in common with vegetables,' grunted William.

Oh, so he *was* listening, she thought.

'One of the boys who picks over the waste outside the Bedford Arms Tavern,' he went on. 'He has a head like a turnip. And there's another one with orange skin. He could pass as a carrot.'

Jane did not want to encourage him. He could go on like this for hours.

'I don't think you can compare Master Fleabane with *those* boys,' she said. 'The scavenging types.'

'Oh, it's *Master* Fleabane now, is it?' he snorted. 'Well, he's still a boy. And they're all the same.'

Jane thought it a pity. Master Fleabane was clearly someone the reserved Miss Hyssop took considerable care of. Yes, there were those who whispered around the Piazza that he was her bastard child. But Jane had always accepted the more generous view. The one that regarded the young man's presence in Miss Hyssop's house as a very visible witness to her Christian charity. Certainly, for one reason or another, the two of them were clearly attached to each other. So it seemed a shame to exclude him. Young Flea might have found a visit to the studio both inspiring and educational.

But no, there was nothing to be gained by pushing the point. William would not change his mind. He was not going to let Master Fleabane anywhere near that painting.

Unless …

Jane smiled at her husband, and it unnerved him.

'What?' he said. '*Now* what!'

She had had an idea.

'No, you're right, of course,' she said. 'There's no reason why the boy should come to the studio. No reason at all.'

She paused and then muttered again, quietly to herself, 'No reason at all.'

'Mind you,' she then said aloud. 'You could always put *him* in the picture as well.'

He looked at her suspiciously.

'Following his mistress,' she added.

He looked at the painting and then back at Jane, screwing up his face. But he said nothing. Instead, he moved to the corner of the studio and began rummaging through a mound of soiled rags in a way that suggested the conversation was over.

Jane waited a few moments. When it was clear he had nothing more to say, she shrugged her shoulders and left him in peace.

Out of the corner of his eye he watched her go. Then he wiped his hands on one of the rags and went back to look at the painting again.

Yes, he thought. It would certainly add to the overall composition.

A scrawny youth would create another contrast with the central figure. William was not going to admit it to Jane, but he had seen a young man trailing round after Miss Hyssop. It was an afternoon when he had been secretly sketching her from the shadows of the arcade. Of course, he could not be sure that the boy attended her on her early morning visits to church. But what did that matter? William was an artist. He could do what he liked. He could make it *all* up if he wanted to.

In fact, he would not even need to be precise about capturing the boy's features. Almost *any* skinny, down-at-heel depiction would create the contrast. After all, this was not real life. And it did not need to be correct in every detail. It was Art. And Art could be true in all sorts of different ways. The main thing was to make the image *work*.

So, yes, it was definitely a good idea to include the boy. He was glad he had thought of it.

§

My first real awakening from childhood occurred when I was fourteen. It was the year in which the old Queen died, and the Elector of Hanover became King George I of Great Britain. Until then I would usually leave the house only in the company of my great-aunt or Miss Greatorex, who was appointed to be my tutor and companion. There was a housemaid, Ruth, and another maid whose name was Ellen. She was a serious-minded young woman, well-suited to a house presided over by my great-aunt. There was also a cook, Mrs Sanders, who seemed to live only in the kitchen.

Every day I attended church with my great-aunt and Miss Greatorex. I would then sometimes be allowed to accompany Ellen, whose duties included buying fruit and vegetables in the marketplace for Mrs Sanders. It was not an adventurous existence and was very different to the lives of the other young people I saw in the Piazza and watched from the windows of the house.

I was largely content at home, applying myself to the tasks Miss Greatorex set me to do, and conversing with her on subjects as diverse as the Thirty-Nine Articles and expeditions to the Indies. When I was not engaged in such pursuits there would always be needlework that required my attention. Occasionally Miss Greatorex would take me to visit places of interest in the wider city. These were often churches, but also included other sites of historical significance. I remember most particularly a visit to the Tower of London and seeing the menagerie there.

My dearest love was to read. I spent as much time

as I could perusing books that were either part of my great-aunt's small library or that were lent to me by Miss Greatorex. Many of these were of a religious nature, but there was also poetry. Miss Greatorex was an admirer of Mr Dryden and said she had once seen him when she had been much younger, and he was still alive, which made me wish to know his works better.

It was shortly before Queen Anne departed this earth that I was given leave to roam alone, although this was most often only to buy provisions in the market on days when Ellen was indisposed. She was never a happy or talkative soul when we shopped together and so I was pleased to be free of her. On my own I had leisure to observe more closely the wonders of the Piazza and found much joy and entertainment in what I saw. I was entranced by the variety of activities, so many of which seemed not to be related to the selling of goods. The old women smoked and shouted at each other about the people they knew. The porters competed in shows of strength, and sometimes fought (which I did not like to watch). The boys who worked there played at football.

It was in my wandering thus through the space of the market that I first saw Sam.

§

When he finally sat down with Jane to eat a pie he was still glowing with the creativity of the notion.

'I've decided to put that Flea boy in the picture,' he said with his mouth full. 'I've sketched him in already – tramping along behind his mistress.'

She stared back at him, a slight smile on her face.

'Have you?' she said.

She very consciously did not say, 'I'm so pleased I suggested it'. She simply added, 'Yes, that's a good idea. More pie?'

There were some things not worth protesting about. One of them was his table manners – or lack of them. Another was the all-encompassing nature of his genius that drew every good idea into its own orbit. It was not that Jane undervalued her own considerable contribution to the partnership. But she had a subtler means of playing her role in the way things got done. And she did not have an ego that needed constantly to be stroked.

Seeing, however, that he had brought the subject up, it was as good a time as any to revert to the central issue.

'So do you think you *will* invite Miss Hyssop. To view the painting?'

He continued chewing in near silence. Either he was being very thoughtful, or the chunks of veal and ham were proving a challenge. Jane decided to add the usual dose of flattery, managing to keep the hint of sarcasm at a level he would not notice.

'It'll be one more demonstration of your great artistic sensitivity,' she said.

He scowled back at her – but she knew the look. His version of self-conscious embarrassment. As usual, he had taken her at her word.

'What if she doesn't like it?' he said, spraying food over the table.

Jane knew it was a distinct possibility. But she hoped

Miss Hyssop would have the good sense to be discreet and diplomatic.

'She doesn't have to like it,' she said. 'The courtesy you're paying her is to let her know, in advance, that she's been the inspiration for the ... form of the lady in the painting.'

He made some noises in his throat that she decided to interpret as agreement. He was still not convinced there was any advantage to be gained by sharing the image at such an early stage. But it occurred to him that there could be some benefit in viewing the lady in his studio. There might be things about her that could only be observed at close quarters. Things that might prove useful. In the painting, perhaps, it did not matter quite so much. The flow of the brushwork and the texture of the oil paints blurred some of the facial characteristics. But in creating the engraving it would be important to render the finer features with more sharpness. He could watch her while she perused the canvas and then make additional sketches once she had left. Those he had been able to do in the secrecy of the Piazza arcades had given him a good basis for her image overall. But they were, well ... sketchy.

And, yes, of course – there would also be some risks in meeting her.

After all these years.

She might remember.

After all, *he* had.

It made him pause.

He was weighing up the pros and cons.

'You're not suggesting,' he said, 'that I go and invite her myself, are you?'

He sounded worried, she thought. Oddly so. But at least it suggested a willingness to accept her plan. And it was also an indication that he wanted his wife to have a continuing role in how it would play out.

'Would you like *me* to ask her?' she said.

He snorted. Again, agreement. Of a sort.

'Not the boy,' he said.

Once more Jane went through her usual thought process. There was what she wanted to say. And there was what she actually said – based on her deep experience and knowledge of her husband.

What she wanted to say was:

'Even though you're now including him in the painting?'

What she actually said was simply a repetition of his words:

'Not the boy.'

And that was that.

Now she could turn her thoughts to how she would manage the matter. How and when she would seek a meeting with Miss Hyssop – which might prove to be of some considerable interest. How she would manage the viewing itself, such that William was not inconvenienced. And how the whole thing might be carried off in a way that would achieve her own ambitions of furthering neighbourly courtesies without adding fuel to the fire of her husband's prejudices. The undertaking was not, she knew, without its challenges. But she became more adept at navigating these sorts of situations as every day passed. All in all, she was feeling pleased with herself. Managing William was not always easy, but it never lacked interest.

She stared across the table at her life partner with a mixture of admiration and toleration. He was not wearing his usual soft cap, so his short bristly hair stood up all over his head. His piggy face was unshaven. There was a trickle of gravy on his chin. He had just removed a piece of chewed gristle from his mouth and put it on the table next to his tankard. Certainly, it was not the most genteel of dinner scenes, but she had taken him on freely. Her parents had thought her mad. But even they had to admit, in the end, that he was something of a one-off. No doubt he would finish his meal and then escape to meet up with the regular crowd at the Bedford Arms in the Piazza.

She meanwhile could retire to her parlour to plot how and when she might engage with the enigmatic figure of Miss Hyssop.

§

Smallow was in two minds about the deal that had been struck.

On the one hand he was sore and not a little intimidated by the fact that Sir Marmaduke Ransome held him personally responsible for his latest dose of clap. Yes, it was true that Smallow had introduced him to Kitty Smith in Tom King's. But that was months ago. He had enjoyed Kitty several times himself – hence his recommendation to the baronet – but suffered nothing other than a minor irritation. And even that cleared up after two weeks of abstinence.

But then he had trained himself to use one of those confounded condoms. Marketed as 'fine leather', they were actually made of sheep's guts – and were clearly not to everyone's taste. Someone like Ransome would probably regard them as unmanly. Smallow also suspected the baronet lacked the manual dexterity to tie the ribbons that kept the thing in place. Certainly after a glass or three.

No, Ransome's assertion was just a means of strengthening his bargaining position. A bargain that was not completely one-sided, of course. For, as Smallow knew, he would be well placed to gain additional business from the arrangement. In the longer term. If everything went according to plan. All being well, it should open several more doors in the wealthy West End of town. And not before time too.

For as an artist Smallow was not enjoying the success he felt his due. Courtesy of his father's liberality he had no financial concerns. But that was not the point. Smallow wanted to be appreciated. He wanted to be recognised. He wanted an eager public beating a path to his door. But the world was so unfair.

Look at that wretch, Hogarth. He had hardly more talent than a sign-writer. An engraver, for pity's sake. And not even a proper engraver at that. He only painted pictures in order to sell his prints. Yet the world could not get enough of Mr Fucking Hogarth. While he, Jonathan Smallow, gentleman painter, was ignored.

Why?

Why on earth was the world so slow to appreciate his attributes as both a painter and a gentleman? You only had to see him to know he was a man of quality. Look at those clothes. That wig. The cleanliness and smoothness of his skin. Surely all those things should count – especially when it came to winning lucrative commissions from well-heeled and noble patrons.

What could Mr Fucking Hogarth offer that could come close? Ugly. Uncouth. Slovenly. And with the manners of a pig. A man who made his money by selling pieces of paper to tradesmen. Yet there were *still* those who wanted him to paint their portraits. It beggared belief!

And, as if the man's unwarranted success were not enough, there was the other thing. The fact the so-called tavern wits thought it such a joke. Ho bloody ho! Such a joke to pretend that they were always confusing the two men. The cur William Hogarth and the gentleman Jonathan Smallow.

'Well, you're both so alike! You're both so short, loud, and full of your own importance. It really is just *TOO* difficult to tell the two of you apart!'

Ho fucking ho!

As if there could really be any mistaking them. One, dishevelled, unshaven, dirty, and crude. The other, a sophisticated man about town. They were poles apart.

So, yes, the world was not only unfair. It was blind. And cruel as well.

It was hardly surprising then that Jonathan Smallow hated William Hogarth with a passion. It was of some comfort to him, of course, to know he was not the *only* person to loath the boorish and cocky engraver. Smallow always derived pleasure from finding someone – *anyone* –

who would join him in vilifying the Hog for the price of a drink.

Rock was an ally in that respect and could be relied upon to say any number of nasty things. It was a store of venom first released when Hogarth ridiculed the complacent Rock four years before. Plate 5 of *A Harlot's Progress* had shown the doctor as a fat, callous quack overseeing the final decline of Moll Hackabout. But there were others who detested the Hog as well. The oaf had been quick to poke fun at people – and quick to make enemies too. If something terrible happened to the great Mr William Hogarth one dark night on his way home from the Bedford Arms, there would be no lack of smiles at his misfortune.

The thoughts gnawed away at Smallow and he began to mutter to himself.

'Nothing can, nor shall, content my soul till I am even with him.'

But then he caught himself speaking aloud and stopped abruptly. Away with such uncontrolled outbursts! Anyone would think he was going mad!

He needed to keep his head.

For there were more pressing matters at hand. And the deal negotiated with Sir Marmaduke Ransome was the most pressing of the lot.

Yes, Ransome had used a combination of threat and innuendo to get the price down to what was a barely acceptable fee, given the scale of the task. But, as Smallow kept telling himself, it would at least provide a route into West End Society. A suitably aristocratic setting within which his talent could be viewed by other potential purchasers.

And, yes, it was a great deal of work.

A whole series of portraits including those of both Ransome and his new wife. Not to mention the additional landscapes. And not much time in which to do them all.

But Smallow was nothing if not a man of ingenuity and pragmatism. Much of the work was being done by assistants for next to nothing. The rest he would knock out in a style that, given the circumstances, would be 'good enough'. The key thing was to have at least one picture that stood out above the rest. One painting that he could point to as a prime example of his true value. Something that could function as his calling card. An image that would be guaranteed to appeal to his new prospective patrons.

But what should it be?

As his thoughts turned back to his ever-present sense of injustice, he began to glimpse a solution. A chance to kill two birds with one stone. And, as the idea became clearer in his mind, the frown on his face changed to a smile.

§

Belinda, Lady Ransome, stared at the largely blank walls.

It would only be a matter of time before they were full of new works of art, including her own portrait. She could hardly contain herself. And, indeed, the dress she was wearing looked as if it too was struggling to contain her. Especially as she continued to puff out her bosom in a proud and magisterial way.

But she would need to be patient. Just as she would also need to be patient – if that was the word – with her husband. Patience was, after all, a virtue. And, heaven knows, the house could do with some virtue.

Sir Marmaduke was living up to the worst side of his reputation in more ways than Belinda had anticipated. She had hardly seen him since the day of the wedding two months before. He inhabited a world entirely separate to her own. When they *did* meet it was usually by chance. The unhappy coincidence of her returning from a supper engagement just as he was leaving the house for an all-night gaming session. He would invariably return from such expeditions as she was rising for a late breakfast. Then he would slide away to his room to sleep off some of his excesses. They had not shared a bed together since their wedding night, when he had been carried unconscious to the marital chamber. Once there he managed to do no more than emit a variety of unpleasant sounds and smells that rendered the air unbreathable.

Belinda tried to convince herself that the separate nature of their lives was for the best. It was now very clear that their interests overlapped in no degree whatsoever. She had viewed the marriage as something that would allow her entry into the hallowed halls of what the world termed 'Society'. He, on the other hand, entered into the partnership with the sole aim of spending even more time drinking, gaming and whoring. The money provided by his wife's father would erase his substantial debts and permit him to embark on a whole new series of precarious adventures.

But there was also the matter of Sir Marmaduke's sexual infidelities. Belinda had not been so naïve as to expect her husband to devote himself entirely to the love of his wife. But she had hoped for some moderation in his conduct. That he might choose his mistresses with discretion and an appropriate respect for her own sensibilities. Such hopes, however, were soon dashed. She hardly needed to hear the town gossip or read the telling expressions on the faces of the servants to know what was going on. It was clear that Sir Marmaduke's appetite was being constantly satisfied by the wide range of strumpets he encountered during his nightly odysseys around Covent Garden.

When Belinda lived with her father, she had been all too aware of the Piazza's darker side. Yes, there were still a few respectable residents there. Her old friend, Prudence Hyssop, was one. But the place had been going downhill for a number of years. And now, having finally made her way into the noble district of St James's, she had lost her husband to the same Covent Garden she had been most happy to escape.

It was all very galling. But it also made her glad that Sir Marmaduke had offered no attempt to consummate their union. For all that she wished to be married in more than name, she shuddered at the thought of her husband's advances. Instead she filled her mind with matters of more importance. The chief of these was her ambition to establish a home that might be seen as a model of good taste and artistic style.

Over the fireplace in the drawing-room hung a French mirror. It was one of the few things of quality to have arrived from Sir Marmaduke's country estate. She gazed into it, admiring the lines of her figure and face that were so handsomely delineated in the soft candlelight. As she did so she imagined how her portrait would look when it was finally hung in the same room. It would surely be the crowning glory of all the new pictures commissioned to transform the house into a temple of splendour and refinement.

But, again, she would need to be patient. Her husband's choice of painter, Mr Jonathan Smallow, had not yet sought an audience with a view to a first sitting. The process for capturing her likeness was not even underway.

She breathed deeply, trying to calm the fears that were beginning to rise in her breast. There was so much going on. So much she wanted to share. But she was feeling very alone. And there was almost no one to whom she could reveal her innermost thoughts.

She looked at her reflection again. What should she say? Which of her friends would listen? Would any of them care enough?

There was only one name that came into her head.

Prudence Hyssop.

§

It had been decided that Jane should call upon Miss Hyssop to invite her to visit the studio at the sign of the golden head.

In saying 'it had been decided', it should be understood that the planning was done by Mrs Hogarth. Whilst her husband made no further objection to what had been agreed, he took no part in bringing it to fruition.

Jane first sent her card and received, within two hours, a hand-written note conveyed by Master Fleabane. Written, so Jane assumed, in Miss Hyssop's own small, neat hand, it said: 'Prudence Hyssop would be delighted to receive Mrs Jane Hogarth at any time tomorrow forenoon.'

On arriving at the house Jane was shown upstairs. The drawing-room was lit only by the weak light of a damp, grey morning that strained to penetrate past high and heavy-curtained windows. Jane noted the dark, wood-panelled walls. She guessed that the room probably retained the same sombre appearance even during the summer, when the north side of the Piazza was burnished with sunlight.

The décor was in keeping with the wood panelling and what Jane imagined to be its owner's old-fashioned character. It appeared to be of a type that was at least thirty years out of date. As Jane's eyes accustomed themselves to the gloom, she could see that the rugs were well worn, the hangings faded, and the upholstery muted by age. There was nevertheless an air of quiet harmony about the whole. As if the room were saying, 'You must take me as you find me.' In that respect the surroundings were in keeping with Miss Hyssop herself. The lady rose from a chair by the fireplace to greet Jane with a smile that transformed her long, naturally dour expression into a genuine show of welcome.

'Mrs Hogarth,' she said. 'You do me an honour. Indeed, you do.'

And from that moment Jane knew that she liked Miss Hyssop.

The only question that formed in her mind was not about Miss Hyssop herself, but why it had taken so long. 'How is it that I lived in the Piazza for as many years as I did and was not introduced to her?', thought Jane. But then, she quickly reflected, perhaps it was not so unusual. This was London after all. It was not a country town where everybody knew everyone else. Where one could do nothing without it being a subject of conversation for every other resident. Moreover, this was Covent Garden. With its constant hubbub and continuous flow of people in and out. The Piazza respected discretion and privacy as much as it celebrated intimacy and excess. It was at the same time the most transparent of places and the most secretive. That was a large part of its appeal and an important aspect of its constant ambiguity. Nothing could be taken for granted in Covent Garden. And nothing could be judged by its appearance. It was a feature of the place evident to any visitor. But it took longer to develop the special empathy and accommodating spirit needed to navigate a path through the mix. Years, some would say. In that respect Miss Hyssop had a distinct advantage over most of those who called the Piazza their home.

Jane was doubly glad of the friendly welcome as it meant she did not have to embark immediately on the essence of her message. It was something that had exercised her mind for much of the previous night. How exactly might she raise the subject? What should she say – and not say? How explicit could she be about the painting?

And what role should she give William in the whole affair? So she was relieved to spend the first few minutes engaged in an exchange of pleasantries. It was the sort of small talk that ranged from the marketplace to the weather – including the merits of wearing pattens to protect against the slush and mud that was a hazard in all but the driest months.

By the time Jane turned the conversation onto the reason for her call, she was feeling more confident. Mr Hogarth's gruffness was surely as well-known as his talents, and Miss Hyssop had already shown clear signs of being a sensitive soul.

'My husband has asked me to speak for him,' said Jane. 'He hopes you will not be offended by that.'

Miss Hyssop intimated that she could not conceive of ever being offended by what Mr Hogarth might wish to say. She stated more explicitly, however, that it was a particular pleasure to meet *Mrs* Hogarth, about whom she had heard only the most praiseworthy reports.

Jane smiled and Miss Hyssop smiled back. There was a sense in which they were already sharing a common language. It was a way of communicating that delighted in being a distinct counter to the male vernacular that was constantly brayed around the Piazza. It encapsulated a joint understanding that said: 'We both know that we are much more likely to have an enlightening conversation without any interference from the male of the species – even an example as eminent as Mr Hogarth.'

Jane began to wonder if Miss Hyssop's status as a spinster was in any way related to such a philosophical outlook. But she quickly put those thoughts to one side. There would, she hoped, be time later for such speculation. For now, she needed to focus on the purpose of her visit and invite Miss Hyssop to view the painting in her husband's studio. There was still, however, the question of how exactly to do that. She had debated with herself whether to tackle the subject head-on or come at it more obliquely. The friendly reception encouraged a more direct approach.

§

Dr Rock's premises were located off Ludgate Hill, near St Paul's Cathedral in the City of London.

The building was about a mile from Covent Garden and Smallow made the journey on foot through the labyrinth of lanes that lay to the east of the Piazza. This route took him over the River Fleet, notorious for its filth and muck. It was in effect an open sewer, carrying away much of the detritus from the cattle market at Smithfield. Plans were in hand to cover the stretch of river from Holborn to Ludgate, but work had not yet begun. Negotiating a path through the mire was therefore something of a challenge. Smallow was beginning to wish he had taken the more obvious course eastwards along the Strand.

He was also still chafing at having been coerced into acting as a courier for his difficult and demanding client, Sir Marmaduke Ransome. He did his best to persuade himself that he was actually a close confidante of the baronet. As such, he was doing no more than might be expected of someone who enjoyed such a privileged position.

Rock was waiting for him and had already prepared a package that he hoped would suffice. It was a small phial of the Very Special Cathartic Venereal Electuary, to be administered orally in small doses over a number of days. He was therefore surprised when the smooth and shiny Mr Smallow informed him of a change of plan.

'Sir Marmaduke only told me last night,' he said. 'As we were sharing a last glass of Madeira together.'

Rock raised an eyebrow.

'But the amount you are now talking about, Mr Smallow, would constitute more than six times the dosage I assumed Sir Marmaduke would require,' he said.

'I daresay it would,' said Smallow. He contrived to look as if the change were just one more expression of the baronet's eccentric and off-hand manner. 'But that's how much he wants. I think he intends giving it to several of his gaming friends in lieu of some of the money he owes them. It shouldn't surprise us that Sir Marmaduke's companions are usually afflicted with the same troubles as himself!'

He made the last declaration with a conspiratorial wink. It said: 'We are all men of the world, my friend – and I'm sure you will not be sorry to see your remedies promoted by someone as well connected as Sir Marmaduke.'

This time Rock raised both eyebrows and took a deep breath. It gave him the appearance of having been inflated beyond the limits of his already prodigious girth.

'But the cost, Mr Smallow,' he said. 'It will clearly be considerably more than what Sir Marmaduke has been good enough to pay in advance. *Considerably* more. Especially as this is a particularly efficacious mixture.'

Smallow had a look of calm complacency on his smooth and shiny face.

'I'm sure I don't need to tell you, good doctor,' he said, 'that such a matter is hardly likely to be a consideration for one as … how might I put it? … as generous and well-endowed as Sir Marmaduke. You are to put the entire figure on his account, and it will be settled with you in due course – as I'm sure is always the case.'

This time Rock looked at him through narrow, suspicious eyes. He much preferred cash in hand. Critics might brand him as no more than a shopkeeper or hawker of recipes, but he knew the value of hard money. There were very few customers with whom he dealt on account. And he had good reason for regarding Sir Marmaduke Ransome as a less than attractive debtor. But to refuse such a proposition risked an even greater negative. The baronet had a mean, vindictive and violent nature. He was not someone with whom Rock wanted to cross swords, even figuratively. He would rather have what might pass as Ransome's good will, as well as his good word amongst like-minded colleagues.

After a few further ruminations, therefore, he decided to comply with Sir Marmaduke's wishes. As he retired briefly to the back room of the premises to muster the additional phials, he hoped he would not live to regret the day his munificence got the better of his good sense.

Meanwhile Smallow looked around the front of the shop and at the range of tinctures and potions that lined the shelves. A goodly selection indeed. And all so readily available. His smirk became a smile, transforming his assumed manly and knowing look into the face of an overgrown infant who was pleased with his own cleverness.

§

Jane adopted her most intimate tone of voice.

'The truth is,' she said, 'William has painted a picture of Covent Garden. And he has included a representation of a woman on her way to church. A representation based on your own good self.'

She paused. That was surely enough. At least to begin with. To see what sort of reaction those few – perhaps startling – words might elicit.

The expression on Miss Hyssop's face was not easy to read. It seemed wistful rather than surprised or offended. But perhaps that was just her way of being polite. Jane decided to press on.

'I believe he has become familiar with your great knowledge and experience of the place and has used it as inspiration for his latest painting – which shows the Piazza in the early morning.'

'How flattering,' said Miss Hyssop.

It was said in a way that suggested she thought it a fitting and proper response. Jane pursed her lips and bit back the urge to say: 'Flattering it is *not*!' Instead, she continued her attempt to navigate a way through the challenges.

'I hope you may forgive him for taking such a liberty,' she said.

She stopped again. It was a long enough pause, she hoped, to suggest that forgiving the taking of liberties was all part and parcel of dealing with Mr Hogarth.

'Sometimes his art blinds him to other considerations,' she went on. 'I'm sure he did not wish to cause offence by using you as a model without your express permission.'

Miss Hyssop smiled. And this time the expression seemed a reflection of what she was feeling rather than what might be expected.

'I can assure you, Mrs Hogarth, I have taken no offence.'

But you have not yet seen the picture, thought Jane!

'I am sure,' continued Miss Hyssop, 'that your husband's talents are focused on things of much greater import than the depiction of a former neighbour. He is, after all, renowned for using particularities to draw out more general themes. The *Harlot's* and *Rake's Progresses* are, in that respect, so much more about the ills of our society than they are about either Moll Hackabout or Tom Rakewell, let alone the individuals upon whom they may have originally been based.'

Jane was impressed. It was a remark which showed that Miss Hyssop was not only familiar with Mr Hogarth's works, but that she also had a distinct point of view as to their artistic purpose. Some people saw the images as simple knockabout humour. Others regarded them as serious moral statements. Jane, of course, knew better – but she was not used to encountering sympathetic observers with a similar cast of mind.

'I'm glad you take such an enlightened view,' she said.

'And your comments have quite rightly brought me back to my primary purpose in calling on you. Which is – on behalf of my husband – to invite you to view the painting. A private viewing before the picture is seen by anyone else. While it is still being worked on, in fact.'

Miss Hyssop's eyes widened. She was familiar enough with Mr Hogarth's method of working to know that the creation of his paintings was usually shrouded in secrecy. Despite the provisions of the previous year's Copyright Act piracies were still rife. Unscrupulous copyists were always looking to steal a march on the production of the official prints. A common practice was plagiarism-by-memory – the copying of an image after the original had been no more than glimpsed in the artist's studio. The combined visual memory and ingenuity of such pirates meant that William always kept his paintings away from public gaze until the last possible moment.

Jane interpreted the wide-eyed look more straightforwardly. A sign that Miss Hyssop felt personally honoured by the invitation. Not that this slight difference of perspective mattered. The result was the same. The ladies expressed their mutual delight that the proposal should have been so thoughtfully proffered – and so graciously accepted. The appointed time for the artistic viewing was eagerly set for the very next day.

There then followed much polite conversation that extended the visit for considerably longer than the simple issuing and acceptance of an invitation. But it was evident that both women already felt something of a bond. And that they were keen to learn more of each other. It was as if the artist himself – by virtue of his absence in all but spirit – had become a positive encouragement for a more feminine and subtle exchange of views. Which was, after all, exactly what Jane had intended.

§

To begin with, Sam Harris was not the sort of young man my great-aunt would have wished me to know. She was, however, less inclined to disapprove than I might have imagined. I believe it may have been because she was losing interest in me. I am now also of a mind to think that she was losing interest in everything else as well. Certainly, she began to be forgetful, even, one day, seeming not to know my name.

Sam was near the same age as I. He was willowy of build but remarkably strong. He carried large baskets of cabbages as if they were nothing at all. But, by virtue of his many guises around the Piazza, he also seemed to be a spirit of the place and not a person of flesh and blood.

When first I knew him he laboured in the vegetable market in the mornings and served in a coffee-house during the evenings. But all that was changed by Mr Tremisgus, an art dealer who lived some few doors from my great aunt's house. Mr Tremisgus saw in Sam someone who might help him in the capacity of a general factotum, and Sam was pleased to change his market and coffee-house duties for a role that everyone regarded as something of an elevation.

Suffice to say that my great aunt felt Sam's change of status of sufficient merit to allow my friendship with him to be condoned, if not exactly welcomed. She maintained until the end a suspicion of what she considered to be Sam's more earthy associations, most particularly as he lived with a woman called Mrs Sparker, who let rooms in her property across the way from my great-aunt's house, and who had a reputation as something of a procuress. It is the same building that is now home to Mr and Mrs Alcazar as well as Jeremiah Potts.

Sam often said things that I found to be very wise even though he had little learning. When I had remarked that he was like a ghost and a spirit of the place, he said it was to his liking, for it made him feel he could be everywhere and nowhere at the same time. Just so long as he could be a strong ghost and not just a thing of the air.

I remember that he said this to me after we had been visiting the church. In those days I sometimes took him into St Paul's Church in the Piazza where we could sit undisturbed by the noises outside. Mr Crum, in those years the verger, did at first greet us with a frown, for although he knew me well, he could not be pleased that Sam was dressed in market clothes. However, after Sam began working for Mr Tremisgus, and was known for an upright soul, Mr Crum was more condescending.

And so it was that I told Sam as much as I thought I could, or as much as I thought he would wish to know, about the Holy Trinity and also St Paul, for whom the church was named. Sam said that his favourite of them all was the Holy Ghost, whom he did regard as altogether more mysterious and powerful than any Father or Son could ever be.

At this time, we were likely fourteen or fifteen years of age, and our understanding was changing from that of children into something else entire. Everything seemed new and exciting, and I had never known myself to be so happy. Sam helped me to see the world afresh. For though I had wandered through Covent Garden on so many days and stared at it from the windows of my great-aunt's house, I had never known the Piazza in the way that Sam knew it. One of his greatest gifts to me was to allow me to see it through his eyes. Through the eyes of a ghost that can go everywhere and see everything.

All the characters he had known in the market and coffee-house were still friends to him, and the work he did for Mr Tremisgus took him into the company of even more divers people and places. He would show me things I had seen a hundred times before, but with Sam I saw them anew. Whether it was the porters balancing baskets on their heads, or the gentlemen who stumbled along the Piazza arcades, too taken with drink to pursue a straight path. Or the genteel folk who promenaded to and fro, more diverted by the way their clothes glistened in the sunlight than they were entranced by the flowers and fruit that hemmed them in on all sides. The pictures in Mr Tremisgus's gallery, and the visitors who came there to nod their heads in a knowing manner. Engravings in print-shop windows. All these things seemed so full of life, and laughter too, when I witnessed them with Sam.

Did I love him? Yes, I did most certainly, in so far as I was able to love anyone, or know what love was. And did he love me also? I feel sure that he did. But then Sam was, in some way or other, in love with a great many things without really knowing why. He was a wonderful person. And I was heartbroken when I lost him.

§

The next day Prudence called at the sign of the golden head with some trepidation.

Jane received her with a wide smile and shepherded her up to a first-floor parlour and a cup of chocolate. It was only after they had refreshed themselves – and passed comment on everything from the colour of carrots to the charming design of a chinaware vase – that Jane conducted her guest down to William's studio. She was very pleased with this arrangement. It meant she could introduce Miss Hyssop into her husband's presence as something of a new friend. She hoped such a stratagem might discourage the show of grumpiness he often exhibited when she interrupted his work.

She also decided to remain in the room for as long as Miss Hyssop was there. She hoped that her presence would ensure that the encounter was managed with maximum politeness and minimum curmudgeonly behaviour on William's part. She had even been contemplating whether to suggest to Miss Hyssop that the two women should be on first name terms. That might, however, be a little premature. Better first to gauge her guest's reaction to the painting. Jane was hopeful that the following minutes might reinforce the basis for a closer friendship. But she was acutely conscious that it might also provoke a more frosty response. Let us wait and see, she thought. There will be time for familiarity later, if circumstances permit.

When they entered the studio William had his back to them. He was mixing something in a bowl on a side table. Miss Hyssop's eyes went from the artist's back to the painting, which stood on an easel in the middle of the room. Jane quickly glanced in her direction, but Miss Hyssop's expression showed no great reaction. Her countenance remained calm. But was she biting her lip?

At the sound of their entry – supplemented by a small cough from Jane – William turned around. There was a definite pinkness about his jowls, presumably brought on by the mixing. But otherwise it was a face that conveyed only deep concentration. His brow was furrowed, perhaps because he was focusing his mind on what was to follow, rather than because he had been interrupted. He did, after all, know the hour of the visit. His wife had made a point of reminding him – twice – that morning.

Jane immediately took on the role of hostess, adopting a formal tone that seemed slightly out-of-place in the chaotic surroundings of the studio.

'William, I should like to introduce to you Miss Hyssop of Covent Garden Piazza,' she said. 'Miss Hyssop, my husband – William Hogarth, the painter.'

As she said it her face also took on something of a pink hue, as if she had just become aware herself of how stilted her words sounded. Any embarrassment, however, was quickly replaced by genuine surprise as her husband stepped forward – not with a frown, but with a coy smile on his face. He held out his hand, having just wiped it on a dubious rag.

'Miss Prudence,' he said quietly. 'It's been a long time.'

§

There was the merest glimmer of sunlight.

It was just enough to silver the edges of the dark clouds that gathered above the Piazza. Flea had bought the items Miss Hyssop had sent him to purchase and was now passing the time of day by watching the world go by.

One of the stallholders in the marketplace had given him an apple. He munched it contentedly as he sat on an upturned basket at the edge of Tavistock Row. It was an excellent vantage point from which to notice things on the south side of the Piazza, where his attention was drawn, once again, to one particular building. The house of the highwayman and the Vampyre, not to mention Mr Alcazar and Jeremiah Potts. It was a place that always seemed to provide Flea with some degree of interest.

First, he saw the old highwayman and his moll very slowly leaving the building for their daily walk. They were easy to notice, as the highwayman was constantly shouting questions into the woman's ear.

'Which way?' 'What do we need?' 'Do you want carrots?' 'No, not *faggots*. CARROTS!'

It was certainly a rum way to carry on if you were trying to avoid detection by the authorities. Surely it was only a matter of time before the highwayman was caught and dragged away to be hanged. Which would be hard on his moll, Flea thought.

Moments later Flea saw Jeremiah rush into the building. Under his arm he held something square. Probably a canvas for painting. When he left again, after no more than a few minutes, he was carrying nothing.

There was, however, no time to ruminate on Jeremiah's coming and going, because almost immediately something of much greater moment occurred. The door to the building opened and two bare-headed, grey-haired men made their way out and across the space that led into the Piazza. They were carrying a small coffin.

Behind the coffin came a woman, white-faced and leaning on the arm of a swarthy man whose bent shoulders told a tale of loss. Flea knew only too well who they were. The news had spread around the Piazza two days before that Mr Alcazar, the painter, and his wife had lost another of their children. It was their second – or was it the third? – such loss in not much more than a year. Flea could not help feeling that such a pattern, though not unusual, was surely unfair. It was not as if children could look after themselves. And there were so many things waiting to knock them down. Flea felt sad for it and was quietly thankful that Miss Hyssop had kept him safe and alive.

The few members of the small funeral party composed themselves before setting off towards the church at the far end of the square. As they made their sorry way past the market workers and shoppers, several men stopped what they were doing and took off their hats. There was no pause in the general activity that marked out the centre of the market space. But as word of the humble cortege spread, a dull and deadening torpor fell over the place. It was only when the group had passed beyond the end of Tavistock Row that hats were replaced and something resembling the normal level of noise resumed.

It all put Flea into something of a reflective mood, and he knew that his mistress would be deeply touched to know what he had witnessed. She was out currently, visiting Mrs Hogarth in Leicester Fields. But Flea knew that someone of her compassionate nature would not leave it long before visiting Mrs Alcazar and offering what support she could. It was another example of what an angel Miss Hyssop was.

Angel? That's probably not the right word, thought Flea.

But it'll do.

§

'What do you mean, you thought it wasn't worth mentioning!'

Jane was cross with him.

'Not worth mentioning that you already *knew* her! Not worth MENTIONING!!'

Extremely cross.

It was not often that William looked sheepish, but he was certainly looking that now. Prudence Hyssop had left the house no more than a minute before. Jane waited until her guest was out of earshot before she let rip at her husband.

He picked up a brush and started to chew the end of it.

'I think "know" is something of an overstatement,' he tried, with less than his usual gusto. 'I haven't spoken to her for years. Fifteen years at least. Probably more. On the odd occasion – the *very* odd occasion – our paths have crossed we've not even acknowledged one another's presence. We're almost complete strangers.'

It was, at one level he thought, a rational response. But he could also hear how lame the words sounded. It was not yet safe to look Jane in the eye.

'Complete strangers!'

Jane's anger had nearly petered out. She was so exasperated that words failed her. She scowled at him once more. He twisted the brush into a corner of his mouth and contrived to look something between morose and contrite. Still no eye contact.

'We'll talk about this later,' said Jane.

And with that she stormed out of the studio.

William waited until she had gone, then threw the chewed brush into a corner. He slumped down on a chair, over which was draped a paint-spattered sheet. Looking up, he peered at the painting of 'Morning' once again. He should not let this little incident deter him. His art must come first. Buoyed up by this retrieved sense of purpose he narrowed his eyes and tried to survey the image with a more objective gaze. Was that enough colour? What – if anything – was missing?

But he could not focus on the picture. Not yet at any rate. His head was too full of what had just happened. So he sat back and reflected on how exactly the meeting had gone.

Once the awkwardness of the introductions had passed – and despite the barely suppressed anger of Jane – things had progressed relatively well. The conversation was, in terms of the aims set, broadly successful. Miss Hyssop did not appear to be upset by the painting. Or at least not too much. Indeed, she seemed more intrigued than offended. Yes, admittedly there had been a few awkward pauses, a couple of indeterminate 'hmmms' murmured quietly. Perhaps even a sharp intake of breath at one point.

So, yes, it cannot be denied – there had been all of *that*.

But once *that* was out of the way …

Well, no – she did not appear unhappy.

'You have included Fleabane,' she said. 'He will be delighted.'

William had screwed up his face. The fact that Flea improved the composition had not improved the artist's view of boys more generally. Jane, maintaining a hold of her temper, was keen to build on what sounded like a positive note. She felt very conscious, however, that the painting presented the youth as a rather under-nourished and shifty character.

'It is not a particularly flattering portrayal of the young man,' she said.

William glared but remained silent. Miss Hyssop smiled.

'Flea has probably never been flattered in his life, I suspect,' she said. 'And, in any case, Mr Hogarth's work is surely not about flattery.'

Jane glanced at William, and William glanced at Jane.

It's all right, his face seemed to say. She's not offended. Honest.

Jane decided to try to move the conversation onto a more chatty level.

'I am sure William would not mind if you called him William – would you, William?' she said through tight lips.

He stared at her from under a heavy brow. Miss Hyssop looked not a touch embarrassed by this implied invitation to be more intimate. Of the three of them, it was she who appeared the most relaxed.

'Thank you,' she said. 'I am very conscious of the compliment you pay me. But, if I am to proffer a humble view on the work of a great artist, it is only appropriate that I address him as Mr Hogarth.'

This had all been said to Jane as if William were not in the room. If Miss Hyssop had looked in his direction, she would have seen an expression of confusion – caught between pleasure, irritation, and bewilderment. For he sensed that it was Miss Hyssop, rather than he, who was in control of the conversation. It was not a situation he was used to, and he felt ill at ease. It also caused him to remember, once again, an affair that he had consigned to a dark corner of his memory.

An incident that had taken place some sixteen years before.

§

If death had taken Sam in 1718, I should have dealt with it better. At least then the divide would have been clear, and I should have known how to mourn. But to have him taken in the way he was, unmade me.

We knew there had been a press gang active in the area and had fallen into the trap of assuming it would focus its attentions on the most drunken and disorderly men who fell from taverns onto the streets around the Piazza. Heaven knows there were always enough of those poor souls for the predators to take their pick.

I suppose I trusted to Sam having his wits about him. But he was curious too, always on a mission to Find Stuff Out, as he would express it. And it was his curiosity that would have led to his downfall, I feel sure of that.

Of course, as things worked themselves out, I could never be sure. It was not as if anyone left a message making clear that one Samuel Harris had been removed to serve in His Majesty's naval command. There were just the rumours, and the reports of those who professed to have seen something. The picture Mrs Sparker and Mr Tremisgus were able to piece together through their many contacts was more complete than any I might have drawn on my own. But it was still unclear. And the only thing I could be sure of was the all-consuming emptiness of a life that had been so full.

§

Jane also spent time reflecting on the meeting between her husband and Miss Hyssop.

She already knew that Miss Hyssop was a thoughtful and intelligent woman. And she could see that she was not overawed by being in William's presence. She might not want to call him by any name other than Mr Hogarth, but perhaps that was just her way of keeping the artist at a discreet distance. A way of maintaining a clear distinction between herself and the image he had created.

Such discretion only heightened Jane's desire to know her better. Indeed, the revelation that she and William had already met made that prospect even more enticing. There was, after all, so much more she needed to understand. And she wanted to hear the story from both sides.

'There are a lot of names that *I* use of Mr Hogarth,' Jane had said, with the sweetest of smiles. 'And you may, of course, call him whatever you wish. But I hope you might at least call me Jane.'

'Thank you, Jane,' Miss Hyssop replied. 'I most certainly will. And you, I trust, will call me Prudence.'

'I will, Prudence,' said Jane, simpering a little. 'Thank you.'

During this interlude William shifted his feet uneasily. He looked from the women to the painting and back again. His face was grim. He had clearly been biting his tongue and now finally felt he could say something.

'So,' he interposed. 'Do you *like* it? The painting.'

The suddenness of the question caused the two women to stare at him. He stared back with a 'What!' expression on his face. '*Now* what?'

At this point Jane was still caught in a state somewhere between simpering and simmering anger, so she pursed her lips even tighter. Prudence assumed his question had been aimed at her.

'I am not altogether sure that "like" is the word,' she said.

Jane saw William's eyes widen and his nostrils dilate. That any person, other than one of his old drinking friends, could have said such a thing – especially within the inner sanctum of his studio – was, to put it mildly, a surprise. She clenched her fists, anticipating a tirade along the lines of 'well, what do *you* know about anything?' Or, even worse, a string of expletives. It was therefore with some amazement that she saw him raise his head, swallow, and pass a grubby hand over his brow. He seemed to be giving the comment an uncommon amount of consideration. His lips made several attempts at forming themselves into a shape calculated to express some words. But these efforts were pre-empted as Prudence continued to develop her theme.

'I think the painting wonderfully establishes the sort of juxtapositions that mark your images as creations of genius,' she said.

William's expression was softening noticeably. Was that a small nod? Jane maintained her stern look. She admired the fact that their visitor seemed so open and honest with William. But it was nevertheless disarming – and something of a shock – to see her husband so relatively tame.

'And there is an intriguing tension,' Prudence continued, 'between what I take to be the satirical purpose of the image and the lyrical mood created by the brilliant use of colour.'

Was that a smile on William's face? Surely not. For

here he was listening to a woman who had the temerity to offer a pronouncement upon one of his unfinished works.

'It is, of course,' Prudence went on, 'difficult to take an entirely objective view when one can see how the model of oneself has been adapted. But that point is not, I believe, central to my response to the picture. I can, I hope, appreciate the fact that the woman has to look like *someone*. But, certainly, the complexity of the concept, and the nuances of execution, take it far beyond anything I could claim simply to *like*.'

By this time William was looking more than pleased with himself. He was positively aglow. Jane thought she had never seen him this way. Other than when he was drunk, of course. Which was – now she came to think of it – quite often. But never in this kind of context. Listening to someone analysing his work in such a particular way. No, this was most definitely unprecedented.

Finally, he managed to utter a few words.

'I'm glad,' he began.

He almost said 'I'm glad you like it' but stopped himself just in time.

'I'm glad you find it so … interesting,' he said, turning away from Prudence to look at the painting again, as if seeing it afresh.

Interesting!

Interesting, thought Jane!

She could hardly believe what she was hearing. Had the man had a fit? Had the genius of creativity finally flipped over into incipient madness?

He turned back towards the women. The look on his

face suggested he was unsure as to whether or not the meeting was over. Jane saw his indecision. She would propose that she and Miss Hyssop withdraw.

Prudence, however, had not finished.

§

It seems that Sam left Mr Tremisgus's house late one night and stumbled into a group of sailors who were baiting some of the drunken rakes in the Piazza with their game of Find the Lady.

It is well known to anyone who is not drunk – or who has his wits about him – that the charade is a simple ploy designed to part a man from his money. Three playing cards are placed face down. The cull is lured into betting on which of the three is the Queen of Hearts, having seen another man, who is also a member of the gang, appear to choose correctly only seconds before. No doubt these sailors were taking the opportunity to extract a few more coins from the less able culls before departing to spend their ill-gotten gains at one of the local hostelries.

It is all too easy to understand that Sam would have been entranced by what seemed to pass as some kind of magic or special skill, and that he would have allowed himself to be drawn within the inner circle of spectators. Such gangs are known to disappear quickly into the crowds and adjacent alleyways as soon as discovery threatens. And so it happened here, when the Watch arrived to disperse the group as being a troublesome nuisance to the peace of the place.

When the sailors took to their heels, leaving just one or two of their victims to feel their empty pockets and rue the fact they had been so tempted, there was no sign of Sam. He had, it was assumed, been secreted away by those who thought they could increase their earnings for the night by turning him over to the press. It would seem that any financial gain for them would have been a mere pittance, and it is painful to think that Sam was worth no more in their eyes.

But then he was both easy prey and in his prime. Young, curious and spirited, but also clearly very able, fit and strong. All the things that made him so attractive to me were also the attributes that rendered him the perfect catch.

So it was that I saw him no more, and I was left with only the ghost of my love.

Since that day my heart has grown around the empty space where Sam once lived. And I have learned to swallow the pain, and to channel my care into other things.

§

'Of course,' Prudence continued, 'if you use the painting as the basis for an engraving, then the lyrical quality will, I suspect, be less evident in the print.'

'It *will*?'

William's first response betrayed bemusement at what she had said. But he quickly corrected his emphasis.

'It will,' he said again. But this time it sounded as if he were agreeing with a fellow connoisseur. 'Yes, it *will*! *Of course*, it will.'

'We, your admirers,' Prudence went on, 'are aware that the precision of your engraver's burin creates a different spirit to that of your painter's brush. But you, of course, will know, so much better than we, how the sharp line and detail of an engraving adds point and edge to your satirical purpose. As far as *we* are concerned, *we* have the great pleasure of receiving from you not one but two magnificent images!'

William must have looked unsure for Prudence continued to develop her theme.

'Forgive me,' she said. 'I am stating what is all too obvious – and, more than that, I am stating it to the creator himself! How foolish you must think me. Please do excuse my very clumsy words, Mr Hogarth.'

Prudence seemed genuinely abashed. But William now appeared entranced rather than simply engaged.

'No,' he said 'That is, yes. I mean, … please go on.'

Jane continued to be astounded by the conversation and her husband's apparent docility.

'You are far too indulgent of me, Mr Hogarth,' said Prudence. 'I know that you must have many important commissions awaiting your attention. But I do very much value the compliment you pay me.'

'Not at all, Miss … that is … Prudence,' said William. 'I hope I am always sensitive to what my public … that is, the discerning viewer … can see in my images.'

Jane was breathing heavily, lips tight. Prudence needed very little encouragement to continue her commentary.

'It is just that – and again please forgive me,' she went

on. 'But I believe I can already discern something of where you will use the point of your burin to such great effect.'

William was craning forward awkwardly, willing her to be more explicit.

'Like …?' he said.

'The woman herself,' said Prudence. 'Her soft lines would likely be harder and more pronounced through the precision of a print. And, as you know so much better than I, her facial expression might even convey a rather more surly and censorious spirit.'

'More censorious?'

It was Jane who had spoken, finally finding her voice. And also finding the conversation as compelling as it was bizarre.

'To heighten the contrast,' said Prudence. 'Between the relative detachment of the female figure and the self-interest of the amorous gentlemen. The sharper definition of her features would allow for a certain ambivalence to be drawn out. Is she condemning what she sees or envying it? It is in such moral ambiguities that Mr Hogarth so excels. And it is precisely what his admirers look forward to in any new work that flows from his genius.'

Once again, the words had been addressed to Jane as if William were no longer present. He was, however, still there – dumbfounded but with an expression on his face that was a mixture of surprise and pleasure.

'And you really are not offended by the image?' said Jane.

Despite Prudence's earlier disavowal, Jane did not

believe such an opinion could sit comfortably alongside her subsequent pictorial analysis.

'I cannot pretend that it was not a distinctly strange experience, Jane,' said Prudence. 'To be confronted by a figure that looks so much like oneself. But now I have become more used to it, I hope I can see it as something else entire.'

She paused. Jane and William waited.

'The painting is so beautifully executed,' Prudence continued. 'And the woman so delicately crafted. However, no one living beyond the Piazza would see in her representation anything other than one of Mr Hogarth's splendidly universal characters. No one, I feel sure, would see the figure as a particular person – let alone as *me*. I am not, I hope, unappreciative of your concern, Jane. But I think it unlikely that anyone viewing this painting – or the subsequent print – would connect such a wonderfully graphic statement of Covent Garden life with the humble individual you see before you.'

William was nodding, a broad grin on his face. He reached out for another brush to chew. Jane looked from him to Prudence, still unsure how she should react. At one level it sounded so rational – if surprising. At another level Jane felt there had to be more to this than met the eye. For there was, of course, the question of how – and for how long – William and Prudence had known each other. This was a subject she did not wish to bring up in Prudence's presence. The first step was to quiz her husband about what on earth was going on. Which was something she would do as soon as their visitor had left.

For the time had now come for her to manage Prudence's exit. Once again, however, it was Prudence herself who took the initiative.

'I must leave you,' she said. 'I have already imposed for too long upon your time and good nature. It has been the greatest privilege to see you in your studio, Mr Hogarth. And Jane, I hope that I might perhaps invite you to take tea with me sometime soon.'

There were a few more pleasantries – mainly from Jane, as William continued to nod and chew in an abstracted way. Then Prudence made her way out of the room, leaving the merest trace of old-fashioned scent in the air.

Jane followed her to the door and bid her farewell, before returning to glower at her husband.

§

When Belinda arrived at Prudence's house later that day she was determined to appear as strong, reserved, and rational as she was able.

Within minutes, however, the warmth and understanding of her friend made such a veneer unsustainable. She was soon giving voice to something that was closer to her most private emotions.

'It's not that I would wish him to be any less independent,' she said, her large bosom heaving as she spoke. 'It's more that I fear he is quite insensitive to the stories that circulate about his behaviour.'

She was trying to hang on to the notion that her

interview with Prudence had been prompted by a wish to preserve her husband's reputation. But it was all too clear that her anguish was due to something else. The fact that she could see her own position in Society being destroyed before it had even been built.

'Have you had an opportunity to discuss matters with him?' asked Prudence as gently as she could.

Belinda sobbed. In keeping with her physique and personality it was a large sob. Prudence felt its impact across the space of ten feet that separated her from the couch on which her friend sat.

'We never speak,' said Belinda.

'Never?' It was the merest of prompts and more an exclamation of surprise.

'Well, hardly ever,' continued Belinda. 'At breakfast, very occasionally – if he has hauled himself from his bed early because of a meeting about money. Or as he's leaving the house in the evening. In either case he's always so short with me. Not impolite as such. He doesn't swear in my presence and plays the part of a much troubled and busy gentleman. But he is cursory. And too often he carries on his clothing the smell of …'

Her words faded away. There was another sob.

This time Prudence did not prompt. She rose from her chair and sat down beside her friend. Putting her arm around Belinda's wide waist she placed her other hand on her trembling fingers.

'Forgive me,' said Prudence once the sobbing had subsided into regular and heavy breathing. 'But do you have anything in common? Just at the moment, I mean.

A common interest or something on which you have need to consult?'

Belinda dabbed at her eyes with an expensive lace handkerchief. She looked to be thinking.

'There is the house,' she said.

Prudence waited, hoping that perhaps her friend might mention something less obviously solid.

'And the pictures,' added Belinda.

'The pictures?'

'The paintings that have been commissioned. Portraits of some of Sir Marmaduke's ancestors. And of Sir Marmaduke himself. And of me.'

Prudence's face took on a more interested expression.

'Might such an enterprise,' she ventured, 'be something that could bring you together. A reason to talk? A subject, possibly, that would enable you both to see your joint heritage anew. Indeed, to see *yourselves* in a fresh light?'

Prudence was struggling to find something to say that might prove helpful in the circumstances. Belinda managed a chuckle. It had a cynical edge to it, Prudence thought, but was at least more encouraging than the sobs.

'I should add a note of caution,' Belinda said. 'For yes, dear Prudence, there are to be paintings. But I suspect they will not be the greatest works of art. We are not talking Mr Hogarth here!'

Prudence was taken aback by the comment but quickly realised it betrayed no knowledge of her earlier visit to the sign of the golden head. It was simply a reflection of the fact that Mr Hogarth was increasingly being talked about as the most talented and commercially astute artist in London.

As such it was almost inevitable that his name should come up in any discussion of the metropolitan art world.

She tried to think of a comment that would be suitably neutral.

'My dear Belinda,' she said at last. 'Mr Hogarth is not the only man in London who paints portraits.'

Belinda just sobbed again.

'No,' she said. 'Sadly he is not!'

Which Prudence felt was a rather odd reply.

§

'It was a long time ago,' he said. 'Before I met you. Obviously.'

'Obviously,' Jane repeated.

They were now in the upstairs parlour and were meant to be sharing a seed cake. William had quickly reduced his piece to a pile of crumbs.

'About fifteen years ago,' he said. 'Longer, I think.' He paused. 'I couldn't have been much more than twenty-two or three.'

He pushed the crumbs around on the table-top. There was a brief silence.

'I'm not asking for a confession,' she said. 'What you did in your youth is of no matter.'

Another pause.

'Well, it *is*, of course,' she went on. 'But you know what I mean. What you did. Who you knew. That was *then*. There's no need for any explanation. No. I'm just surprised, that's all.'

He looked up at her.

'That you hadn't mentioned it,' she said.

She did not want to sound as if she were interrogating him. But she *was* surprised. It was not often that she did not know what was going on in William's life. Or in his mind. This was different.

'I don't think I knew what I'd done, to be honest,' he said. 'Choosing to put her in the painting, I mean. I know I'd sketched her. But I sketch a lot of people – and I don't use them all in my pictures. No, I don't think I realised what I'd done – not consciously – until you pointed it out. And I've been trying to think *why*.'

She made a few movements, brushing down her dress, as if she were about to leave him in peace.

'I really don't need to know,' she said. 'And you don't have to tell me anything. Nothing at all.'

He stood up. His face had softened. The sensitive husband that so often lay hidden inside the rough cast of the painter's exterior was struggling to get out. A crumb of cake, still attached to his bottom lip, emphasised his helpless expression.

'But I want to,' he said. 'I *want* to tell you. Because Miss Prudence – that's how I knew her – well, she saved me. And it's time I told someone. Told *you*.'

'Saved you?'

'Yes,' said William. 'And I don't think I've quite forgiven her since.'

§

Once Belinda had left, Prudence went in search of Master Fleabane.

He was in one of the small parlours, polishing silver. Flea was in no regard a servant, and this was not a task that had been allotted him. But he liked doing it and had claimed it as his own. He said it gave him a good feeling, making precious objects sparkle. Prudence had replied by saying that the objects were not precious at all. That they amounted to no more than the most basic silver a woman such as herself might possess. The pieces were utilitarian rather than decorative and should be judged by their usefulness, not their aesthetic qualities. But Flea was not to be dissuaded. In his mind he had cast the bowls, plates and jugs as veritable treasures. Moreover, he placed the highest value on the fact that his mistress was happy to entrust him with their care.

As Prudence walked into the room Flea put the silver down in the expectation that she would have another mission for him. But she asked him to continue. Then she moved to the window and looked down into the stable-yard that abutted the space at the back of the house.

'You recall Mrs Hogarth, Flea,' she said. 'The lady who visited two days ago. Whose house you took the message to in Leicester Fields.'

'House with the gold head up outside, miss?' said Flea. 'Gold head of a cove with whiskers. Not easy to miss, miss.'

Prudence smiled.

'The very one,' she said. 'It is the head of Sir Anthony van Dyck.'

Flea paused briefly in his polishing. He looked vaguely concerned by this piece of information.

'Foreign gentleman, miss?' he said. 'Sounds like a foreign name. Dike. Sounds like he could be a Hollander, miss.'

'A Fleming, I believe,' said Prudence. 'But you are essentially correct, Flea. An artist of the Low Countries.'

Flea pulled a face. He was pleased to have been essentially correct. But he was unclear what a Fleming might be, and how it differed from a Hollander. He channelled this slight confusion into more rigorous rubbing. Prudence continued to stare out of the window.

'Dead, I take it?' Flea ventured at last.

'Sir Anthony van Dyck?' said Prudence, her brief reverie punctured by his comment.

'Miss,' he added by way of affirmation.

'Yes,' she said. 'He died about a hundred years ago, I should think.'

'Ah, *very* dead,' said Flea. 'And did he have a gold head, miss?'

Prudence laughed.

'Probably not,' she said. 'Although his reputation *is* golden. For some people certainly.'

There was another pause.

'Mr Hogarth is most definitely of that opinion,' she said. 'Have you seen Mr Hogarth, Flea? Perhaps when you delivered the card?'

'No, miss. Not then,' he said. 'But I know who you mean. I notice him a lot around the Piazza. Drinks in the Bedford Arms. Short cove. Wears a long, russet coat most days. And a cap. No wig. Difficult to miss him, miss. Just like his gold head.'

Prudence smiled more broadly as she looked down at a man who was leading a horse out of the stable-yard. Yes, Flea's powers of observation were clearly as keen as ever. He had summed up the figure of Mr Hogarth very well.

She turned from the window and gazed at him. She liked to watch him work. And she could see the pleasure he derived from his total absorption in the task. Now aged thirteen, Flea conveyed an impression that was neither child-like nor adult. His slight frame suggested someone younger than his years. Yet his deep-set eyes and often intense expression hinted at someone considerably more mature. Prudence reflected that he had always had this quality. She could easily imagine him retaining the same worldly-wise visage through the rest of his life.

Watching him polishing the jug also reminded her of the young silver engraver she had first met all those years ago. When would it have been? 1720? Sixteen years before. She was glad he had done so well for himself. First as an engraver of silver pots, then of copper plates, and now as a celebrated painter. She would never, of course, have sought him out again. It was not her place to do such a thing. Indeed, if the truth be told, she had spent much of the intervening years purposely avoiding him. And avoiding his wife as well. But now the connection had been renewed – and not at her behest. She was hopeful it might prove to be an association of interest.

Especially as Mrs Hogarth had struck her as such an amiable and intelligent woman. She would most certainly like to know *her* better. But where to begin? Perhaps, thought Prudence, Jane might like to attend a meeting of the Green Group.

§

'So, when you say "saved", what do you mean?'

Jane was no longer cross. Just puzzled.

'Saved from damnation?' she said.

The expression on his face was wry.

'It wasn't my soul at risk,' he said. 'It was my body. And, no, before you start getting the wrong idea, it was nothing like *that*! I may have had a few *amours* before I was delivered into your lap, my love – but Miss Prudence was not one of them.'

Jane pulled a face.

'She's not your type, is she?' she said.

It was a throwaway line rather than an attempt to add to the substance of the dialogue. William looked at her askance, not sure whether she was baiting him. He opened his mouth to ask but then thought better of it. Best to stick to the point.

'It was just after Tom and Moll first opened their place,' he went on. 'About 1720 I'd guess. *1720!* So, there! That ages me. 'Sblood! I wonder how many other old devils can remember Tom King's just after it opened!'

Jane nodded and sat down again. What he was recounting was history. A time well before she met him. A time when she would have been only ten years old. It was around 1720 that her parents moved into the Piazza.

She could remember the busy-ness of everything. And the noise. All the things she had become so used to in the years that followed. But in 1720 it was all very new.

'I'd had too much to drink,' William continued. 'So, no surprise there. Except it made me outspoken. More than usual. About everything. I was probably showing off.'

He gazed into the distance, a wistful expression on his face. Jane pursed her lips. Showing off was what her husband did. What he had always done. He stirred himself and carried on with his story.

'There were some ... some fellows who took exception to what I was saying,' he said. 'Vile sots who'd pitched up hot-foot from creating mayhem around town.'

He rubbed his hand over his scalp a few times before going on.

'To cut the story short, they took against me. They pushed me about. Then they picked me up. Carried me outside and threw me on the ground.'

He rubbed his upper arm and shoulder as the ghost of a pain passed through his body.

'Then they stood around,' he went on. 'Talking about what to do to me. I'd fallen on my elbow and was hurting. I was certainly in no fit state to put up a fight. So I curled up into a ball, expecting a kicking.'

He looked at Jane ruefully. He was embarrassed but knew he could rely on her support. She watched him as if he were a small boy admitting to a misdemeanour.

'It's all a bit of a blur,' he said. 'But I was worried. Worried they might do more. Something a lot worse.'

There was another pause, more scalp rubbing.

'A lot worse,' he said again. 'Truth is … I thought they might kill me. Or maim me.'

The colour had drained from his face.

'You have to remember,' he went on, 'this was only a few years after the Mohocks.'

She had vaguely heard of the Mohocks, but it was so long ago. She could have been no more than a baby. He saw the question in her eyes.

'Gangs of so-called gentlemen,' he said. 'They terrorised London for a while, attacking people for no reason. And doing horrendous things to them. Like slitting their noses.'

He raised his hand to his nose and felt it before going on.

'In 1720 there were still enough numbskulls around who thought it fun to act like a Mohock. Stupid fellows who reckoned it good entertainment to maim an innocent Christian.'

Jane looked hard at him. Was he making light of it? Or seriously suggesting that he had been an innocent Christian?

'There's no doubt I was in peril,' he continued. 'And I was in fear of my life. Or perhaps I should say my death.'

He rubbed his arm and shoulder again. Jane was frowning. Had he not been so deadly earnest she would have smiled. There was an oddly dramatic tone in his voice and a note of absurdity in his telling. Together they created a tension that needed puncturing. But there was no way she could do that. He was speaking with a depth of feeling she had not heard for a long time. She did not want to do or say anything to suggest she was not listening to him with the utmost seriousness.

'As for my friends,' he continued. 'Well, they were no help. I can't recall who was there. I can't even remember who my friends *were* in those days. But whoever they were, they were either dead drunk or had made themselves scarce as soon as the other fellows started rattling their swords. And I mean that literally! That I *do* remember. That they had swords. Swords that they rattled. Swords that could be used for slitting noses. Or stabbing people through the heart.'

Jane was touched by the fact that her bluff and headstrong husband was betraying a less than confident side of his character. But he seemed to be distressing himself more than was necessary. She wanted to calm him, to let him know that he was safe. She moved her chair closer to him. One of his paint-stained hands lay on the table, while the other roved over the bristles of his scalp and the stubble of his jowls. She reached out and touched him.

'So what happened?' she asked.

He seemed lost for a moment or two but then recovered and gazed at her. His eyes looked tired, she thought.

'What happened next,' he said, 'was that *she* came along. She could only have been about twenty at the time. A few years younger than me. She just loomed up out of nowhere. On her way to church, I suppose. It was, after all, about seven o'clock in the morning by then. Yes, I know. *Seven!* Can you believe it! I must have been out all night.'

He almost laughed.

'I could do it then, of course,' he said with a shrug. 'We *all* could. Stay up all night.'

Jane smiled. Yes, she thought. We were all younger then. Some more than others. Some of us would have been getting up and preparing for a day's schooling!

'She just walked up,' William carried on. 'Walked up and told them – the brutes with the swords – told them in no uncertain terms to leave me be. And do you know what? They did. Without even giving me a farewell kick, they withdrew. I'm not sure I saw it all, to be honest, because I was still on the ground. But when I sat up, I could see two of them dragging the other one back to Tom King's. There was some shouting – a few more curses flung at my head, and some choice words aimed at her as well. But otherwise, I'd been left alone.'

He squeezed Jane's hand.

'Well, you can imagine,' he said. 'I got to my feet – unsteadily, I dare say – and started to say something. But she waved me away. Told me to have a care. That I should learn from this. And that she would pray for me. Ha! Learn! Pray!'

He laughed again and shook his head.

'I didn't know what to say back,' he said. 'But I *did* ask her name. I do remember that. I don't think she wanted to tell me. So I asked her again. And she said it was Miss Prudence. That was all. Miss Prudence. Then she went on her way. To church. And I was left to count the cost of what might have been.'

He paused and smiled sheepishly.

'That was my morning,' he said. 'Back then. My

morning. The first morning in Covent Garden when I felt that life was … well, you know. The first morning I realised I needed … help, I suppose.'

Jane pursed her lips and looked at him with love.

'So you see,' he went on. 'Miss Prudence saved me.'

§

Jonathan Smallow sat back in his chair, a smug smile on his face.

He was staring at five phials of liquid that stood next to each other on the table in front of him. The sixth phial had been passed to Sir Marmaduke late the night before when the two men met at Tom King's.

Ransome had been gruff and awkward. He had put the phial in his coat pocket and immediately turned away from Smallow, saying not another word. Instead he marched – or rather swayed – over to a table on the other side of the room. Behind it sat a woman who had just removed her breasts from the confines of her dress. Smallow decided he should get to know her at some point. He heard Ransome call her Slippery Sal.

Smallow played the scene through again in his head as he stared at the phials. The link between the lure of Sal's flesh and 'remedies' such as the Very Special Cathartic Venereal Electuary seemed only too clear. For a few moments his mind wandered as he considered the cost of temptation. The impossibility of saying no. And what it might mean to forego the kind of indulgence that often led to distress and even death.

The fiend is at mine elbow and tempts me.

It was ever thus.

At the same time, both a stimulating and a dispiriting prospect.

He poured himself another glass of wine. Then he tried to look at the phials in a different way.

There they stood, side by side, like soldiers lined up for inspection. Taken together would their consumption be enough to kill a man? Who could know for certain? Other than by trying. Such a dose would surely be sufficient to cause significant pain or at least irritation. One step along the way to murder itself.

Which clearly begged the question of how exactly it should be done. How was the medicine to be administered? And when?

There was no immediate rush. That much was clear. He had waited this long. What did a few more days matter? Because, after all, it was not just murder that was on his mind. Death was a dog that would certainly have its day. But first there had to be humiliation. Without the humiliation, much of his joy would disappear. So it would require him to think it through. He needed a plan.

A plan that would allow him to witness at first hand the ignominy he intended to heap on his victim's head.

§

When William retired to his studio it was not to continue working on the image of Prudence – which suddenly felt rather too close for comfort.

He would work instead on something else altogether. His newest and most secret endeavour. A project about which he was still feeling unsure.

The idea had come to him only recently. On the day he walked the two hundred yards from his studio to view Leicester House. The building which – if he could believe the rumours – would soon become the main London home of Frederick, Prince of Wales.

For some time William had been nurturing a degree of resentment at what he considered to be a snub. He may have become the city's most popular engraver and a painter of renown, but he had received not a single royal commission. Indeed, he had heard from more than one source that His Majesty, King George II, had a particular antipathy towards him. Well, so be it. What did the stupid, old, German fart know about *anything*? It was not a point of view likely to impede the unstoppable commercial success of London's most celebrated print-maker. William had therefore put it out of his mind.

Until, that is, he heard the stories about Leicester House.

It was well known that the Prince of Wales and his regal parent held bitterly opposed views on almost everything, and that they could hardly bear to be in each other's company. If that were the case, was it not likely that the Prince might delight in supporting an artist so disliked by his father? Most especially an artist who lived just yards from the newly appointed princely residence.

It was this idea that had put such a strange look on William's face when his wife found him wandering back across Leicester Fields only days before. The simple yet inspired idea that he might cultivate royal patronage not by courting a disinclined king, but by making himself the peerless champion of an antagonistic son and heir. It was with such a brilliantly astute scheme in mind that he had begun work on a new and covert experiment aimed at currying Frederick's favour.

Nothing less than a portrait of the man himself. The Prince of Wales.

He had shown it to no one, not even Jane, and was feeling more than a little awkward about that. But he continued to cling to the notion that it was just an experiment. No more than an initial sketch in oils that he might abandon at any point. Because he really was in two minds about it. *At least* two minds.

For the challenge of producing a princely portrait did not fill him with enthusiasm. Not as a work of art. Regardless of the benefits of securing the Prince's patronage, William knew the picture itself would hardly excite anyone other than its subject. Artistically it would be nowhere near as innovative as his new series on *The Four Times of the Day*.

As he attempted to review the canvas more dispassionately, however, he could see that the emerging portrait had its merits. And, yes, he had certainly captured something of the Prince's courtly presence. But did that also make it too much like every other royal portrait he had ever seen? Was the treatment sufficiently individual for it to be recognised as *his*? It was easy for *him* to regard the brush-work, for example, as characteristically his own. But would other viewers see it that way? Did it contain enough of his especial qualities to render it *truly* unmistakable as the work of William Hogarth? Because, if it did not, then why do it at all?

What was at stake, after all, was his artistic reputation. Any picture by William Hogarth had to have something unique about it. But in this case – and with a genre so defined by tradition and expectation – what could that uniqueness be? Could he make more of the background? Or would that simply be a distraction? Perhaps he should concentrate solely on the figure of the Prince, making him a shining example of royalty against a dark setting. He could change the clothes he had sketched in. Make them silver perhaps.

At the same time, however, he did not want to be novel just for the sake of it. So could he create something different without departing too far from the bounds of convention? Another way of showing the world that there was, indeed, no subject that was beyond the genius of William Hogarth.

But he needed to bide his time. There was nothing to be gained by revealing his hand too soon. No point in giving his critics a chance to lampoon him. He could do without all the cheap jokes. All the barbs they would throw in his face simply out of spite and envy.

'Mr Hogarth, known for his *Progresses*, seems now obsessed with his *OWN* progress, and is clearly working his way up the social ladder – from Harlot to Rake … and now to *PRINCE*. Is there no height to which he does not aspire? And no depth to which he will not stoop in order to get there!'

Yes, it was all too easy to imagine how the hacks would enjoy scribbling such lines.

So he would wait. Until the canvas was finished. And then the painting would speak for itself.

In the meantime, it should remain hidden from view. Even Jane's view.

His little secret.

He was pleased. Well, sort of.

For there was still a small, nagging murmur at the back of his head. An annoying little voice that would not be put off from insisting that this whole hare-brained scheme was really the worst idea in the world.

§

They had known each other as Covent Garden neighbours for ten years.

It could hardly be called a friendship, but Miss Hyssop and Jeremiah Potts rarely passed one another in the Piazza without several signs of animation, often accompanied by a few words of inconsequential conversation.

Jeremiah felt honoured by the slight attentions Miss Hyssop paid him. There was, after all, a gulf between them in terms of their social standing. He was a humble courier who lived in a garret. She was a lady of some means who occupied the whole of one of the grander houses opposite. It was perhaps partly this distinction that caused Jeremiah invariably to assume a somewhat theatrical mode of behaviour in her presence.

For her part, Prudence found his exaggerated bows and

flourishes charming. As she grew to know a little more of him, she realized that much of Jeremiah's expressive show could be traced to his earlier ambitions as a performer. She began to see that, even in his day-to-day existence, he lost no opportunity to strike a pose. And, as the years passed, she could appreciate how such a 'character' created certain expectations. It seemed clear to her, for example, that the market sellers would have been disappointed had he not conducted himself in this way. Any flagging of his energies in this regard would have been interpreted as an indication that Jeremiah was under the weather.

As Prudence looked out of her first-floor window onto the Piazza below, Jeremiah was always one of the easiest figures to recognise. No one else managed to walk in that prancing way. No one waved his arms about quite so much whilst standing still and talking. Sometimes she would see him darting about in the course of his deliveries, crossing the square with packages of different sizes. Often it was only too clear what they were. Canvases and boards, for example, which were not always wrapped. At other times he carried a clutch of smaller items that were not identifiable from such a distance. Occasionally he employed a large sack that he swung over his shoulder.

Not that it was any business of hers, of course. And she would not have wanted anyone to think that she was prying. But this was the second time in two days that she had seen Jeremiah take what looked like a canvas into the house where he lived. Surely such a thing could only be for Mr Alcazar. Which was a good sign, Prudence decided. For it meant that he was painting again.

When the Alcazars lost one of their children the previous year, it had been several weeks before the grief-stricken father had felt able to pick up his brush. And perhaps Prudence was reading too much into what she had just observed. But she was encouraged by the strong possibility that the practice of painting had been resumed in the house across the square.

Such an observation was also, however, another prompt for her to visit *Mrs* Alcazar. The artist might well be capable of immersing himself in his work again. But Prudence's instincts told her that his wife would have no similar activity through which to channel her loss.

She would call on her without delay.

§

When Jane suggested she invite Prudence to take tea with her, she was expecting her husband to scowl.

Given what he had told her about the incident all those years ago, she assumed he would want to draw a line under the more recent meeting. His response therefore caught her by surprise.

'Good idea,' he said. 'And while she's here she can take another look at the picture.'

At first Jane thought he was being sarcastic. In fact, she waited to see if he was going to follow up the comment with something less subtle.

'Actually, why not ask her to move in? Then she can be here to torment me every single day.'

Something like that.

But no. There appeared to be no such intent in the face he pulled as he wrestled with a chicken bone.

'Good,' said Jane. 'I shall arrange it.'

For all his difficult moments – which were many – William was a complex being. His ability to surprise Jane, along with his flashes of sensitivity, had been important in making their marriage the success it was. She knew very well that his personality was far more variegated than his bluff exterior suggested. In fact, she found it puzzling that so many people never thought to question the persona he presented to the world. Surely a careful reading of his work made it only too clear that it was the product of a mind that was anything but simple and straightforward.

Nevertheless, there was something different about the situation with Prudence. It was not just the courtesy he had shown her. For all his rough edges, there had always been a charm and a twinkle in his eye. Or so Jane thought. No, it was more to do with the circumstances. For one thing, there was the whole business of exposing an unfinished work in progress to someone he appeared hardly to know. Yes, the image portrayed a woman who was modelled on Prudence. But that might have been enough for him to be even more guarded than usual.

Then there was the story about her 'saving' him from what sounded like real physical harm and possibly worse. With most people one might have expected such a saving grace to mark the beginning of some kind of relationship, even if not a close one. But it was very much in character that William should regard the incident as an embarrassment rather than a blessing. What was it he had said? That it was difficult to forgive Prudence for saving him? That must surely be tied up with some silly masculine sense of honour. If it had been one of his old drinking friends who had stepped in, then it would presumably have all been fine. But a woman! And a young, frail, church-going, prim young lady at that! Well, it wasn't good for a chap's reputation to be saved by such a guardian angel, was it?

So what had changed? What was it that made the once ignored Prudence now a more acceptable – even desirable – presence around not only the house but the studio as well? Jane was not sure she understood. But then that was William Hogarth for you. Just when you thought you knew where he was going, he would swerve off in a different direction and surprise you with something new. Something you were not expecting at all.

Anyway, it was all to the good. If William was happy to have Prudence back on the premises, then Jane was even more delighted. She had developed a liking for the intriguing Miss Hyssop and wanted to know her better.

§

I shall engage once more with the recollections of my life at some point. But I have today had some reminder that it is the present and not the past in which I must live. In which we all must live. And die.

I have for some time taken an interest in Mr Alcazar, the painter who lives across the way. It was some two or more years ago that I first met his wife at church in the Piazza, and I knew she was then grieving for the loss of an infant.

And then last year I became aware that she had lost another child. What a tragedy to visit on a young family. But, oh, how familiar. It was then that I first visited her within her own dwelling, which is both family home and the studio of her husband. Such is the practice with several painters, it would seem. There are few who can afford to live and work in separate spaces.

Mr Alcazar is a man of some character and strength. He is tall and dark and bears his troubles with great dignity. I believe his origins may be Spanish, but he is very familiar with our English ways and paints in a style like the Flemish artists who have made Covent Garden their second home.

Certainly, the painting I saw him at work upon last year was a masterly thing. A view of the Piazza itself, from the east end looking towards the church, and most elegantly done. I complimented him upon it, but he was most humble and quiet in his response. The death of a child surely puts everything into perspective, even one's most cherished creations. He told me then that he had not been able to paint for some weeks after the loss, and I was most sorry for that, hoping that his art may have brought him some relief.

I had not thought to have such a conversation with him and his wife again and have spoken to them of more happy matters several times during my walks around the Piazza. But I grieve to say that the misfortune of death has come upon them once more and carried off yet another of their children, leaving but one. It is too sad for words, yet I feel I must record it in my journal, for where else will there be a record of such a small life lost other than in the parish records?

I called upon them two days after the funeral, in the

hope that Mrs Alcazar had been able to rest and perhaps be calmer in her spirit. She is a woman who was once robust but who has been worn down by the trials of this life. Her skin seems unnaturally pale when seen next to that of her husband, and her hair prematurely white in places. The scene of the two of them, with their remaining child standing by, made a deep impression upon me. I wanted to help but knew not how. Except to pray. But suffice to say the grace of God is mysterious to behold and cannot always be discerned by the grieving eye.

I had again hoped that Mr Alcazar might have found some support and distraction in his work. For I remember when we met in the marketplace some weeks before he told me of his plans to embark on more images of the Piazza. The painting he created the year before had elicited much interest and he wished to repeat its success. And so I did enquire on this matter and looked about me in expectation that I would see signs of his work.

But he sighed at this and put his arm tenderly about his wife. Alas, he said. I can never paint when the pain is so raw. I must allow more time. And our grieving must be a shared grieving, and not one I can escape from in the things of this world.

It was, I do believe, a most tender speech and showed his great care for his wife. But it did perturb me also. For I knew I had seen Jeremiah delivering canvases into the house, and had cherished the notion that they, and what they should become, would be a comfort to both Mr Alcazar and his wife as they do whatever they are able to find solace in this all too difficult world.

I will call again, for Mrs Alcazar seems barely alive. And I will perhaps suggest that a change of air may strengthen her constitution.

§

Prudence arrived at the sign of the golden head on foot.

It was a short distance from her home, and she liked walking in London. This was despite the bustle, filth, noise and ever-present threat of unbecoming behaviour. On this particular morning she left her house unaccompanied, exiting the Piazza by Henrietta Street. Turning into Bedford Street and then Chandos Street, she made her way down to St Martin's Lane, before crossing into Hemmings Row. A short distance further on, over Castle Street and via the short stretch of Green Street, she entered Leicester Fields at the south-east corner.

Jane welcomed her warmly, buoyed up by her husband's enthusiasm for the visit.

'William has requested that you spend some time with him in his studio,' she said. 'But I think it only right and proper that you refresh yourself first. And we can get to know each other a little better.'

Prudence was most gracious in her response, and Jane was charmed with her guest. She noticed how Prudence's more frequent smiles transformed her whole appearance. It was not a face that could be called pretty or handsome, but it was by no means unattractive. Certainly a lot more becoming, so Jane thought, than its representation in William's painting. Moreover, she decided, it was a face that indicated a depth of understanding, a distinct hint of wisdom, and not a little boldness. Perhaps a face, she mused, that had seen more of life than one might have imagined.

As these notions passed through Jane's mind, she caught a glimpse of herself in the mirror that hung opposite where they had seated themselves. Her face was what the world called comely, but with clear lines of determination and business acumen. It did not have the austere or ascetic qualities that made an unsmiling Prudence appear as a cross between a saint and a duenna. Jane's face was characterised by its almost constant expression of good-natured tolerance, conveyed by the creases around her twinkling eyes. Not for the first time, she reflected that she could not have made a success of her marriage without deep reserves of good humour.

'You are very much a woman of the world, Jane,' said Prudence.

Jane took the comment as it was meant – an unalloyed compliment.

'You must see so much of the artistic and cultural life of London,' Prudence continued. 'Indeed, I imagine that much of it passes through your doors. It must give you a unique perspective on the nature of the metropolis and its characters.'

'Certainly the diversity of London life is all too apparent every day of the week,' replied Jane. 'But then you must find the same in Covent Garden. I can't pretend that I don't miss the Piazza. Yes, it has its challenges. But its sheer spirit of movement, theatrical show, and constant performance – even in the market – make it one of the most vibrant places I've ever known. It was not always the sort of inspiration my parents valued. But I never regretted their choice of the Piazza as home.'

'I could not agree more, Jane,' said Prudence. 'There has never been a time when I have thought at all seriously of living anywhere else. It is true that, in part, my decision to stay was prompted by the terms of the lease. Although, if I had had half a heart to move away, the matter of property could surely have been resolved. But where would I go? A woman of a certain age may wish to hide in a quiet closet somewhere less active. Such a decision, however, would simply hasten my slow decline into somnolence! Much better to be poked and prodded by the bizarre variety that life throws up every day. And, yes, it may include the odd raucous comment or inappropriate remark. I am not, as you may imagine, totally immune to the stories that are bound to circulate about a lady who maintains herself in some comfort in the Piazza. But that, it seems to me, is a small price to pay for the benefits of such constant stimulation.'

Jane could not be more pleased with this and resolved immediately to count Prudence amongst her most valued companions. It was only a conundrum that so many years had passed without there being anything other than the most fleeting contact between the two of them. Yes, one could blame the anonymity that characterised much of bustling London life. But there were surely other factors as well. Growing up as the daughter of the renowned painter, Sir James Thornhill, and then transitioning into the wife of the equally famous William Hogarth, had cast Jane in a decidedly public role from her earliest years. In many respects it was the very antithesis of the quiet independence around which Prudence had modelled her own life.

As the conversation continued to bloom, the tea was largely ignored. But then, as both ladies acknowledged, the taking of tea was hardly ever indulged in for the delights of the sour brew itself. Jane's preference was for the more manly drink of coffee, whilst Prudence's choice was usually chocolate. Tea, however, provided a more obvious social platform. And its rituals encouraged a measured exchange of opinion. Just right for a tentative and slightly formal conversation.

They continued to talk for some minutes about the pleasures of the town and of Covent Garden in particular. And then Prudence raised the question of the Green Group.

§

Jeremiah stared at the canvas he had mostly covered in dark paint.

He did not pretend to understand it. In some respects, he was frightened by it. But it was what it was.

A featureless mass of black and grey that said …

What?

Night? Shadow? Despair?

He was confused. He wanted to ignore it, to run away from it. But at the same time he wanted to talk about it. To try to explain it. And to have it explained. But who could he turn to?

Not someone who was a painter. That would be ridiculous. Mr Alcazar was a good man and always so friendly. But no. He was a *proper* painter. And he had too many troubles of his own.

Clearly not Mr Hogarth. That was unthinkable.

Then the thought of Mr Smallow came into his mind, much as he tried to keep it out.

Jeremiah held his head in his hands. He could feel himself shaking.

No, away! Away!

It was not a thought he wanted in his head. He was at least half sure that Mr Smallow was a devil. That it was mostly because of Mr Smallow that he was having these nightmares – and painting these … these … things.

He waited for the terror to subside. Outside the sun was shining weakly. He shook his head and tried to think of sunnier thoughts.

Who else?

There was Catherine, of course.

He had first met her at her father's business, close by the Strand. Mostly on account of the deliveries he made on behalf of Mr Bickham, Pargeter's print-shop had become one of Jeremiah's regular destinations. In the year since that first meeting he and Catherine had become close. One might even say more than that. Very close.

But that did not mean he could tell her everything, did it?

He had not been able to talk to her about Kitty, for example.

Well, how could he? How could he possibly talk to a tender and innocent lady friend about ...

About all that.

Jeremiah had made a point of never mentioning Kitty's name while she was alive, let alone after ...

After her fall.

So talking about this ...

What were they? Worries? Fears?

He could not begin to think of bringing those sorts of things to Catherine.

No matter that he would have been overjoyed to lay anything else at her feet.

But, no. Catherine had to be protected. Kept separate. And cherished as something different.

So who else?

Miss Hyssop?

Was that even the thought of a rational man?

Except that she always seemed to take an interest in those less fortunate than herself. You only had to speak to anyone around the Piazza to know that. Yes, there were some who said cruel things about her. But most said the opposite. He had even heard her described as an angel.

Now Jeremiah was far from being a religious cove ...

But all the same ...

He did believe in God. Sort of. So might an angel like Miss Hyssop be able to help?

He wrung his hands and wished he were a child. At

least then he would be able to cry. Whereas being a man meant …

Well, it meant he could not cry. He could only rail. And at what?

He left the house and headed out into the Piazza. He needed to lose himself in the ebb and flow of life out there. Staying inside was not good. He needed to keep moving. He needed to keep telling himself that everything was all right.

Even though it wasn't.

§

'You are a person of such insight and experience,' Prudence said.

Jane demurred. Prudence carried on.

'They are qualities which I know would be appreciated by a broad range of people, most especially women of maturity and discernment.'

This time Jane bowed her head slightly.

'I was wondering,' continued Prudence, 'if you might consent to join me and a few friends with a view to sharing some of your thoughts on the nature of Art and Home.'

Art and Home? That's a rather large subject, thought Jane. But what an intriguing idea. She was used to being asked to talk about matters of a more distinctly feminine character, or about nothing much at all. But Art and Home sounded more interesting. Just so long as it was not simply code for 'Tales of my Life with Mr William Hogarth'. But then the very idea did not do justice to

Prudence. She was certainly not the sort of woman who would speak in code. These thoughts passed through Jane's mind in a flash. She smiled while Prudence developed her invitation.

'We have a little group of friends – we call it the Green Group – who meet occasionally to discuss matters of substance. Like art or politics. We are all women with enquiring minds and enjoy the opportunity to express views and exchange ideas within a small and closeted environment, free from the constraints of public scrutiny or judgement.'

Jane was charmed – both by the concept and the way Prudence expressed it.

'That sounds delightfully ...'

She stopped herself from saying, 'Charming'.

'Delightfully independent,' she said.

Her smile was, she hoped, broad enough to show that she meant it in a wholly positive way.

'Independent is a good word, Jane,' said Prudence. 'We like to think our small discussions broaden the mind and create perspectives that might otherwise not be available to ourselves. But it is not always easy to find sympathetic contributors. As you would expect, we are none of us ever short of opinion. But opinion is not of the essence without sufficient stimulation by way of new information on which the mind can reflect. As well as welcoming you as a friend and interested party, we should so much value the depth of knowledge you would bring into our little coterie. But I do not wish to put you under any pressure, Jane. Perhaps you may regard it as something to which you might give your consideration at some point and let me know if it is of interest.'

Prudence's character was such that she always approached matters in a considered and sensitive way. Her remarks were also, however, couched in the careful language of those who have only recently found themselves to be on friendly terms.

Jane was more inclined to strike while the iron was hot.

'I have already considered,' she said. 'And I'm pleased to say I would most certainly like to accept. But tell me – why is it called the Green Group?'

Prudence smiled, both at Jane's prompt agreement and also the question.

'You will think us foolish, I dare say,' she said. 'But on the first occasion when there were just three of us together – discussing, I believe, the origins of the Piazza and the architect Inigo Jones – we noted that, quite coincidentally, we were all wearing something green. One of my colleagues suggested we should refer to ourselves as the Green Group and the term stuck. It is, I hope, something of a neutral colour. The Whigs have their blue and buff, while the Tories seem to choose any colour that suits them. Green, however, is unclaimed and makes no statement of political allegiance.'

Jane was delighted.

'And do you still wear green when you meet?' she asked with a broad smile.

Prudence laughed.

'Perhaps we should,' she said. 'No, the name has now

detached itself from any sense of who we are and why we meet. If the concept were to go on past the lives of the current group, I suspect new members might waste several hours debating the origins of the name!'

'Well, I can say with great enthusiasm,' said Jane, 'that I look forward to being introduced to the Green Group whenever you are next pleased to meet. And I'll make sure that I do *not* wear green for the occasion!'

Another laugh from Prudence. The two women were clearly enjoying each other's company. But Jane was also conscious that the visit had been arranged so that Prudence might see William – and his painting – again.

So it was that, after a few more minutes, Jane conducted her guest downstairs to the studio where her husband was working on a canvas that was *not* 'Morning'. It looked to be the portrait of a man who was dressed in silver. But neither woman was able to see it clearly because William quickly took it off the easel and placed it out of view behind a box in the corner of the room.

§

The young woman – or Vampyre – had hardly been seen by her fellow tenants.

They would certainly have struggled to say what she looked like. But each of them was grateful to have her there.

The room had been unoccupied throughout January and February, reminding them all of Kitty's former presence and deathly absence. Even the old tailor, Mr Flint was surprised by how much he missed the familiar creaking of floorboards. He thought he would have preferred the space to remain empty. But the eerie quiet had filled him with ghostly and uncomfortable thoughts. He wanted the house to be inhabited by living souls, even if that meant being inconvenienced by noises from upstairs.

So, when the new young lady moved in, the feeling amongst the residents was that something approaching normality might return. Jeremiah in particular welcomed the fact. He could now at least try to associate the room with someone other than Kitty. Although it was proving difficult.

However, the new tenant turned out to be more mysterious than anyone had foreseen. Her name was only known at all because someone called with a letter for her. Miss Bell. Miss Sarah Bell.

She had neither introduced herself nor been observed more than very occasionally during daylight hours. Jeremiah and Mr Alcazar had glimpsed a spectral presence leaving the building late in the evening and returning early in the morning. So, was she another prostitute? It was a reasonable assumption, thought Jeremiah. There were, after all, very few opportunities available to women who were looking to survive the mean conditions of Covent Garden. But if that were the case, she must surely conduct her business elsewhere. Unlike when Kitty was alive, there were no men tramping heavily up and down the rickety stairs every night.

As with most things in the Piazza, however, there was little to be gained by prying. The place was a hub for the diverse and the unexpected. Most things, no matter how unusual, were quickly absorbed within its variegated mix.

And so, after the initial bloom of curiosity, nobody in the building took much notice of the tenant who was never seen – but whose soft step could be heard during the day, tracing a path back and forth across the bare boards where Kitty Smith had once lived.

§

Jane had already played it through several times in her mind.

Should she stay in the studio on this occasion or leave William and Prudence to discuss matters without her? When she asked her husband over breakfast he had shrugged and made a snorting noise. Probably a sign that he did not care one way or the other. Jane therefore decided to concoct some excuse and leave the two of them together.

Alone with his new visitor, William tried to adopt a casual air. He ventured a comment about Prudence needing to take him as she found him. Then he invited her to sit on an old, leather armchair that was bespattered with paint. Seeing the questioning look on her face, he ferreted about in a corner before finding a grey, muslin sheet which he draped over the chair. The sheet was almost as stained as the chair itself but Prudence, unconcerned, sat down on it. His attempt at gallantry was, she decided, a token of gracious welcome and she was grateful. Even so, she was still not sure why he should be treating her in such a way. Nor indeed why she had been invited back into the hallowed space of the studio.

William perched on a wooden stool next to the easel. He cleared his throat and looked around the room. Indeed, he looked at everything – other than Prudence. Finally, however, his eyes came to rest on where she sat, bolt upright, lips pursed.

'Miss Hyssop,' he said. 'Miss Prudence, I mean. That is, … Prudence. I owe you an apology.'

It was not what she was expecting. From what she already knew of the celebrated Mr Hogarth, apologies were not what he did. There was a distinct sense in which to apologise – for *anything* – would have been to undermine the bluff exterior and devil-take-the-hindmost attitude that was key to his public persona.

'It is overdue I know,' he added. 'Very overdue.'

He pulled a face that could only be described as contrite. Prudence's instinctive politeness and cultivated upbringing could not let such a remark pass without comment.

'I am sure you can have nothing to apologise for, Mr Hogarth,' she said. 'Certainly not to me.'

He pulled another face. It might have been a smile. It was difficult to tell.

'William, please,' he said. 'Call me William. Or Will. Billy, even. You see, I'd very much like to remove the barrier that the words Mr Hogarth might mean.'

Prudence looked puzzled.

'I am not sure I understand … William,' she said.

William she could just about manage, although it took

some effort. She could never have called him 'Will'. And 'Billy' was, well, quite unthinkable.

He stood up and moved about aimlessly before resettling himself on the stool.

'On that morning, many years ago,' he began. 'When was it? 1720? I seem to recall Tom King's was still very new in those days. Well, on that morning you did a very noble – and a very brave – thing. You almost certainly saved me from something of a drubbing – and possibly much worse. But what did *I* do? Instead of acknowledging your act of self-sacrifice, instead of visiting you and thanking you properly, ... instead of that, I made a point of acting as if it had never happened. I ignored you. Even when I passed you in the Piazza, ... I ignored you. And I continued to ignore you.'

He paused and appeared genuinely galled by the memory.

'It was unconscionable,' he said. 'Ungentlemanly at so many levels – and I say that as someone who has never been known as a gentleman. But I also say it as a man who is nowhere near being the lout he's often considered to be.'

It sounded more like a plea than a matter of opinion. The fact was that Mr Hogarth had always taken every opportunity to reinforce the common perception of his genius. To some extent his behaviour all those years ago was just one example of what had become a self-fulfilling prophecy.

Prudence pursed her lips tighter. She also had memories of that night – and of what followed. And they were even less pleasant than his. But he was not to know that. And she was not about to tell him. She would continue to listen to *his* story – and keep her own story hidden.

'The trouble is,' he said, 'the longer it went on, the harder it became. For me to say anything at all, I mean.'

He seemed to be offering this as some kind of excuse. Almost as if the demon Time had been the one at fault, rather than the great artist himself. Time had turned what was undoubtedly a failure of good grace into an intractable error. And one from which no simple mortal could have escaped.

'So,' he went on. 'I want to say sorry. And to thank you. Properly, that is. And … beg your forgiveness.'

He frowned, having surprised himself by the way his little speech had developed. Apologising was one thing. But asking forgiveness?

She wanted to be able to smile at him, but she was still wrestling with the memories he had stirred. When it was clear, however, that he was waiting for some kind of response, she tried to reflect quickly on what she might say. She could say that it did not matter – except that it did. She could say they could start anew – although that sounded as if they were estranged lovers. Given William's preference for straightforward talking, she decided to take the conversation back to how this new revelation had begun. Back to the picture. Back to 'Morning'.

'Is that why you modelled the woman in your painting on me?'

He was taken aback. He started to speak. Stopped himself. Looked at her again. And then he began to laugh.

And fortunately – or so he remembered thinking – so did she.

It was perhaps a nervous laugh on both their parts. But it did at least put the more difficult memories to one side. At least temporarily.

'It's funny how things can appear so preordained when you look back at them,' he said, as the small laughter ran its course. 'Whereas, at the time, everything seems much more random. So, no, it'll probably not surprise you that the painting was not undertaken with apology in mind. And, to be honest, I'm not sure why I modelled the woman on you. Except that *something* must have been going on in this dense little space.'

He tapped the side of his head with a paint-stained finger.

'Something to make me do it,' he said.

He was not sure why, but he was finding it oddly comforting to talk to this woman who was still almost a complete stranger to him.

Prudence waited a moment or two, not sure if he had finished. She was feeling privileged that the nervous laughter had initiated what appeared to be a new connection between them. It was clearly not the intimacy of close friends – they did not know each other well enough for that. But perhaps that was the very thing that made this conversation possible. Prudence was outside William's usual sphere of activity and experience – but with just enough of a link to his past to create a bridge of sorts.

It looked as if he wanted to say more. But just at that

moment the quiet mood of their tête-à-tête was broken by the intrusion of a third person.

§

'Oh lawks! Sorry, Mr H!'

The words were spoken by a lank, angular man.

'I didn't know you was in conference, so to speak,' he went on. 'I wouldn't have taken the liberty, if you know what I mean. Not wanting to be in the way, if you get my gist.'

'What is it, Jeremiah?' said William, with something more like his usual gruffness. The soft tone that marked his conversation with Prudence had disappeared. He would, he supposed, need to make some kind of introduction.

'This is Miss Prudence Hyssop,' he said. 'A near neighbour of yours in the Piazza.'

'Miss Hyssop,' said Jeremiah, taking off his hat and letting his hair fall about his face. He bowed low in a manner that suggested someone far less awkward than the character who had fallen so unceremoniously into the room.

Prudence could not help smiling.

'Jeremiah,' she said. 'I hope I find you well.'

'Thank you, miss,' said Jeremiah with another small flourish. 'Tolerably so, I must say.'

William looked from one to the other.

'Oh, of course,' he said. 'You know one another already. Well, I suppose that's only to be expected. It's difficult *not* to know someone who lives so close by you in the Piazza.'

For all William's wish to show greater sensitivity in Prudence's presence, he did not note the oblique look she cast in his direction. A look that said, 'You may be right – but then *you*, Mr Hogarth, are a prime example of how one can live alongside near neighbours for years and not know them at all!'

'Jeremiah and I have been acquainted for some time,' she said aloud. 'And I am aware that Jeremiah plays a role in our great metropolitan art world.'

Jeremiah oozed pleasure at what he took to be a commendation. William pulled a face. It suggested that he thought Jeremiah's contribution to the artistic life of London was rather more marginal than Prudence was implying.

'You have the oils I asked for?' he said.

'Indeed, Mr H. I have the oils,' said Jeremiah.

He bestowed a knowing look on both William and Prudence as he handed over the package. As if the concept of 'oils' could be understood only by those people most intimately connected with the art world.

William mumbled an acknowledgement and jerked his head to suggest that his courier need tarry no longer. Jeremiah was quick to take the hint but did not wish to leave without making what he hoped would be a double compliment.

'Wonderful painting of the Piazza, Mr H,' he said, nodding towards the canvas of 'Morning' on the easel. 'And a captivating picturing of the lady too, if I may be so bold.'

There was a final flourish of his hat, and he left the room displaying decidedly more decorum than his entry had promised.

Once he had gone William caught Prudence's eye and they shared a chuckle. Although, in William's case, it was more of a snort and shake of the head.

'Well, at least *some*one likes it,' he said.

Her smile recognised his self-deprecation.

'I suspect Jeremiah sees a great many paintings in various stages of completion,' she said. 'He may have as good an eye as many a connoisseur.'

William nodded but looked less than convinced.

'You presumably know,' he said, 'that he's mostly a fetcher and carrier of artists' materials. But he's also been helping me out in other ways too.'

He paused, reflecting that this was perhaps not the sort of thing to tell a new acquaintance. But there was something about Prudence's open face that encouraged the sharing of confidences.

'It may just be my imagination,' he went on. 'Or the fact that I'm not as good at remembering as I used to be. But I've been losing track of what I have here in the studio. To put it more bluntly, some of my materials appear to have gone missing. A canvas here, some brushes there. A couple of pigments. Now you might suppose, with all the stuff I get through, there's no way I can know what's here and what's not. And you'd be right. So I thought I'd do something about it. Which is why I've asked Jeremiah to keep an eye on things in the studio. A sort of audit of my stock. Like in a shop. After all, he probably knows more than I do about what comes in and what runs out. And he needs the extra money too.'

He pulled another face. She was getting used to the fact

that his facial expressions were every bit as communicative as anything he might say.

'And who knows,' he went on. 'Perhaps I *did* just imagine it. The whole idea that someone might want to rob me. Rob me of my ... my living. It's a damned stupid thought, I know – excusing my language. But once it crept into my silly noddle, I couldn't get it out.'

He slapped his hand against the side of his head as if rebuking himself. Prudence listened in silence. Once again, she felt it a privilege that William should admit so much in her company.

'What's more,' he said, 'I can't help thinking it's connected to *this*.'

He signalled over his shoulder towards the canvas of 'Morning'.

'The painting,' he said. 'And the memories it's stirred up.'

Prudence continued to sit in silence. Her body had tightened, and the blood had drained from her face.

Memories.

Yes, memories.

But none of that was noticed by William who, too full of his own thoughts, was looking for a brush to chew.

ACT II

The Missing Portrait

'Flea?'

The way she said the word – in an elongated and thoughtful fashion – suggested a question lay behind it.

'Miss?' the young man replied.

His voice had not broken completely. Sometimes it sounded frail and reed-like – the voice of a small child. At other times it was deep and scary in the way it boomed from such a meagre body. And then there were those occasions when it wavered uncomfortably between the two. For all that 'miss' was only one syllable, it conveyed a distinct ambiguity.

'Flea,' Prudence repeated. 'What do you make of Jeremiah Potts?'

'Make of him, miss?' said Flea.

'As a person, Flea,' continued Prudence. 'Is he someone you know at all well?'

Flea pulled at his chin as if trying to wrench it away from the rest of his face. There were one or two hairs on its tip and, for a moment or two, he was distracted by them.

'He does a lot of bending, miss.'

'Bending?' said Prudence.

'A lot of stretching too,' said Flea. 'And waving his arms about. Like he's acting.'

Prudence mused on this. Master Fleabane was not

always the most loquacious of individuals, so when he made a statement of this kind it was worthy of consideration. It was also the case that Flea's assessment complemented her own. There was, Prudence felt, less than a complete match between Jeremiah's outward persona and what she surmised his more private self to be. William's comment about him needing 'the extra money' had also piqued her curiosity.

'Flea,' she said again.

'Miss?'

He looked at her with the eagerness of a puppy keen to demonstrate a mixture of respect, obedience and affection.

'I know you have a particular talent for noticing things,' she said.

Flea tried to keep the glow of pride from his face.

'Would you be uncomfortable,' she went on, 'if I asked you to observe Jeremiah for me? From a distance, I mean. As part of a discreet enquiry into the state of his … wellbeing?'

'You want me to spy on him, miss?'

There was no hint of disapproval, surprise, or even humour in Flea's words. It was a simple matter-of-fact summary, to confirm that he had understood correctly. Prudence suppressed a smile and pursed her lips. She should have anticipated such a straightforward response. And there was no point in denying her purpose by trying to dress it up as anything other than what it was.

'Spy is not the word I would have chosen, Flea,' she said. 'But, yes, essentially you are right. I would like to ascertain if Jeremiah may be in need of some … support.'

'I like the word spy,' said Flea.

There was the shadow of a grin around his thin lips.

'I think I should like to be a spy, miss.'

This time there was no way Prudence could keep the smile from her face. And it conveyed both pleasure and approval of what Flea had said. It was only days since she had been reading excerpts from Ned Ward's *The London Spy*. The accounts – which provided a wry and satirical commentary on city life – had originally been written at the end of the previous century and published before Prudence was born. Such was their popularity, however, that they had been reprinted several times, only very recently appearing once again in the London press. It was stretching a point perhaps, but Prudence felt it provided the merest justification for allowing the word 'spy' to be used in the current context.

'What is it especial, miss, that you wish observed of the gentleman?' said Flea. 'Or is it a more general sort of noticing?'

'I am interested,' Prudence continued, 'in how Jeremiah provides for himself. And what he takes home for his … sustenance. I know he runs errands for a great many people. I have seen him carrying packages and parcels at all times of the day and night. But I am most especially interested to know how well he caters for *himself*.'

She hoped she was choosing her words carefully enough to suggest that she had nothing other than Jeremiah's welfare at the front of her mind. Which was how Flea understood it. Although, to be honest, he was not that interested in *why* Miss Hyssop should want him to keep an eye on Jeremiah. And anyway, it was not in his nature to question anything his mistress asked of him. His implicit trust in her goodness meant that, as soon as the task was clear, his only concern was to carry it out to the best of his ability. The fact that it involved 'spying' simply made it all the more compelling.

It was a vocation for which he felt a deep and instinctive calling.

§

The Green Group was about to meet.

Jane felt oddly excited and arrived at Prudence's house early, hoping to be the first. It would be easier to remember who was who if she observed them arriving one by one. As Master Fleabane ushered her into the hallway, however, she could hear a characteristic voice that she recognised. So she was not surprised by the sight that greeted her as she entered the first-floor drawing-room.

'My dear Jane,' said Prudence. 'We were just talking about you.'

Before Jane had a chance to acknowledge the comment, another woman launched herself forward.

'Jane, dear! What joy! What perfect joy! To know you are to grace our little set.'

Jane smiled back, reeling slightly. It was difficult to think that any set might be described as little if it included the considerable presence of Belinda Parrish (as was). As a physical figure she was everything that Prudence was not. Large, florid, effusive and loud.

Their paths had originally crossed years before, when the young Miss Jane Thornhill was living in the Piazza with her parents. Belinda was the only daughter of a successful man at law who plied his trade in a quiet corner of the Inner Temple. For a while father and daughter rented one of the arcaded houses a few doors away from both Prudence and the Thornhills. Mr Parrish had acted on behalf of Sir James in a legal dispute and Belinda attached herself to the artist's daughter with an enthusiasm that Jane found somewhat stifling.

The friendship was never close. Certainly, when Mr and Mrs Hogarth moved out of the Piazza in 1732, Jane made no attempt to keep up the connection. Shortly afterwards Mr Parrish and his daughter relocated around the corner to a substantial house in Bow Street. Jane heard nothing more of her former friend until just two months before the meeting of the Green Group. It was then that she read of Belinda's marriage to a baronet of dubious reputation – Sir Marmalade Ronson, or something like. She had not actually seen Belinda in the flesh for some three or four years.

Time, however, did not appear to have muted Belinda's enthusiasm or volume. Indeed, if anything, the cloistered atmosphere of Prudence's drawing-room seemed hardly expansive enough to contain her.

'Belinda,' said Jane in a purposely quiet voice. 'How delightful to see you again. You look so full of ...' There was the merest pause, before she completed the sentence. 'So full of life.'

'Of course, my dear Jane,' replied the fulsome Belinda.

'How could one be anything other? Aeons may have passed before the brief flickering of our own existence – and, no doubt, aeons will follow our demise. So it is incumbent upon us all to be as alive as we can possibly be!'

It was a remark, Jane felt, that contrived to be both philosophical and trite at the same time. The sort of statement that marked Belinda out as someone who, for all her charm and intelligence, could also be a mite trying.

Jane quickly cast a sidelong glance at Prudence, whose face wore a non-committal smile. It seemed to imply that it was as well in this world to be prepared for every manifestation of human life. That not to do so would inevitably lead to a sense of frustration with one's fellow human beings. But the smile also hid a more deeply felt admiration for her voluminous friend. Given the domestic turmoil she knew Belinda was enduring, it said something for her spirit that she should appear so self-assured.

'And are you still … alive … in this part of town?' said Jane. 'In your elevated state?'

The words were more than a little barbed. But Belinda seemed not to notice. Or, if she did, not to mind. In fact, she took the question as an opportunity to launch into a brief synopsis of her current situation.

'Lord, no!' she said. 'Had you not heard that I have resided in St James's Square for more than six weeks now. Since very soon after I became the wife of Sir Marmaduke Ransome.'

At this, Belinda burst into a fit of laughter. It seemed to indicate that nothing could be more humorous than the name of her husband – and the fact that she had aligned herself with it for the rest of eternity. Prudence looked on with an expression in which sadness shadowed her admiration.

'So, you are Lady Ransome!' said Jane.

She was now remembering some of the stories she had heard about the baronet.

Belinda raised her eyebrows, nodded her head, and laughed again in a way that seemed to assert, 'Lord, yes! Isn't that a thing!'

'I am so glad that Belinda wished to remain part of the Green Group after her withdrawal to the West End,' said Prudence with evident warmth.

She very much hoped that Belinda would find the shared company of the group supportive. It was just then that two other women were shown into the room by Flea.

The first to enter had a slight figure and an angry face. She was introduced to Jane as Mrs Louisa Crust, wife of *Mr* Crust. Jane seemed to remember Mr Crust as being someone associated with the Covent Garden Parish Council and local Watch – but had never met either him or his wife. The second woman was younger. She was pale and had a distracted air about her. It was as if she had just remembered that she was supposed to be somewhere else but could not for the life of her remember where.

'I'm sorry,' she said. 'So sorry!'

Jane smiled back, unsure what the young woman was sorry about but feeling it was not her place to enquire.

'May I introduce Miss Catherine Pargeter,' said Prudence. 'Catherine is the daughter of Mr Pargeter, the print-seller.'

Ah, of course, thought Jane. She did not know Catherine but had certainly heard of Pargeter's print-shop.

'No doubt,' said Prudence, addressing Mrs Crust and Miss Pargeter, 'you will already be aware of Mrs Jane Hogarth, even if you have not yet had the pleasure of meeting.'

Belinda wheezed and made a noise that sounded like 'Lord-yes!' Mrs Crust nodded sharply and repeated Prudence's words, 'No doubt'. Miss Pargeter contrived to look immensely awkward.

'Oh yes,' she said. 'I'm sorry. I really am.'

Jane did not know why another apology was called for, but she decided it must just be Miss Pargeter's way. There followed a few more inconsequential comments, a little small talk, and several non sequiturs. Prudence then managed to shepherd her guests towards a carefully arranged circle of chairs.

'Please be seated, ladies,' she said. 'We are complete. Or at least as complete as we shall be today. Mrs Woakes has sent word that she is incapacitated with an ague.'

There was much murmuring that implied the assembled company wished Mrs Woakes a speedy recovery. There was also some muttering, however, to the effect that it was a long time since Mrs Woakes had been seen at the Green Group. Or indeed anywhere else. Jane remained silent. She had no idea who Mrs Woakes was, and had the distinct impression that she was unlikely ever to find out.

'And so, to our topic for today,' said Prudence after a calm had settled on the group. 'Mrs Jane Hogarth, daughter of the late Sir James Thornhill, wife of the eminent artist Mr William Hogarth, and a former resident of this Piazza, has very kindly agreed to share with us a few reflections under the heading "Art and Home".

And with that, amid an expectant hush, Prudence turned and smiled at Jane.

§

In resuming my recollections, I shall endeavour to focus on only a few circumstances from my earlier years, as I believe there to be little merit in recounting the details of what was a fairly unadventurous life.

Yet I am prompted by those events that presently surround me to reflect upon instances that, with the benefit of hindsight, I now know to be of some interest, at least to me, in the context of my current life.

Losing Sam drove me towards an even more insular life than I had had before I met him. I spent most of my days in the house, using that time as gainfully as I was able in reading and also drawing, which I had taken to with some delight, and to which I still resort in my most private moments. It was another loss that prompted me into a more active engagement with the world.

That was the death of my great aunt in 1720. She had been unwell for some time, and her slipping away was as unremarkable as had been most things about her life. It was only after she had gone that I really became aware of what she had been for me. That is, a source of stability and, I needs must say, comfort for the whole of my childhood life.

It is true that I had a somewhat sheltered upbringing but, compared to the lives of many of those I saw around me in the Piazza, it was doubtless a life of great privilege and consideration.

The blessings of that upbringing continued after her death, for just in the same way that the house had been bequeathed to her for the duration of her life, so I was informed that the same provision now applied to me. Whether this was due to the great and kind foresight of some now distant family member, or whether it was a matter of chance or even legal complexity, I still do not know. But I hope I have been ever grateful for it, and the continuity it has afforded me.

Miss Greatorex left soon after my great aunt died. Ellen stayed with me for a further two years, before meeting and marrying a sour-faced drover, and decamping with him to the west country. Ruth and Mrs Sanders followed soon after. Ruth went to a grand house north of the Oxford Road. Mrs Sanders retired to live with a sister, I believe, in Kent. Such is the way things go.

I have been fortunate enough to have a series of good and homely maids over the last twelve or more years, and the one who now tends to many of my needs, and who is called Abigail, is a perfect assistant about the house, being almost silent and often invisible. She also likes to cook, and so I am spared the expense of employing a separate cook, which would in any case be an unnecessary indulgence, given my simple habits and tastes.

The other member of the little group that I suppose I should refer to as my establishment is Master Fleabane.

But then I should mention him in his proper place, and not insert him too early into the pages of this journal. For he is an individual worthy of more attention than just a passing line, if only because of his notable arrival.

§

Jane had been determined to say nothing that was not generic and uncontroversial.

She certainly did not want to say anything that risked compromising either her or her husband. What followed over the next twenty minutes, therefore, was relatively bland, slightly quaint, and occasionally humorous. A brief account of what it had been like to grow up in a house of art and artist's materials, only to escape into a very similar environment when she married. Despite her failure to engage with several unspoken questions – like how on earth do you manage to live with such a man? – the group members seemed delighted by what she was prepared to share.

Prudence then thanked Jane and invited a wider discussion of the topic, Art and Home.

They began by observing that art increasingly appeared to feature domestic settings. This was followed by a discussion about conversation pieces – which had become very popular amongst those who could afford to commission paintings depicting family groups and other informal social scenes. There was a lively exchange about the nature of drawing and painting undertaken by women in their own homes. Was that also art? Or was art in the modern age defined by commercial purpose? Or the need to have an audience? And were those two things essentially the same? Then there were the issues around displaying art in the home. If one could not afford paintings, were the very good quality prints that now existed a fair substitute? Or did they constitute something else entirely?

As the discussion progressed Jane realised that most of the artistic debates she had witnessed in the past had been conducted almost entirely by men. If nothing else, the comments of the Green Group were a clear indication that the creation of images was a subject of far greater scope, and more general interest, than was often assumed. The exchanges also gave Jane the opportunity to observe her new companions more closely.

Belinda was equally loud in everything she said, and Jane was aware of a good deal of name-dropping. Sometimes it was a nobleman or his lady that lived close by her new home in St James's Square. Sometimes it was the name of an architect or interior designer who had been recommended for the development of the Ransome residence.

'I know I am most fortunate to be in such a position,' Belinda said. 'One must do what one can to enhance beauty wherever it may be found.'

Jane could see that comments of this kind made Louisa Crust frown very hard. They also reduced Catherine Pargeter to her most apologetic. Perhaps not surprisingly, Prudence navigated a path through the debate without appearing to be ruffled by anything that anyone said. At intervals she threw in her own small comments, each of which seemed to Jane to be deceptively provocative or quietly ironic. In fact, Jane had the impression that, for all Prudence's obvious respect for her Green Group friends, she also found them distinctly amusing.

When Louisa entered the fray on her own account it was always with the air of someone who knew. There was no room for doubt. An example was her view that 'Art in England should be English. It must be a statement of national character. And I won't hear a word said against it.' Jane smiled, knowing she had heard the very same sentiment from her own husband on several occasions.

In contrast with Louisa's stern conviction, Catherine began her contributions with the usual contrition.

'I'm sorry,' she said. 'But I do think women should be allowed to paint more than just flowers.'

Given that the same point had already been agreed by the rest of those present, Jane thought it difficult to understand what Catherine was sorry for.

Whenever the conversation became too conceptual Belinda could be relied upon to bring it down to earth. This usually involved references to things she was planning to do to her house and the people she was hoping would do them. She made reference to a certain Mr Smallow. He had been engaged to create a series of portraits, including those of herself and her husband. It was not a name that meant anything to Louisa. Catherine had heard the gentleman mentioned more than once at her father's shop – and by another person as well. Prudence developed a slight cough at this point and left the room for a glass of water.

Jane's ears, however, pricked up. She knew that Smallow was a man for whom William had nothing but loathing and contempt. She was not sure exactly *why*, never having met him herself. But she had heard stories. Apparently because both men were of short stature, some wags had insisted that Messrs Hogarth and Smallow looked alike. Jane found it hard to believe that anyone could possibly look anything like the squat, awkward, grumpy, badly dressed Mr Hogarth she knew and loved. But she could easily understand how her self-important husband would have chafed at such a comparison. A reaction which would simply have encouraged those who wished to bait him. There were more than a few people who enjoyed making jokes at William's expense. And his prickly nature could be counted on to fan the flames of their wit.

Another name that came up was Jeremiah Potts. It was when the discussion turned to the fact that it was becoming easier for artists to combine work life with home. Unlike times gone by, when commissions were often large pieces for stately buildings, many artists now worked on smaller pictures like portraits. There was no longer a need to house vast canvases and employ large numbers of assistants to procure and prepare materials. Supplies of pigments, oils and other requisites could be fetched quickly from a range of specialist shops around town. Jeremiah was cited as one person whose livelihood depended on this constant to-ing and fro-ing between suppliers and artists.

At first Louisa was not sure who Mr Potts was. But once he had been described as 'a local Piazza character'

– in some detail, it has to be said, by Belinda – Louisa nodded sternly.

'Ah, yes,' she said. 'I know *exactly* who you mean!'

The mere thought of Mrs Crust's hawk-like face stonily scrutinising Jeremiah's flamboyant gestures made Jane smile. She suppressed any expression of humour, however, as soon as she saw Catherine's face. It had turned even paler than it was before. Had Belinda's vivid description of Jeremiah perhaps prompted some worries or fears? If it did, she managed to recover quickly.

'I'm sorry,' she said. 'Yes, I think I know who you mean. Jeremiah Potts. Yes. I'm sure I do. He comes into the shop now and again. To make deliveries. Yes, I'm sorry.'

It was this combination of interesting subject matter and intriguing companions that kept Jane fully engaged for some two hours. And when the group finally broke up, she was more than ever pleased that Prudence had invited her to attend. It also confirmed in her mind what a mature and fascinating person her new friend was.

As the five of them parted it was, predictably, Belinda who was most effusive in her comments to Jane, making it clear that she hoped they 'might be friends once again'. In some respects, it was no more than a courtesy. But at another level Jane felt that Belinda really meant it. And that – for all the great show Lady Ransome put on as she stepped into her sedan chair – the words had been a cry from the heart.

§

When Master Fleabane reported back to his mistress, he declared an intention to divide his account into two sections.

The first section would concern itself with Jeremiah's personal and domestic purchases. The second would concentrate on his business as an artist's courier. Prudence nodded her approval of this very ordered proposal and composed herself to listen.

Flea began by providing details of the bread, meat and few pieces of fruit that Jeremiah had brought back to his room over the course of two days. For some items Flea even specified their weight and how much they had cost. Prudence managed not to smile too broadly at the thought of the young man recording these particulars with such obvious relish. Indeed, she listened with an enquiring look on her face, which encouraged Flea to elaborate on the quality of the meat and fruit. At the conclusion of this inventory of provisions Prudence professed herself pleased that Jeremiah should be feeding himself relatively well.

It was, however, when Flea began the second part of his report that her face took on an altogether more concentrated expression. Noting this, Flea methodically recounted that, during the same two days, Jeremiah had collected from suppliers and artists a total of twelve packages. They included everything from canvases to brushes, pigments and oils, plus a range of other items, including a wooden board, a bottle of arrack and a savoury pasty. Most of these things were taken straight to the premises of various artists. Deliveries were made to four different gentlemen, the most prominent of whom was Mr Hogarth. The other three were Mr Joseph van Aken, Mr George Bickham, and Mr Jonathan Smallow.

Of these three, only the last was familiar to Flea, as it was the same surly gentleman who had accosted him two weeks before in Tavistock Row. The other two names meant nothing, although they were clearly well known to Miss Hyssop. Mr van Aken, she said, had painted several views of Covent Garden Piazza and Mr Bickham she knew as a print maker of some renown. She said nothing at all about Mr Smallow.

Flea's report combined a dispassionate sense of order with the odd conspiratorial nod. Moreover, it was, Prudence decided, a narrative that demonstrated both acute observation and a remarkable memory. Its conclusion was that, in most cases, the deliveries appeared worthy of no great note. There were, however, two exceptions to which Flea wished to draw attention.

One was where he had been unable to track an item all the way from its place of origin to its final destination. It was on the first day, when Jeremiah collected a blank canvas and took it back to the house on Tavistock Row.

The second exception occurred the following day. Flea observed Jeremiah leaving Mr Hogarth's house carrying a package that was smaller than the previous day's canvas. The item, which was wrapped in sacking, Jeremiah had first taken back to his room. Then, later that afternoon, he left the house once more, carrying what looked like the same object. He delivered it to Mr Smallow's studio before returning home.

Prudence thanked Flea for this very thorough account and gave him some small monetary reward. From the look on his face, he clearly regarded the gift as a badge of honour, akin to receiving a medal for a well-executed military manoeuvre. Thanking her in his usual taciturn way, he added a remark to the effect that if Miss Hyssop were disposed to undertake any further acts of surveillance, he was most certainly her man.

Left alone to ponder what Fleabane had told her, Prudence had to admit that any evidence – if that is what it amounted to – was at best circumstantial and open to various interpretations. Taken by itself it was hardly worthy of further consideration. Yet it also needed to be viewed in the context of what William had told her. Especially in terms of his notion that things had gone missing from his studio.

She might be wrong, of course, but it did seem possible that Jeremiah may have purloined some of the items he was being paid to keep watch over. Given that his only income came from his courier work – which clearly did not pay well – Prudence could imagine him being subject to temptation. The opportunity to keep back a canvas here, or some brushes there, may have proved difficult to resist – especially if they could be sold on to other clients. It was, she knew, a distinctly uncharitable thought on her part. But she had to consider it as at least a possibility. Certainly, with respect to Mr Hogarth, she could envisage Jeremiah perhaps thinking that the odd ingredient would not matter. After all, what was one more brush to the most successful artist in London? Not that such thinking made it acceptable, of course. Particularly given the position of trust Jeremiah enjoyed in William's studio.

And perhaps none of it was true anyway. It might all be no more than uninformed speculation. There was almost certainly a perfectly good explanation for what was going on. Or perhaps *nothing* was going on at all!

Except that she had the distinct feeling that something *was*.

In fact, Prudence had a quite specific sense of foreboding. And a little voice inside told her that she should do something about it. She was, after all, likely to be one of only a few people for whom the wellbeing of *both* Mr Hogarth and Jeremiah mattered. William was, admittedly, a new acquaintance – but Jeremiah was a longstanding neighbour. As Belinda had put it, he was a local 'character'. It would be an abdication of responsibility to let him fall victim to his demons if something could be done to help.

Thus it was that Prudence persuaded herself that she should act. Not only for Jeremiah's sake – but for William's as well. And one thing was clear. There was no time to lose. She took up her quill and penned a short note.

Going down to the kitchen, she found Flea eating a fruit tart and basking in the success of his excursion into the world of espionage. Insisting that he should not move a muscle until the last crumb of the tart had been consumed, Prudence gave him the note. It was addressed to Jeremiah, requesting him to call at his earliest convenience on a matter of business. She assumed he would be keen to discover what 'business' Miss Hyssop might have in mind.

And she was right. For it was no more than two hours later when Jeremiah presented himself at her front door, wishing to know if now might be a convenient time.

§

The bawd had warned the young woman not to ask too many questions.

But, spending almost every night at the house, she was curious. She wanted to know about the clients' lives, not just their sexual preferences. She knew the place attracted men who ranked amongst the highest in the land. The ruling class, she had heard them called. It was already clear, however, that their grand titles, airs and graces testified to nothing but the very lowest and meanest of natures. It was one of these so-called noble men she most wanted to see.

It seemed only reasonable that she should ask her fellow workers about such things. Which clients were the most frequent visitors? Who were the more occasional guests? What were their names? A few of the girls were prepared to share such knowledge. Others were more protective of what they knew. Perhaps they feared this newcomer might use the information against them.

One of the older women seemed happy enough to discuss the merits of the various men she had entertained during the preceding weeks. It seemed best to ask her the question directly – especially as the individual's name had not arisen in any other context.

'Have you come across a man called Sir Marmaduke Ransome?' the young woman said.

The other woman pulled a face.

'Friend o' yourn?' she said.

The young woman said no, she had never met him. But she had heard him spoken of. By others.

The older woman looked suspicious but continued to talk.

"E's been 'ere more than once,' she said. 'Rough bastard, so they say. I ain't been wiv 'im. Wouldn't want to.'

She lit her pipe and smoked in silence for a while. Then she started up again, as if she had just remembered something.

"E's married now, so I 'eard.'

It was said in a flat tone that betrayed no particular opinion on the matter. The younger woman assumed it was stated simply as a dull fact – something unlikely to have any bearing on the gentleman's attendance at the house. Such a view was reinforced by what the older woman said next.

'Pity 'is poor missus, eh?'

There was a pause while she continued to smoke.

Then she spoke again.

'Pity us all, for that matter. For we're all in the same boat.'

§

Jeremiah regarded the note from Miss Hyssop as a message sent from above.

Perhaps she really *was* an angel and had already seen into the torments of his soul.

Far from being a comfort, however, such a notion simply made him more nervous. As did the thought of being introduced into one of the Piazza's grand old houses. He decided that such a setting required his most theatrical persona.

Having been shown into Miss Hyssop's drawing-room, Jeremiah bowed low in a fashion that would have done justice, Prudence thought, to the Theatre Royal itself.

'Jeremiah,' she said.

Her tone was calculated to fall somewhere between friendly engagement and business-like propriety. Jeremiah bowed again but seemed unable to utter a word. His eyes flickered as they tried to take in what he could see around him.

'Jeremiah,' Prudence repeated. 'Do please be seated.'

He made a show of brushing some dust from his breeches. Then he perched himself on the edge of an upright chair with an air of trepidation.

'Jeremiah,' said Prudence yet again, this time with firmness.

She was determined not to beat about the bush.

'You must understand that what I am about to say is in complete confidence and shall be known to no one other than we two.'

Jeremiah drew his face into a tight smile, unsure how he should interpret this opening. Was complete confidence a good and business-like thing? Or should he be worried?

For her part, Prudence was resolved to stick to her plan. She felt sure Jeremiah would respect her more if she took the matter head on.

'Jeremiah.'

She was using his name as a way of taking a run at the subject.

'It is a known fact,' she said, 'that you are a carrier of packages. However, it is perhaps a fact known only to *me* – simply by virtue of our closeness as neighbours – that such packages are sometimes conveyed into the house in which you live.'

She knew the statement was vague and somewhat enigmatic.

'Packages, miss?' he said.

'Packages, Jeremiah,' she repeated.

She kept her eyes on him. Her expression was neutral. He stared back. What followed was rather strange. As could be read on the faces of both participants.

There was a silence of at least a minute. Perhaps longer.

During that time Prudence and Jeremiah looked each other in the eye, not glancing away even for one second. Jeremiah's face at various points suggested that he was about to speak. His eyebrows moved up – and then down. And then up again. His wide lips formed themselves into shapes preparatory for speech – only then to relax, before tensing again.

Across the room from him Prudence sat very still. Her only movement was a slight downward tilt of the head, so that she was able to look up at him from under her brow. And then a tightening of the mouth, before her lips parted slightly. To an unknowing observer it was a silence that may have indicated two people who were equally at a loss as to what they might say to each other. But to the individuals themselves it was something else entirely. For whatever reason, and despite their great differences, Prudence and Jeremiah were very much of the same mind.

The minute that passed was not therefore a period of nothingness. Instead, it was pregnant with every thought that passed through their connected consciousness. In several respects, this time of quiet facial contortion stood in for many more minutes of conversation. For, in the silence, Jeremiah could read Prudence's astuteness, determination and goodwill. While Prudence could see in Jeremiah's face the consideration of multiple stories that might explain or excuse the implications of what she had said. In other words, it was a silence that spoke volumes. And when the two of them finally *did* speak, it was to acknowledge the bond already formed by what they had *not* said.

'It's not what you think,' said Jeremiah at last.

Prudence had to smile. She was delighted he had not run from the room. There was, after all, no reason on earth why he should stay to be accused of anything. And she was only too aware that she might be overstepping the mark by speaking in such a way. His continued presence was encouraging.

'And what *do* I think?' she said as gently as she could. 'And please forgive me, Jeremiah. I have not offered you any refreshment. Would you take something to drink?'

These last words were added to reinforce what she hoped was the good nature of the discussion. If nothing else it would demonstrate that she had not invited him there in order to berate him.

'Thank you, miss,' he said. The ghost of a smile curled the edges of his mouth as he acknowledged both the offer and the sentiment. 'Nothing for me, thank you. But I appreciate your kindness.'

He paused and smiled more openly. Then he breathed deeply, as if preparing to give a speech.

'When I say it's not what you think,' he went on. 'What I mean is that it's not what it may *appear* to be.'

'And what *is* that, Jeremiah?'

'The gathering up of goods. For financial gain, miss.'

The words were delivered as if they had been prepared for a court of law. As perhaps they may have been.

'Jeremiah,' said Prudence. 'I may not know you well, but I hope we are acquainted enough for me to judge that you are not a dishonourable man. You are a near neighbour and a long-standing member of this community.'

She wanted to provide him with some degree of emotional security. Jeremiah looked bashful.

'You are very kind, miss,' he said. 'And I appreciate your attention. But, in the spirit of confidentiality to which you have alluded, miss, I want to be clear that …'

He paused.

'There is more to this than meets the eye.'

§

Dr Rock halted his one-horse chaise at the eastern end of the Piazza.

It was his favoured spot in Covent Garden, and where people expected to find him if they wanted one of his tinctures or patent medicines. He stood up on the chaise and looked around, surveying his estate. At the far end of the space the august portico of St Paul's Church dominated the scene, as it had done for the last hundred years. In front of the church the horticultural market had now engulfed the sundial column that marked out the centre of the square. At this time of year there was little colour to be had in the displays of potted plants and small trees, although they still attracted folk who came to gaze rather than buy.

To the left, from Rock's point of view – between the horticultural display and Tavistock Row – was the main vegetable market. Two lines of brick-built shops and wooden sheds ran the length of the Piazza, hemming in an array of smaller stalls and willow baskets. One of the more familiar structures of the inner row was Tom King's coffee-house, itself little more than a shed.

His eyes looked back to Tavistock Row, lingering for a while on one of the buildings towards the east end of the terrace. It was a house that had twice been visited by death in the past few months. First had been the unfortunate fall of a young lady who broke her neck on the stairs. More recently, the sadly afflicted Alcazar family had lost another of their children to a fever. Death and disease were everywhere and could not be denied for long. The challenge was not how to avoid them – but how to face them. Every experience of Rock's life had made that simple truth ever more evident. And he had, of course, played his own small part in trying to alleviate the suffering that life inevitably involved.

Yes, it was true that he was known to many as a quack – castigated as a charlatan, a manipulator of people's fears. But such a verdict simply betrayed a misunderstanding of the human condition. For none of his potions made people worse than they already were. None of his cures inflicted pain. There was nothing he sold that, used responsibly, would not aid a recovery of sorts. What did it matter if not every tincture or treatment could be proved to be, in itself, efficacious? That was not the point. Death and disease respected natural philosophy no more than anything else. The important thing was to give people hope. To raise their spirits. To put them in a frame of mind from which they could start to see the positive side of life. Surely that was a great deal better than wallowing in a slough of despond.

So, there was nothing at all shameful in what he did. If only the same could be said of everyone else he dealt with.

He turned to his right and surveyed the northern side of the Piazza. The space of the square was more open here. Just a few traders had their wares set out on the ground, which left enough room for other activities. Two people were walking their dogs. Some children were playing tag. Rock had often stopped to watch boxing matches in the same place, although they seemed less common now. His eyes took in the elegant arcade and row of houses that was still, in his view, the architectural highlight of the square. Inigo Jones's overall design had lost none of its symmetry and splendour. Despite the presence of the market, the terrace retained an Italianate style and grandeur that could be found nowhere else in London.

As his gaze moved from one house to another, he

ruminated on the people who had lived there during the many years he had been providing his service. And he paused for a few seconds as his eyes alighted on the mid-terrace house he knew to be the home of Miss Prudence Hyssop. He had sometimes glimpsed her from his chaise as he moved around the Piazza, but he always resisted the urge to look in her direction. From out of the corner of his eye he had tried to ascertain the nature of her expression and speculate upon the workings of her mind. But she had always been as keen to avoid his gaze as he was to escape hers.

§

Prudence looked at Jeremiah in her calm and composed way, inviting him to say more.

He clearly liked his last set of words, and so repeated them.

'In all honesty, miss, there really *is* more to all of this than meets the eye.'

Prudence was puzzled.

'I am afraid you are going to have to say a little more, Jeremiah,' she said. 'Certainly, if I am to comprehend the full extent of your meaning.'

He shifted on his chair and looked distinctly uncomfortable. His face tried out several more expressions before finally settling on one that was a combination of contrition and confidentiality. If Miss Hyssop really *was* an angel, there was no point in being anything other than totally open with her, was there? After all, wasn't that what *he* wanted as well? The opportunity to share his secret.

Not *all* of it, of course. But at least some of it.

'You see, miss,' he continued, 'the truth of the matter is that I have taken to … painting. That is, I have made a beginning.'

Prudence's mouth opened but she closed it quickly. It was a spontaneous indication of her surprise. And she was not sure how to respond. Before she could think of anything to say, Jeremiah continued.

'*But*,' he said, making the word sound quite final. 'I lack the means.'

He stopped and looked at her. His mobile face pleaded in ways more articulate than his words.

'You lack the means,' said Prudence, playing back the words as a prompt for him to say more. Was he referring to a lack of talent? Or materials? Space perhaps? She could not be sure.

'I know it's a terrible thing, miss,' he said, 'but I couldn't afford to buy the things I needed. And I didn't want to draw attention to what I was doing by asking. I wanted to keep it secret, you see.'

He stopped to bite the side of a long finger before going on.

'That's why I started borrowing,' he said. 'Borrowing from Mr Hogarth. It was only ever Mr H, miss. And I *will* pay him back. One day. I'm not sure how. Not yet. But I *will*. And in the meantime, I thought perhaps he might not notice. Except he did. And then, of all things, he asked me to keep an eye on the stocks!'

Jeremiah slapped his palm across his brow in a dramatic fashion and looked mortified.

'I didn't know if it was good luck or bad luck,' he went on. 'Or whether it was God saying it was all right. To borrow things, I mean. For a while at least.'

Prudence frowned.

'I do not think you can bring God in to support your case, Jeremiah,' she said.

He looked embarrassed. Even if Miss Hyssop was not exactly an angel, she was most certainly a pillar of the local church. If *any*one knew what was in the Almighty's mind when it came to things like borrowing, it would be her.

'You're right, miss,' he said, shame-faced. 'Begging your pardon. And His as well, of course. But it was all rather odd, if you see what I mean. Mr H asking me to look after the very things I was borrowing.'

Prudence did not know what to say. She did not want to reprimand him. Or inhibit him from telling her more. So she decided to leave to one side the matter of whether Jeremiah's 'borrowing' was defensible at any level. She would focus instead on his painting. This might at least encourage him to explain why he had made the decisions he had.

'We should speak more of this … borrowing … in due course, Jeremiah,' she said. 'But first – perhaps you could say something more of your painting. What sort of painting is it?'

It was, she thought, the mildest of questions. Straightaway, however, she saw the blood drain from his face, and he appeared to be lost for words. Perhaps she should take an even gentler approach.

'Well, whatever it might be,' she continued in her most

encouraging tone, 'I imagine it must give you a great deal of … satisfaction.'

Jeremiah's expression was difficult to read. But it certainly did not convey anything approaching satisfaction. Faced with his continuing – and increasingly awkward – silence, Prudence had no alternative but to keep talking. She did not wish to make him any more uneasy than he already was. But she sensed the discussion could only progress if they found a way to focus on the nature of his artistic endeavour. Perhaps the paintings themselves would say more than their creator.

'Might I see something of your work?' she said.

She hoped her smile would be interpreted as supportive, but she was feeling distinctly tense inside.

'I have always been interested in art,' she went on. 'And it may be easier to continue our conversation if I have some idea of how you have been using … the things you have … borrowed.'

Jeremiah's look of white-faced mortification was replaced by a red flush that suggested embarrassment underscored by despair. Prudence was distressed that her comments should have occasioned such obvious pain. So she coloured a little herself and resolved to remain quiet while her visitor regained his equilibrium.

He stood up. But then, changing his mind, sat down again and perched even closer to the edge of the chair. Finally, with his eyes fixed firmly on the floor, he began to stammer out some words.

'That, miss, is the thing I most want,' he said. 'In the whole world. To be able to speak about it. But, at the same time, it is the very thing I dread. For my work is poor and broken and not what you would expect a painting to be. It is all as poor and broken as am I!'

Prudence was desperately thinking what she might say.

'But you are just beginning,' she said. 'You said so yourself. I am sure that even Mr Hogarth's first paintings were … poor. And perhaps a little broken too.'

These words, with their implicit reference back to the 'borrowing', seemed only to increase Jeremiah's anguish. It therefore took some time – and a good deal more talking – before Prudence was able to find a way forward.

§

I remember the very first time I felt myself beginning to be interested in the art world of Covent Garden. It was some years before Sam's disappearance.

I have mentioned that the premises of Mr Tremisgus, the art dealer for whom Sam worked, were no more than a few doors away from where I lived. It was about the time of Queen Anne's death in 1714 that Mr Tremisgus announced that a painting of Covent Garden Piazza might be viewed in his rooms for a few days prior to its being sold. The painting was by an artist called Jan Griffier.

It was the first time I had seen a painting of the Piazza, and I was entranced by it. I have no idea who bought it at the auction which followed, but I remember thinking that I would love to have such a picture. To buy a painting of this quality, however, I knew to be beyond my means, and so I began to frequent some of the nearby print shops in the hope that I would find a representation of the Piazza that I could afford. My efforts were largely unsuccessful (they have been more successful since), and the images I found did not, I felt, do justice to the vigour of the place. I do recall that the first image I bought was a map showing the square as it was at the end of the last century.

It was about this time, however, that I first began to take a wider interest in those artists who were painting the Piazza. I was especially intrigued to find that the only names mentioned were from the Low Countries, as Mr Griffier had been. Indeed, my impression was that most of the painters hereabouts were of foreign origin, and I heard mention of no one who was English.

That has largely remained the case, and poor Mr Alcazar is another example of the very proficient foreign artists who excel at depicting the manifold spirit of Covent Garden. It is only in recent years that the names of English artists have become more prominent, with Mr Hogarth the most renowned. But even he has not, so far as I know, attempted to portray the Piazza in any serious way.

Until now, that is – with his painting of 'Morning' being perhaps the first picture of the marketplace by an Englishman to be prepared for public view. It makes me very conscious of the privileged position I have enjoyed, simply by being able to see the picture during its creation, quite apart from the fact that the woman is modelled upon me.

But the first mention of Mr Hogarth in these remembrances must needs prompt the recollection of the first time I saw him. Although he was at that date no better known than was I.

For as I think further on these matters, I am aware that it was because of this first meeting that I spent much of the last years staying out of his path. And also the path of his dear wife.

It is a blessing to record that this, I trust, is now no longer the case. And I am thankful that Mr Hogarth's 'Morning' has perhaps begun to heal the hurt engendered by that dark dawn so long ago.

§

Much against her better judgement, Prudence agreed to continue the conversation by visiting Jeremiah in his room on the following morning.

The decision did not give her an easy night's rest. She was putting herself in a situation well beyond what might legitimately be regarded as Christian charity. She was also not clear as to how it could be reconciled with the relationship she now enjoyed with Mr and Mrs Hogarth. In such a context, might her contact with Jeremiah be perceived as naïve or even duplicitous? Was it morally just to be in receipt of Jane and William's trust whilst lending support to someone who had admitted purloining his employer's materials?

Even more immediate than that, however, was the fact that she would be venturing alone to the room of a single man who had already confessed to being poor and broken. She must have taken leave of her senses. Most especially as it was such a long way up.

She had visited the house before – and recently – when

calling on the Alcazars. But the higher storeys were surely not so familiar. The way up from the ground floor to the first floor was easy enough, but the ascent to the second-floor landing was decidedly hazardous. She tried not to think of how that young woman had lost her footing on the same stairs just three months before. From the second floor up to the garret was, by comparison, somewhat easier. The narrow stairwell was boxed in, and she was able to support herself against the retaining wall. It reminded her …

But no.

Just concentrate on the climb.

And a very steep climb it was. Especially for a woman in middle age – and in a dress not suited to such a precarious expedition.

At the top of the final flight there was a small space that was little more than a bare wooden platform. Ahead of her a door stood open. It led into a well-proportioned loft that was flooded with light from a south-facing casement window.

Jeremiah stood in the middle of the room, his arms outstretched, looking both proud and embarrassed.

'Miss Hyssop,' he said. 'Welcome to my humble abode. My … home.'

It was not just good manners that made Prudence smile warmly back at him. She realised that the personal concerns she had so recently been rehearsing needed to be put to one side. At least for a while. Because here in front of her stood a man who was so obviously baring his soul as well as his home. How else was she to interpret his ambiguous expression? Yes, this was difficult for her. But it was clearly not easy for him either.

He smiled back nervously and swapped his pose of vulnerability for one of his more usual low bows.

'Please to be seated,' he said.

He moved to one side and waved his arm towards a chair. She expressed her thanks and sat down carefully. In front of her was what appeared to be a makeshift easel, constructed from a small table and two pieces of wood. It only declared itself as an easel by having a canvas balanced upon it. The whole contraption faced away from her, towards the far end of the room where the casement led out onto the roofs beyond. It made her feel as if she were sitting for her portrait. But it also reminded her of being in William's studio and seeing the painting of 'Morning' displayed on a real easel. The two spaces were worlds apart. It was as if the two easels represented the huge divide that separated Jeremiah from William. Prudence started to feel insecure once more.

'Can I offer you a very small glass of shrub, Miss Hyssop?' said Jeremiah. 'It was a gift to me from Mr Pargeter, and I should be honoured if you would partake of some.'

Prudence paused. She did not want anything to drink. She particularly did not wish to imbibe something of a spiritous nature at ten o'clock in the morning.

'That would be delightful, Jeremiah,' she said. 'Thank you.'

It was the right thing to say, and her acceptance made him visibly relax. It also gave her a chance to look around the room while he made a show of fetching the flask and polishing two very small, thick-stemmed glasses.

Ahead of her, on the other side of the improvised easel, was where Jeremiah had made his studio. The high casement window provided a good amount of light and there was space for an aspiring artist to move about in the course of his work. A few canvases stood along the edge of the floor with their fronts turned towards the wall. The other end of the room, which was behind her, appeared to be Jeremiah's domestic space. Prudence turned and quickly took in what was there. A small window, a low bed, a table and another chair. There was also a mess of small items, randomly placed.

A shiver ran down her back. It was not that she had allowed herself to come alone to a man's bedroom – although that in itself was not without its terrors. It was more that she realised in that moment what she had mostly managed to avoid thinking about up to this point.

The memory of having been here before.

The knowledge that she was sitting in what had been Sam Harris's room all those years before.

The thought perplexed her more than she was willing to admit. Very briefly her imagination conjured a ghostly presence where the easel now stood. It was the figure of a young man, bashful, with his arms stretched out. Much as Jeremiah had been standing there just moments before.

The vision no sooner appeared than it vanished again.

It was replaced by the very corporeal presence of Jeremiah as he held out a small glass of shrub. He was smiling but his mobile features took on an expression of concern when he saw the cloud that passed across his visitor's face.

'Are you quite well, miss?' he said. 'I hope the climb has not wearied you. We're almost on the roofs here. Nearer the stars – or the angels, as I like to think of it. Nearer than I'm ever like to be again.'

He was trying to lighten the mood and put Prudence at her ease. But he was also worried that she might be having second thoughts about being there. He had intended to sip his own glass of shrub in a genteel fashion, but instead he gulped it down in one.

'I am well enough, Jeremiah,' said Prudence. 'Thank you, I am fine. It is just that the thought came upon me that this house holds a degree of sadness. I was thinking of poor Mr and Mrs Alcazar.'

She did not want to mention Sam. Or Kitty Smith.

Jeremiah's face had grown longer.

'You're right there, miss,' he said. 'There are ghosts aplenty hereabouts. I feel sure of that.'

§

Mid-morning was always the quietest time inside Tom King's.

The last nocturnal reveller had left some two hours before. The focus was now on providing a service to the market traders. That, and restoring some kind of order to the place after another rowdy night. Moll busied herself behind the bar, supervising the washing of glasses and directing the two girls who were sweeping up and putting the chairs back in their usual places.

The stranger who sat in the corner – his hat pulled low over his face, and his great coat wrapped closely about him – was keeping himself to himself. He had ordered a second bowl of the gritty coffee that the place served up for the market folk and sat silently reading a newspaper. Moll glanced in his direction. It was difficult to see much of him, so shrouded was he by his clothes. But she guessed he was not much more than forty years of age. One of the girls had come behind the bar and whispered that he had a wooden leg. But Moll could not see from where she was standing. An old soldier, she reckoned. They often came back from campaigns with bits missing. She kept her eye on him. It was not that common to have someone in the place who did not look familiar. Certainly not at this time of day.

He may have felt her eyes upon him, for he finished his drink, folded the newspaper carefully, and pushed it into the pocket of his great coat. When he stood up Moll could see him better. A well-built man. But, yes, a wooden leg. As he made his way over to the bar it announced itself by thumping on the bare wooden floor. Moll could now see his face. It was handsome and tanned by the sun. Almost as brown as the cheeks of the oldest market stall-holders. Yes, almost certainly an old soldier, thought Moll. Back from the colonies.

He dug in his pocket and put a coin on the bar.

'That will suffice, I trust?' he said.

'That'll do handsomely,' said Moll.

It was too much for two bowls of coffee. He would want more for his money. She knew how it worked.

'Perhaps a question then,' he said. 'As these parts are foreign to me.'

So, what *was* he then? What had the soldier become with his one good leg? A bailiff? A thief-catcher? Or just someone paid to spy on one of her clients? The place was well-known as a magnet for a very mixed kind of company. If you were trying to track down a noble debtor, general trickster, unprincipled attorney, or average scoundrel, you could do worse than try your luck at 'Kings' College'. But, from Moll's point of view, if they paid for their drinks and did not wreck the place, they were as welcome as anyone else. No matter that some of her customers may not have been the most honourable gentlemen in town. It was not for her and her husband to stand in judgement. After all, you could even find men of the cloth at Tom King's. For did not our Lord say that he would rather spend his time with tax collectors, drunkards and whores than with hypocrites? Or something like that.

'Depends what it is,' said Moll.

Her voice made clear that he was not beyond suspicion.

The stranger pushed his hat further back on his head to show more of his face. He wanted to disarm her wariness and was now smiling. Yes, a good-looking face, she thought. Nice eyes. Perhaps not a spy at all.

'Just some local information,' he said.

'Like?' said Moll.

She knew all the best local girls. And she knew several who would be very happy with a gentleman this handsome. Even with only one leg.

'I was wondering if you knew of a person who used to live hereabouts?' he said. 'A lady. A Miss Prudence.'

So he *did* want a woman. Choosy though. He wanted a particular one. But the name was not familiar to Moll. Certainly not one of the ladies who frequented Tom King's. Certainly not with a name like Prudence.

'Can't think that I do,' she said at last.

He looked disappointed.

'But if it's a *lady* you're looking for,' said Moll, determined to cheer up such a handsome and generous cove. 'If *that's* what takes your fancy, I knows a fair few who are particularly ladylike in their ways.'

She gave him one of her most appealing leers.

'*Particularly* ladylike.'

§

Prudence did not want to think about ghosts.

She tried to concentrate her mind on the here and now. On why she was there in Jeremiah's room. On what she was hoping to achieve. On how she could move the situation forward in as positive a way as possible. She sipped the shrub that had, until that moment, remained untasted. It smelled of peaches. She drained the glass and held it out to Jeremiah.

'Another one, miss?' he said.

He was pleased the drink had proved acceptable. Prudence waved a finger in the air.

'Thank you, but no,' she said, feeling a warm glow in her chest. 'I am sufficiently refreshed.'

He looked relieved.

'It had not been my wish to speak of misfortune,' she went on. 'But, for the briefest of moments, the sense of loss was inescapable.'

'I understand, miss,' he said. 'Mr and Mrs Alcazar are not deserving of such as has been visited upon them.'

He was standing before her, wringing his hands. He wanted to say something to bring comfort to them both but could not find the words. She could see his helplessness and decided to press on towards the matter in hand.

'So where shall we begin?' she said.

She looked around, implying that now was the time to move the discussion on to the subject of his painting.

'I should very much like to see some of your work,' she continued.

Even though this was the stated reason for her visit, the words seemed to take Jeremiah by surprise. He suddenly stood bolt upright, shoulders back, chin raised. Prudence was not sure whether it made her think of a lawyer preparing to address the court, or a condemned man going stoically to his death.

§

Just as the stranger was leaving Tom King's, a more recognisable figure entered.

He was short, well-dressed and had an undoubted air of self-importance. He strode up to the bar and spoke to Moll, who was writing something in an order book.

'Who's peg-leg?' he said, tipping his head back towards

the man he had passed on the way in. 'I haven't seen him around here before.'

'Ah, now, Mr Smallow,' said Moll. 'There's a *lot* of folk you haven't seen. Not at *this* time of day, that's for sure. We gets all sorts in here during the day-time. Porters. Traders. Strangers. Even the odd painter.'

He glanced at her. Was she baiting him?

'It's a different world to when you night owls come in,' she went on. 'A lot quieter. People drinking coffee, don't you know? 'Cos this *is* a coffee-house after all, Mr Smallow. So would you like a bowl? Just to celebrate your calling upon us at this very unexpected hour?'

'A pox on your coffee,' said Smallow. 'I want some information.'

Moll laughed.

'*Another* one!' she said. 'I could set myself up as a blessed Horacle at this rate!'

Smallow did not know what she meant – and was not interested enough to ask.

'Was Ransome in last night?' he said.

'And what if he was, Mr Smallow?'

He would like to have torn her off a strip for her impertinence but did not want to forego her good will or compliance.

'I need to speak to him about his current commission,' Smallow said. 'But he seems to be lying low.'

He paused and puffed out his chest, before adding, 'I am creating a series of paintings for his new establishment.'

He could never resist the urge to boast.

'I know you are,' she replied. 'He told me just the other night.'

Smallow looked at her suspiciously. Was she goading him again? Surely his artistic commission was hardly the stuff of coffee-house tittle-tattle.

'Really, Mrs King?' was all he said. 'I find it hard to believe that Sir Marmaduke would discuss matters of art ... in here.'

'It was less to do with the art,' said Moll. 'If you take my drift, Mr Smallow. It was more to do with the money he said he was saving.'

She looked at him in a provocative way. He blushed at the thought that Ransome might have actually been talking about these things in such low company.

'He said that?' he growled.

Moll did not like Jonathan Smallow and was determined to rile him as much as she could.

'Well, not in so many words,' she said. 'But he *did* say he'd worked out how to get the best deal from a painter.'

Smallow wanted to walk away but he felt trapped. Either Moll was piling lie upon lie just to annoy him, or there was some truth in what she was saying. One way or another, he wanted to know.

'And what did he suggest was the way to do that?' he said through tight lips.

He feared he was simply playing into her hands and setting himself up for a bout of derision.

'Payment in kind,' said Moll, trying her hardest to keep a straight face.

At that moment her husband appeared behind her,

carrying a small barrel of brandy. Smallow was about to ask for further clarification, when Moll went on.

'He said he'd kept the price down by letting you fuck his wife whenever you fancied.'

Tom had picked up enough of the conversation to realise that his wife was having fun at Mr Smallow's expense, and that she had probably made up the whole thing. He put the barrel down on the counter and burst into laughter.

Smallow turned bright red with ill-concealed rage, his lips twitching. Finally, he managed to spit a few venomous words in Moll's direction.

'Thou art a boil, a plague sore!'

The effect of the strange curse was simply to add to the general air of mirth that now gripped the Kings. Smallow turned on his heel and stormed out of the coffee-house. If Ransome was temporarily staying away from Tom King's, it could only be because he had found distractions elsewhere. No doubt he would be lounging in some other dive or brothel. Smallow would find him.

In the meantime, he would call again at the house in St James's Square and see Lady Ransome. And no, not to fuck her – even though the thought was not wholly unattractive. But to move the commission forward. The fee might not be of the size he was seeking – but there were now *other* reasons for wanting to use the Ransome residence to good effect.

§

There was a nervous look in Jeremiah's eye.

He stood on the other side of the makeshift easel and grasped it with both hands. Then, turning it round to face Miss Hyssop, he took a step back so that she could see what was on it. The canvas was no more than two or three feet wide, and slightly less high.

'This one,' said Jeremiah. 'This one is nearly finished. It is, in that respect, my latest work, and perhaps the best place to begin.'

Prudence's muscles had tensed. She realised that she had been holding her breath. She made an effort to relax. And to breathe.

'It's …,' he began, moving towards it.

But then he took a step back again. Silence.

'It is …,' Prudence repeated after a few moments.

Her mind was filling up fast with new thoughts, one of which was sheer relief. It was not as awful as she had feared. It was not a representation of nakedness, abomination, or something unimaginably indecent. It was …

It was shapes of colour.

Bold, primary colours. Squares and rectangles mostly. But a couple of circles too. They all had the look of being freely painted. As if a child had done them. Most were outlined with a thick black line of paint. All on a white background. Nothing else. No people, no animals or birds, no landscape, no imagined scene. Nothing real. Nothing at all. Nothing except bright blocks of colour, butting up against each other. All held together in a kind of web by the black lines that flowed around them. Like dark, grey, lead bonding small panes of coloured glass in a church window.

'It is …,' she tried again. 'It is very colourful. A very colourful … pattern.'

She paused. She wanted him to say something. Anything that would indicate what was meant by it. But she could see that Jeremiah was waiting. She needed to say more. Enough to prompt him. Except that this … this … painting was like nothing she had ever seen before, and she had no idea what she might say. It was, after all, nothing other than marks of colour. No subject. No composition.

'Does it have a title?' she said.

She turned away from the canvas and looked at Jeremiah. He was moving his weight from one foot to the other but seemed pleased by her reaction.

'I call it "Number Four",' he said. 'It's not a very good title, I know. I thought I might call it something that was closer to what was in my head. Something like, "Market on a Sunny Day".'

Prudence looked back at the painting. There was nothing on the canvas that said either market or sunny day to her. Nothing that would say that to *any*one.

'I rather like "Number Four",' she said. 'It has an air of … mystery about it.'

She was trying her best to sound neither condescending nor patently inauthentic.

Jeremiah waggled his head, as if weighing up the alternatives.

'I know the market doesn't look exactly like that,' he said. 'But it seems like that to me – if I just listen to it. Or imagine it. Or think about how it works. All the bits. Together.'

He kept his gaze on the canvas, afraid to look Prudence in the eye. He knew that what he was saying probably made very little sense, but he felt compelled to keep going.

'Would you like to see some more?' he said.

The skin around Prudence's eyes tightened. How could she say anything other than yes?

So it was that, over the next few minutes, Jeremiah showed her three more paintings – placing each one in turn on the makeshift easel.

The first was a series of vertical stripes. Encouraged by Prudence's interest in what the paintings were called, Jeremiah said he thought of this one as 'Daybreak'. The second looked, so Prudence thought, like someone had spilled paint – mostly brown spots and grey dribbles – across the canvas. Jeremiah called it 'The Crowd'. The third was the most worrying of all. It was a single block of grey and black that covered most of the space, with only a thin border of unpainted canvas around the edge. Jeremiah paused before announcing its title.

'I'm not sure I can name it,' he said quietly. 'But I think it should probably be called "Despair".'

Prudence bit her lip. She was staring at the canvas, caught up by its mesmerising spell. How could she get out of this? How could she move the conversation forward without suggesting that Jeremiah was talking like a madman?

But, no. She should not be so judgemental. She was here to help. If she could. And if one thing was already clear to her, it was that the poor man hopping from foot to foot in front of her was a deeply disturbed individual. Nothing could say that more plainly than these so-called pictures. She was determined to give them – and Jeremiah – as much consideration as she could muster. But she also knew that anyone who saw them other than herself – anyone less concerned with trying to save his troubled soul – would ridicule them as the work of a lunatic.

All of which made it that much more important that she attempt to be as supportive as she could. If she was likely to be the only person not to laugh outwardly at what Jeremiah had done, she needed to use that position in a positive way. She may have come to see him primarily to talk about his 'borrowing'. But that now appeared less of a concern. Yes, she would need to deal with it in due course. First, however, she had to protect Jeremiah from the derision of others. And from himself.

She began tentatively.

'I can certainly see that there is much of despair here,' she said of the last picture, which was still on the easel.

He said nothing. Just more shifting from one foot to the other.

'And I think your ... canvases raise important points,' she added slowly. 'Questions, indeed.'

She could not bring herself to think of them as pictures. They were canvases – little changed from their original state, except by the addition of some crude daubing. Her comments were, she knew, vague and unlikely to be greeted with enthusiasm. When she turned to look at Jeremiah, therefore, she was surprised to see delight and relief on his face.

'Oh, Miss Hyssop,' he said. 'I cannot begin to tell you what that means to me. For that is *exactly* what I have wished to do. To ask questions. Questions of myself. And questions of what I *see*. Out there.' He pointed towards the casement. 'Over the roof tops. In the market. Across the town. But also what I see in *here*.'

He tapped the side of his head with a long finger.

Prudence stared and tried to smile.

'And please don't misunderstand me, miss,' he said. 'I don't *only* want to paint these ... these ... *questions*.'

'You don't?' said Prudence

She felt that a giant hole might be about to open up under her feet.

'Lawks, no, miss,' continued Jeremiah. 'I want to paint *other* things as well. Buildings. And people. Beauty. And ... Love.'

He paused and looked at his feet.

'I want to learn, miss,' he went on. 'Really I do. I want to learn how to paint *proper* pictures. But before I can do that, I have to clear out what's in *here*.'

He tapped the side of his head again.

'Once I've done *that*, miss, I hope I'll go on,' he said. 'Go on and paint more. And better.'

It was a useful thing to have said, because it provided a basis for Prudence to get back to her reason for wanting to engage with Jeremiah in the first place. His 'borrowing'. If his intention was to paint more – of *anything* – she needed to make sure that it did not involve taking things from Mr Hogarth.

It was time for her to make her proposal.

§

As the stranger stepped back into the marketplace, he pulled his hat low over his face again.

There was still a good deal of activity on show. He spent several minutes watching the traders at work, and the medley of customers making their way up and down the main avenue of vegetable stalls. The greater part of the morning had passed and several of the sellers were packing up for the day. A trio of porters stood about joshing a fourth. Two men were loading the back of a cart under the gaze of an old woman who sat smoking a clay pipe. A small dog started to urinate against a basket of cabbages and was chased away by a youth in a leather jerkin. A lady customer in a long pink cape was inspecting what remained on display. She pointed to some artichokes and spoke to a woman who looked to be wrapped in a brown blanket. The stranger noted all these details with the fascination of someone for whom they had a special meaning.

Two small boys were running along trying to pull each other's hair. They stopped briefly to look at the man with one leg. The stranger scowled at them, and then laughed to himself as they ran off. For one reason or another, there were plenty of folk who found him intimidating. It had not always been that way, he mused.

Across the square, on the north side of the Piazza, a carriage was picking its way slowly towards Russell Street. He could see a few empty sedan chairs lined up along the arcaded walkway. A milkmaid passed in front of him, a churn of milk balanced on her head. She slowed her pace and gave him a seductive look. But then, noting his leg, moved swiftly on. People often found his face engaging.

But his peg-leg could be unsettling. He might be a beggar about to ask for alms.

He approached nearer to the terrace of houses that spanned the short distance from James Street to the Covent Garden theatre in the north-east corner of the square. As he did so he pulled his coat collar up about his ears, even though the wind was now less strong.

This had been the place, he thought.

At least it *was*.

Then.

But that was so long ago. Everything would have changed.

Everything *had* changed.

He stepped back behind one of the columns that formed the arcade. A house door had opened, and someone was coming out. It was a woman.

She closed the door behind her and started walking towards the corner of James Street. A voice called after her. Another woman. A girl really. Not more than twenty.

'Abigail!'

The first woman turned and smiled. They must be friends, he thought. Ladies' maids perhaps. If, indeed, ladies still resided in these houses. *Real* ladies, that is.

But that was something he did not know. He pushed his hands into his pockets, his face grim with frustration. There was so much he did not know. He would have to be patient. It could hardly all be discovered so quickly.

Not in just one morning.

§

Prudence adopted a business-like tone.

'Jeremiah,' she began.

Picking up the new note in her voice, he made a show of seeking her permission before seating himself on the second chair.

'Jeremiah,' Prudence repeated. 'There are two things which I should like to put to you. Two things which I hope you will feel are an appropriate and considered response to the privilege you have afforded me in showing me your canvases.'

He said nothing but leaned forward, eager to hear what she might say.

'The first,' she said, 'is that these paintings should not leave this room. I am certainly no expert in these matters – but I would suggest to you that the world is not ready for your ... work.'

She paused and then corrected herself.

'That is to say, the world is not ready *yet*.'

He looked at her intently and nodded solemnly. Almost regardless of what she might say, he was enthralled by the fact that someone of her standing was prepared to comment on his paintings. Prudence decided to interpret his silence positively.

'The second thing,' she went on, 'is that I will support you in your endeavours to paint. So long as the secrecy around your first canvases remains intact. *And* so long as you continue to pursue your objective of painting ... of painting what you yourself described just now as proper pictures. I think it will be a great benefit to you if you can widen your approach and embrace other more ... more recognisable subjects.'

She hoped her words would be heard as both an encouragement and a clear recommendation to diversify.

'What I mean by that, Jeremiah, is that I shall provide you with a small allowance,' she said. 'A sum of money. It will not be extravagant – but it should be sufficient to furnish you with a moderate supply of canvases, paints and other materials.'

His face was a picture of amazement but still he said nothing.

'As I have intimated, Jeremiah,' Prudence continued, 'such an allowance would be conditional on the two points I have mentioned already. But there is also one other very important condition.'

He nodded slowly. The look of amazement changed to one of intense concentration.

'The third condition,' she continued, 'is that you immediately stop ... *borrowing* things from Mr Hogarth.'

Jeremiah nodded enthusiastically. He even managed a smile that he hoped would be seen as a serious expression of his deep gratitude and sense of blessedness. For he could not quite believe what he was hearing. That he had acquired a patron. Or should that be a patroness? Well, *what*ever it was, it was ... wondrous. *That's* what it was. Wondrous!

He threw his arms out in a show of bewildered excitement and cast around for some words that would do justice to the momentous nature of the occasion. But Prudence had not finished.

'In fact,' she went on, 'I think you could provide Mr Hogarth with some much needed peace of mind. You could let him know that, having now monitored the situation, you feel confident in recommending that he might dispense with your services as a guardian of his materials. That you feel sure the stock levels are stable. And that nothing is … missing. Nothing at all.'

Nothing at all.

At these words, Jeremiah turned pale, bit his lip and looked distinctly more nervous. Prudence was surprised by this sudden and visible change in his expression but thought she might know its cause.

'You can rest assured,' she added, 'that my small allowance will compensate for any additional earnings you may forego as a result of such a step.'

Jeremiah nodded although his face was still taut. And he appeared to be shaking slightly. Prudence decided it was time to go. She thanked him once again for his openness in sharing the fruits of his labours, and he tried his level best to regain his former sense of blessedness. But as Prudence made her slow and careful way back down the challenging flights of stairs, she could not help being distracted by the sudden change that had come over Jeremiah during the final seconds of their interview.

By the time she regained the comfort of her own drawing-room, she felt exhausted. She was also worried. Had she done the right thing? Should she be indulging a man who was clearly not in total command of his faculties – and who seemed prone to such strange shifts in mood? Should she encourage him in the undertaking of what might be nothing less than an unnatural road to madness?

Then she tried to look at it from a different point of

view. If Jeremiah had been drinking himself into a state of insensibility, would she have provided him with an allowance to buy himself yet more spiritous liquor? No, clearly not. But then that was different, wasn't it? Art was not as inherently debilitating as drink, was it?

In any case, was she not acting simply out of Christian duty and kindness? Thanks to her own good fortune, she had the means to dispense charity in a number of ways. And what, after all, was the alternative? She could not allow Jeremiah to fall prey to any one of the uncomfortable fates that might still await him even now – including those of a proven thief and madman. Not if she could help it.

In her heart she knew that what she had done was compassionate and not without reason. But she still felt a deep sense of unease.

§

Jane was feeling despondent.

William was more than usually out of spirits. In fact, she was not sure when she had last seen him quite so obviously upset. And whatever its cause, he did not want to discuss it. Which made her even more concerned. It was not often there was something going on that he was not happy to share with her.

He was, after all, a largely transparent man. At least to *her*. In most situations she felt she could read him like a book. Even when he started off being secretive and sheepish about something, he normally came round to talking about it in the end, one way or another. But on this afternoon, he seemed particularly withdrawn and uncommunicative. All she could tell was that something was missing – from his studio. And she only knew *that* because she had heard him shouting in frustration.

'Where is it? What on earth have I done with it?'

The sentiment had been expressed in more colourful language than that – and the basic message punctuated with various oaths and profanities. But that was the gist of it.

However, when she attempted to calm him and enquire if there was anything she could do to help, he closed down completely. She would not understand, he said. And he added – as though he thought it would make things better – that *no one* would understand. Then he stormed off to Covent Garden, presumably to drown his sorrows at the Bedford Arms with Frank Hayman and the others. That was usually the solution when things were not going well. Or even if they *were*.

Once he had gone, Jane felt compelled to go into his studio. Why, exactly, she was not sure. It was certainly not to look for whatever he had lost. Although she did want to reassure herself that it was not the painting of 'Morning'.

And so she stepped tentatively into his special space. It was never tidy at the best of times, but now it was clear that William had turned the room upside down in his search for whatever he had lost. She was relieved, however, to see that 'Morning' was there. It was positioned proudly on the main easel, as if making a clear statement about what he considered to be his best work.

But then that made her all the more intrigued.

If the painting on which he had spent so much time was still there and in apparent good order, what else could have provoked him to such a rage?

She could think of nothing.

Nothing at all.

§

'Smallow can produce landskips by the yard,' her husband had said.

Belinda had thought he was joking. Until she discovered that three of the landscapes done for her new home had been painted as one twelve-foot-long roll of canvas, and only then cut into sections. Hence the need to practise a commentary that would explain the all too obvious similarity of the three countryside views.

'Yes,' Belinda could hear herself saying to guests. 'We have several prospects that show adjacent grassy swards at Sir Marmaduke's estate. The land there is so uniformly captivating, don't you know.'

Except that there had been hardly any visitors to the house in St James's Square. And none who were even remotely interested in freshly executed and dull landscapes.

But that was not the worst of it.

For there were the portraits.

Her husband had agreed to pay Mr Smallow for twelve portraits in all, with two aims in mind. The first was to capture retrospectively the faces of Sir Marmaduke's forebears from the last hundred years. Most of those worthies had drunk, gambled or hunted themselves to death before taking the trouble to sit for their likeness. The Ransome family preference had been for dreary pictures of dead game (especially stags and pheasants), robust livestock, and muddy fields. That was all very well for the crumbling pile in Herefordshire, but the house in St James's Square was a different matter altogether.

The second objective was the creation of two larger paintings. Portraits of the current baronet and the woman who had consented to be the latest Lady Ransome in a long line of imposing beauties. The brief had therefore been very clear – at least in Belinda's eyes.

Of course, she was neither so naïve, nor so deluded, as to expect the finished artworks to rank amongst the finest in London. Any such aspiration had been dashed by Sir Marmaduke's insistence on appointing Mr Smallow in the first place. But Lady Ransome had clung desperately to the hope that the final array of portraits would at least pass muster. Such faith, however, was proving difficult to maintain. For the first pictures had started to arrive – and they were not auspicious.

The first problem was that they all looked the same.

Yes, the badly painted hair, hats, wigs and costumes differed, one from another. But the facial features of the various extinct Ransomes were almost identical, regardless of their sex or age. During a rare, and notably short, matrimonial exchange on the subject, the baronet voiced his opinion that it mattered 'not a jot'. Indeed, he suggested that it might be considered a positive advantage – to be able to show how the family's physiognomy endured steadfastly unchanged over time. But essentially he did not give a fig. For Sir Marmaduke, portraits simply demonstrated that there had been Ransomes before – and that there were Ransomes still. What the dead ones may actually have looked like was of no interest at all. Indeed, the only one of the new portraits to which he had given more than a cursory glance was that purporting to be his great grandmother. It was rumoured that she had been one of Prince Rupert's favourites, and Smallow's painting showed her exhibiting a generous amount of flesh. Certainly enough to distract attention from her face.

So, no, it was only Belinda who felt the pain. She had dreamed of showing off her house to elegant and well-connected ladies of the town. But as each of Mr Smallow's canvases arrived, she felt ever more devastated by the array of images that were mostly drab, mediocre at best, and grossly inelegant at their worst. For, regardless of anything she might say to the contrary, the pictures would all reflect on *her*. And she had not taken the very risky step of marrying Sir Marmaduke Ransome only to be considered drab, mediocre or inelegant.

It only added insult to injury when the artist began submitting his exorbitant accounts for the ornate gilt frames that proved, if nothing else, that sows' ears cannot be transformed into silk purses. The fact that he had sent the bills to her rather than to her husband presumably meant that the cost was quite separate to the fee agreed for the paintings. Sir Marmaduke would, no doubt, take a different view. So, yes – the whole thing was a terrible mess. But it was too late now to change course. The work was more than half done. Belinda would have to make the best of it.

She tried to focus on the very few positives that could be taken from the whole sorry saga. One was that Mr Smallow had been able to complete most of the work without troubling her personally. Meeting him at the beginning of the process had been enough for her to know that she did not like him. The fact that he had been able to do the landscapes and the dire ancestral portraits without having to call on her again, was a positive blessing. The finished pictures that had so far been delivered arrived courtesy of a courier. Belinda had at least been spared the physical presence of the odious, puffed up, little man.

However, she knew that was about to change. For the last phase of the tortuous affair was now to be undertaken. The two final portraits of the commission. Those of herself and her husband.

These would require Mr Smallow's most particular and personal attention. He was therefore due to visit them individually to begin the first of his studies for their faces. It had been decided that the clothes and bodies, as well as the background scenes, would be painted by assistants. In his original brief to the artist, Sir Marmaduke had agreed that the use of a 'lesser hand' for such details would be 'immaterial'. More importantly it would further reduce the cost. Mr Smallow contracted to ensure that all aspects of the faces, 'and the fleshly parts most intimately connected thereto', would be executed by himself.

Belinda had resigned herself to the arrangement.

Having subsequently seen several examples of Mr Smallow's portraiture, she was not sure it was possible to be a 'lesser hand' than he had already shown himself to be. Having said which, as she kept telling herself, perhaps it might work in everyone's favour. For Mr Smallow would be able to concentrate all his own personal efforts on what would be the most critical parts of the whole commission. He, more than anyone else, would surely realise that making a good job of the final two pictures would improve his chances of attracting further wealthy patrons. Lady Ransome had to believe that the artist's own self-interest would ensure that these two paintings would be of a different order to what had gone before.

It was therefore with mixed emotions that Belinda prepared herself for the visit she was about to receive. She was unhappy with everything Mr Smallow had produced thus far. But there still remained this tiny glimmer of hope. The hope that the best was yet to come. And that the artist – for all his personal unpleasantness and irritatingly bumptious behaviour – would excel himself in this, the climax of the commission.

She drew her shoulders back, lifted her chins, and looked at herself in the French mirror. She was Lady Ransome of St James's Square. And she was worthy of a portrait that could hold its own alongside a painting of … the highest in the land. Alongside royalty, indeed. It was perhaps an extravagant and unrealistic ambition. But she needed to bolster her confidence in every way she could.

There was a clumsy knock on the door, followed by the appearance of the mealy footman whose name was Boyd.

'Scuse, ma'am,' he said. 'Gennelman – Mr Smellie – is 'ere, ma'am.'

Belinda rolled her eyes and sighed. The auguries were not propitious.

§

I should like to recount the incident that first threw the paths of Mr Hogarth and myself across each other. It had been consigned by at least one of us to the dark recesses of memory. But recent circumstances have brought it back into a certain amount of light.

It was, I think, in 1720. Mr Hogarth was unknown to me as an artist then, and indeed it is only subsequently I have learned that, at the time, his work was mostly limited to the engraving of silverware and the production of trade cards. That he was known to me at all was simply because of his physical characteristics. I had seen him around the Piazza and noted him largely because of his stature, which was noticeably shorter and squatter than that of those others with whom he kept company. He seemed always to have a confident air about him, and a loud voice that made him appear somewhat brash and vainglorious. I could no more admit it to him now than I could have done then, but his figure made me smile.

It is perhaps not surprising that such a character was always likely to make himself enemies, and it was in this respect that my meeting with him – if such it can be called – did occur.

It was early one morning, and I was on my way to

church for Morning Prayer. It has been my habit to traverse the square on these occasions, and my route took me past not only the market stalls that were, by then, already trading, but also past Tom King's coffee-house, which had opened no more than a year or so before. Even in those days the place was known to stay open all through the night, and so it was not unusual to see late signs of revelry being played out around its doorway. Even if there was not much to be seen, I could frequently hear the shouts and ribald comments that flowed from inside. On this particular morning, however, there was more activity than was usually the case. I looked towards the place and caught sight of a small man who was being physically ejected from the coffee-house by three other men. They had him by the collar and were casting curses and more than a few blows in his direction.

The small man who was the subject of this attack – for so I took it to be – stumbled as he was almost thrown from the doorway, and he fell forward onto his face. His body sprawled after in a most inelegant way.

It was only then, by the light of a nearby fire, that I recognized the person to be none other than Mr Hogarth.

§

The man who entered Belinda's drawing-room with a package under his arm had the rubicund appearance of an overgrown cherub.

He was short, plump, and – on the evidence of his cheeks – shiny. He wore a coat that reinforced this shininess with its radiant turquoise sheen. The smile that played across the cherubic features was oddly contorted, as if trying to express both pleasure and condescension. Smallow was nothing if not proud, and Belinda had the impression that his pride had been especially polished for the occasion. No doubt he had made a show of arriving at the house in the hope that news of his visit would spread around the square. The Ransome commission was a West End connection he intended to turn to his advantage.

This was the figure that advanced across the carpet to greet Belinda. She looked at him again, noting the full wig that added to his general air of newness. She had heard some people say that Mr Smallow resembled the great Mr Hogarth – at least physically – but she could not see it herself. Admittedly, this might be partly because Mr Hogarth did not sport a wig most of the time, preferring his artist's cap. But even so, Belinda mused, the comparison could hardly be considered. To the eye of someone who had seen both men at fairly close quarters, there was surely far more that separated them than otherwise. Mr Smallow's lustrous smoothness contrasted sharply with Mr Hogarth's rough and stubbly exterior. Where Mr Smallow preened and paraded, Mr Hogarth slouched and was slovenly. And as for Mr Hogarth's clothes … Well!

But then Mr Hogarth was a great artist – whereas Mr Smallow most manifestly was not.

'Lady Ransome,' he said, bowing slightly.

'Mr Smallow,' said Belinda in a flat tone. 'You have come to paint me.'

It sounded like a statement of fact but was actually

a question. The package under Smallow's arm, and the nature of his dress, suggested something other than work.

'Alas,' he said, adopting a strained look of disappointment. 'That delight will only be mine in a few days' time. You recall that we set your first sitting for the day after tomorrow.'

Belinda had no recollection of the date, having clearly not wanted to dwell on such details any longer than necessary.

'Of course,' she said with as little enthusiasm as she could manage.

Smallow was smiling now. In Belinda's eyes it made him even less attractive than when he was endeavouring to be serious.

'As for today, ma'am,' he said. 'I begged leave to call with a view to making you a personal and most delicate proposal.'

For a brief moment Belinda was taken aback and found herself more than usually grateful that she was a married woman. Her expression obviously conveyed something of this confusion, for Smallow immediately took it upon himself to expand upon the matter.

'I am very conscious of the great honour that you and Sir Marmaduke have done me by commissioning so many of my paintings for the adornment of your splendid new residence,' he said. 'I am equally conscious that there are some notable parts of your house where the walls will have to wait some little while longer before the portraits intended for them are quite ready.'

He waited to see her reaction. She simply pursed

her lips and made an 'ummm' noise. It did not sound supportive, but rather communicated her unease. He decided to press on.

'I therefore thought that perhaps I could loan you a picture which you and your guests might find to be something of a talking point, and which could therefore provide an additional focus – and perhaps even something of an engaging diversion – in the intervening period. It would be a gesture of good will on my part and would also, I hope, provide you with some comfort in the days during which I shall, of course, be working on your own glorious image.'

Belinda was intrigued and not a little suspicious. Smallow was not the sort of man to do anything out of a sense of generosity. So what was he up to?

'It is another picture by your own hand, Mr Smallow?' she said, forcing herself to be politer than she wanted to be. She was recalling all too vividly the paintings he had already completed.

'It is, indeed, my lady,' he replied.

Belinda was now bemused. Why would Smallow feel that yet another one of his paintings might provide an 'engaging diversion' whilst he was completing the Ransome commission? It was bad enough having his mediocre works on the wall when they were depictions of long-dead relatives. Why should she want the loan of a picture that had nothing to do with her new status as a baronet's wife?

'If I may,' said Smallow.

He was clearly keen to dispel any further puzzlement by revealing what was obviously the picture to which he had been referring. He loosened the string that held in place the brown wrapping. As the paper fell away it revealed a painting, no more than eighteen inches across and about two feet high, in a simple but elegant gilt frame. The artist held it out in front of him for her close perusal. It was the portrait of a man.

Belinda gazed at it, her face now expressing a combination of surprise and incomprehension.

§

Catherine Pargeter put down the book she was reading.

She had made a resolution. It was time to move on.

Not necessarily physically. She found it impossible to envision a future that did not see her continuing to support her father and his business. To imagine something outside of that familiar arrangement was quite literally unthinkable. For all that some of the novels she read posited futures full of change and adventure, she knew that real life was a much tamer affair. Every time a bold or exotic thought crept into her mind, she banished it. She could no more give up her father and his print shop than she could relinquish her trust in the inherent goodness of the world's natural order.

But it was time to move on in other respects. She was not getting any younger. And there were some aspects of life that required refreshment. The meeting of the Green Group had prompted her to review some of these.

Mrs Hogarth had spoken so engagingly about the relationship between home and art, and it raised several questions in Catherine's mind. In terms of her own experience, home and art – by which she meant the business of selling prints – had been inseparable. Which was fine. She knew she had gained much knowledge and fulfilment from living above the shop. But she had also become conscious of a range of diverse ways in which home and art might be intertwined.

At one end of the spectrum was the figure of Belinda, Lady Ransome. By virtue of her very fortunate marriage, Belinda had managed to break out of the mould which had shaped her life in Covent Garden. She was now presumably enjoying an extremely contented home life, whilst also commissioning great artworks for what sounded like a very grand house in St James's.

At the other end was her close friend Prudence Hyssop. Yes, she was indeed a true and dear friend, and Catherine could not conceive of a person ever being truer and dearer. Prudence was also extremely knowledgeable about artistic traditions and styles, and in that respect was a rarity among women. Indeed, she was probably the only woman with whom Catherine could have a meaningful conversation about the finer points of engraving.

But then Prudence had, for whatever reason, chosen not to pursue the ways of love and marriage. She had dedicated herself instead to cultivating her own taste and to helping others. It was, Catherine thought, an almost saintly life. Prudence had never appeared unhappy with her lot – and who was Catherine to suggest there had been anything other than a confident single-mindedness behind her friend's decision to remain a spinster?

So, where did that leave Catherine?

Belinda's excess of affluence and conjugal bliss was way beyond Catherine's wildest dreams – which were not very wild at all. On the other hand, Prudence's superior intellect and selfless dedication to charitable causes represented a moral high ground as impractical as it was unattainable.

But these surely were the extremes. And Catherine understood herself well enough to know that she was not extreme in any sense. Instead, she would retain her faith in the natural order. More specifically, she would trust to a middle way that would provide the emotional stability her heart desired, whilst also supplying the tangible security her sense of duty could never forego.

Art. Home. Love. Continuity. It was a humble list. Not much to ask.

She turned back to her book. The heroine had just been saved from a life of drudgery by a handsome suitor. For some reason Catherine imagined him to look something like Jeremiah Potts – but with more expensive clothes.

§

'It is the Prince of Wales,' said Belinda.

Smallow's smile widened and, if possible, appeared even more hideous than before.

'Of course,' he said, as if the represented presence of King George II's eldest son in Lady Ransome's drawing-room might be considered the most natural thing imaginable.

'Remarkable,' said Belinda.

Her succinct response conveyed no sense of enthusiasm – just a pronounced ambiguity. Did she *mean* remarkable? And, if so, pertaining to *what* exactly? The picture itself? Its subject? Or the fact that Smallow had managed to paint a portrait that actually looked like someone in real life!

'As I was saying,' said Smallow, 'I thought it might serve as something of a curiosity. A portrait designed to draw the eye of your guests until such time as the beautification of your impressive home has been consummated by your own fair likeness – which will, of course, be more lovely and more temperate than even a summer's day.'

Belinda remained mute. So Smallow waited for the merest sign of interest to appear on his patroness's face before continuing.

'*And* …,' he added.

The word and a sense of incompleteness both hung in the air. Belinda had no option but to prompt.

'And?' she repeated.

'I thought that perhaps, if it suited you,' he continued, 'you might be inclined – if your guests felt the picture to be sufficiently diverting – to mention that it was the work of your humble servant, Mr Jonathan Smallow.'

He coughed politely into his left hand while he continued to hold the painting in his right.

'It might,' he expanded, 'encourage them to conclude that the artistic sophistication of the esteemed Lady Ransome is perhaps something to which they too might aspire.'

Ah, so *that's* what this is all about, thought Belinda. A

simple and selfish ploy on Smallow's part to promote his work amongst the great and the good of St James's!

She was not sure whether she was outraged by his proposal or simply staggered by his nerve. If she had felt herself capable of emitting a sardonic laugh, then this would have been the moment to do it. But such a response would hardly constitute the sort of good breeding one would expect of a lady in her position.

His barefaced cheek, however, also made her pause. And it encouraged her to look at the painting more closely.

It was undoubtedly a depiction of the Prince of Wales. There was no doubt of that. The face showed the features which had become familiar to anyone who had glimpsed His Royal Highness around St James's Palace or in the royal parks. However, what Belinda noticed as much as the characteristic face was the fact that it had been done with a great deal of artistic competence. Certainly, a great deal more than Smallow had shown in his portraits of the dead Ransomes. She was not sure how she should react to such a disparity, except that her first instinct was to take it badly. For it seemed to suggest that the artist deployed far more effort – not to mention skill – in the pictures he painted for other noble clients.

Although she then checked herself. This was, after all, a portrait of the Prince of Wales, no less. The heir apparent to the throne of Great Britain. Given Smallow's clear self-regard and naked ambition, it was hardly surprising that he should reserve his best work for such a portrait. A painting presumably meant to curry royal favour, as well as act as an advertisement for his talent across the wider reaches of St James's. Not that this made it easier to accept the fact that the faces of her husband's ancestors were so badly done. If he could manage something as proficient as this painting of the Prince, why could he have not done something at least half as good in depicting a dusty old Ransome?

But of course, she reflected – it would all come down to money. Part of Smallow's reason for showing her this painting was surely to demonstrate what could be achieved if his talents were fully appreciated. And rewarded. In other words, if he was paid a proper fee rather than the knock-down terms Sir Marmaduke had forced him to accept. Was this simply Smallow's way of saying, 'Pay me better – and I will devote the same amount of care to your *own* portrait?'

Well, if such a covert message was at least *part* of his plan, then she would answer in kind. She would deliver a coded response calculated to keep him guessing.

'The painting is most certainly a fair likeness,' she said. 'A *very* fair likeness. And I am sure Sir Marmaduke will be delighted to see it – and to be reminded of your abilities, Mr Smallow. Your proposal to loan the picture to us is most agreeable. It is also one that I trust my husband might be persuaded to view as worthy of his personal consideration.'

She paused, expecting Smallow to make his apparent stratagem rather more explicit. But he simply smiled and gave a slight bow.

'Are you happy then?' Belinda continued. 'Happy to leave His Royal Highness here, with me – so that I may acquaint Sir Marmaduke with your proposal? Or would you prefer to speak to my husband in person?'

Smallow adopted his unattractive grin again. No, he most certainly had no wish to trouble Sir Marmaduke. And, yes, of course, he would be more than delighted to leave the Prince in the noble and sensitive care of Lady Ransome.

And without further ado, Smallow bid farewell and left her alone.

Indeed, such had been the speed of his exodus that Belinda was left feeling confused. But at least he had gone. That was the main thing. She allowed herself a smile. Because, of course, there was more to be pleased about. A small ray of light in what she had convinced herself was an almost entirely dark prospect. The possibility that, if her husband could be persuaded to increase the terms of the commission, there was still a very real chance that *her* portrait at least might be rendered in a manner worthy of its subject.

She moved across to the table on which Smallow had placed the painting of the Prince of Wales.

Yes, it was not only good – it was dazzlingly good. And, surprising as that may be, it was surely a sign of better things to come.

§

During the days that followed the meeting of the Green Group, Jane and Prudence spent an increasing amount of time together.

It was just as they were arriving back at Leicester Fields after a shopping expedition that Jane raised the matter of William's latest upset. She followed it with the suggestion that he would almost certainly benefit from Prudence's calm and considered counsel.

'He's less vexed about it than he was,' said Jane. 'At first he didn't want to talk about it at all. He and I have discussed it since. More than once, as it happens. But I know it's still gnawing away at him.'

Prudence was concerned.

'I'll leave him to tell you himself,' Jane continued. 'He's expecting you. I hope you don't mind. I'll wait long enough for him to get it off his chest. Then I'll come and rescue you!'

In the studio William was busy with what looked like a fresh canvas. He waved Prudence towards the old leather chair and then pointed back at the canvas.

'If it works out,' he said, 'this will be the next one. After "Morning". The second in my *Four Times of the Day* series. Although I already know the central figures won't be so compelling!'

She smiled at the compliment and sat down self-consciously. 'Morning' was not quite finished, and she felt that she might still be sitting for the artist to make a final study of her profile.

'I don't suppose Jane said much, did she?' said William. He put down his brush and wiped his hands on a cloth.

'But she thought it might help,' he went on. 'Help *me*, I mean. If I talked to you again. About things going missing. I know you must think I'm obsessed by it. Losing stuff. But there we are!'

He leaned back against a work-bench and picked at the paint on his hands. He was trying to make light of it, but Prudence could see the worry on his face. It made her nervous. But she did not want to say anything until she knew which way his remarks were tending.

'Jeremiah's now released himself from spying on my stock,' he continued. 'He said he'd not noticed any problems. For more than two weeks now. So he thought it probably wasn't worth it. Checking everything every day.'

He paused before going on.

'I wasn't paying him enough, I suppose!'

He chuckled, suggesting he was making a joke at his own expense. Prudence felt it safe to venture a tentative remark.

'That's good,' she said. 'But you still want to talk ... about it?'

She was not sure where this might go. He scratched his head and sighed.

'It's probably not related,' he said. 'Not at all. But all the same ... I now seem to have ... lost a painting.'

She waited to see if he would say more. But when he leaned back again with a rueful smile on his face, she realised that she would have to ask.

'When you say "lost" ...,' she began.

He pulled another, more enigmatic face.

'I mean I don't know where it is,' he said. 'That is, I don't know if I truly lost it. Or if it's been taken. But how can you lose a painting – in a studio? I've looked everywhere. Under everything. It was only a small picture, you see.

I thought I might have covered it up. Hidden it. But it's certainly not here. So, ... it must be ... somewhere else.'

Prudence's mind was racing. Surely Jeremiah would not have taken anything that William was working on. Other than by mistake. Could he have borrowed it and – heaven help us! – painted over it, thinking it was just a spoilt and discarded sketch? But, no. That was unthinkable. And absurd. Why on earth would Jeremiah do such a thing when he had access to *new* canvases?

The thought prompted a more expressible question.

'Was it a finished painting?' she said.

'Not entirely,' said William. 'It was mostly done – but it needed more work. Why? Do you think that's important?'

'I am not sure,' she said, trying to keep her voice as steady as she could. 'Except that I imagine a finished painting might have more ... more value. Than a work in progress.'

He nodded.

'Yes, I see,' he said. 'For a thief, you mean. Except there's no question of anyone breaking in. The place is always locked when there's no one here. Which is why, even now, I can't really be sure.'

Prudence was still thinking of Jeremiah. He was, so far as she knew, the only person with free access in and out of the studio. But, again, he would surely not have taken a nearly finished picture – would he? It simply made no sense.

'What does Jane think?' said Prudence.

He pulled another face.

'She thinks I might have given it to someone,' he

said. 'Or sent it to the framers and not remembered. I hadn't shown it to her, you see. It was … well … it was an experiment. Just something I was trying out. Which made her think I might have got fed up with it. Painted over it. Or thrown it out. It wouldn't be the first time. So she has a point, I suppose!'

He made another chuckling noise. But it was a sorry sound and suggested only embarrassed confusion.

'It is a small painting, you say?' said Prudence.

She was desperately hoping that Jane was right. And she was thinking about the canvases she had seen in Jeremiah's room. None of them had been particularly small.

'Yes,' said William. 'Twenty-four inches by eighteen. Or near enough. Smaller than anything I've done for quite a while. Certainly small for a portrait.'

'A portrait?' said Prudence.

'Yes,' said William with another weary chuckle. 'There's no point in my being coy about it now. Jane was surprised when I told her. And I dare say you will be too. It was a sketch in oils. Of our friend across the way.'

He waved his arm vaguely in the direction of Leicester House.

'The Prince of Wales.'

§

When Ransome came in, accompanied by another man, the young woman was sitting on the scarlet couch.

Her older companion came and stood next to her.

'Well, ain't it your lucky day!' she said. 'You said you wanted to see 'im. And 'ere 'e is!'

The young woman looked across at the two men who were both very drunk. They were dallying with a few of her new colleagues close to the door. One of the men was tall with a cruel, flat face. The other was short and had a shiny expression of barely concealed contempt. Both were well dressed and wore expensive wigs.

The young woman made room for her companion on the couch.

'Which one is he?' she asked, although she already knew well enough from the descriptions she had heard.

"E's the big bastard,' the older woman said. 'The small un's just a fawner. A great painter apparently. Or so 'e'd 'ave you believe.'

The young woman stared.

'Mr Hogarth?' she asked quietly.

She named the only artist she had heard mentioned as 'great' during her short time in the city. Mr Hogarth's *Harlot's Progress* and *Rake's Progress* were much talked of.

The older woman laughed under her breath.

'Hah!' she almost spat. "E'd *like* to be!'

So not Mr Hogarth then.

The younger woman felt she had perhaps sounded naïve and decided to say no more on the subject. If the short, pompous little man was not the famous Mr Hogarth, then it hardly mattered *who* he was. Her interest was focused on the taller one. He was now surveying the room, a sneer distorting his already unattractive face.

So this was him then. The baronet.

She made a concerted effort not to attract his gaze. It was too early for that. She needed more of a plan first. But at least she now knew what he looked like. And that he came to this place.

Now she had to concentrate her thoughts on what she would do. And when.

Most specifically she needed to focus on how exactly she would kill Sir Marmaduke Ransome.

§

As Mr Hogarth lay on the ground, unable through intoxication or injury to raise himself, the three men who had propelled him from Tom King's gathered around him.

One was long and thin, one of average height but exceedingly wide, and the third was short and stocky. It was this third man who appeared to be the ringleader as he stood between the other two. He it was whose voice dominated the scene, and who seemed to be directing events.

He stood over Mr Hogarth, pouring a torrent of verbal abuse in his direction, which he then followed with a kick to the body of his prostrate victim. It was this that provoked me and made me act. For although I am no stranger to the arbitrary violence that men perpetuate one upon another, I could not stand idly by and watch this man suffer the blows of a bullying gang when it was perfectly clear that he had already been rendered helpless and incapable of defending himself.

And so it was that I made a deviation in my route and walked towards them.

The thin man and the wide man were the first to notice my approach, and they had expressions on their faces that betrayed their confusion. Did this woman – this rather plain young lady – really mean to solicit their attention whilst they were so obviously engaged in an act of correction over one of their fellow men?

As I drew closer, however, they could have been only too sure that such an interruption was exactly what I intended. The two of them stepped back to stare at me, and in so doing, each grabbed an arm of the short, squat man who was still pouring out a stream of abuse on Mr Hogarth's head. For he looked to be readying himself to take another kick at the body that now hardly moved on the ground in front of him.

I am not sure how I was able to speak the words, my heart was beating so. Yet speak I did, managing to say in as strong a voice as I was able:

'I order you to desist. You are exceeding the bounds of human conduct. This man has suffered enough.'

I cannot, of course, be certain that those were the exact words I used, but I am sure it was at least the intent behind my intervention. It was all so long ago now – more than fifteen years – and many of the details have been lost in the recesses of my mind. But some things remain all too clear, and I must admit that, as I write this, I have begun to tremble with the thought of them.

I had liked to think I was beyond that. That time, the great healer, might have put sufficient distance between then and now for me to be able to recall and record the incident without succumbing so obviously to the tremors that now affect my frame.

But perhaps it is not so unexpected, knowing what was to follow so soon afterwards, and how it was such a blight upon my body and my soul. But I can only treat of these matters in their correct order. And one at a time. Certainly, in recalling that fateful morning in the Piazza, the things that make me shiver most are the remembrances of the two faces which were at the centre of the scene. Those of the thin man and the wide man are lost to me. They have faded into the fog of anonymity that engulfs so many of the men who come and go in the Piazza of Covent Garden.

But I have always remembered the face of Mr Hogarth, looking up at me with a clear incomprehension of what was happening.

And I have also always remembered the hate on the face of the short man who was his tormentor, and who would perhaps have been his slayer. Hate for Mr Hogarth. And now also hate for me, as the other two men pulled him away with the words:

'Enough. Come off now, Smallow. Or you shall swing for his death.'

§

Flea had seen a one-legged man before, for it was not so unusual.

But then Flea always noticed people who were missing something. They were almost always men, he concluded. He could not recall having seen more than one lady with only one leg. But then he decided that a lady with one leg would probably not get out much. Men had more of what

Flea might have called a roving spirit. A restless need to move around, regardless of how many legs they had.

He had no conception of how a limb might be lost other than as the result of enemy action. This was due more to the bent of his imagination rather than any clear evidence to the effect. But it certainly coloured the way he viewed the world. He held to the idea that across the seas were foreign lands noted for the large number of arms and legs that had been given up in the course of their conquest. The lack of a limb was therefore something he took to be a badge of honour. A man with only one arm or leg was not to be shied away from. Rather he was an individual to command respect.

There were, however, things that made *this* one-legged man worthy of Flea's particular notice.

The first was his sun-tanned skin which stood out even alongside the tawny, weather-beaten faces of the market sellers. It suggested he had only recently arrived from whichever foreign land had custody of his leg. Then there was his habit of pulling his collar up around his ears and pushing his hat down over his eyes – even on a warm day. It was a habit Flea found both curious and attractive – and was exactly the behaviour he would expect of a spy. In fact, for the next day or so Flea adopted the same styling with regard to his own collar and hat. It both suited his character and aided his ability to skulk through the market with a heightened sense of stealth.

Once he had perfected this new skulking routine, he decided to put it into practice by following the one-legged man. It was all part of Flea's ambition to hone his own spying skills to the point where they could be applied to some suitable vocational calling.

When Flea first observed him in the Piazza the man had been wandering slowly through the marketplace, looking at the sellers and porters with a keen interest in what they were doing. It made Flea wonder if the man had thoughts of entering the market trade himself. Perhaps he was familiarising himself with how it all worked. Identifying where he might fit in. It has to be said, however, that there were no other one-legged men working in the market. Flea could not help thinking that the red-faced porters who did most of the fetching and carrying would have made a strong case for two legs being an indispensable qualification for the role.

Flea had also seen the man walking around the Piazza and looking at the buildings, most especially the house in Tavistock Row where the Vampyre lurked. He had then gazed across the square towards where Flea lived with Miss Hyssop. Surely that had to betoken *some*thing, Flea thought. It was distinctly uncommon that anyone should spend quite so long looking at the buildings in that way. And then the answer came to him. Of course. The one-legged man was an officer of the law who was closing in on the arrest of the old highwayman and his moll.

But if the one-legged man's movements around the Piazza could be characterised as slow and steady, it was another matter altogether when he headed away from the market. For when Flea followed him along Russell Street towards Drury Lane, he was immediately impressed by the man's speed. It was all the more remarkable given the busy-ness of the thoroughfare and the need to weave between a medley of pedestrians, carts, horses, and sedan chairs. Flea was concerned that this acceleration was perhaps an indication that the man knew he was being followed. But one thing made that unlikely. The simple fact that he never glanced over his shoulder. For, as Flea knew well, fugitives *always* look back at their pursuers.

The route the man was following was a winding one, down towards the Strand. It was just before arriving there, however, that he stopped to look at the window of a print-shop. There were several other people looking at the various prints on display, and Flea was able to join the small crowd without drawing attention to himself. He was just getting into a position to see what had caught the eye of his quarry, when the man opened the door of the shop and went in.

Flea stayed outside, pulling thoughtfully on the few hairs that were still attached to his chin. His curiosity was now well and truly piqued, for it was a shop he knew well. Indeed, it was a building to which he had delivered letters from Miss Hyssop on a number of occasions. And the name of the shop-owner was blazoned above the door in letters of gold against a black background.

Pargeter.

§

Clearly something was going on.

The last two times Prudence had caught sight of Catherine – once in the market, through a throng of people, and once from her drawing-room window – the print-seller's daughter had been in conversation with Jeremiah. Prudence wondered whether this was something new or whether she was only now noticing it. Was it perhaps a professional arrangement? After all, Jeremiah's courier duties often took him to Catherine's father's shop.

There was no disguising the fact, however, that the meetings did not suggest business. No packages changed hands. And on the second occasion Catherine followed Jeremiah into the house where he lived in Tavistock Row. So, did that mean that Catherine knew about Jeremiah's efforts as a painter? Prudence had made stipulations about his strange and demonic daubs remaining a secret. But was Catherine already privy to Jeremiah's inner struggles?

Prudence's mind was full of questions. Might her friendship with Catherine actually provide another avenue through which she could understand and support Jeremiah? For the more she thought about it, the harder it was to avoid one particular conclusion. At some point, she was going to have to talk to him about the latest thing to have gone missing from Mr Hogarth's studio.

So how should she do that? There were, after all, no other clues as to what might have happened to it. If, as Jane had suggested, it had accidentally been dispatched to the picture framer or cast away, then surely such a mistake would have been discovered by now. But if the painting really had been stolen – or borrowed – there could really be only one suspect. And his name was Jeremiah Potts.

Prudence's head told her that the most efficient way of pursuing the enquiry would simply be to ask him.

Given her new position as his benefactress, that should at least be easier than if she were no more than a casual acquaintance. Or might Catherine be able to help? But even as the thought occurred to her, Prudence knew it just added another level of complexity. For Catherine might not wish to acknowledge any kind of relationship with Jeremiah. She might even be complicit in whatever Jeremiah was up to.

But no!

Prudence erased the idea immediately. It was unworthy of her. And it was not the sort of thing a true friend would allow herself to think. She had to stem the flow of such a ridiculously overheated imagination. It was so unlike her. She asked Abigail to make her some chocolate. Something to sooth her troubled mind.

Sitting quietly with her cup, she was more reflective. She could, she thought, see why it was happening. Why she was getting herself worked up in this way. It was partly because she wanted to help Jeremiah, whose life was so clearly tinged with madness. And it was partly because she wanted to help William, who had so determinedly taken her into his confidence.

But it was also because she was struggling with the memories that had flooded her mind. Memories she was trying to address through her journal. Memories which were proving to be more painful than she had anticipated.

There was no doubt that what was going on around her was intricate and involved. And, for the first time in a long while, she was experiencing feelings of real stress and strain as she attempted to make sense of it all.

Whatever else she might manage to do, she should try to avoid making the situation any more complicated than it already was.

§

St James's Square was an ideal address for an aspiring woman of the world.

Positioned between Piccadilly and Pall Mall, it was no more than a few hundred yards from St James's Palace, the primary London residence of the British royal family. Sir Marmaduke Ransome had taken over the lease of a house on the east side of the square once it was known he was to marry Miss Belinda Parrish. It was assumed by most observers that the arrangement had only been made possible with the financial support of Sir Marmaduke's future father-in-law. Indeed, there were some who were of the opinion that the alliance was hardly more than a marriage of convenience. Several commentators suggested that it must have been ambition that blinded Miss Parrish to the less obviously attractive aspects of becoming Lady Ransome.

As the first weeks of the union unravelled, the scales fell from Belinda's eyes. She became aware of the horror she had embraced. It was some comfort that she had not been forced to embrace it physically. But the mental and emotional distress still caused her to question why she had chosen to embark upon such an unhappy course. The result of this introspection was usually the same. She bolstered her spirits by telling herself that, whilst she might not change the character of her husband, she most certainly *would* change the character of her new home. The house would be rendered so inviting that visitors would flock to her door despite there being any numbers of reasons why they should not.

Key to her decorative scheme were the paintings commissioned from Mr Jonathan Smallow. And although Belinda felt nothing but discomfort in the company of the artist, his latest work had at least provided the very slenderest shred of hope. If his portrait of the Prince of Wales were truly more representative of his abilities, then she might retain some confidence in the two paintings he had still to complete. Those of herself and her husband. The picture of the Prince – albeit that it was only on loan – had therefore taken on a symbolic presence in the house. It signalled Belinda's social aspirations, whilst also pointing the way towards a similarly outstanding portrait of Lady Ransome herself.

Her first thought was to have the princely portrait hung in the entrance hall, where it might greet expectant guests. But this raised two issues. The first was that it might be too immediate a distraction from the overall splendour of the house. The initial impression of her home should be one of scale and grandeur, and there was a distinct danger that the delicate proportions of the portrait would encourage too narrow a focus.

The second issue was that she did not wish to make such a feature of a painting that would be no more than a temporary inhabitant of the space. Better, she decided, to hang it where her own finished portrait would eventually grace the wall of the drawing-room. In that way her image would, in due course, be seen as a fitting and expansive replacement for what was, after all, a rather small portrait of the Prince.

It would be only after the total scheme had been completed, and all the pictures in place, that she would persuade Sir Marmaduke to engage more fully with polite Society. Until then she was content to entertain a more limited range of visitors, including a select few from her years spent close to Covent Garden. The recent personal and intimate conversation at the home of Miss Hyssop had convinced Belinda that Prudence was her most compassionate and dependable friend. She was most definitely someone to be welcomed into the hallowed halls.

Additionally, the meeting of the Green Group that followed soon after had reintroduced Belinda to Mrs Jane Hogarth, whom she had not seen for some considerable time. As the daughter of the late Sir James Thornhill, Serjeant Painter to King George I and a Member of the Royal Society, Jane was also someone who could most certainly be received within the exclusive quarter of St James's Square. Moreover, she was married to one of the most brilliant stars of the current art world. Yes, it was true that William Hogarth had a reputation for being often uncouth and difficult. But, as Belinda was finding out, such manly traits were not uncommon. Mr Hogarth was, most importantly and regardless of his flaws, a genius. Just as Sir Marmaduke was, regardless of *his*, a baronet.

The idea of inviting Prudence and Jane to view the

house in its current, advanced state of redevelopment therefore seemed a good way to proceed. It would mark a first step on the road towards a wider throwing open of the Ransome doors.

§

Louisa Crust lived in Bow Street, just around the corner from Covent Garden Piazza.

Prudence did not call on her as often as their geographical proximity might have suggested. This was partly because Louisa could sometimes be what the world termed 'hard work'. In fact, 'hard' was a word that suited her in more ways than one. Her hard-edged and hawkish exterior was matched by the hard-nosed mentality of a woman who felt herself confronted every day by the sad truths of a sinful world. It was a state of mind all too clearly justified by the empirical evidence of the local environment. But it was also a disposition that rarely made for an uplifting chat. Prudence therefore regarded Louisa as a good friend to be consulted on a selective basis.

On this occasion, however, Louisa's invitation to tea had been seized upon with eagerness. For Prudence hoped that the redoubtable Mrs Crust, wife of the even more daunting *Mr* Crust – stalwart of the Parish Council and local Watch – might contribute some insights on the matter of crime in the art world.

'Do you think, Louisa,' said Prudence once they were past the initial pleasantries. 'Do you think your husband's parochial duties are made more challenging by his being responsible for an area like Covent Garden? As compared to a parish that is more … that is to say, less … miscellaneous, I mean.'

Louisa's expression betrayed no sense of surprise at the question.

'*He* would say it makes for a more predictable routine,' she said.

Her husband was always characterised simply as '*He*' – as if his word might be considered second only to that of his Creator.

'You'd almost think they were lining up to have their heads broke every night, so regular are their habits,' she went on, not feeling it necessary to explain exactly who 'they' might be.

'In some parts of town, the Watch have a more fitful time of it. But hereabouts, it's all too predictable,' she added.

Prudence felt that such a declaration, in the mouth of anyone else, might have been accompanied by a sense of irony. But Louisa delivered the words as dull statements of fact.

'You can almost set your watch by them,' she said.

'Really?' asked Prudence.

She just managed not to smile at the unintended pun.

'In what way?'

'They have their routines,' continued Louisa. 'They come out of the theatres and gaming houses just before midnight and start the serious drinking. The Kings' place is the most notorious venue. But there are many others, as I'm sure you know only too well. Given where you live, you must hear them every night.'

There was almost a note of accusation in her voice. 'If you will insist on living in the Piazza, Prudence,' she seemed to be suggesting, 'then you can hardly complain about the noise.' (Not that Prudence ever had.)

'The drinking goes on for a couple more hours,' continued Louisa. 'Then they take themselves off on what *He* calls one of their *progresses*.'

Again, it was difficult not to smile. Mr Hogarth's choice of the word 'progress' for his print series had been astute at several levels.

'And a *progress* is …?' prompted Prudence.

'The terrorising of good folk by rampaging around the streets, breaking windows, watchmen's lanterns, and people's heads – most especially their own. Then they stagger back to the Piazza, usually between four and six o'clock. By that time they're in a very unpleasant state. So, they go back to Tom King's where they try to stay upright until the market's underway, when they finally slither off to the dark holes whence they came.'

Another suppressed smile from Prudence at Louisa's choice of words.

'*He* says that's when they're most troublesome,' Louisa went on. 'But also least capable.'

Prudence nodded. It was difficult to believe that Louisa could say all this without the merest hint of mischief.

'If they cause a real breach of the peace,' she continued, 'then *He* sends them up before the magistrate. But if they're just disorderly, the watchmen give them a whack round the head and send them off with their tail between their legs.'

Prudence bit her lip. For it was, of course, no laughing matter. And as a long-time resident of the Piazza, she knew only too well what sort of disturbances 'they' could cause.

'There are many artists living and working around Covent Garden,' she ventured. 'Do *they* give any trouble, so far as the Watch is concerned?'

'No,' said Louisa, with great authority. 'Your artists are not so troublesome. They get drunk quicker and fall over sooner. And are mostly a danger to themselves rather than to other people. That's what *He* says. And *He* should know. *He* is acquainted with most of the artists, and they're a sorry lot in the main. Whereas the arrant troublemakers …'

'The ones you can set your watch by,' added Prudence, unable to stop herself.

'Indeed,' said Louisa. '*They* tend not to be artists. It's only the artists who fancy themselves as gentlemen who cause *that* sort of trouble. Most of your artists mix in different circles.'

Prudence nodded slowly.

'But are the artists troublesome in other ways?' she asked. 'Does your husband have to deal with disputes, for example? Or anything else that might contravene the law?'

'*He* would say no, I'm sure,' said Louisa.

She was fully confident not only in *His* view but also her own ability to convey it – and indeed anticipate it – succinctly.

'*His* role is all about maintaining the peace of the parish. And your artists mostly stay the right side of the line. Quite a club, you might say. They look after themselves and tend not to break each other's heads.'

It was, Prudence thought, a rather bizarre conversation – and she was not sure it told her much she did not already know. Certainly, if one artist thought another one had purloined his work, it was not a matter for the parish authorities. An aggrieved artist could take his case to the magistrate if his property had been stolen. But overall, the theft of finished or near-complete paintings was limited by the practicalities of how they were created. Many were the result of collaboration, with artists sharing out the different jobs – landscape, fabrics, animals, people – based on their respective talents. It was particularly prevalent in portrait painting, with the face, hands, clothes, and background features often being done by several different hands. In that context the theft of a canvas made little sense.

None of this added much substance to Prudence's speculations as to what might have happened to William's missing painting. Everything Louisa had said about the connected nature of the artists' community made it even less likely it would have been taken by another painter. So whilst Jeremiah had to remain a potential – indeed, probably the *only* – suspect, there appeared no logical reason why he should have put his relationship with William at risk in such a way.

The time spent with Louisa, however, had proved more entertaining than expected – and it put Prudence in a positive frame of mind about the value of friendship. So, on her return to the Piazza, she was even more delighted to find a note from Belinda inviting her and Jane to call at the house in St James's Square. There were many reasons to welcome such an invitation, not the least being a chance to admire Lady Ransome's new home.

§

I have been troubled by what I have just written, and by what I must soon come to write. And so I will now take time to remember something that brings me only joy and a feeling of fulfilment, even if its relation is not strictly in the order in which events occurred. I speak of the advent of Master Fleabane, who has been a constant support to me for the last eight years.

I had lamented the state of my life with regard to the lack of children, and time will tell – and I will tell, if I am able – the reasons why such an apparent loss was felt so keenly. I had not inured myself to a life without family, but had undertaken it with something of a will, venturing to pronounce that I would perforce make the best of what God had been pleased to provide as my lot. When, however, the Lord himself saw fit to deliver an infant who needed succour, I could not but submit to His will.

To tell the truth, Master Fleabane was not an infant, but an urchin. His age was as uncertain then as it is, unsurprisingly, now. But it was agreed by all concerned that he had the physical traits and demeanour of someone who might be six or seven years old at most, and perhaps no more than five.

His first appearance – a word which makes him sound a spirit and not human at all – was during Morning Prayer one Sunday early in 1728. There was a quiet moment in the order of service when those of us who were there as worshippers became aware of a snuffling sound which, at first, we thought might be the whimpering of a dog that had wandered inside from the churchyard or market beyond.

When, however, we turned to view the origin of the sound, we found a creature of a different kind. A small child – we knew not whether boy or girl – in filthy rags and showing every sign of having come straight from the lowliest of places. It was sucking upon two of its dirty fingers, whilst a stream of rheum proceeded from its nose. Our gaze strayed along the aisle and across the back of the church, in the expectation that it would discover a mother, or even father, of similar sort. It is not unusual for beggars to loiter about the doors of the church, although it is rare for them to enter into the building, such is the attention given by the verger and his man to prevent them.

At the end of the service the child remained there, and was still alone, and there were those of us who asked what should be done. Some were for ejecting the poor wretch back out into the cold, and several more who stared suspiciously, saying it was a devilish plan by some dissolute parent to elicit alms. The verger was all for dragging the child away to a place of correction, like the Bridewell hospital, on the sure assumption that it was the progeny of some demented person, 'for mad they must be to thrust such a thing upon good Christian folk'.

I was like to regard the vision as more angel than devil and felt it incumbent upon me to be a little accommodating on behalf of my fellow worshippers. I cajoled the child into sitting with me, much to the discomfort of some of those who still remained in the church, and I took it upon myself to ascertain whether the angel be boy or girl, which was easy to do given the small and ragged nature of its covering.

I then asked the small boy if he had a name, and if he knew to whom he belonged. To both questions he answered that he knew not, although suffice to say that he was not so articulate as to express these thoughts clearly but was rather overwhelmed by our attention and his apparent state of being lost.

I knew I could not allow the boy to be subject to further hurt, and that, if nothing else, I should be the cause of providing some security for him as attempts were made to identify a parent or guardian to whom he could be returned. I therefore pledged to wash and feed the boy whilst such enquiries were made, and returned to my house with his small, grimy hand clasped in mine.

My maid at that time was not Abigail, but a large and pink lady who was never known by any other name than Mrs Turnbury. Mrs Turnbury was a woman who, being much my senior in years, had always the air of knowing more than I did about almost everything. Confronted with the boy, she made a show of indicating how improper it was that I should remove a child of the streets from its natural environment. Nevertheless, she showed by her careful handling of the waif that she was pleased to be of some support to the lost soul.

Between us, therefore, Mrs Turnbury and I fed the boy on porridge, biscuits and milk, which he did eat with a voraciousness I have not witnessed in many humans since. And we also washed him in a large tub. I can still remember that his body turned the water grey, and that when he emerged his skin was of an altogether different and pale nature.

And so it was that I determined I should hold onto him for the day or two that were needed before his parents or friends could be found, and that such respite would at least provide the opportunity for me to feed and refresh him as best I was able. During that short period we should, of course, have need to call him something, and I suggested that we should call him Paul, after the saint for whom our church is named. Mrs Turnbury, however, protested that this did sound too permanent, and that, as he would be with us for so short a duration, we should prefer a term that was more specific to the marketplace, from which he had no doubt wandered.

I smiled at her thinking, but felt that it was really of no matter, as whatever we chose would not be the boy's real name. I remember, indeed, making a small jest of it and insisting that he should be called after a flower rather than a vegetable!

To my surprise, Mrs Turnbury suggested the name of Fleabane, by reason of its being a small flower that was not altogether unattractive. I smiled at the suggestion, and indeed the word Fleabane made me laugh – which Mrs Turnbury took as agreement.

And so the child was to be called, for the short time of a day or so, Master Fleabane. With that, Mrs Turnbury set off to speak to her friends in and around the marketplace with a view to our finding as soon as possible the people to whom our so-called Master Fleabane belonged.

A year or two later, Mrs Turnbury left me to return to

the country where she had an ageing mother who needed nursing, and I acquired a younger maidservant in her place.

But, of course, the mystery surrounding Master Fleabane was never solved and, eight years on, he lives with me still.

§

In St James's Square, Boyd – the mealy footman – had been briefed.

Two ladies would be arriving, and he should be on the lookout for their carriage or sedan chairs.

Lady Ransome was therefore taken aback when she peered out of her front window and saw her two visitors arriving on foot. Fearing that Boyd might not provide a sufficiently elevated welcome to such travellers, Belinda swept into the entrance hall just as he was about to open the front door.

'That's all right, Boyd,' she said. '*I* shall receive the ladies.'

Boyd said nothing, slinking back along the hallway with the air of someone for whom everything in life is rather too much trouble. Belinda looked crossly at his back before opening the door.

'Dear Prudence, dear Jane,' she crowed. 'Did you leave your carriage around the corner? It is uplifting, I agree, to amble into the square and feel its presence.'

Prudence and Jane glanced at each other and then back at Belinda.

'Dear Belinda,' said Prudence, smiling broadly. 'Carriage indeed! We walked, of course. And very pleasant it was too.'

'We hardly stopped talking the whole way,' said Jane.

Belinda continued to smile but the tightness around her eyes made clear that she was aghast. The thought of walking through the heart of London! It was less than a mile from Covent Garden to St James's Square and little more than half that distance from Leicester Fields. But walking the streets, at any time of day or night, was just not something a lady did. And it was certainly not seemly to be having an extended conversation about it on the doorstep. Without further ado Belinda waved them both into the entrance hall.

As she did so, she decided there was, after all, some merit in receiving her guests herself. For now she had the opportunity to begin her guided tour with a short introduction to the hallway. She began by flinging open her arms.

'Welcome to …'

There was a brief pause. Please not 'my humble abode', thought Jane.

'The Ransome residence!' said Belinda.

Prudence and Jane dutifully looked about them with wide eyes and appreciative smiles.

'What a delightful hall,' said Prudence.

'A beautiful effect,' added Jane. 'Such elegance and purity of line.'

The pale colours and intricate gilt mouldings were not to Jane's taste and made the place look, she thought, more like a palace than a home.

'I'm glad you think so,' said Belinda. 'I am particularly pleased with the architraves, which I feel add considerably to the overall harmony of design. They are the very latest style. Quite unique in London just at the moment, I am led to believe.'

Prudence and Jane simpered and smiled back. Prudence's own home had hardly anything in it that was less than thirty years old. Jane and her husband's property was too much a working space for either of them to take anything other than a cursory interest in its decoration and furnishings. Nevertheless, both visitors wanted to show enthusiasm for something that was clearly so important to their friend.

Jane felt it appropriate to extend her comments to include the paintings on the walls – even though the images appeared to be of an unexceptional quality and remarkably dull in terms of their subjects.

'The pictures add to the overall balance,' she said. 'They bring their own sense of … heritage to the contemporary styling of the walls.'

This was all the encouragement Belinda needed to launch into her presentation of the house's artworks. Starting in the hallway gave her the chance to begin with some of the less distinguished specimens. It was better, she reflected, to build up from this low base. She therefore spent more time than was justified in pointing out a muddy view which she claimed was a faithful representation of her husband's family estate in Herefordshire.

Prudence and Jane nodded politely, both of them thinking that a more sombre prospect could hardly be imagined. If that were indeed what Herefordshire looked like – and neither of them had any idea – then it was a blessing their friend did not have to spend many hours there. This, however, was a sentiment they kept to themselves.

But Belinda's effusions over the Herefordshire countryside were nothing compared to her commentaries on the two portraits that hung on the other side of the hall. The first was the current baronet's great, great uncle Roderick who had been an admiral of the fleet.

'Sir Marmaduke always says Sir Roderick would have made a better pirate!' squealed Belinda. 'He does look rather upset by it all, doesn't he?'

This was clearly meant as a jest, and Prudence and Jane made a show of laughing.

The second portrait was of Sir Marmaduke's great grandfather, who had been a Lord Lieutenant somewhere or other at the time of the Restoration.

'Sir Brandon Ransome-Thrope married Lady Laetitia Ticklee-Thrope and thereby acquired the Thrope name and estate in Leicestershire,' said Belinda. 'But unfortunately lost both of them soon afterwards.'

Prudence and Jane caught each other's eye. Belinda's words made it sound as if the unfortunate Sir Brandon had accidentally mislaid his Thrope name and estate.

Quite apart from the circumstances that may have explained the doleful expressions on the two gentlemen's faces, what Prudence and Jane noticed primarily was that Sir Roderick and Sir Brandon looked exactly alike. Prudence made a tactful comment about their strong facial characteristics. Jane was not so sure. For all that Belinda's words implied that the portraits had been painted from life, Jane had the distinct impression that they were of a rather more recent vintage.

'The frames are very beautiful,' she said.

Belinda took this remark as a prompt for them to move on, guiding her visitors the short distance into the drawing-room. She explained that she was expecting to receive new portraits of both herself and her husband 'any day now'. Whilst she could not expect those to rank amongst the greatest of paintings, she humbly hoped they might take their place alongside the 'old masters' that showed her husband's ancestors to such good effect.

For *now*, however, she wished to show her friends a picture that had been loaned to the house by the same artist. It was hanging in the very place that would soon receive the unassuming image of her own good self. It was, she made clear, a much smaller picture than the one which would replace it. But it might nevertheless prove of some interest – and provide a glimpse of the quality of work she was hopeful would soon be seen in subjects that were, quite literally, closer to home.

And so saying, she stood to one side to allow Prudence and Jane to see the compact portrait that hung in an alcove on one side of the marble fireplace.

There was a stunned silence, which Belinda took to be a good sign. Her guests were obviously impressed.

No one said a word. Even Belinda remained quiet, not wanting to distract her friends, who were so clearly entranced by the image. For their part, Prudence and Jane glanced at each other again, eyes wide, before turning back to look at the painting.

The silence continued and Belinda began to feel a little uncomfortable. Perhaps they did not know who it was, she thought. After all, Prudence and Jane did not move in such august circles as herself. She therefore ventured to provide some assistance.

'You know whom it portrays, of course,' she said.

'Yes,' breathed Prudence.

'It's the Prince of Wales,' said Jane in a very quiet voice.

'It is indeed,' crowed Belinda. 'And by an artist whose name I hope will soon be on the lips of many.'

For although Lady Ransome had nothing but loathing for the horrid toad, she would rather he be seen as a reptile of some renown.

She therefore paused for dramatic effect before adding the words:

'Mr Jonathan Smallow.'

Jane's face was tight. Prudence had turned deathly white.

§

Mr Alcazar was staring at the wall in silence.

He felt hurt, aggrieved, insulted. But he did not have the spirit or energy to show his displeasure. The offer had perhaps been made with worthy intentions, but it left him feeling abused. He looked across at his wife who had hardly spoken since the recent loss of their child. She was a pale imitation of her former self. How much longer could she endure this kind of grief? They were a proud family. He knew she would feel the same as he, even if she did not express a similar sense of anger.

The visit of Mr Smallow had been a surprise. They both knew him – not simply because he was a local artist. He had been a fairly frequent visitor to the house. He called on Jeremiah occasionally to berate him about something or other. And he had spent time with Kitty Smith. Mr and Mrs Alcazar had heard his voice on the stairs more than once.

There had also been times when Smallow was accompanied by one of his rakish friends. Mr Alcazar recalled meeting a tall, imperious man in the hallway one night. The man had demanded to know if 'the girl' was upstairs – as if Alcazar had been the housekeeper, and the house a brothel. It was small comfort that, after Kitty's sad death, the tall, flat-faced man had not been seen again. The young lady who now inhabited Kitty's room had only been glimpsed on a couple of occasions. But it was already clear that she did not invite the same sort of company.

Smallow's unannounced arrival at the Alcazar residence did not, therefore, rekindle happy memories. To be fair, he had paid his respects and made some elegant comments of commiseration on the family's loss. 'All that lives must die,' he had said, 'passing through nature to eternity. I trust you shall be joined with your loved ones again in eternal bliss.' Mr Alcazar was touched by the remark. But it soon became clear that Smallow's visit had been prompted by something other than the delivery of condolences.

When Smallow finally broached the real reason for his visit, it left Mr Alcazar as troubled as he was angry. How could he explain it, even to himself, without it sounding at best manipulative and at worst fraudulent? Yes, it followed on from encouraging words about wanting to help the Alcazars sustain a more reliable income in the face of their loss. Yes, there had been some indication that Smallow might be able to help a fellow artist. But, at the heart of the proposal was duplicity and conceit.

If Mr Alcazar understood him correctly – and he kept replaying the conversation in his head – Smallow was proposing to buy some of his paintings. That specifically he wished to purchase two copies of Mr Alcazar's most recent view of Covent Garden Piazza. Paintings which he would then adapt slightly, before selling them on as his own work.

Smallow had seemed so cocksure about the soundness of the proposition.

'You lose nothing, Al,' he had said, adopting an overly chummy tone. 'The paintings would be mere copies of a work you've already created, so, in that respect, not "originals" at all. They'll be bought by clients to whom you would otherwise have no access. And I pay you a fee, no questions asked. It would be a truly collaborative venture that guarantees you money for pictures you've not yet painted, and which, on your own, you could not sell. You literally have nothing to lose by it – and everything to gain.'

Mr Alcazar had stared back at him, lost for words. This was absolutely not what he understood by artistic collaboration. This was daylight robbery – and conspiracy to defraud.

But Smallow had taken the silent response as an indication of interest and so continued to talk. The 'copies' should not be identical to the original, he said. Each should contain sufficient difference in the detail for them to be justifiably described as individual views. They should not be signed by Mr Alcazar but given over to Smallow as anonymous works. And, needless to say, Mr Alcazar should tell no one about it. No one at all. It must remain their own little collaborative secret. Were those terms to be breached, then the commercial arrangement would clearly be terminated forthwith. Finally, Mr Alcazar would be required to sign a document – 'no more than a note, really', Smallow assured him – relinquishing any rights to the paintings.

Mr Alcazar looked back at Smallow. The visitor stood before him, calmly passing a walking cane from one hand to another. There was a complacent smile on his shiny face, as if his only thought were to perform a charitable act in order to benefit a fellow artist and his family.

'I am slow, Mr Smallow,' Mr Alcazar said at last, maintaining a formality of address that made no allowance for their shared calling. His halting voice also betrayed more than a trace of his heritage. 'But you are saying I sell you my work. To be *your* work.'

Smallow's smile grew wider.

'As I say, Al – it would all be in a spirit of collaboration,' he said. 'I would take your vista of Covent Garden and add a few touches of my own. You would be well rewarded for your work – by *me*. And I would receive *my* recompense from the final buyer. Everyone wins! What do you think?'

In principle, perhaps it really was not so different to the more accepted forms of shared endeavour. But even

Smallow knew that this latest proposal overstepped the line that divided legitimate collaboration from illegal collusion. It was a strategy not without its risks. But it was always difficult to prove that any canvas was the work of only one artist.

Mr Alcazar's face, however, had taken on a dark and serious expression that told of his recent difficulties. Perhaps, thought Smallow, he should have waited longer before laying out his proposal. But then, given the prevalence of death in this house, it was more than likely that Alcazar himself would not be around for much longer. One had to take one's chances while they were there.

'Mr Smallow,' said Mr Alcazar at last. 'You find me at a sorry time. I hope you will excuse if I say no more. My head is not ready to …'

He was struggling to find appropriate words.

'To deal with another commission at this moment?' suggested Smallow.

Mr Alcazar stared at him and nodded slowly.

'Then I shall leave the proposal with you,' continued Smallow. 'Just something between we two – I mean, *three*.' He nodded towards Mrs Alcazar, as if to include her in what was beginning to sound like a conspiracy. 'Do let me know when you've had time to consider the matter further, and I shall be delighted to call upon you again.'

And so saying, Smallow bowed to Mrs Alcazar and made his way out of the still, sad space into which he had blustered half an hour before. As the door closed behind him, Mr Alcazar hoped he might never hear Smallow's voice in the house again.

§

On the way back from St James's Square there was only one topic of conversation.

Was the portrait of the Prince of Wales the one William had 'lost'? And, if so, what on earth was it doing in Belinda's house?

So far as the first question was concerned, Prudence and Jane were convinced the answer had to be 'yes'. Neither of them had seen William's canvas but he had described it to them. That knowledge, plus the style and brushwork, surely made it unmistakable.

But then, just as quickly, they had to revise that view. For it was only 'unmistakable' because of what they already knew of the picture and its creator. To anyone else the painting would not necessarily have declared itself as the work of the famous Mr Hogarth. Its royal subject matter and delicate scale both made it highly unlikely that even an informed viewer would associate it with the artist of *A Rake's Progress*.

And with that thought in mind, they suddenly became aware of how difficult it might be to prove that the painting was, in fact, by William and not Smallow. In many respects its creation had been an experiment – the result of William trying to paint in a fashion that was purposely unlike his usual style. Jane decided to approach the subject from another angle.

'It's doubly strange that it should be Smallow who seems to be at the bottom of this,' she said. 'I'm not sure if you're aware of the fact, but William loathes him. And I daresay the feeling's mutual.'

Prudence had gone very quiet.

'Have you come across him by any chance?' added Jane. 'Smallow?'

They were about to cross a busy street. Prudence gripped her friend's arm tightly while they waited for a break in the traffic. Safe on the other side, she answered the question.

'I had some dealings with him,' she said. 'Many years ago. But that is all in the past. I do not know him now.'

'Well, I've never met him,' said Jane. 'But I gather he's something of a popinjay.'

She paused and then added:

'Not to mention a thief and a cheat by the sound of it!'

This led on to the question of how the painting had found its way onto Belinda's wall. Had Smallow stolen it himself? Or had it come into his hands via a different route? If William had indeed sent the canvas to the framer – or left it somewhere – had Smallow simply made off with it? It was, after all, a small canvas – small enough to be hidden under a coat. The only thing Jane felt she could say with any confidence was that William would not have let Smallow anywhere near his studio. The only artists allowed that privilege were his closest friends, like Frank Hayman and Samuel Scott.

'And Jeremiah, of course,' added Jane as an afterthought.

Prudence's stomach turned over. She pursed her lips and tried to stay calm. For she knew that she needed to broach the subject with Jane. Not to do so would compromise their friendship. Particularly in the context of this current challenge. She would have to tell Jane about

Jeremiah. She needed to share what she knew. And what she had done.

But how?

To tell Jane about the 'borrowing' would not only break the confidence she had established with Jeremiah. It would also risk undermining her relationship with Jane, who would surely wonder why Prudence had not spoken about it before. It was making Prudence's heart ache as much as her head. For she knew full well that Jeremiah's past actions meant that he was still the person most likely to have removed the princely portrait. She had to give some voice to that view.

'I think you are aware, Jane,' she said, 'that I have known Jeremiah for some years. As fellow Piazza dwellers, we have had at least the space between us as a common bond. I would like to feel that I understand him a little.'

'You think Jeremiah might be involved?' said Jane with a directness that unsettled her friend. Then, seeing the look on Prudence's face, she changed the emphasis.

'That is, you think Jeremiah may know something about it?'

Prudence was thoughtful.

'Jeremiah is the only person,' she said before pausing. 'The only person who has had unlimited access to William's studio in recent weeks. If he did not move it himself, he may have some thoughts as to what might have happened.'

'But William trusts him implicitly,' said Jane. 'He even had him keep an eye on all his materials.'

Prudence bit her lip. This was not getting any easier. Knowing what she did, it was unbearable to hear Jane speak in this way. There was only one thing for it. She would need to take personal responsibility for discovering whether or not Jeremiah was involved in any way at all. It was important that she uncover the truth first, rather than indulge in further speculation. Even so, a small voice continued to urge her to be more transparent. And to tell Jane everything. The knots in her stomach tightened. She was confused and not at all sure what to do.

'I understand,' she said at last when Jane began to look concerned at her friend's strained silence. 'And Jeremiah will have earned that trust, I am sure. But the fact remains that he has been in and out of William's studio more than anyone else. Perhaps he saw something. What I suppose I am suggesting is that my relationship with him may be enough for me to seek his … his point of view. Confidentially.'

Prudence was not happy with such covert wording. What she had said was not untrue, but she knew she was being less than honest.

'Would you like me to come with you?' said Jane. 'When you see him.'

Prudence paused again as she struggled to keep her emotions in check.

'I think it could put Jeremiah on his guard, if I might be so bold, Jane,' she said. 'That is not to suggest that your presence is in any way intimidating …'

She forced a thin smile to show she was purposely making light of the matter. Then she continued.

'But if two ladies of a certain age descend upon him in concert, he may feel a little … unnerved.'

Jane smiled back. In the absence of anything better it was a reasonable plan, and she was content to endorse what her friend had proposed. There were, after all, other important questions that she needed to address.

Like how and when to tell William.

§

I cannot avoid for much longer writing what I must write.

It pains me beyond words to even contemplate something I have spent so many years exorcising from my mind. But circumstances seem now to be conspiring towards what may be some kind of revelation. And perhaps, in my heart, it was the need to make my confession that prompted me to undertake this narration in the first place.

Is confession the right word? Perhaps yes, perhaps not. Time will tell. There is truly nothing of which I feel I need be regretful in respect of my own behaviour. But there is no doubt that I have been much ashamed by what happened, and have therefore remained silent on the matter, even to myself, for almost fifteen years, pretending in my relations with others that it did not happen.

But it did happen. And I must confront that now. Not to do so will leave me even more hurt and also compromised by what I currently see happening around me.

§

It was not difficult for Prudence to arrange another interview with Jeremiah.

She did not even have to employ the services of Flea. She simply watched from her window and noted Jeremiah's comings and goings. He usually spent time in the marketplace towards the end of the afternoon. The market selling had ended some hours before, but there was still a good deal of activity around the square. Clearing up, preparations to store items for the morrow, plus the general scavenging that went on during the latter part of the day. A time when any porters and stall owners who were still around were most at their leisure and inclined to chat. It was therefore a daily opportunity for Jeremiah to catch up on the local gossip and carry away a few wilted vegetables at the same time.

Prudence crossed the Piazza and intercepted him just as he was freeing himself from the blustering company of two porters. They looked to have been teasing him about something they found funny but which Jeremiah regarded as only embarrassing.

'Jeremiah,' she said rather more loudly than was her custom. 'How good to see you.'

He was surprised to find himself addressed quite so boldly by Miss Hyssop but recovered quickly. Bowing low, he asked in his most formal voice how she found herself on this pleasant afternoon.

'I am very well, thank you, Jeremiah,' she replied. 'And how have *you* been since we last had the pleasure of each other's company?'

Jeremiah appeared to give the question deep thought. It was obviously deserving of more than a routine answer.

'I have been very changeable, miss,' he said at last.

'Ah,' said Prudence, unsure. 'And is that a *good* thing?'

'I believe it *is* good, miss,' he said. 'And *for* the good too.'

Prudence was puzzled. Was he being purposely enigmatic? Or was this just another of his idiosyncrasies? It was not clear. She decided to stick to her plan.

'I was hoping, Jeremiah,' she said, 'that we might have another little talk. In your ... studio, if that suited you. It would give me a chance to acquaint myself with how your work is progressing.'

Such a direct proposal, she knew, might well perplex him. She was therefore not surprised when his face exhibited a medley of expressions ranging from amazement to doubt to, finally, something resembling a smile.

'I *thought* you might,' he said, contriving to show off his teeth to good effect. 'It is your right, of course. As a lady patron – whose patron-ing is so well appreciated.'

He paused and look confused. That wasn't the right word, was it? Best to carry on though. Keep going.

'But I feel I should warn you, Miss Hyssop ...'

He stepped an inch or two closer, looked about him in a conspiratorial way, and lowered his voice. Prudence felt herself tense.

'You see, Miss Hyssop,' he said. 'There have been some changes.'

He paused before saying again, 'Some ... changes.'

Prudence tried to read what was going on behind his mobile face, which showed a mix of pride, fear and timidity. It was, she thought, not unlike the figure he had cut at their previous meeting and betrayed a lack of self-confidence no amount of posturing could disguise.

'Changes in your work, you mean?' she ventured. 'In your style of painting perhaps?'

'In all *sorts* of things, miss,' he said mysteriously.

He was now waving his arms about in a way that suggested it was difficult to be more precise in his explanation. Prudence bit her lip and wondered how she might turn the conversation onto the subject of the missing picture.

'May I see them?' she said tentatively. 'The ... changes.'

She gave him time to think and then added:

'It would be good to talk again about paintings in general – and what specifically you have been doing.'

Jeremiah sighed. But was it resignation or relief?

'You may see the changes indeed, miss,' he replied at last. 'Of course, you may. For I believe that you, of all people, might understand.'

§

Dr Rock was a more reflective person than people gave him credit for.

And he was also so obviously misunderstood.

Much of the world might call him quack, impostor, charlatan. But that simply showed how little they appreciated the close relationship between mental and physical wellbeing.

His cures and remedies were specifically designed to address the complexities of the human condition. Yes, of course those products had a direct impact on the body itself. Head, teeth, gut, nether regions. But, most importantly, they encouraged belief and positive thinking. Wellbeing was largely a matter of one's state of mind. If one believed strongly enough in the efficacy of a remedy, it was much more likely to work.

Dr Rock knew that only too well. And so did many of his customers. Even if they were less inclined to make such a distinction.

It was just so unfortunate that an ignorant world insisted on casting aspersions.

Even in the face of such ill-considered prejudice, however, Dr Rock maintained his dignity and sense of purpose. If one entered the public arena – as he had done – one had to be prepared to endure the vicissitudes that such a position inevitably entailed. If Sir Robert Walpole could tolerate the insults of the vulgar crowd, then so too could Dr Richard Rock.

Being the provider of patent medicines was, after all, not so different from being a leading statesman. Both positions required a certain disinterestedness in the exercise of power. One could not expect to command the support of all the people all the time. But that should not lead one to deviate from one's endeavours to serve the common good.

So whilst it might be more comfortable *not* to be the subject of satirical squibs, one had to accept that such public commentaries came with stature and reputation. As they did for the king's first minister. And because Dr Rock was as wise as he was true, he knew that adverse publicity was not without its benefits.

Even his unflattering depiction by Mr Hogarth in Plate 5 of *A Harlot's Progress* had been less than an unmitigated disaster. For it was yet another recognition of his social standing and professional eminence. And if one was going to be satirised by *anyone*, Mr Hogarth was clearly the rising man. So much better than being lampooned by a lesser artist.

Dr Rock had therefore always faced the slings and arrows of outrageous fortune with equanimity. Such a state of mind was important for one's own wellbeing. The alternative was anxiety and, ultimately, self-destruction. It was all too easy to succumb to such demons. Frankly, he found it troubling that some of his acquaintances took the challenges of life rather too negatively.

Mr Smallow was a case in point.

There had been more than one occasion recently when Dr Rock had witnessed Smallow at Tom King's working himself up into a feverish temper about Mr Hogarth. It was far from rational behaviour, even for a man in his cups. Indeed, it betokened something akin to incipient madness. And it had every sign of manifesting itself in violent and probably ruinous tendencies. Passions which, even if they harmed no one else, would almost certainly be detrimental to the health of the individual himself.

It would therefore be as well to keep an eye on Smallow.

Dr Rock nodded wisely to himself as he continued to reflect, glass in hand.

Now might be a good time to create a new Special Electuary. A remedy specifically designed to alleviate Melancholy Madness.

Just so long as he insisted on being paid cash in hand.

§

Jeremiah's mood had changed.

Only moments before he had looked uneasy, borne down by his own thoughtfulness. But now he was radiating a confidence Prudence had not seen before. It was encouraging and disconcerting at the same time. Prudence was left wondering whether these sudden changes of mood were just another sign of his particular lunacy. Her curiosity and compassion, however, overcame her doubts. So, when he waved her in the direction of his home, she smiled graciously and walked with him to the house in Tavistock Row.

At the door Jeremiah felt in his pocket for a key and then led the way up the several flights of stairs. Once again Prudence was conscious that it was not an easy ascent. It was with a decided sense of relief that she finally arrived safely in his garret.

Change was evident as soon as she stepped over the threshold, most obviously in terms of the tidiness. The space still seemed to be serving as both home and studio, but the distinction between the two was now more marked. At the domestic end of the room a sense of order prevailed. At the small window were curtains that had almost certainly not been there before. The bed was neatly made. A few books had been placed on a shelf fixed to the wall. A vase of flowers stood on a small table. It almost looked as if the place had been furnished in expectation of Prudence's visit. But that was not possible, was it? Jeremiah had not been totally surprised by Miss Hyssop's wish to see him again – but he had surely not made these changes simply in anticipation of another visit.

When Prudence turned to the other end of the room the change was different but just as clear. Instead of haphazard pictures facing the wall, there were only two canvases to be seen. One stood on Jeremiah's makeshift easel next to the fireplace. It was in the process of being prepared for use and was covered by a layer of white ground. It might have been a new canvas but was more likely a discarded picture that had been painted over. Some marks were still visible beneath the white ground. Prudence's heart fluttered. This was one of the fates she had first imagined for William's painting of the Prince of Wales.

She put a stop to these thoughts by looking at the other canvas. It stood in the centre of the room on a proper easel – perhaps something that Jeremiah had bought with his new allowance.

This picture really did take her breath away.

It showed a scene set against a Covent Garden background. In the distance was the familiar shape of St Paul's Church. To the left, a couple of rakish men were dallying with two young market women. But, most importantly, in the centre of the picture was the representation of a woman. She seemed bewildered by what was going on around her. And she was accompanied by a young male attendant.

Prudence could not believe her eyes and was genuinely lost for words. For the picture was – and was *not* at the same time – a copy of Mr Hogarth's 'Morning'. The main elements – church, rakes, market girls, and the central pairing of a woman and boy – were essentially the same. But they had been treated quite differently. The composition was less a 'copy' of the original, and more a new and strange configuration of the same components. To Prudence's eye, the treatment gave the whole image a naïve and innocent air. A simpler and untutored version of William's far more accomplished scene. For, not surprisingly, the quality of Jeremiah's painting – assuming it to be by him – was hardly such as could be compared with Mr Hogarth's work. It was at best a crude experiment in trying to relay the essence of 'Morning'. But the overall impression was not without charm. And the artist had captured an enigmatic expression on the face of the woman – who was most certainly not modelled on Prudence. There was, however, a familiarity about the features that reminded her of *someone*.

All in all, Prudence found the experience unsettling. Like looking at something that was at the same time oddly comforting and deeply disturbing. It was a great deal to take in. Neatness and order in the room. The spectre of over-painting. And now *this* …

This unnatural and baffling version of reality.

She was aware that she was staring. Standing and staring. Silent and still. Jeremiah must wonder what on earth she was thinking. But he appeared unsurprised by her reaction. When she turned towards him, she could discern both calmness and pride in his face. It was the quiet and patient expression of someone who fully expected her to spend some time taking it all in.

Prudence felt it her duty to make an appreciative

comment, even if only to acknowledge what she could see around her. Changes which, she presumed, signalled other developments.

'Your room, your studio, Jeremiah,' she began tentatively.

He was shifting his weight from one foot to the other.

'It is all so different,' she went on. 'I know not where to begin.'

Jeremiah looked pleased, although he continued to shuffle about like a nervous schoolboy. He clearly interpreted Miss Hyssop's remarks as suggesting positive change. And that she was, in effect, commending him on the transformation.

'Thank you, miss,' he said, smiling more broadly now. 'I cannot claim responsibility for all of it, of course. Much is due to the lady.'

As he said this, he pointed bashfully towards the woman in the painting.

Now Prudence was even more bewildered. Did he mean *her*? Was he suggesting that it was the painting that had made the difference? What on earth *did* he mean?

Jeremiah saw the confusion in her eyes and chuckled, recognising that he was being less than clear.

'I'm sorry, miss,' he said. 'I'm sorry. I will explain.'

§

Earlier that day the young woman left the house in Tavistock Row and made a rare excursion into the marketplace.

It was, after all, quite literally on her doorstep, and she was conscious that she had given it hardly any attention at all. And so it was that she circled the square, looking at the many stalls and shops, taking a keen interest in what she could see around her.

It was, however, a very particular eye that she brought to her tour. Had anyone been bold enough to enquire what most intrigued her – and if she had been plain enough to reply with the truth that burned in her heart – the answer might have proved unsettling.

Is it the flowers you're most fond of looking at, miss?

That might have been one question.

Or is it the vegetables? And, if so, which ones in particular?

Or is it some of the other things that can be acquired around the place at different times of the day and night? Bread or cakes? Bacon or pork? Combs or pocket-books? Earthenware or glass?

Had the young woman been apt to respond, she would have needed only a slight shake of the head to show how unmoved she was by all these things.

Then what can it be, miss, that your brow should be so furrowed?

Ah, I see now. Ironmongery perhaps?

Had she been open, she might have owned to the tools and other diverse devices that caught her eye.

So, it's them, is it, miss? Would that be the scales? The weights? The rules and measures?

Not at all, might have come the quietly breathed answer.

The knives then? Some of the very best you can buy anywhere in London.

But what might have been her answer – had such a conversation been possible?

Or even dreamed of?

§

The explanation required Prudence to be seated.

Jeremiah moved across the room, picked up one of the chairs, and placed it in front of the new easel. He then waved his arms about to indicate how honoured he should be if Miss Hyssop would kindly sit down.

Prudence was grateful to accept the seat, but her mind was racing. Why had his repetition of the words 'I'm sorry' served only to confuse her even more?

'It is you, yourself, Miss Hyssop,' he said, 'who have been the prime mover in all this. I think it is not too strong a sentiment to say that you have saved me. That you have saved me from myself.'

Another smile from him, wider this time.

'When you visited me two weeks ago, miss, you could see I was lost,' he said. 'And you provided, out of your great generosity and Christian spirit, the means for redemption. I'd taken myself off into a dark place, and you gave me the light to emerge into something new. And to do things I'd not been brave enough to do before.'

He looked dramatically towards the picture, clearly wishing to lead her eyes there. The painting was evidently the thing that, for him, most clearly encapsulated the sense of what he was trying to say.

'You will, miss, no doubt recognize the inspiration

for my humble composition,' he said. 'What I might be so bold as to call an example of my more natural style of depiction.'

She nodded, continuing to watch for signs of what he might mean. She wanted to ask him about the paintings she had seen the last time she was there? Was he still producing those expressions of madness? Or had he really transformed his style so quickly into one that at least *looked* as if it represented a more sane disposition? She did not, however, want to risk upsetting him with such potentially difficult questions.

'It is, I admit, not so accomplished as I would like,' he went on. 'But I'm still finding my feet, as it were. Or should I say my hands!'

He waggled his fingers in the air. It was a very small jest – and he was obviously trying to put his guest at her ease. For all her outward calmness, Prudence's stiff exterior must have betrayed the turmoil she was experiencing within.

'But it is …,' he continued, pausing briefly. 'It is … not so bad. As almost a first go at it. If you see what I mean.'

Again, Prudence felt she had to say something, even if only to let him know that she was paying attention.

'Its subject is indeed very like Mr Hogarth's painting,' she said.

'Yes, miss,' he said. 'And that has been my model. Mr H's work is a most memorable vision in so many ways. "Morning" I believe it is called, miss. And I understand that the lady depicted is herself modelled on someone who currently graces my humble dwelling, much as she graces Mr H's wonderful picture!'

Coming from anyone else, the compliment might have sounded awkward or insincere. But Jeremiah's respect and warmth shone through the courteous flourish with which the line was delivered. Prudence relaxed noticeably and allowed herself to smile at his gallantry.

'What you say is essentially true,' she said. 'Although I feel sure that "grace" is perhaps too generous a term.'

Jeremiah acknowledged the remark with a bow.

'Well, you'll have seen straightaway, miss,' he went on, 'that my poor picture is a very meagre impression of that glorious scene. And there's been no attempt in this slight work to emulate the marvellous capturing by Mr H of your own exemplary character and carriage, miss. But I wanted to try painting a picture that showed our remarkable Piazza and some of its life. And I also wanted to paint a picture of a lady. And so I thought I could do no better than to borrow from Mr H's great work.'

Prudence was once again disturbed by Jeremiah's choice of words. The last time he had talked about borrowing from Mr Hogarth it had been in connection with something else entirely.

'So, I remembered as much as I could of Mr H's painting, and then tried to set it down – but in my own simple way,' he said. 'A way more suited to a man who is so much less of an artist than the great Mr H. But a way that might also give me comfort and some sense that, in the end, it might not be just a poor copy of something that's beyond me – but an expression that's really my very own. And special to me only.'

Prudence nodded and looked back at the painting. As

she did so, she felt she could almost hear the beating of Jeremiah's heart. She did not comprehend what he meant but his composed voice clearly cloaked a deep passion. And it was now evident that the painting conveyed a heartfelt sincerity. For all its naïve touches, including the representation of the boy (who was most definitely not Flea), the treatment of the woman's face showed a peculiar sensitivity. So, was it meant to represent a particular individual?

Prudence decided to ask.

'And the lady?' she said.

Jeremiah's face had taken on another of his ambiguous expressions. Somewhere between pride and embarrassment, confidence and affliction.

But, at that very moment, the lady herself entered the room.

§

Mr Pargeter had been thinking for some time that he could do with more help in the shop.

His daughter had always been a great support. But business was growing. So he had put an advertisement in the window. There was certainly scope for taking on an extra pair of hands.

And that was really the point. It was difficult to think that anyone could provide the necessary assistance without two hands. But there was no reason why the job could not be done by someone who was otherwise not fully endowed with the usual number of appendages.

Certainly, a missing leg should prove no great drawback – particularly as it did not appear to limit the man's mobility. And especially as he possessed a quite extraordinary memory and an almost obsessive sense of order and tidiness. He was also very strong. Look at the way he had lifted that heavy box of paper onto the counter. Mr Pargeter knew that he would have struggled to do it himself. He would have needed to wait until young Potts dropped by – although Jeremiah was not what you would call brawny.

That was even before you took into consideration the one-legged man's obvious love of pictures and prints. He had more than a passing knowledge of how they were made and what their qualities were. And he had a particularly good grasp of maps.

The testimonials he carried, assuming them to be genuine – and Mr Pargeter would check, of course – bore the names of military men. So it was likely the individual was well-drilled in terms of discipline and respect. Overall, then, the prospect of employing Mr – what was his name again? Samson? – seemed quite attractive. At least for a trial period.

Mr Pargeter pushed his wig further back on his head and allowed himself a satisfied smile.

'Samson,' he thought. 'Good name for a strong man. And he wears his own hair too. I must make sure he doesn't cut it!'

He chuckled at his wit. And at his business acumen.

For the fact that Mr Samson had only one leg would presumably mean he could be paid that much less.

§

'I'm sorry,' said Catherine, as she came into the room. 'I really am sorry.'

It was not immediately clear whether the apology was because she had walked in on a private conversation or simply because she was always sorry. One way or another, however, her entry caused a degree of disquiet. Catherine appeared genuinely agitated at seeing Prudence. Jeremiah looked equally perturbed. Prudence was perhaps the most startled of the three, although she had assembled the pieces within a matter of seconds.

And it now made some kind of sense.

The woman in Jeremiah's painting was Catherine. It was far from being a perfect likeness and had been executed in a naïve style. But it was close enough to be recognisable now that Prudence had the flesh and blood original before her. And the changes in the room and studio more broadly? They were presumably also due to Catherine's influence. But then such a conclusion involved so much other speculation.

For a few seconds there was an awkward silence while each of them looked at the other two, trying to work out what had happened – and what should follow. It reminded Prudence of a comic scene at the theatre. The sort of stilted situation when a character bursts in upon an activity that she or he is not supposed to know about – and on which the plot then turns. Perhaps a similar thought had also occurred to Jeremiah, for he was now nodding and bowing in an overtly dramatic way.

'Ah, yes!' he said, as if everything were exactly as one might have expected. 'Of course. You two ladies are already more than a little acquainted. Friends, in fact.'

Prudence was the first to respond.

'Indeed, we are,' she said. 'Catherine is a valued member of the Green Group – a gathering of ladies I have the pleasure of hosting at my house.'

'I'm sorry,' said Catherine again. 'Yes, dear Prudence. How very nice to see you. Charming, I mean. Not nice. That is, ... I don't mean just nice. I'm sorry for interrupting.'

'Not at all, Catherine,' continued Prudence. 'Jeremiah was just showing me his painting of the Piazza – and the fine delineation of a woman who is clearly drawn from your own dear likeness. Am I right? And are you perhaps here to resume your role as artist's model? I must apologise myself for imposing on your professional appointment.'

Prudence suspected there was far more at issue than a simple modelling arrangement, but it seemed an appropriate way to move the conversation forward without appearing to assume too much. It was also apparent that she would be unable to raise the subject of William's missing portrait now that there was a third person in the room. She therefore decided to make a tactical withdrawal. Perhaps she could invite Jeremiah to call on her later during the day.

She rose from her seat with a comment to the effect that she was overstaying her welcome and would leave them to conduct their business together. However, Jeremiah stepped forward with an earnest look on his face.

'Please, Miss Hyssop,' he said, his breath catching

in his throat. 'I should be – that is, *we* should be – most grateful if you could spare us a little more of your valuable time. Please.'

The tone of the supplication was so grave that Prudence sat down again without a murmur. Jeremiah began to breathe more easily. He fetched the second chair and placed it for Catherine while he remained standing.

'Forgive me,' he said (while Catherine mouthed 'I'm sorry'). 'Forgive me, Miss Hyssop. I know you and I did not plan to meet this afternoon. I know it was chance that brought you here today.'

Prudence said nothing to hint at her own premeditation.

'But Catherine and I have discussed the possibility of talking to you,' Jeremiah continued. 'And this is too good an opportunity. At least for *us*. Especially as you've now seen … the changes.'

There was another 'I'm sorry', but quieter this time.

Prudence composed herself and smiled. Her compassionate nature could not refuse their request, and her curious mind was eager to know the facts. What is more, she was now considering whether she might be able to extend any exchange of confidences to include the subject that continued to dominate her thinking. The missing portrait.

Both Catherine and Jeremiah appeared consoled to see Prudence exuding evident signs of support and interest. Jeremiah crossed the room, took a cushion from the bed, and placed it on the floor so that it formed a triangle with the two chairs. Then he sat down on it and crossed his legs.

Looking towards Catherine, he said:

'Shall I begin?'

An unspoken 'my dear' was left hanging at the end of the question.

'Please do, Jeremiah,' Catherine replied.

Prudence could clearly discern another 'I'm sorry' which, if not actually voiced, was etched across Catherine's face.

§

Had the young woman been in the market for knives, there may have been one that suited her purpose.

But it was difficult for any onlooker to know what that purpose might be.

It may have been that the knives were not of the right type. Or that they were too expensive. Or simply that she did not wish to discuss the matter with the old woman who was selling them. Or the old man who was sharpening them.

Or perhaps she simply did not want to draw attention to herself. Or the fact that she had even been looking at the knives at all.

It might have been all of these things. Or none of them. And almost certainly nobody noticed. Not even Flea.

For the young woman from the house on Tavistock Row was very discreet. Almost invisible. And she gave no impression of being someone who was in the market for knives.

§

Jeremiah cleared his throat.

'Catherine and I have known each other for some months,' he began. 'We met at her father's print shop. Pargeter's. You must know it, of course, miss. Down towards the Strand.'

'I do indeed,' said Prudence.

'We've been meeting quite regularly,' Jeremiah went on. 'You might even say that we've been … courting.'

He paused and looked at Catherine with love tempered by incomprehension. Catherine returned his gaze. She muttered something that sounded like, 'It's probably my fault. I'm sorry.'

'When you provided me with the means to go on with my work, Miss Hyssop,' Jeremiah continued. 'Well, it did my confidence a power of good, and I decided to ask Catherine more directly. If she would consent to be my guide and helper, that is. It's all been a bit quick, I know. But there's been no time to lose. For Catherine's like you, miss, She has a very sensitive nature.'

Prudence smiled.

'You see,' he went on, 'I was worried that, without Catherine, I might continue to … to wander.'

'To wander, Jeremiah?'

Prudence did not want to interrupt but was anxious to know what he meant. Was he aware of his incipient madness? Or was he talking about something else? His 'borrowing', perhaps. Even his life more generally. A shadow had passed over his face. Prudence looked towards Catherine, but she was staring at the floor.

'I'd rather not go into all the details, if you don't mind,

miss,' he went on. 'At least not now. But I've been keen to follow a more straight and narrower path. Than in the past. Your confidence in me helped. It helped me to open myself. To Catherine.'

Prudence once more looked towards the other chair, but Catherine was still studying the pattern of the one small rug.

'I'll make this telling as brief as I can, miss,' Jeremiah said. 'But the thing itself ... well, it grew up between the two of us almost without us knowing. Until we *did* know it.'

He sighed.

'I'm not making much sense, am I, miss?' he said.

'You're making complete sense, Jeremiah,' said Prudence. 'Please go on.'

'Well, miss,' he said. 'I asked Catherine to look at my pictures. After *you* had. It was wrong of me, I know, because you said I shouldn't do it. Show them to anyone else.'

Prudence made a movement with her hand to dismiss the thought. Jeremiah sighed again.

'But Catherine was different,' he said. 'Very different, very gentle. But also very clear. In the way she saw things. I had to let her see into my heart. And my head. I wanted to know what she thought. I needed to know if the pictures were truly ... troubling. And troublesome too. You'd been very good to me and said nothing bad. But I knew you were worried. You're a very intelligent person, Miss Hyssop. The fact that you told me not to show them to other people ... well, it made me think. And I'd already been told by … no matter. I'd been told by someone that they were … evil.'

Prudence raised a hand to her lips. Where had *this* come from? Who could have said such a thing?

'*You* would not say that, miss,' said Jeremiah.

'Jeremiah, I do not *think* it,' Prudence added quickly. 'You must not suppose that I do. Not for one moment.'

'No, miss,' he said. 'Thank you, miss. No, I don't suppose it at all. But I wanted to hear what Catherine said as well. Because … I couldn't bear to keep anything from her. If she was going to be my …'

He came to a halt. Prudence was keen that he should continue.

'And what was Catherine's view?' she said.

In one sense it was odd to be asking Jeremiah when Catherine was sitting next to her. But it seemed the only way to proceed without causing further distress.

'What did Catherine think?' Prudence said again, giving him more time to consider the question. 'What did she say about your …?'

She was not sure which term might best describe his paintings, so she made one up.

'Your … abstract pictures?'

Jeremiah thought some more and then started chuckling quietly.

'That's a good word, miss,' he said at last. 'Abstract. I like that.'

More chuckling. Prudence was not sure whether it was encouraging or unnerving.

'Well, miss,' he went on, 'Catherine suggested I should

try painting something less … *abstract*, I suppose. She said I should paint those things that I loved the most.'

Catherine looked up briefly and nodded. The hint of a smile trembled around her lips. There then followed a pause while Jeremiah and Catherine gazed at each other. For the first time Prudence began to feel a little embarrassed.

'So, you decided to paint the things that you loved,' she prompted. 'Like the Piazza. And Catherine.'

There was much nodding and an air of almost adolescent self-consciousness between the loving couple.

'Yes, miss,' said Jeremiah. 'I particularly wanted to paint Catherine. Most especially in the Piazza. And Mr H's picture was a special inspiration.'

This comment encouraged them all to look again at the painting on the easel. In doing so, Prudence was finally able to catch Catherine's eye and smile.

'But I should like to do a proper portrait of Catherine too,' continued Jeremiah. 'So I've been thinking how to go about it. Mr H has done some very good faces, and I'd love to learn how he builds up the layers so that the skin looks real, rather than just … pink.'

Prudence's attention was suddenly of a different order. This was too good a chance to pass up. She did not want to drive the conversation towards her original aim if it risked inhibiting the current revelation. But Jeremiah himself was suggesting a link to William's portraits. She had to follow that up. But how? Could she ask him to say more about what he knew of Mr Hogarth's method? Or should she be more direct and ask specifically about the picture of the Prince? The former approach would be more in keeping with the tone of the conversation. But she should not allow herself to be deflected from her purpose. There was too much at stake – for both William and Jane. She surely had to put their interests first. So, she decided to be direct.

'Did you see the portrait that Mr Hogarth was working on most recently?' she said. 'Before it disappeared?'

It was not simply direct. It was blunt. Clumsy even. But she needed to know.

She was hoping that Jeremiah would simply nod and make some unexceptional comment about the picture's subject. Or the fact that he had only seen it weeks before. Perhaps he might look alarmed and ask what she meant by 'disappeared'. *Anything* – rather than convey the slightest sense that he knew what was in her mind.

But no.

The look of horror that instantly transformed Jeremiah from loving artist to terrified victim could mean only one thing. Prudence was dismayed by what appeared to be nothing less than a confession of guilt. He stood up and began to pace about the room, wringing his hands. Catherine started saying how sorry she was, which – in the circumstances – now seemed entirely appropriate. Meanwhile, Prudence tried to stay calm and anticipate what Jeremiah might say.

Finally he stopped his pacing and threw his arms wide. His face was that of a tortured soul.

'I couldn't help it,' he cried. 'I *had* to do it. He forced me. He said he'd report me as a madman if I didn't. And he said other things as well. Worse things. *Terrible* things. He said they'd take me away and lock me up. And that I'd never see ...'

He glanced at Catherine.

'And that I'd never see *anyone* ever again.'

Prudence needed to pacify him, for he was clearly distraught. But she also had to understand what he was trying to say.

'Jeremiah,' she said quietly. 'Please settle yourself. Catherine and I are both here with you. You have nothing to fear from us.'

Jeremiah screwed up his face in anguish.

'Nothing to fear from you, miss,' he said. 'No. And I'm so, so grateful for it. Believe me, I am. But from *him*, ... from *him* ... *Everything* to fear. Everything in the world!'

'Him?' said Prudence. 'I don't understand, Jeremiah. Of whom do you speak? Who can have frightened you so much?'

Jeremiah's face was drained.

'Who else?' he said in a broken voice. 'Who else, but Mr Smallow!'

ACT III
The Fraudulent Copy

Prudence did not want to keep it to herself.

Yes, there were matters of confidentiality to consider. Jeremiah and Catherine were owed a level of protection. It was the least they might expect, given their frankness. But matters were getting complicated. And Jeremiah had, in effect, made a confession. That certainly needed to be shared with Jane.

'The meeting with Jeremiah was easy enough to arrange,' said Prudence, once the two of them were seated in her drawing-room. 'But it took a course I did not expect and raised issues that neither of us could have anticipated.'

'You have my full and undivided attention, dear Prudence,' said Jane.

'Well,' said Prudence, her voice seemingly close to breaking up, 'the first and most important thing I have to disclose is, I am afraid, not a pleasant business. Not at all. And I daresay we shall have to think very much about quite what we do with the information.'

Jane's face was tight, her eyes alarmed.

'For, dear Jane,' Prudence went on, 'I am very sorry to say that it was indeed Jeremiah who removed William's painting.'

Jane was watching her friend closely. Prudence's exhausted expression conveyed only too clearly the huge strain she was under.

'Yes, it was Jeremiah who stole it,' she continued, breathing hard. 'There is no escaping the fact that it was theft. For I have heard it from his own lips.'

Jane was stunned. Since their last conversation she had convinced herself that such a familiar, and erstwhile loyal, assistant could in no way be the culprit.

'But why on earth would he do that?' she said. 'And how did the painting end up in Belinda's house?'

Thoughts were tumbling through her head quicker than she could count them. And she was not sure which of the many questions was the logical place to start. Fortunately she knew that, in Prudence, she had a calm and sensible counsellor. Even though her friend was clearly labouring under great stress herself, Jane knew that Prudence would already have had time to consider the matter in depth.

'Let us take one thing at a time,' said Prudence. 'I shall begin with why Jeremiah removed it in the first place. Or at least the reason as he explained it to me.'

Jane sat forward on her chair. Prudence, straight-backed, perched on a couch. Her face conveyed a determined seriousness, but the way she moved her hands – clutching and unclutching her fingers – suggested that what she had to say was causing her some considerable torment.

'It concerns the painter, Mr Smallow,' she said.

'Ah,' said Jane. 'Of course.'

'Mr Smallow appears to have some power over Jeremiah,' said Prudence.

'Some power?' echoed Jane. 'What can you mean? It sounds quite unnatural.'

Prudence grimaced.

'And perhaps it is,' she said. 'It is certainly not something into which I should wish to enquire too deeply, my dear Jane.'

There was, Jane thought, a distinct tremor in her friend's voice.

'In fact,' Prudence went on, 'I think it serves our purpose best if I focus only on as much of the story as is absolutely necessary.'

Jane nodded slowly, although she was not sure what her friend meant by this.

'I'm in your hands, my dear,' she said.

Prudence took a deep breath.

'We cannot allow ourselves to be distracted by all the attendant circumstances, Jane,' she went on. 'But it needs to be acknowledged, at least by we two if not by the wider world, that Jeremiah has been dabbling in painting. He took up the brush some time ago. And what he produced, at least initially, were pictures that exhibit some … unearthly tendencies. Pictures that, were they to come before an unsympathetic audience, might be sufficient to condemn him as … mad.'

Jane's eyes were now wide with bewilderment. No, this was certainly not the sort of disclosure she had anticipated. The fact that Jeremiah had painted any pictures at all was a surprise. The thought that such pictures were strange enough to drain the blood from her friend's face was deeply worrying. For Prudence was now looking very pale indeed.

'Unearthly tendencies?' Jane repeated, unclear as to what such a term might refer.

'As I say, my dear Jane,' Prudence went on, 'it is as well we do not look too closely. But they were pictures that, if nothing else, could only be the result of an unbalanced mind.'

Jane did not know whether to be aghast or sympathetic.

'I can tell from your face that you've seen … them,' she said. 'The … pictures.'

For all her friend's resolve not to delve too deeply, Jane could see how upsetting Prudence was finding her narration. Was that simply because of the pictures? How unearthly *were* they? How unbalanced *was* the mind that had created them?

But Jane was also spurred on by more than curiosity or compassion. For at the root of this whole sorry business was a crime. Theft. A capital offence. And they were talking about the man they now knew to be the thief. A thief who had used his position of trust in order to steal an important artwork from her husband. If Prudence was suggesting that Jeremiah's mental state might have been a mitigating factor, then Jane had to know more. For as things currently stood, they were discussing a matter that might well result in a man – a man they both knew well – being hanged by the neck. Perhaps *this* was why Prudence seemed more agitated than Jane had ever seen her before.

'Yes, I have seen the pictures,' Prudence said after a pause. 'It is not a form of expression to which Jeremiah is now attached. I believe he has painted over the offending works in his efforts to progress towards … something new. But the fact remains that such bizarre representations were, until very recently, part of his … work.'

Prudence was speaking slowly, choosing her words carefully.

'I think it is understandable,' she continued, 'that an aspiring artist should try his hand at different methods. The pictures I have seen from his ... his darker period ... I have chosen to see them as ... experiments. Attempts to explore unusual ways of expressing his ... feelings. But clearly not everyone who saw them took such a view.'

'You mean Mr Smallow, I presume,' said Jane.

She brought her mind back to what her friend had said about the other man. William's painting had been taken by Jeremiah. But he had been acting, it was suggested, under the 'power' of Jonathan Smallow. But what did that mean exactly?

Prudence sighed. Her face looked very tired. The dull light in the room exaggerated the greyness of her skin.

'I fear so,' she said.

Jane waited for her to say more. But it took Prudence some seconds to compose herself.

'Mr Smallow is one of Jeremiah's clients,' Prudence continued at last. 'He employs Jeremiah much as William does – as a courier, running errands. Although Jeremiah's relationship with him has always been less close than with your husband. For I know that Jeremiah has enormous respect and admiration for William.'

'Respect and admiration!' said Jane. 'But clearly not so much that it stopped him from committing a capital crime on his property!'

Prudence knew the words were more than justified by what was being revealed. Yet she also recognised the absence of malice in her friend's voice. Jane had given expression to an obvious thought – but had managed to make it sound more like a wry observation than a bitter riposte. It was another confirmation that Mrs Hogarth was a wise confidante who was able to listen with an open mind. Even when the case touched so very personally upon herself and her husband.

But it was also a prompt for Prudence to get to the crux of her account more quickly.

§

It was about a week after the incident that first brought Mr William Hogarth to my attention – the incident that left him sprawled across the space in front of Tom King's, with his three enemies standing over him.

I had assumed the matter had ended there, and I gave it no great consideration over the following days, other than to wonder whether Mr Hogarth, in a more sober state, might acknowledge me or even remember the incident at all, given that he had been very taken with drink at the time.

What I had given no contemplation to was the vengeful and vindictive passion that had been brewing in one of his persecutors. A malevolent spirit that was, as I soon learned, concentrated upon me.

I had been nearly home and was approaching the Piazza along King Street. It was growing dark, and I was anxious to be back before night fell entirely, and so my steps were hurried. Whether he had been following me and rushed ahead, or just seen me appearing and acted on impulse, I cannot say. All I know is that he was suddenly before me, barring my way, having stepped out from one of the alleys that link King Street to the churchyard.

It was the small man whom I had seen belabouring Mr Hogarth with his two associates. On this occasion, however, he was alone. He stood glaring at me, a cruel smile on his smooth face, and I could smell the liquor on his breath.

'Well, if it isn't little Miss Do-Good,' he snarled, or words to that effect. 'And where might you be going? Off to save some other poor, demented soul from his elders and betters? Eh?'

I stood quite still, petrified by this evil apparition, and lost for words. For what could I say, when the last thing on earth that I desired was to engage in any kind of conversation with him?

I looked about me for help, but there were only a few passers-by. And what might I tell them, other than that a man was talking to me, and that I would rather he did not. It seemed beyond me to utter any such thing, and I could see out of the corner of my eye that, on the other side of the street, a couple were passing arm-in-arm. Except that they were not respectable, and that she showed every sign of being a harlot who had just attached herself to her beau. That was, after all, the nature of meetings around the Piazza, especially at this hour. It was such a common sight to see men and women appearing to meet and exchange some words in these streets, that the scene of myself confronted by a small, well-dressed man in full wig, and looking for all the world as if he wanted to purchase his pleasure, was all too familiar a view.

But as I stood there saying nothing, he continued to leer and to make cruel and suggestive remarks that were meant for me only to hear. I began to be truly afraid for myself, as the darkness was now falling by the minute, and I feared that, if I did not break away from him immediately, I would be lost in the shadows.

I opened my mouth to make some sort of protest, but he grabbed my arm roughly and pushed me towards the even darker recesses of the alleyway.

§

Prudence drew herself up.

'You are right, of course,' she said. 'Whatever else Jeremiah may have done he has betrayed William's trust. And it is so much more agonising that he did it at the behest of someone whom he could only ever regard with disrespect and disgust.'

Again, Jane could sense the real distress in her friend's voice.

'You should not tax yourself so, dear Prudence,' she said. 'The responsibility for none of this rests upon *your* shoulders. We'll discuss how to proceed in due course. But first you must calm yourself and finish your telling of Jeremiah's testimony. You are the dearest of souls and the most compassionate of companions. But believe me, dear friend, you must not take the world's troubles as your own.'

At these words, whatever was left of Prudence's composure crumbled. Jane rose from her chair and sat on the couch next to her friend, taking her hand and squeezing it gently. Prudence was close to tears, but she took a deep breath and continued with her tale.

'If Jeremiah is to be believed,' she said, 'Mr Smallow came upon him unexpectedly in his room. He saw Jeremiah's attempts at painting and mocked him. The pictures were, he said, abominations in the sight of God. The Devil's work. They were enough to have Jeremiah committed to Bedlam.'

'Oh, my dear Prudence,' said Jane.

She put her arm around her friend's shoulders. For a minute or so they sat in silence. Then Prudence wiped a drip from the end of her nose and Jane disengaged her arm.

'Thank you, Jane,' said Prudence. 'You are a great comfort. And so understanding. Especially when this all concerns a crime against your husband. You would be quite within your rights to call for the magistrate and have Jeremiah immediately apprehended.'

'Dear Prudence,' said Jane. 'We shall come to everything in good time. My only thought now is to hear your story. For I can see that it lies heavy on you, and I want to share your burden.'

It was Prudence's turn to squeeze her friend's hand.

'Thank you,' she said. 'I shall continue presently.'

She rose from the couch and called Master Fleabane, requesting that he bring some sherry wine. Then she looked from the window into the Piazza before returning to the couch where Jane was still sitting.

'Jeremiah said he pleaded with Mr Smallow,' Prudence said. 'To show some mercy. But the man was implacable.

He declared he would have Jeremiah detained. He said the word of a respected artist would be sufficient to condemn him. But Jeremiah continued to plead. Was there nothing he could do?'

Prudence was breathing heavily. More squeezing of hands.

'You will have guessed the rest, dear Jane,' said Prudence, who was trying to keep from shaking. Jane put her arm around her again.

'I assume Smallow made a demand,' said Jane. 'That he subjected Jeremiah to what I believe is called extortion.'

Prudence bowed her head.

'Was it specifically aimed at William do you think?' Jane asked.

'I fear it was,' said Prudence. 'Jeremiah said he did not know if it was in Mr Smallow's mind when he burst into the room. Probably not, he believes. He thinks it was not so considered. Rather the grasping of an unlooked-for opportunity – once it was clear he had reduced Jeremiah to a state of ... subservience. You have said yourself that there is no love lost between William and ... that man. And I know ... that man ... to be ... vindictive.'

Jane pulled Prudence closer for she was still shaking visibly. They sat in silence for some minutes as Prudence's breathing slowed in harmony with Jane's. Finally, Jane opted to edge the conversation forward as gently as she could.

'So,' she said, 'Smallow presumably made it clear he'd do nothing – so long as Jeremiah stole something from William. Is that right? That Jeremiah should steal a painting. A painting that Smallow would then ... *what*? Try to pass off as his own work? Yes, I know that's exactly what he *has* done. But it just seems so ... nonsensical. How long can such a falsehood be maintained? I know we may not be able to prove the picture really *is* William's work. And, for all we know, Smallow may have repainted some of it. But, in the end, surely everyone must recognise it for what it is. An imposture. So, yes, I can see *how* it happened. But I still don't understand *why*. The fact is that Smallow is *not* William Hogarth. And he can't possibly sustain the pretence that he *is*. Not with one small painting that's not even typical of William's work!'

Jane's speech gave Prudence time to recover herself. When she next spoke, her voice exhibited more of its usual strength and good sense.

'You are right, Jane,' she said. 'I cannot think of two people who are more different than William and ... that man. But I do not think that this is about the appropriation of William's art. I am not sure it is even about using the picture for fraudulent purposes – even if that appears to be the logical conclusion of what we witnessed at Belinda's.'

Jane pulled a face.

'Then what *is* it about?' she said.

Prudence looked her friend squarely in the face.

'I think you said it just now, Jane,' she said. 'When you declared that Jonathan Smallow is not William Hogarth. I suspect *that* is the crux of the matter. Mr Smallow wishes he *were* Mr Hogarth. He is deeply jealous that William is everything he is not. And he wants to make William suffer. Taking the painting is connected to that, I feel sure. Part of a malicious campaign. An attempt to undermine William's success and aspirations. Yes, Mr Smallow may derive some passing benefit by claiming the work as his own. But the nature of the man suggests that this is more about spite and vengeance than it is a calculated fraud.'

Jane was thinking quickly, replaying in her mind anything William might have said in the past about Smallow. The idea that what she and Prudence were now discussing was something other than just theft and fraud was an entirely new thought. Heaven knows, theft and fraud were serious enough! Serious enough to get a man hanged. But what Prudence was now suggesting was even graver than that. And certainly more personal. It represented a real threat to William's state of mind, if not his very being.

'I should add, Jane,' said Prudence, 'that Jeremiah does not know that we have seen the painting. And that we have seen it in Belinda's house. There seemed nothing to be gained by telling him – especially given how distraught he was.'

Jane was nodding, almost mechanically, and still thinking hard.

'But I'm now totally confused,' she said. 'Did Smallow coerce Jeremiah into stealing that picture specifically?'

Prudence exhaled deeply. She had recovered something of her usual serenity, but her face was still drawn and tired. There was a gentle tap on the door, and Flea entered carrying a tray on which were a flask of sherry and two glasses. The women smiled their thanks as he set the tray down next to the couch, before leaving as discreetly as he had entered.

Prudence poured the wine and handed a glass to Jane.

'The *short* answer to your question is – yes, he did,' said Prudence.

'But then I don't understand,' said Jane. 'How did Smallow know about it? That it even existed, I mean.'

'Because Jeremiah told him,' said Prudence.

Jane's eyebrows were raised. Prudence carried on.

'Mr Smallow wanted to know what William was working on,' she said. 'Jeremiah did not want to mention *The Four Times of the Day*, for fear the information would find its way to a pirate print maker. Talking about the portrait was Jeremiah's way of diverting attention onto something he assumed was far less important. Something he had only glimpsed in the studio. Something small and hidden away in a corner, as if William had half discarded it. But it was the portrait's scale and subject that sparked the other man's interest. Jeremiah believes it was only then that the idea suggested itself to Mr Smallow.'

Prudence and Jane looked at each other, their eyes expressing a host of unspoken questions. Jane started to sip her sherry, but then downed it all in one go. She was not sure whether she was upset, worried, angry, surprised, or simply puzzled.

'Heavens,' she sighed. 'What can I say? This is all far more ... tangled than I'd ever imagined.'

Prudence smiled for the first time since they had begun their earnest conversation. It was a tired smile but it warmed Jane's heart to see it. She smiled back and, in that brief exchange, the two women conveyed a shared sense of resolution in the face of life's complexity.

'It is certainly complicated, Jane,' said Prudence. 'And I have not even told you about Catherine yet!'

§

Later that day Jane sat alone at the sign of the golden head reflecting on what Prudence had told her.

There were, she felt, several loose ends.

For one thing, it had not been resolved how and when to tell William. Jane had purposely postponed saying anything to him about what they had seen at Belinda's, in the hope that some of their speculations might prove groundless. But Jeremiah's confession to Prudence meant that the evidence was now conclusive. William had to be told. And soon.

There were also, however, other things which troubled Jane. One was Jeremiah's fear of Smallow. It appeared to hinge on Smallow's threat to expose the courier as the creator of strange and misguided paintings. Expressions of madness sufficiently menacing to have him committed to Bedlam. Prudence had seen the pictures herself and her reaction seemed to endorse such a view. But Jane found the whole notion puzzling at several levels.

She had grown up in a world of painters and paintings. And, yes, she knew full well that there were standards and expectations that framed the way the art world worked. What *was*, and was *not*, acceptable. But there were also a great many amateurs and experimenters out there. A significant number of people who were just daubing – enjoying their right to put paint onto board or canvas.

She also knew from personal experience how odd and macabre her own husband's pictures could be. Some of his published prints were quite bizarre – and she had seen other sketches and early versions of works that even *he* considered too outlandish to be made public. Pictures that, had they found their way into the wider world, would have seen him accused of defamation or profanity. Most of those he had destroyed or painted over.

In such a context, it seemed unlikely that any of Jeremiah's scrawls could possibly be considered as dangerous – not in comparison with designs that were manifestly libellous or even blasphemous. Prudence had, of course, viewed them with a gaze of Christian sensibility. Perhaps that was why she saw such expressions as the work of dark forces. But even that could not account for what sounded like Jeremiah's all too apparent fear. Jane had no doubt that Smallow must certainly be one of Jeremiah's more unpleasant taskmasters. But the man was also well-known as a pompous ass. Was it not more likely that Jeremiah would have shrugged off Smallow's threat as just one more proof of his brutish and drunken bullying?

It did not add up. And Jane began to wonder if perhaps Prudence had been just a little too easily persuaded by what Jeremiah had told her. Even if he did feel himself genuinely intimidated by Smallow's comments, was that really enough to make him steal from another artist who was so obviously far more important as both a client and sponsor?

No, there had to be more to it than that. Jeremiah's fear of Smallow had to be rooted in something else. But what?

§

Mrs Alcazar heard the knock at the door – and it worried her.

She was frightened it might be that horrid man again, come back to repeat the proposal that had put her husband in such a bad humour. But then it had been a very gentle knock. She thought it unlikely that such a man would be capable of gentleness. So she rose from her bench and walked slowly towards the tall door that led out into the passageway. She felt more stable now. Not quite so in need of her husband's arm to lean on. He was out, at one of the local auctioneers, and had left her alone with their one remaining child.

When she opened the door, she found herself staring into a very pretty face. It was a young woman who could not have been older than twenty, Mrs Alcazar thought. She was dressed soberly in black. Was she too perhaps in mourning? Or was this her customary attire?

'Mrs Alcazar?' said the young woman.

Mrs Alcazar was entranced by her face, which seemed oddly familiar, especially around the eyes.

'I'm Sarah Bell. Your neighbour. From two flights up.'

The young woman looked up at the ceiling, as if to reinforce the meaning of her words. Perhaps she felt it necessary. Mrs Alcazar's face did have a certain blankness about it.

'Miss Bell,' said Mrs Alcazar, so quietly that it hardly made a sound.

'Miss Bell,' she repeated, this time trying to inject

some volume into her voice. Her eyes darted between the pretty face and the small bunch of daffodils the young woman was holding in front of her bodice. The contrast of the yellow and green against the black was startling and added to the overall prettiness of the vision.

'Please to come in, Miss Bell,' she said, standing to one side.

The young woman moved forward into a room that was so much higher and lighter than her own shadowy quarters two floors above.

'I would not wish to disturb you, Mrs Alcazar,' she said. 'So you must please turn me away. If you would prefer to rest. But I wanted to express my condolences. Late, I know. But I was not aware. Indeed, I've not been aware of much at all since I moved in here. And I have been preoccupied. So I ask you please to excuse me. And to accept these flowers. As a small token. Of my sympathy.'

The voice carried an accent. It was not from London, but Mrs Alcazar could not put her finger on its origin. The young woman also spoke in short breathy sentences. It gave her, so Mrs Alcazar thought, a very engaging demeanour.

'You are very kind,' said Mrs Alcazar. 'Very kind to think of someone – to think of a family – whom you do not even know. The kindness of strangers is, however, a precious thing, and I bless you for it.'

The young woman stared at Mrs Alcazar who now held the flowers as if they had been a gift of great worth, rather than one of the cheaper bunches being sold off in the marketplace only a few yards away.

By the time Mr Alcazar returned an hour later, Miss

Sarah Bell had disappeared back into the anonymity from which she emerged. Mrs Alcazar, however, derived great pleasure from retailing the details of the visit to her husband. It seemed to him that the young woman's call had given some life back to the grey and worn face of his wife. He was deeply grateful for that.

Mrs Alcazar told her husband what she had learned of the young woman. She had arrived from the country only shortly before taking up residence in the house. She had found a position as a night-nurse for a frail old woman who lived on the far side of Drury Lane. The hours were very unsociable, but it was at least a job. A way of maintaining life and limb. At least for now. Due to the nature of the work, she spent much of the daytime trying to sleep and had made no effort to introduce herself to the house's other residents. She had briefly seen the man who lived in the garret as he passed quickly by her room. But she had not spoken to him. She had tried to speak to the old lady who lived on the first floor as she stood at her open door. But the old lady had withdrawn in some confusion.

'She's mostly deaf,' Mrs Alcazar had informed the young woman.

'I realise that now,' Miss Bell had replied, with a smile. 'I saw her husband shouting at her a few days later!'

Mrs Alcazar also told her husband that Miss Bell was looking to equip her room more fully and had asked for advice. Was there anywhere nearby where she could acquire things for preparing food?

Mrs Alcazar said she had given the young woman a

few suggestions. And that she had also lent her one or two essentials to tide her over.

'Not very much,' she said to her husband, fearing he might think she had been overly generous with some of their few possessions.

'Just two of our older earthenware bowls. And that sharp carving knife I'm always worried about cutting my finger on. The one with the bone handle. She seemed very pleased with that.'

§

Jane and Prudence agreed that they should tell him together.

William's response was immediate and positive when his wife asked if they could speak with him on a matter of some importance. But, as they took their places in his studio, it was already clear that he had something on his mind.

'You seem distracted, my dear,' said Jane. 'Can we help? Or would you prefer we spoke another time?'

William leaned against the table, pulled a face and shook his head mournfully. Then he crossed his arms.

'It's nothing,' he said. 'Nothing that should surprise me.'

The two women quietly waited.

'Frank was here,' he went on. 'He was at the Bedford Arms last night. And that ... poltroon, Smallow ...'

He paused, as if the mere mention of the poltroon's name would explain everything. As he chewed his lower lip he did not see the startled glance that passed between Jane and Prudence. They had rehearsed what they would say and had tried to anticipate how he might respond. But neither had imagined that William would be the first to mention Smallow's name.

William noticed the tight look on Prudence's face and assumed she might not know whom he was talking about.

'Smallow is a devil,' he said. 'A devil sent to torment me. Frank said he was sounding off at the Bedford – going on about how he was picking up one client after another in the West End, and how that set him apart from certain print-makers he could name. As if it mattered that an incompetent sot like him should be showered with tedious commissions from the numbskulls of St James's Square …'

Another glance between the women.

'We *all* know that's no sign of artistic merit,' William said. 'But then to have the gall to suggest that *I* myself would be chasing such customers if I could. The barefaced cheek of it! That he should even *mention* my name when I'm not there. And at the Bedford too!'

He shook his head again. Deep down, of course, he knew that he should not be upset. But he was struggling to throw off the irritation. His prickly nature meant that his skin was nowhere near as thick as many imagined. He was acutely sensitive to negative comments, and they nagged away at him for days on end. At one level he knew that he was already the foremost London artist of his time. And he also knew that Jonathan Smallow was, at best, a jobbing portrait painter – someone only kept in work because the demand for dull faces outstripped the supply of talent available to produce them. He knew all that. But he still could not shrug it off. For Smallow had been an unpleasant thorn in his flesh for far too long.

But enough.

His wife was waiting patiently. And she was accompanied by the calm and insightful presence of Prudence Hyssop. They were presumably here to let him know if there had been any news of the missing picture. So he should bestow on them his full attention. He gave his bristly head one last, almost brutal, shake – as if to throw off any last remnant of Smallow – and addressed his guests.

'But my dear ladies,' he said, managing a smile of sorts. 'I vex myself unnecessarily. Forgive me. I am at your service.'

Jane and Prudence looked at each other again. The last couple of minutes had disrupted the calm preparedness that each had brought into the studio. There would need to be some adjustment to what they were going to say. But the look they exchanged also managed to convey an element of tacit agreement. It said, very well – we need to respond to the circumstances of this latest piece of information. But we must also stay true to the key elements of our plan. Those elements were three in number.

First, they would state their belief that the disappearance of the painting was the work of Mr Smallow. Second, they would say that they had discovered this by virtue of a fortuitous visit to their friend, Lady Ransome. Third, they would make no mention of Jeremiah unless it was absolutely necessary. They hoped this approach would be sufficient to convey a proper and true account of who was responsible for the theft – and where the painting now was – without straying too much into the more complex narrative of how exactly it had got there.

As their report unfolded it was, Jane thought, difficult to categorise her husband's reaction. It seemed to differ from moment to moment, and to include everything from disbelief to laughter. The colour of his face changed from white to almost beetroot red and then back to a more normal shade of dirty pink. His expression did not stay the same for more than a few seconds at a time. And he peppered the whole of the telling with a series of noises that were either exclamations or grunts.

When he found his voice sufficiently well to string some words together, it was to express what Jane and Prudence had anticipated. Disgust that Smallow should be involved at all – and outrage that the man should have had the temerity to steal one of his paintings. But even that paled by comparison to his astonishment that Smallow should then try to pass the picture off as one of his own works. The very suggestion that anyone could possibly confuse the work of the two men was 'Beyond belief – quite beyond belief!'

It was perhaps this total exasperation that eclipsed any questions he may have formed about exactly *how* Smallow had acquired the painting in the first place. William was much more concerned with focusing his fury on the perpetrator than on unravelling the details of how the deed was done.

'Well, we must get it back,' he said, once his initial

explosion had subsided. 'We must go to Lady Ransome and demand that she return it to its rightful owner.'

Jane and Prudence glanced at each other again.

'You can leave that to us,' said Jane.

She and Prudence had already discussed the matter and convinced themselves that Belinda would be nothing other than horrified when she learned the truth. Horrified – and also extremely keen to avoid any public scandal. If the picture could be quickly reclaimed from her wall, then perhaps a line could be drawn under the whole unhappy episode. It might even be possible to conclude the business without the need to involve Jeremiah at all. He could not be absolved of his part in the crime, of course – but Prudence and Jane could at least try to move things forward without making him even more culpable than he already was.

Such a course of action did not, however, address the issue of Smallow himself. And it was this that continued to gnaw away at William once the two women had again left him alone. He slumped onto a chair, his mind racing with angry thoughts. Yes, he would be relieved to get the painting back. Not just because it was his – but because he was not sure it was something he should have painted at all.

But it was not the painting that was the real problem. It was the fact that it had fallen into the hands of Smallow. To call out the blackguard for theft and fraud was not without its risks. William's critics would enjoy the chance to ridicule him. They would revel in the fact that a jobbing artist had passed off one of the great Mr Hogarth's paintings as his own.

But then what was the alternative? To ignore the imposture, and to – in effect – let Smallow get away with it?

No. That would be intolerable. And it would simply be licence for Smallow to continue being what he had always been. A boil on the arse of English art.

So, yes, it was one thing – and a good thing at that – to have his wife and Prudence recover the picture. But that did not deal with the man himself. What William wanted was an end to the raillery. An end to the laughter at his expense. And an end to the deceit and abuse of such a third-rate nobody.

What William wanted was an end to Jonathan Smallow.

§

The day had arrived in St James's Square.

The day when the portrait of Belinda, Lady Ransome, was to be delivered. The day when it would finally adorn the alcove currently occupied by a small and more modest portrait of a certain gentleman.

Belinda was delirious with nervousness. Such a state of frenzy was perhaps to be expected. She had never had her portrait painted before. Indeed, this would be the first time she had ever seen an image of herself that was not the familiar face she admired in her mirror. But the feeling of apprehension had been multiplied several times over by the nature of Mr Smallow as an *artist*. That she retained any faith in his professional competence was due solely to his portrait of the Prince of Wales.

She had now been able to study the picture at close quarters for some considerable time. There was absolutely no doubt that it showed significant ability and not a little genius. For one thing, it most certainly looked very like the heir to the throne – even if it did perhaps flatter the Prince in parts. It also exhibited the flourishes and details she was so keen to see in the portraits of herself and Sir Marmaduke. The gentle light on the Prince's wig, the elegance of his posture, the informality of his smile, and those oh-so-pink lips. She had to believe that Mr Smallow had purposely reserved the best of his talents for those of his clients who were still eminently alive. Even so, her tremulous state betrayed the fact that such an analysis did little to put her at ease. For all that she considered herself and her husband to be illustrious members of Society, they were clearly not on the same level as the Prince of Wales.

There was also, of course, the nature of Mr Smallow as a *person*, which hardly improved Belinda's state of mind. She had never found him anything other than insufferable. Perhaps abhorrent was a better word. He was pompous in the extreme, and his efforts to accommodate his ways to the requirements of polite society served only to make him even more unbearable. It was therefore something of a mixed blessing that he had been so cursory in his preparations for the final two portraits. Belinda had imagined that he would require her to attend several sittings, but he seemed satisfied to spend no more than an hour sketching her. This, he claimed, was a perfectly usual practice. He would be best able to translate the work of his pencil into the sumptuous art of oils within the privacy of his studio.

The preparation regarding her husband had been even more perfunctory. Mr Smallow made his preliminary drawings on the basis of an earlier painting of Sir Marmaduke which had been executed some five years before. A portrait that Belinda had never liked.

While this casualness of approach added to her nervous state, she was thankful that it did at least spare her the strain of enduring Mr Smallow's attentions for any more time than was absolutely necessary.

When, therefore, the hour of the much-anticipated delivery arrived, she was all aflutter. The prospect of seeing the pictures for the first time – and having to suffer the presence of the man himself – was almost too much to bear. She was to receive him alone. Sir Marmaduke was still abed and had announced the night before that he was rapturously content for his dear wife to take personal receipt of the infernal faces.

'You have a dashed better eye for these things than do I,' he rasped. 'Though I daresay no phiz painter on earth could possibly come near the beauty of the actual article, m'dear.'

It was meant as a compliment. But, even as he said it, Belinda could smell the reek of cheap perfume on his clothes. Thus it was that she was alone when the mealy Boyd announced the arrival of 'Mr Shallow, ma'am, and some other gennelmen'.

The 'other gennelmen' were porters. Under Mr Smallow's direction they bumbled into the drawing-room carrying two framed canvases, each covered in green baize cloth, and two easels, on which the shrouded pictures were positioned. All this while, Belinda stood in front of the fireplace trying to calm herself and suppress the fluttering in her chest and stomach.

Mr Smallow pranced about, issuing orders to the porters in a peremptory manner, and bestowing on his hostess a series of oleaginous smirks and ingratiating smiles. His mode of dress, she thought, made him look like a peacock. And his wig was too big for his body. He peppered his movements with low bows and sweeps of his hand, in which he held a large, lace handkerchief.

Finally, everything was in place. Mr Smallow waved away his two attendants with the irritable gesture of a man who clearly thought that no one could do the job as well as it should be done. Once the porters had gone, the footman closed the double doors behind them. Lady Ransome was left alone with her portrait painter.

Smallow bowed again and bestowed upon her a most ominous smile.

Belinda bit her lip.

§

Smallow had spent the first part of the morning being creative in a different way.

He had been mixing five phials of Dr Rock's Very Special Cathartic Venereal Electuary with a bottle of the best brandy he could find. When he put the final concoction to his nose, he could smell only the brandy.

That's good, he thought. That's *very* good!

But then he started to worry that the potion might not be strong enough to do its job. He had some ratsbane in the cupboard downstairs. Perhaps he should add some of that. But then that would surely be detectable. And, what's more, the act would lose its subtlety. Its artistry.

The idea of at least severely injuring a man by administering a remedy for venereal disease was in itself delightful. The thought that it might also prove fatal was that much more beguiling. Especially as such a death would almost certainly be attributed to misadventure rather than murder. After all, if one simply wanted to kill a man by poisoning, there were other and cheaper options available, were there not? No, he was right. The ratsbane should be avoided. It was far too obvious.

For there really was something incredibly attractive about ending a man's life with a cure. Death would most certainly have his day.

It had put Smallow in a particularly good humour ahead of his visit to Lady Ransome.

§

She wished he would stop showing off his teeth in that obsequious manner.

'Lady Ransome,' Smallow crowed, bowing low and waving the lace handkerchief several times in the air.

His gaze took in the very large figure of the woman who stood in front of the fireplace. Moll King's jibe – about Sir Marmaduke granting certain liberties with his wife if it brought down the price – had lodged in Smallow's mind.

And now that he looked at her, with the morning light glinting on her necklace and her breast heaving with ill-concealed excitement, he decided it would not be the worst thing in the world. Perhaps the portrait would be a way of gauging the lady's sentiments towards him. It had, after all, been executed with a view to capturing what he took to be her latent passion.

'Mr Smallow,' said Belinda flatly, trying to keep the tremor out of her voice.

'Lady Ransome,' said the painter again.

She resisted the temptation to say, 'Oh, for heavens' sake, Mr Smallow – get on with it!' Instead she turned her eyes towards the shrouded shapes that lurked like two guests who had not yet been introduced.

'Is Sir Marmaduke to join us, ma'am?' oozed the painter.

He glanced around the room, as if half expecting to see his host step out from behind a screen or curtain.

'Sir Marmaduke is indisposed,' said Belinda, stopping herself from saying more. Why should she even attempt any kind of apology or explanation?

Smallow pulled a face, expressing a degree of surprise. But then he smiled. It suggested that the presence of anyone other than Lady Ransome herself would be entirely superfluous to such a meeting.

'In which case, my dear lady,' he said. 'Perhaps I should bring Sir Marmaduke into the room by unveiling his portrait.'

Belinda returned him an unenthusiastic nod. Smallow then minced towards one of the two easels and drew back the covering with a theatrical flourish.

If he was expecting an exclamation from his hostess, he was to be disappointed. Belinda simply stared. It was not terrible, she thought. And it did at least bear a passing resemblance to her husband. Or at least to how he looked on a good day, when he was not carrying the debilitating marks of drink and a long night. What was most noticeable, however, was that it appeared to be hardly more than a copy of the earlier portrait – the one Smallow had taken as his primary reference. Yes, the clothes and wig had been updated. But the pose, and the flat, curled-lip expression, were exactly the same. Instead of classical columns in the background, this new version showed Sir Marmaduke against some indeterminate muddy shapes that Belinda assumed were meant to represent a forest.

There was an awkward pause, interrupted only by the sound of Smallow's feet as he shuffled about, adopting a series of artful poses. Finally, Belinda spoke, maintaining the same flat tone that she hoped masked her feelings.

'It is very like,' she said.

'Very like Sir Marmaduke,' said Smallow.

He nodded keenly, like a giant bird pecking.

'Very like ... his last portrait,' said Belinda.

'Ah,' said Smallow, not quite sure how he might respond to the comment.

'Sir Marmaduke has such a classic and timeless face,' he continued. 'And he has, I perceive, changed very little over the years. Age has not withered him.'

He stopped and dispensed another of his gruesome smiles, inviting Lady Ransome to say more. But Belinda's mind had already moved on. She had seen enough to make her fear the worst. What did it matter, after all, that her husband looked exactly the same heartless cur in this portrait as he did in the last one? She suspected he might prefer it that way.

It was all of little consequence compared to the big question.

What of *her* portrait?

Her eyes were now peering at the cloaked frame that stood on the second easel. What should she expect? How should she react? Her heart was pounding so hard that she thought it must be visible to Smallow. He had indeed noted the palpitating bosom and the anxiousness in Lady Ransome's face. But he assumed that both signs simply indicated his client's great excitement at the prospect of seeing herself revealed to the world's gaze.

Whilst all his instincts were attuned to making the most of the moment in theatrical terms – dragging out the revelation for as long as possible – he now felt it would not be appropriate. He would instead move to a swift consummation and exult in the profusion of thanks that Lady Ransome would shower upon his head. He therefore said nothing, but instead moved slowly and with great purpose towards the easel. He grasped the edge of the cloth that hid the painting from view. And then, with a great sweep of his arm, he threw the covering into the air, as if it offended those present by continuing to mask the beauty that lay below.

The green baize fell in a heap a few feet away. Mr Smallow stood back, his legs apart in a classical style, his arm outstretched, pointing the way to the vision that was now exposed, displayed on a canvas that glistened with newness in its very ornate gilt frame.

Belinda stood very still, staring.

And then she gave vent to the most enormous shriek.

§

Upstairs Sir Marmaduke stirred slightly in his large, unkempt bed.

He thought he heard a woman cry out. But then that was something he was used to. He smiled a lascivious smile, turned over, and drifted into a state somewhere between sleep and wakefulness.

Dreams, desires and recollections coalesced into a fog of lust, as he picked his way through the cesspit of his mind.

Lucy had been very obliging. Most accommodating indeed. The way she had flourished those birch twigs was nothing short of perfection. And then the great dexterity of her fingers. After her third set of administrations, he was well and truly spent. It had been another good night.

But he still had his eye on that other girl, the new one. What was her name? At first, she had told him it was Caroline, but he had heard Lucy call her Sarah.

Well, whether she was Caroline, Sarah or the Queen of Sheba, he would have her, there was no doubt about it. And she obviously wanted him too. He could tell by the way she kept giving him the eye across the room, even when she was being roundly fondled by that old bishop. She knew what she liked, and she clearly liked the look of Sir Marmaduke.

Well, she would have him. But not at old Mother Nonsuch's. No, that was too constraining, too decorous an environment. Fine for the birch twigs, the teasing fingers and the fondlings. Fine even for the sort of rutting that suited the old farts who could barely stiffen up long enough to make a visit worth its while. But Mother Nonsuch was far too protective for what *he* craved. He needed to get the girl out of there. Get her over to Tom King's and get her drunk. Then he could take her back to a room somewhere nearby, tie her up, and mercilessly plunder her every way known to man.

The smile widened on his half-sleeping face, and he fell back into unconsciousness, deaf to the sounds that continued to come from somewhere else in the house.

§

Boyd, the footman, was the first to enter Lady Ransome's drawing-room.

He had been reluctant to do so. The last lady he worked for, just a few streets away, was often entertaining men alone. She was also in the habit of shrieking and screaming a great deal in their company. Boyd had learned to his cost that she did not welcome having her entertainment interrupted. Her words – if he remembered correctly – were, 'No, thank you, Boyd – I most certainly do *not* require any assistance.' Given the circumstances, he was grateful she had provided him with such a fulsome reference.

Matters were, however, likely to be different at the

Ransome residence. Certainly, the view below stairs was that neither Sir Marmaduke nor his Lady were particularly taken with the shiny-faced artist fellow – Smellie or Shallow, or whatever his name was. Indeed, Lady Belinda never looked anything other than crestfallen at the prospect of his visits. The baronet himself invariably kept to his bed (although it had been rumoured by the groom – and he should know – that the artist cove had pimped for his master on occasion).

When Boyd heard the scream, therefore, he felt reasonably confident that his entry into the drawing-room would not interrupt any intimate encounter. The sight that met his eyes confirmed the fact.

Lady Ransome had collapsed onto a chair, her recumbent posture suggesting that she had suffered an attack of the vapours or something equally feminine. The gentleman artist, a concerned look on his face, stood over her, flapping a lace handkerchief. This was presumably meant to create a delicate draught to cool the lady's fevered brow.

Boyd was followed into the room some seconds later by the bony figure of Murfitt, her ladyship's maid. Murfitt grasped the situation immediately. She rushed straight out of the room, only to reappear a minute later with a glass of water which she administered to her ladyship with a good deal of simpering. By this stage, Belinda was showing signs of recovering from her affliction. Both Boyd and Murfitt noticed, however, that she kept her gaze resolutely on the carpet. She clearly wished to avoid raising her eyes to anyone or anything in the room.

'Help me away, Murfitt, if you will,' she said feebly.

Murfitt threw an accusatory glance at Smallow. In her estimation at least, there could be no reason for her mistress's distress other than that absurd little man who made such a show of himself. It was hardly surprising that Lady Ransome could not bear to look at him.

Then, with her bony head held high, and with the substantial bulk of Belinda leaning on her bony arm, Murfitt led her lady away to the quiet of a small parlour at the back of the house. Once safely ensconced there, Murfitt supplemented the glass of water with a drop of something stronger and was encouraged to see a rosy bloom return to her mistress's cheeks.

Meanwhile, in the drawing-room, Boyd was left alone with a red-faced Smallow, who was now showing signs of considerable unease, and a determined eagerness to make his escape.

'Thank you,' said the hapless artist, although it was not clear what he was thanking Boyd for. Boyd looked totally baffled by the situation. There followed another awkward silence, during which both visitor and footman gazed around the room at anything but each other.

'I must away,' said Smallow at last, as if remembering some pressing engagement. 'Duty calls. I shall see myself out.'

He turned to go, but then stopped.

'I am forgetting,' he said, turning round again to face the footman. 'I am to take back a painting I lent to Lady Ransome. She will have no further use for it.'

So saying, he moved towards the fireplace and removed

the small portrait of a man that hung in the adjoining alcove. Then, with a slight nod in Boyd's direction, he strode manfully out of the room. A few moments later Boyd heard the front door close behind him.

Left alone in the drawing-room, the footman gave vent to a long exhalation of breath, as if to say, 'Well, I'll be blowed. These high and mighties have some funny ways about them. And not a care for those as has to listen to their screechings and their squawkings.'

But then, he quickly reflected, that was exactly what being a footman was all about. Being available. Hearing and seeing almost everything. And treating all of it with a mixture of disdain and discretion. He had to admit to himself, however, that he was galled at seeing Lady Ransome distressed. She was usually so perky and loud, so big and robust. Indeed, he had had the odd fantasy about his lady more than a few times, being rather taken by her large and (in his imagination at least) inviting persona.

With that thought lingering in his mind, he was about to leave the room when it occurred to him to peruse the two paintings that had stood there, ignored throughout the commotion. Boyd found the one of his master somewhat unexceptional. The recognisable features of Sir Marmaduke did little to offset the dark and dull setting that was mostly brown. Was that a dog painted into the corner? A brown dog? It was difficult to see.

The picture of my lady on the other hand …

Well, … goodness!

How had he managed not to notice it before? Except that so much had happened in the last few minutes.

But now that he was able to look at the picture properly ...

It was, he felt, quite wonderful. At least to *his* eyes. There she was, recognizably his mistress, Lady Ransome. Although it had to be said that it was a representation which was more as he imagined her, rather than as he saw her on a day-to-day basis. She was dressed – if dressed was the word – in some kind of sheer garment that showed every curve of her ample body. Indeed, it barely covered one of her breasts, which seemed to strain against the fabric for release, the nipple making a noticeable imprint that he found quite entrancing.

Then there was her face. Yes, they were most definitely her features. But the expression was not one he had seen on her face before. Indeed, he very much wished he *had* seen it. But then he assumed it was an expression reserved only for Sir Marmaduke. Or her lover. For it showed a veritable pout. Or perhaps leer was a more accurate term. It was certainly the kind of look that Boyd had seen on the faces of the drabs and trulls he encountered on his evenings off, walking around Covent Garden Piazza.

In fact, so engaging did Boyd find the image that he stared at it for some time in a state of reverie. His hand wandered to his breeches, where he noted evidence of his passionate admiration. Judging that his presence would not be missed for a few minutes, he therefore took himself off to his very small room in the eaves of the house where he hastily gave expression to his new-found love of painting.

§

He dragged me into the churchyard and pushed me against the wall of the church, where the place is darkest and furthest from the path.

And then ...

I do not know that I can write this, my hand trembles so.

§

Flea showed Catherine into the shadows of Miss Hyssop's drawing-room soon after five o'clock.

The first two candles of the evening did little to lessen the gathering gloom. But there was enough light for Prudence to see that her visitor's face was marked by tiredness and strain. It was certainly not an expression to encourage small talk.

'Dear Catherine, I can see that you have something of import to communicate,' she said. 'Will you take some refreshment? A small glass of sack, perhaps?'

'I'm sorry. You are always so very kind, Prudence,' said Catherine. 'But no, thank you. I am fortified simply by seeing you. And seeing you looking so well.'

The quality of light in the room was not such as to make anyone look well. But Prudence smiled to acknowledge the courtesy. Her visitor was crouching forward with the air of someone who wished to disburden herself as soon as possible.

'I'm sorry,' Catherine said, 'but I have come to you, Prudence, to beg a favour.'

She emitted a small cough before continuing.

'It is my dearest wish that you will consent to be a witness to my marriage.'

Prudence smiled more broadly now.

'To Jeremiah, I assume?' she said.

Catherine looked at her feet.

'I'm sorry,' she said quietly. 'That is, yes. My father is determined to close the shop in order to be there. But Jeremiah felt I should be accompanied by a lady also. He knows that I am fortunate to count you as a friend, and he believes you to be a paragon among women.'

Prudence bowed her head. Another polite compliment. But Catherine's words also conveyed much more. They told her that Mr Pargeter must be pleased with his daughter's choice of husband. The print-seller had a reputation for being very protective of both his business and his daughter. Then there was what Jeremiah had said about her being a 'paragon'. Whilst it was gracious of him to have said it at all, Prudence felt compromised. She was, after all, complicit in the knowledge that he had committed a serious crime.

'I am flattered, my dear Catherine,' she said. 'It will be a privilege and a pleasure to be with you on the happy day. Love is a blessing, wherever and whenever it chooses to light up our lives.'

The two of them had maintained an air of formality up to this point. But Prudence's words touched Catherine deeply, and she burst into tears. Prudence quickly rose from her chair and sat down next to her friend.

'I trust these are tears of happiness,' she said.

'They are! Oh, they are! I'm sorry,' sobbed Catherine, who looked as if a weight had been lifted from her.

'It's just that I've been so nervous about asking you,'

she went on. 'And so desperate to share the news with someone other than my father.'

'And so, you have been holding it as a secret,' said Prudence. 'And one close to your heart.'

Prudence did not wish to imply it was wrong to hold a secret. Given her own predicament, that would hardly have been credible. But she did want to know more of the circumstances that had brought about this union. Apart from anything else, it might have a bearing on the broader situation with regard to Jeremiah and the theft of the painting. For it still seemed more than likely that he would be required to pay a heavy price for his part in the crime. And Catherine had been present when Jeremiah confessed to his role in the whole affair. So, had all of that played a part in their determination to marry – and to marry now? Was Catherine staying true to her beau in spite of the impending challenges? Or had Jeremiah's precarious position, and potential fate, perhaps even prompted her decision?

'Secrets are troublesome,' said Catherine.

'Troublesome?' said Prudence.

'I'm sorry, but they are,' Catherine went on. 'They eat at you from inside, until there's nothing left. Once they're out they are so much easier.'

Prudence looked at Catherine, a profusion of thoughts and memories clamouring for attention in her own mind. She put them to one side. For she did not want to think about secrets. Not now.

'But *then* they're not secrets at all,' continued Catherine. 'Once they've been shared, I mean. I'm sorry. I'm talking nonsense. I think perhaps I'm not quite myself.'

Prudence decided to lead the conversation back to the practicalities of Catherine's relationship with Jeremiah.

'Your father is clearly supportive of the marriage,' she said.

Prudence suspected that Mr Pargeter may have been only too happy to see his daughter finally wed to a man like Jeremiah. Whilst most fathers would have wanted to pass on the upkeep of a daughter to a better-provisioned husband, Prudence knew that Mr Pargeter relied on Catherine's help in the print shop. Jeremiah may not have been a man of independent means, but he was very familiar with the London art world.

'Yes,' said Catherine. 'Although I have to admit there was a time when he found Jeremiah to be ... I'm sorry – what do I mean to say? A little too eccentric, I suppose. But now he's come to know him better, he's seen that Jeremiah's ... energy is much to be admired.'

Prudence was moved by Catherine's devotion. But she was still mostly worried by the unresolved issues that were circling around the head of her friend's husband-to-be. In the circumstances, it was difficult to be optimistic about what the future might hold. She decided to glance back at the past before venturing a look forward.

'If you are at your ease, dear Catherine,' she said, 'it would be most enlightening to understand something of how the two of you arrived at this point.'

'I'm sorry,' said Catherine. 'Of course, I should have done that already. It is right that you should know as much as possible.'

Prudence listened intently as Catherine described

how the relationship had developed over a period of months. Whilst Catherine clearly derived comfort from telling her tale, Prudence was nevertheless perturbed. Did her friend understand the dangers that still lay ahead? Or had she retreated into a fantasy world where the realities of Jonathan Smallow and the implications of Jeremiah's culpability did not exist? In the candlelight, Catherine's wan face had taken on a fairy-like quality. Her eyes were brighter now. But there was also a sense that, in her desperation to be happy, she was prepared to ignore anything that might threaten such an outcome.

For her part, Prudence felt that she had been thrust into the midst of someone else's story. She could also not help reflecting that Jeremiah, as muddled as he was, must surely consider himself fortunate in the number of people – women specifically– who appeared to have his best interests at heart.

By the time Catherine finished her narrative, Prudence's drawing-room was in near darkness, lit only by the two candles that flickered by the couch where the two women sat, haloed by a small glow of golden radiance.

Catherine looked towards the fitful flames and thought how unbelievably happy she was. Prudence, however, was more conscious of the number of shadows that lay beyond the close circle of light.

§

Flea was used to treading the familiar path from Covent Garden Piazza to Leicester Fields.

Once again, he had been dispatched by Miss Hyssop with a letter for Mrs Hogarth. It was a note communicating the fact that Prudence had arranged for the two of them to call on Belinda the following morning. The visit had been organised – so far as Lady Ransome was concerned – with a view to discussing a topic for the next meeting of the Green Group.

As Flea left the house, Covent Garden was in the process of transforming itself from a marketplace into an arena of night-time entertainment. In the centre of the space a few scavengers were raking through the mounds of market refuse that still remained. One or two stallholders were making preparations for the following day's business. A number of young gentlemen could be seen, but mainly heard, making their noisy way towards one of the local inns. Along the walkways there were already noticeably more ladies loitering than there had been an hour before. A queue was beginning to form for the theatre. Sedan chairs lined up under cover of the arcade, adding to the general congestion immediately outside Miss Hyssop's house.

Flea therefore headed into the middle of the square. He was hoping to run into one or two of his boon companions. They often hung about the place at this hour, congregating somewhere between Tom King's coffee-house and the church. By this time of the evening Tom King's was usually quiet. The day-time custom of the market traders had ended some while before, and it was still too early for any nocturnal visitors. Most of those would arrive much later, having finished their business at theatres and gaming dens.

Flea knew full well that 'King's College' (as the place was sometimes known) only really came to life after midnight. He was therefore surprised to hear shouting coming from the coffee-house doorway. A single voice only – but it was making enough of a din to catch Flea's attention.

He stopped and listened.

No – he had not been mistaken. There it was again.

The name of Hogarth. Or, if truth be told, something that sounded more like 'Hog Art'. But he was sure it was meant to be the same thing. And it was being shouted in none too respectable a manner.

'Hog Art!' cried the voice. 'William Fucking Hog Art! Thou art unfit for any place but hell! A face like a pig! And paintings to match! Hog Art! That's what it is!'

This declamation was being made by a small, smartly dressed man in a full wig. His shiny red cheeks, coupled with the nature of his outburst, suggested an extreme state of drunkenness, even at this relatively early hour.

He was standing half in and half out of Tom King's, giving expression to his thoughts in a way that could be heard by anyone passing. Flea could see the bulky presence of Tom King himself starting to bundle the small man back into the confines of the coffee-house. It was one thing to have defamatory words expressed within the privacy of the place, but quite another to have them bellowed across the surrounding neighbourhood. It was certainly not the kind of sideshow the proprietor wanted to encourage at this stage of the evening.

Flea stood and stared for a moment or two and consciously added it to the things he had noticed that day. Then he had a quick glance around. None of his confederates appeared to be there. So he continued on his way to Leicester Fields.

But it was rum, he thought to himself. Rum that he should be heading towards the house of Mr Hogarth – and hear what clearly sounded like that gentleman's name brayed across the Piazza. Very rum indeed.

Flea pulled at the hairs on his chin and ruminated briefly on the concept of coincidence, before turning into King Street.

§

Prudence and Jane discussed their plan again on the way to St James's Square.

They would be as sensitive and subtle as possible. But in essence there was only one objective. To inform their friend that the painting of the Prince of Wales was not the work of Mr Jonathan Smallow.

Lady Ransome received them in a small parlour they had not seen on their last visit. In such a confined space Belinda seemed more monumental than ever. Even so, her two friends could discern signs of worry and fatigue around her eyes. They enquired about each other's health and then seated themselves around a table. Prudence and Jane planned to begin by talking about the Green Group. They were therefore surprised by Belinda's next remark.

'You're both being extremely polite in not mentioning the painting at once,' she said.

Prudence and Jane looked perplexed.

'The painting?' said Jane.

Belinda sat up straight and assumed a look that was imperious and understanding at the same time.

'The portrait of me,' she said, as if the subject were only too obvious. 'I imagine it is rapidly becoming the talk of the town.'

Prudence and Jane quickly scanned the walls of the parlour, but the only artworks on display were a few floral watercolours – probably the work of their hostess.

'It's not in here, of course,' Belinda went on. 'It's far too big! Come along. Let's go and get it over and done with!'

So saying, she led them back along the passageway and into the drawing-room. The impact was immediate and immense.

A new painting adorned each of the alcoves either side of the fireplace. One was a muddy picture of a haughty man they assumed to be Sir Marmaduke. What drew their attention, however, was the image on the other side. The very spot where they had previously seen the portrait of the Prince of Wales.

Prudence and Jane were not sure whether their sense of shock was due to the Prince's absence or because what had taken his place was so … so … arresting.

'You can say what you like, dear friends,' said Belinda.

A tiredness in her voice suggested that she had already endured every emotion possible on the subject. There was clearly nothing further to be said about it – or its subject – that could surprise or hurt her.

'I wanted to consign it to an attic,' she said. 'But Sir Marmaduke says he likes it.'

Despite being clearly troubled by the picture – and for all that she did not usually hold her husband's opinion in high regard – there was no disguising the slight note of pride.

'He says he finds it … warming,' she continued.

The comment was made as if it were nothing other than a sign of the gentleman's undying love for his wife, notwithstanding all the evidence to the contrary. Prudence and Jane tried not to look at each other. They felt that their friend's remarks betrayed several degrees of ambiguity. There was a brief silence, punctuated only by the sound of Belinda's breathing while she waited for her visitors' verdict.

Jane wanted to ask immediately about the other picture – the image of the Prince. But she knew she could only progress to such a topic after having provided some opinion on the portrait that hung before her.

'You are a very fortunate woman, Belinda dear,' she said.

The remark surprised Prudence as much as Belinda.

'I could only *dream* that someone would wish to paint *me* in such a fashion,' continued Jane. 'Whereas *you* …'

She left the words floating in the air for a moment or two.

'Whereas *you*,' she repeated, 'are one of Nature's timeless nymphs. The painting represents you as such, and will, I'm sure, give both you and your husband much pleasure in years to come.'

She stopped suddenly, realizing that the words were now outrunning her thoughts. In fact, she had little idea of what she was trying to say. Other than to avoid any suggestion that the woman in the picture looked like a whore who was trying her damnedest to lure the viewer into bed.

Belinda was not sure whether or not Jane's remarks constituted a compliment, and the confusion showed on her face. Was it a *good* thing to be a timeless nymph? What *was* a nymph anyway? As the question began to form on her lips, Prudence stepped in with a comment designed to steer them away from both Nature and nymphs.

'If I might speak intimately,' she said, 'as we are three women together ... I must say that I have always admired – envied even – your fullness and beauty, dear Belinda. And in viewing this picture, I can see even more clearly the differences between us. If people in a hundred years' time were to stumble upon a faithful representation of me, they would see only a thin and somewhat austere person. When, however, they gaze on *this* – as gaze they must – they will delight in an artistic age that was ripe in its representation of womanhood. For this is not just a portrait of you, dear Belinda. It is the picture of a modern woman. A woman of our age.'

Prudence stopped as abruptly as Jane had done. And for the same reason. For she too was not sure how to extricate herself from the difficulties raised by the painting. But she need not have worried. What Belinda chose to hear were clear statements of support and admiration, both for the portrait and for her as a human being.

'You are very kind,' she said, her face showing relief more than anything else. 'And perhaps you are right in looking at the image from a more objective point of view.

I am clearly too close to it to be able to form such an opinion. I've not had my portrait taken before, and I must admit that it has been a more unsettling process than I could ever have imagined.'

Jane and Prudence made a few further small and reassuring observations. Both, however, were also reflecting on the nature of 'Morning', the painting William had based on Prudence. It was, of course, a very different style of work, with a completely different objective. But it was nevertheless a reminder of the complexities involved in the presentation of someone's likeness. Particularly a woman's. And most especially in an art world dominated by men.

When the two of them next had the opportunity to catch one another's eye, it was with a view to moving the conversation forward. Jane was the more impatient and it was she who spoke first.

'But what of the Prince of Wales?' she said. 'What of the portrait that hung in this very place the last time we were here? Is that now in another room perhaps?'

Belinda looked briefly concerned that the discussion of her own portrait – which had been more encouraging than she might have hoped – should now turn to a different topic. But at the same time, it was perhaps no bad thing that her own likeness be considered in a broader artistic context that included His Royal Highness. Over time the art world might be persuaded to view *both* portraits as fine examples of the painter's best work.

'Heavens, no,' she said. 'I've no idea where *that* might be. Very likely in one of the state rooms at Leicester House, for all I know. Mr Smallow took it away with him when he delivered the portrait of me.'

Belinda turned once more to look at the picture of herself that leered down at the three of them. So she did not see the taut expressions on the faces of her two visitors.

§

It is difficult. But I must try to do it.

He forced me against the wall, so hard that the back of my head hit against the stonework and I felt as if I might pass out.

I could feel him pulling up my skirts, and the cold on my legs, and I was numb with fear and amazement, as if it were all happening in some other place and to someone else.

And the fumbling, the ceaseless fumbling that seemed to go on forever, while his hot and stinking breath was on my face, making me feel sick.

And then the pain, in my heart, but most severely in my stomach and in my tender parts as he forced himself on me, and in me.

And when it was over, the disgust, and weariness, and fright, and loneliness in that dark, hard place that was so close to my home, and was my church, but was also the scene of my nightmares, and where I have not wanted to be in my waking thoughts for so long that I had almost persuaded myself that it did not happen.

And yet it did.

And as it was then, so now.

When I would wish so much to cry.

But the tears will not come.

§

Evening – and early by the standards of Tom King's coffee-house.

But the drinking was already well underway. Moll was not complaining. The price of arrack was the same whether it was six o'clock or midnight. Although that was not quite true. The drunker you were, the more it cost. A prompt start was therefore propitious – at least for the proprietor and his wife.

Certainly Dr Rock had consumed more than was usual, such had been the encouragement of those around him. He sat in a half-unconscious state at one end of a long table. His large, wigged head was propped against the wall and his eyes flickered intermittently. One of the place's regular sirens, who went by the name of Slippery Sal, attempted to lift his spirits with a show of affection and allure. But she soon gave up trying to raise any amorous interest in the good doctor.

At the other end of the table sat Jonathan Smallow. He was noticeably quieter than he had been the previous night – which was when Flea heard him shouting 'Hog Art' to all and sundry. So, yes, calmer perhaps – but still distinctly morose. For all his bright and shiny apparel, a gloomy and nervous air hung about him. When Slippery Sal realized that Rock would provide neither entertainment nor sustenance, she edged closer to where Smallow was sitting. He reacted instantly, clutching an open satchel that lay on the bench beside him.

'It's all right, dearie,' said Sal. 'I'm not after your bag. You're safe with me.'

She ogled him, showing off a set of uneven teeth, and pulled down her bodice to reveal an ample cleavage.

'What you got in there anyway?' she said, feigning interest in the one thing that seemed to hold the man's attention.

'Artists' materials,' he said. 'You wouldn't understand. It is the stuff as dreams are made on. The base metals from which we conjure gold.'

Seeing the glint in her eye, he added a note of clarification.

'I speak figuratively, of course,' he said. 'There is no real gold in there. Just magic. The magic in the web we weave. The magic of art.'

Sal appeared no more enlightened by this information than she had been by his former remarks. Men talked such drivel when they were in their cups. Well, to be honest, they mostly talked drivel even when they weren't.

She pointed to the open bag. Protruding from the top was something wrapped in brown sacking and tied with string.

'Let me guess, then,' she said. 'That's a picture.'

'Your powers of observation are truly amazing,' replied Smallow, with a curl of his lip. 'But you are wrong. It is nought but a crude canvas that requires more work. And more ... artfulness.'

His face had taken on its usual lofty, self-important expression. He was speaking in riddles and cared not one jot whether the siren understood his meaning.

'Is that so?' said Sal.

She was barely able to contain her contempt for the

cocky little prick. Although he was unfortunately all too typical of the bumptious dolts she had to deal with every night. She knew who he was, of course – and that, as a common painter, he was not amongst the most elevated of Tom King's clients. But he always wore the finest clothes, so he had to be a man of some means. Which meant she was prepared to put up with his pompous, drunken claptrap if there was something to be gained by it.

'And what's in the bottle?' she said, pointing at what looked to be the only other thing in his bag.

'Nothing for you,' spat Smallow. 'Another artist's material. Especially formulated for removing unpleasant stains. So keep your hands off.'

The last comment was prompted by seeing Sal lick her lips, as if she wanted a taste. Smallow pulled the satchel closer.

'Don't even think of it,' he said. 'For you will sorely rue the day. It is a strong brew and will not only remove your many unpleasant stains – but your skin as well!'

Sal drew back. She was curious, but no more. And anyway, what was it to her what an artist chose to carry in his knapsack? She was interested in money. Or, failing that, a drink to help get her through the tedious minutes of trying to engage the fellow's attention further.

She decided on a different approach, sliding her right hand under the table and onto his thigh. He started slightly at the touch but made no attempt to push the hand away. Once he was convinced that she was not after his artist's materials, he appeared more relaxed. The ghost of a smile flitted across his pink, smooth face.

'You would like a drink, I daresay,' he said.

Sal licked her lips again.

'Well, now,' she said. 'There's a thought! Arrack, I think, if you'd be so kind.'

Smallow called to a young, dark-skinned woman who was passing the table.

'Arrack for the lady,' he said.

He made the word 'lady' sound anything but ladylike.

Sal managed another grim smile herself. It was, after all, a start. And at such an early hour she was prepared to try a few tricks that would cost her little. Black Betty brought the arrack and set it before them. Sal picked up a glass in her left hand, took a sip and made a point of licking her lips once more.

'I trust it is satisfactory,' said Smallow, with a sneer.

'It'll do,' said Sal, replacing the glass on the table. 'For now.'

And with that she moved the fingers of her right hand across the artist's crotch, rubbing at the lump she could feel hardening under her touch.

At the other end of the table Dr Rock stuttered into life. He looked about him as if he were unsure where he was, before sinking back into a state of somnolence.

'It's just as well he's still alive,' said a sharp voice from an adjacent bench. 'We might all need his ministrations later!'

The comment was made by a tall man with an ugly, flat face, who was sitting just a few feet away. A stout woman sat astride his lap.

'You're right, Sir Marmaduke,' said Smallow. 'He is indeed the Rock to which we cling.'

So saying, he sat back, resting his own head against the wall while he curled his arm around his satchel. Below the table Sal continued her slow and rhythmic work.

§

On leaving St James's Square, Jane and Prudence returned at once to Leicester Fields to relate the news to William.

Francis Hayman was in the studio with him. But when William saw the look on the women's faces, he sent his drinking companion on his way.

'You go ahead, Frank,' he said. 'I'll come and find you at the Bedford Arms as soon as I can.'

Hayman left with a puzzled and worried look on his face. As soon as he had gone, Jane and Prudence recounted what they had discovered.

When William heard that Smallow had reclaimed the painting, he was both shocked and upset. In the time since the women had left to see Lady Ransome, he had convinced himself that the picture's recovery would bring the unfortunate episode to a swift and timely end. He paced up and down, snarling, while Prudence and Jane watched warily from the side of the room.

'I have to get it back,' he said through tight lips.

He was trying to keep the lid on what was now a boiling temper.

'Where does the scoundrel live?'

Jane and Prudence shook their heads. They didn't know. Did *anyone* know? Well, *somebody* must! But wait.

William scratched at his stubbly chin. Of course.

Jeremiah would know. He delivered things to Smallow, didn't he?

Jane and Prudence stayed quiet.

'Right then,' said William sharply. 'I'll find Jeremiah – damn me if I don't!'

Then he quickly changed his tone.

'Forgive me, ladies,' he went on, removing his old, soft cap in a gesture of apology. 'I'm forgetting myself. And I can see from your faces that you'd counsel more consideration. More composure. So be it.'

He stopped his pacing and stood still, breathing deeply for a moment or two.

'I'll join Frank at the Bedford,' he said. He replaced his cap on his head and pulled on his long, russet coat. 'And then we shall see what we can see.'

Jane was anxious. In all their years of marriage she thought she had seen every expression that his very mobile face could produce. But she had not seen this one before. The fury and irritation had largely disappeared. In their place was a look of steely determination and the marks of an implacable spirit. However, there was also something new and unearthly about the glare in his eyes. He mumbled a few words under his breath.

'This must end. *He* must end. And I am the one to do it.'

He looked around the studio, letting his eyes rest on several things. His paints. His brushes. The easels. His engraving tools. Jane's fear increased. For it was as if he were gazing at all of those things for the last time.

Then he rushed out of the building into the night, where a storm was brewing.

§

'You're a queer cod!'

Ransome stared contemptuously at Smallow before continuing.

'Yesterday you were the most choleric coz in town, bawling the place down with your curses on that Hoggit cove. Then today you act like a miserable sot and don't say a word to no one. And *now* look at you, you dreamy-eyed bastard! You look ready to pop!'

Smallow gave no sign of replying, so Ransome changed the tack of his banter. This time it was directed at the siren who was cosying up to the painter.

'You'd better watch out, Sal,' he called, his voice conveying a certain familiarity with the slippery female. 'If I were you, I'd get some more arrack in before he's done. You need to make him pay up while he's still under your thumb!'

Ransome brayed loudly, pleased with his wit. Slippery Sal returned him a gruesome smile.

'You'll stand me another one, won't you, dearie?' she crooned into Smallow's ear, at the same time waving her free hand at Black Betty.

Smallow muttered, 'Yes! God, yes!'

Betty brought the drink quickly.

'So let's make it a large one then, shall we?' Sal said to Smallow, as Betty set the bottle down.

Smallow shuddered and let go a desperate sigh, before closing his eyes. A glow of calm pleasure settled across his shiny cheeks.

Sir Marmaduke leered at his sometime companion with a face that was half amused and half disgusted. But before he could give voice to any more vulgar remarks, his eye was caught by something else. He dislodged the stout woman from his lap and stood up.

'I thank you, Susan,' he said to the woman, who looked disappointed by the turn of events. 'I thank you most bountifully,' continued Ransome, bowing to her, 'for the delightfully inventive stories that you have been so good as to whisper in my ear. For their diverting details have gone some considerable way towards renewing my appetite. That, and also seeing Smallow here expend his foul sap. But I am afraid I have spied another. And she, I fear, must trump you tonight.'

Susan feigned a pout but appeared less than crestfallen when Ransome lodged a coin of some value in her ample bosom. She was used to his capricious ways, and it was not the first time she had made her story-telling pay without cost to her person. Her eyes then followed the baronet's gaze across the room towards the door, through which a young woman had just entered. The new arrival was looking about herself intently, as if she were unfamiliar with both the place and the company.

'My dear Caroline,' Ransome called to her. 'Or should I call you Sarah? For I believe that is your true name.'

The young woman looked towards him, her expression showing a degree of relief, if not pleasure, at seeing a face she recognised. Then she threaded her way around the small crowd that clustered by the bar, her roving eyes taking in the various scenes that were playing out in different parts of the room. Ransome made no attempt to move towards her. He simply stood waiting by the bench on which he had previously been sitting.

'So you decided to come,' he said in his usual sneering tone. His look made clear his view that it was hardly a surprise. As if anyone – least of all a woman – could resist such charm and authority.

Sarah said nothing but puckered her lips in a way that gave her face an ambiguous air. Yes, she had come. But having stepped out from the comfortable arena of Mother Nonsuch's place, the gentleman had better make it worth her while.

Ransome was not a man for subtleties. He pulled her roughly towards him and planted a kiss on her mouth. She felt her body tense but tried not to reveal her disgust as she reeled from the combination of bad breath, tobacco, and onions. He sat down on the bench, pulling her onto his lap, so that she sat where Susan had been only a few minutes before.

Again, she tried to hide her loathing as she felt him swelling, hard and impatient, against her backside. It was not that she was prudish or unused to such attentions. Heaven knows, she had endured multifarious and abhorrent abuse over the last weeks. But there was something about Sir Marmaduke Ransome that filled her with the most intense revulsion. It was all she could do to maintain the merest hint of acquiescence.

He insisted that she drink. What was it to be? Brandy? Wine? She agreed to some wine. She knew she would need something to fortify her, but she must not allow herself to drink too much. While the wine was being brought, Ransome kissed her again, squeezing her against his body. The kiss was fuller this time and she could feel his hot, rough tongue in her mouth like a rape. She wanted to spit it out but, again, managed to control herself. He drew back and looked at her through narrowed eyes, suspicious that she was making him work too hard for these initial favours. She saw the question in his face and knew she needed to be clever and more compliant. Certainly if she was going to achieve her aim.

She stroked his hideous cheek before inserting a finger into his repugnant mouth. His wig smelled of animals and sweat, and she made a move to push it off and away. He seemed pleased by her aggression and tore the wig from his head with a smirk. Now you can see me properly, the look said. And get at me more easily. And I will see you better too.

Without his wig, he was even uglier and utterly charmless, she thought. His face was that of a man with no soul. She looked at it as closely as she dared and knew instantly that everything she had heard about him was true. His cruelty and his total want of gentleness. He was now fumbling with the front of her dress. She breathed deeply and manoeuvred her body to allow him easier access. Let him do what he likes, she said to herself. At least for now.

It took him some time, while he continued to slide his lascivious mouth across her face and neck. But at last he freed her right breast from her bodice, and then her left, exposing them to the foggy air of the coffee-house. And his own lecherous gaze.

'A veritable pair of beauties, my dear girl,' he slurred through dribbling lips.

He swivelled her on his lap, making her gasp, while she forced herself to adopt an amorous and appreciative bearing.

'Are they not a fine pair, Smallow?' he said, calling across the table.

Slippery Sal had been whispering something into the artist's ear and appeared annoyed that her lewd proposal might be eclipsed by a newcomer's tits. Smallow had now recovered some of his spirit. He smiled back, admiring his patron's good taste. It reminded him of something Sir Marmaduke had said weeks before, when briefing him on the execution of Lady Ransome's portrait. The exhortation to 'make the most of my wife's bubbies.'

Even Dr Rock had regained a state of consciousness and seemed mesmerised by the way the baronet was now chafing the young woman's nipples in a clumsy and brutal way. Ransome licked her cheek, choosing not to see the look of pain that flickered across her face as he pinched her teats between his fingers.

'Do you have a room hereabouts?' he said gruffly, his mouth pressed against her ear.

She tried to heave herself away from him, for he was making her sore. She nodded energetically, hoping it would make him stop his rough pawing. Which it did – but only because he had put his hands on her hips so that he could move her around.

'It's just across the way,' she breathed, trying to free herself. 'Tavistock Row. Near the corner.'

He leered at her, triumph oozing from his pores.

'It could hardly be closer,' he panted. 'Capital! Just time. For one more drink Then you will show me where. And I will show you *how*!'

She was about to say:

'You will know the place. You have been there before.'

But the words died on her lips as he thrust his right hand roughly under her skirts.

§

William's hunt for Jeremiah could wait.

The Bedford Arms, on the south side of the Piazza, was warm and welcoming. Hayman had organised drinks. Samuel Scott was there – as well as someone William had not seen for some time. It was that pleasant foreign fellow, Alcazar. William knew him as a gentle soul. He had also heard that his family had suffered another tragedy only a short time before. For all that William was pent up with emotion and aggression, the sight of Al Alcazar, looking drawn and full of pain, touched something in him. William was not known for his sensitivity, but a small voice inside his head whispered that the theft of his painting was nothing compared to the loss of a child. It was a sobering thought, and when he sat down at the table with his fellow artists – none of whom knew about his missing canvas – it was a relief not to be the focus of the conversation.

'It's good to see you here again, Al,' he said.

'Thank you,' said Alcazar. 'It is comfort to be again with friends. Artists.'

His halting voice still carried a hint of the Spanish accent that had been stronger in former years.

William watched him closely. The Spaniard had a serious and lined face that looked sad at the best of times. But now, settled across his features like a shade, was a tired but noble resignation. It would be a privilege to paint such a face, William decided. And, as the thought came to him, he knew he was always most contented and philosophical in the company of his fellow painters. Not *all* of them, of course. But he forced himself to keep the spectre of Jonathan Smallow at the very back of his mind. At least for the few minutes it would take to sympathise with Al.

'And how is Mrs A bearing up?' said Hayman.

Alcazar hunched his shoulders and shrugged in a peculiarly Mediterranean way.

'It is hard,' he said. 'Harder for her. I have worried. She not left the house, except for the funeral. But thankful now, she is gone to visit cousins. In the country. Barnet.'

He made a sweeping motion with his hand. An indication that he had no great idea where Barnet might be, but that it was certainly some way off.

'I think country air is good,' he continued. 'Her cheeks should be the colour of coral. Not ash.'

It was the simplest of expressions but, in the company of painters, it conveyed a great deal.

'Is good for me also,' he said. 'For I come here again.'

And so saying, he did his best to smile. The faces of the other three artists showed their relief, and Scott slapped him on the back. William could feel his own pain draining away. He was breathing more steadily now. But there was still a nagging ache in his gut. And he knew it would not leave him so easily.

§

Suddenly the young woman was on her feet.

She had pushed the man back against the bench with more force than she knew she possessed. Now it was *her* turn to fumble under the dress. And when her right hand emerged from below the folds of cloth, it was brandishing a six-inch kitchen knife that glinted in the glow of Tom King's newly-lit candles.

The sight of the knife changed everything.

Ransome was suddenly alert. His frame no longer marked by torpor and lust, but by a quickness that belied his drunken state. Smallow sat bolt upright. He had pushed Slippery Sal to one side and held his bag close to his chest. Dr Rock was also wide awake and edging himself away from the scene of conflict. Those who had clustered at the bar were now watching the affray. Behind them Tom King could be seen moving forward, intent on defusing the situation.

But it was Sarah Bell who held centre stage. With her breasts still exposed, she pivoted on one foot, the knife held at arm's length, grasped tightly in both hands. As she turned from right to left, she pointed the weapon at all and sundry, though her main focus was Ransome. The message on her determined face was clear. Approach at your peril. I will cut anyone who comes near.

Even when Tom King pushed his way to the front of

the small crowd, his palms raised as a sign of appeasement, she flicked the blade in his direction.

'Stay where you are!' she said in a voice that was steadier and louder than she could ever have imagined. 'You may take me down – but I will mark you!'

It was not a threat anyone was taking lightly. Tom King certainly had enough experience of altercations and scrapes to bide his time. It was not uncommon for coffee-house rows to escalate into full-blown scuffles. Tom's priority was always to shepherd the protagonists out into the open space of the Piazza before any serious harm could be done. But this was different – and at its centre was a woman he did not know. He could remember only one other occasion when a woman with a weapon had taken against someone in his place. And that had not ended well. So he was prepared to allow for some give and take. Blood was not easy to clean up.

For his part, Ransome seemed to find the scene increasingly amusing. He was now leaning back against the wall and smirking.

'Oh, I do like spirit in a bitch,' he said loudly. 'And your lovely tits are even more alluring when there's a flush upon them.'

The assembled company were unsure whether to laugh or not. Some had expressions that showed several degrees of confusion. What exactly was going on? Who *was* this woman? And isn't that Sir Marmaduke Ransome?

Sarah continued to hold them at bay, although the hopelessness of her position was beginning to dawn on her. One small woman with a knife, facing a room full of people, most of whom were men. And drunken men at that. The odds were not in her favour.

If she was going to say her piece, this was the time.

If she left it any longer, she would be disarmed and carted off to prison. Or possibly worse.

It was now or never.

§

Jane did not want to stay in Leicester Fields.

She had a presentiment that she should be closer to wherever her husband was. So when Prudence suggested that her friend return with her to the Piazza, Jane happily agreed. The Hogarths' maid was briefed as to where her mistress might be found, and the two women left the sign of the golden head no more than half an hour after William.

As was their custom, they made the journey on foot, even though darkness had now fallen. But with their arms firmly linked, and their necks and shoulders well wrapped against the biting wind, they covered the half-mile quickly and in good heart.

The weather had taken a definite turn for the worse, and the drizzle had become a driving rain that the wind was whipping up into an ugly squall. As they shook themselves off in the hallway of Prudence's house, the prospect of drying out in each other's company before an open fire warmed them considerably. First, however, they went through to the kitchen.

Abigail was making pastry. Flea was poring over a

newspaper with a slow eye, as his finger moved carefully across the crime reports. Prudence asked Abigail to heat up some of the soup she had prepared earlier in the day. She then gave Flea a mission for the evening that involved him leaving the comfort of the stove. Jane expected the young man to grimace at such a task, given the nature of the weather. So she was fascinated to see his expression take on an unexpected keenness. He pulled at his chin and cocked his head on one side, while his face made a spasm that might have been a wink.

Mr Hogarth was, Prudence told him, most likely to be in the Bedford Arms, just across the way. Could Master Fleabane please observe him there – as stealthily as possible, of course – and let the ladies know if he appeared to be at his ease?

Flea gave Miss Hyssop a very meaningful nod before pulling on his hat and heading out into the gathering tempest. The two women then retired to the drawing-room for a glass of sack while they awaited their soup.

§

The mood in Tom King's had changed in the last minute.

Sarah's initial flourish with the knife had caused alarm. Now, however, everyone seemed to be enjoying the spectacle.

The young woman continued to hold centre stage, her face a picture of determination. Her arms were still outstretched as she levelled the knife at those closest to her. But there was a new sense of fascination in the air. It was now clear to everyone that the bare-breasted Amazon could not prevail over a room of rowdy louts. As long as she was prepared to pose so dramatically, however, they might as well relish her performance.

Ransome continued to lean against the wall, a sneer on his face as he looked her up and down. He knew he could disarm her. It might cost him a scratch but nothing more. What was such a drab compared to a lion-heart like him? No, he was taking delight in the fact that this sprightly trollop was livening up the place. He was in no hurry to end the show.

Much the same went for most of the onlookers, who were happy to gawp. Even Tom and Moll King were now watching with less concern on their faces. If they were worried about anything, it was the interruption in the ordering of drinks. The sooner normal service was resumed, the better it would be all round.

The one person who was acting as if his life might be in danger was Dr Rock. This was due less to any apparent intent by Sarah – who had no idea who he was – and more to the good doctor's naturally timid character. Whereas drink was known to embolden a great many men, it had the opposite effect with Rock. Indeed, it drained any semblance of courage that he might have summoned up when sober. He therefore continued to sidle surreptitiously around the edge of the table. His small movements only halted when Moll stepped forward to address the young woman. Mistress King had decided that the unprofitable situation could be mediated only by another female.

'What is it, my dear?' she said in a tone that was not

without sympathy. 'Who's ruffled your pretty feathers? Come on, lovely. Let's put that blade down, eh? I'm sure we can sort this out without any mischief.'

Sarah looked at Moll, recognizing a figure of authority and a voice of reason. But she also knew that no one could possibly understand what she was feeling, and why she was there. She shook her head in a demonstrative way. Then she started to speak.

'Forgive me,' she said. 'It was not my course to do it here. To impose on you all. But he was feeling under my petticoats. And would have found the knife.'

There was a ribald shout to the effect that it was not a prick Ransome was after. Even the baronet laughed.

But Sarah was not to be put off.

'I was to do it later,' she said. 'When I was back in my room. With *him*!'

She spat out the last words, throwing a look in Ransome's direction that was as sharp as her blade. The references to Sir Marmaduke had captured everyone's attention.

Moll took another step forward. She made a sign with her hands to indicate that she should be left to deal with this alone.

'Do *what*, my dear?' said Moll. 'What was you to do back in your room with this ... gentleman?'

Her question gave rise to more earthy remarks. Moll ignored them, although her scowl would not have been out of place on the face of a schoolmistress scolding a class of unruly rascals.

'What was it you was to do?' she repeated slowly.

She was trying to make clear she wanted a woman-to-woman conversation, and that the young girl should ignore the distractions.

Sarah was breathing hard. It looked as though the effort of keeping her arms stretched out was beginning to tell. Ransome thought that now was perhaps the time to bring the matter to a close by jumping the jade and throwing her to the floor. Like everyone else, however, he was intrigued by what she might say. What *exactly* did she want to do to him? And more importantly, *why*? It was something of a puzzle. He had never exchanged more than a few words with her at the Nonsuch bawdy house. Tonight was their only pre-arranged meeting. She had not even had a first taste of his very particular habits, let alone a reason for taking exception to them. So what was all this about?

Sarah glanced in his direction, and then at Moll, as she continued to speak.

'I was to kill him, of course,' she said.

This comment drew not so much a gasp as rather an awkward silence. There was something about the icy way she delivered the words that made everyone take note. It was not the outburst of a fiery woman who felt herself affronted. It was the simple statement of someone who had set her heart on a cold-blooded act, only to be foiled by how things had played out. At the word 'kill' Dr Rock pulled an anxious face as he began once again to inch around the table.

Ransome's eyes were now fixed on the girl. What did she mean? What could she possibly have against him? Other than what any number of slatterns might have.

Moll's face tightened. Perhaps this was more serious than she had thought. She was about to ask when Sarah, unprompted, carried on speaking.

'To pay him back,' she said.

Her voice was now trembling.

'To pay him back,' she repeated. 'For killing my sister.'

The room filled with murmurs. Ransome's eyes had narrowed. He stood up straight. Part of him wanted to end this nonsense – which is what it surely was. To silence this unstable, rambling slut – and get on with the evening. But to do that might imply guilt. If he threw her to the ground now, it might look as if he had done what she claimed. That he had indeed killed her sister – whoever *she* was. No. He should not allow himself to be made an accessory to her delusions.

And yes, he was curious as well.

He therefore checked the movement his body had made in her direction. Instead, he leaned back against the wall again – this time crossing his arms while he shook his head slowly. Oh dear, his posture seemed to say – the sad depths to which people will stoop just to gain attention.

Sarah was quiet. She had said her piece and did not know what more she could add. They would no doubt arrest her and commit her for trial. For threatening behaviour and possibly more. But at least she had declared her vow to avenge her sister. Even if it made no sense to most of those present.

The fact was, however, that what she had said made no sense to *anyone* – least of all Ransome, as his face clearly showed. For his assumed look of piteous derision had been replaced by what appeared to be a genuine expression of incomprehension. He held out his hands as if to say, 'I've really no idea who this person is, or why she might have fixed her sad and twisted madness on me.'

Moll decided to continue as chief inquisitor, though she was wary of encouraging the girl to disclose more than might be helpful in bringing the scene to an end. The sordid background did not matter if it had no bearing on Tom King's. Moll's common sense told her it would be better for any details to be recounted in some other place, away from the main coffee-house space. On the other hand, she needed to keep the young woman talking.

'And who might your sister have been, my lovely?' she said, trying to inject a note of tenderness into the bald question.

Sarah's face was showing intense strain. Her lip quivered as her arms began to shake. She glanced at Ransome in a way that showed the horror of what she must now say. Then she looked back at Moll.

'Kitty Smith,' the young woman blurted out. 'Kitty Smith, whose room is now *my* room. And whose neck was broke. Broke by *him*!'

This time there *was* a gasp from those who stood around. All eyes turned towards the baronet.

§

I cannot say for certain that I was with child. But I knew that I was with fear.

Fear both for myself and for any creature that might grow inside me from that man. I wanted no trace of him in my body, and such was this feeling that it overcame whatever else I might have felt in terms of my Christian responsibility towards an unborn child.

But then I did not know that there was any such child. And what I did next may well have been for nought, if I was not indeed pregnant.

For I acted out of fear. And selfishness also. I put myself above the possible needs of someone, something, else. Which is why, at last, I have to confess it.

Dr Rock was not so well regarded in Covent Garden then, but he was already known to me because my great aunt had been a user of his tincture for the teeth, which she acquired from his premises near Ludgate Hill.

And so it was to that place that I travelled, as quietly and anonymously as I could, to seek from him a substance that would make me lose anything that might be inside me.

It was not difficult, for I had money and was determined. But I remember the look on his face as he stared at me, despite that I tried to keep my gaze down. And the sense that he seemed to know me, even though I had not spoke my name.

When he said, 'Have I not seen you in the Piazza?', I nodded weakly, glad to put his questioning mind at rest. For whilst my answer was true, I knew that he must surely deal with other women who would claim the Garden as some kind of home, and that I had identified myself with those sisters, rather than provided a clue to my own position.

Since then, of course, I have spied him oft in the

marketplace, but would like to think that he no more remembers the timorous young woman of fifteen years since, than he would do the many others who have sadly sought his remedies.

The potion was foul indeed and made me very sick. But, by one means or another, it did cure me of my unrest, and I no more sought to tax myself with the worry of what had overtaken me on that terrible night.

§

Ransome looked around at the many enquiring faces and then started to laugh.

It was the only sound in the room. Dr Rock stopped his slow movement along the edge of the table. Everyone was waiting.

When Ransome's laughter finally spluttered to a halt, he shrugged and turned to the young woman with the knife.

'So, I am accused of killing someone I did not even know,' he said. 'Is that it? Is that the sum of your complaint, my dear deranged beauty? Well, I have to tell you, you sharp-tongued little whore, that I have broken no one's neck in my life. But I *am* perhaps persuaded to break *yours* if you persist with these spiteful lies.'

He looked about him as if he were canvassing support.

'You pushed her down the stairs,' said Sarah, her face now aflame with passion. 'Down the stairs. Just across the way. In Tavistock Row. She told me you were cruel. She told me you beat her. And then you killed her.'

Ransome was now nodding slowly and smiling again. Everyone else was entranced by the exchange. No one moved – not even Rock.

'So *now* I know who you're talking about,' said Ransome. 'We *all* know who you're talking about. The little trull that sadly met her end on those treacherous stairs. Stairs where I have nearly fallen to my *own* death on more than one occasion.'

'She was my sister,' repeated Sarah, her red cheeks now wet with tears. 'Kitty. My dear Kitty. And you killed her!'

'Dear Kitty, indeed,' said Ransome with a sneer. 'Yes, I *did* know her. And I did visit her. Much to my discomfort, I should add. But I can assure you, my dear deluded girl, that I most certainly did not kill her. No matter what she may have said about me.'

'It was no accident,' Sarah continued between sobs.

She was moving her arms now, trying to keep the feeling in them.

'Don't tell me it was an accident,' she went on. 'I know it wasn't. Kitty wasn't like that. She was careful. Very careful. She was pushed. I know it. She was murdered.'

Ransome again looked around at the surrounding faces as if he were in a court of law. His expression seemed to say: 'I ask you, gentlemen of the jury – can you honestly countenance such a flimsy fabrication as this? Against *me* – a worthy and honourable member of the community!' Then he puffed out his chest and said aloud something that changed the course of the wrangle.

'Well, perhaps you *do* know it, my dear,' he said. 'And yes, now that I recollect, I do recall the lady's demise. But

I have to tell you ... I really do have to tell you ... that you have the wrong man. I was nowhere near the wretched place on the night of which you speak. Although ...'

He paused dramatically before going on.

'If you look around you, my girl, I suspect you may indeed cast your eyes upon the person who put his mark upon your dear sister.'

His words cut through the air of Tom King's like a scythe.

There was a sudden silence. And then everyone began to talk at once. The hubbub was matched by a general movement of bodies, as people pushed forward to get a better view. Was Sir Marmaduke looking at anyone in particular?

In that general surge of activity, Dr Rock saw his chance to get free of the table. He made one last, quick move to propel himself away from the wall and towards the door. But in doing so, he stumbled over Smallow's outstretched leg. A second later Rock found himself falling towards the floor and, more worryingly, towards the woman with the knife.

Sarah was caught off guard by seeing the bulk of the doctor crumpling forward in such a precipitate and unexpected way. She stepped back and to one side as nimbly as she could, recoiling from the mass of his body as it collapsed wigless at her feet. And, as she did so, Ransome stepped swiftly behind her and disarmed her of the knife.

Seeing how the scene was developing, Tom King pushed past his wife and grabbed at the girl, encircling her waist with his large hands by way of restraint. But Sarah had nothing left. Her strength and resolution had been drained, and she slumped in Tom's arms, her face ashen and her spirit crushed.

§

Within fifteen minutes Flea was back at Miss Hyssop's house with his report.

Mr Hogarth was indeed drinking at the Bedford Arms. Flea rehearsed the names of Mr Hogarth's drinking companions. Mr Scott, Mr Hayman and Mr Alcazar.

Mr Alcazar? Prudence was surprised, until Flea informed her that he had observed Mrs Alcazar and child departing earlier in the day. He had been reliably informed that she was visiting her sister in the country – although he could not be sure which especial or peculiar country it was. Probably somewhere in the north, if he could rely on the way his informant had waved an arm in the general direction of St Giles.

Despite their continuing concerns about William's state of mind, both Prudence and Jane smiled at the news. The obvious delight that Master Fleabane showed in garnishing his report with such detail was all too clear. In fact, there was not much that passed him by. In his very short excursion to the Bedford Arms and back again, he had noticed two other things of some interest.

One was seeing a very wet and bedraggled Jeremiah letting himself into the house on Tavistock Row. Jeremiah was accompanied by a lady – although Flea could not see her face, which was hidden beneath a rain-soaked hood.

The second thing he noticed was the unusually large number of people in Tom King's coffee-house at such a relatively early hour. Perhaps they were all seeking refuge from the very inclement conditions outside.

These two things were not directly relevant to the mission on which he had been sent, of course. He therefore made no mention of them to Miss Hyssop, but simply stored them away in his mind as further indications of the increasingly stormy night.

§

Ransome drove the point of the knife into the wall.

It should stand there as a warning – and a testament to his manly skill in disarming the bloodthirsty bitch. He was all for dragging her before the magistrate there and then on a charge of attempted murder. But Moll talked him down with a conciliatory speech that blended compassion with common sense.

'There'll be no need for that,' she said. 'You just take another drink, Sir Marmaduke. That's what you need. Then you leave the girl be. Look at her, poor thing. She's hardly alive.'

'Poor thing!' exclaimed Ransome. 'Why, the she-devil tried to kill me!'

'No she never,' continued Moll. 'She just said she *wanted* to. And if we took before the magistrate everyone who came close to doing what they dream of, Sir Marmaduke, the poor justice wouldn't get a wink o' sleep from one week to the next! All's well that ends well. That's what I say. And as far as I can see, you're no worse off than you was half an hour ago. Whereas *this* poor mite looks fit to expire.'

Tom carried the young woman into the small, curtained closet the Kings kept as their private space behind the bar. Moll continued to deal with Ransome, who was now keen to resume his evening of drinking and whoring. There were a few more grumbles about harlots taking respectable people's names in vain. But the baronet soon adopted the condescending air of a wronged man who had, for the time being, chosen to overlook an injustice.

'Thank you, Sir Marmaduke,' said Moll. 'You always said you was an honourable man. And now you deserve a drink. A very big and a very strong one.'

Moll never missed an opportunity to market her liquor.

Ransome sat down next to Smallow, who was white-faced and looking very worried. Slippery Sal had left his side and was helping Dr Rock to dust himself down – whilst also slipping her hand inside his pocket to relieve him of his lace handkerchief.

'You shouldn't have said that,' said Smallow through tight lips.

'*Now* what?' growled Ransome impatiently.

Yes, he most definitely needed that large and very strong drink.

'You shouldn't have said what you did. About who might have killed the girl.'

Smallow's shiny face was taut. He was trying to speak so that only Ransome could hear.

'And why might that be?' said Ransome, who was beginning to find his companion rather tedious. 'Do you perhaps have something to hide?'

'You bloody well know what I mean,' insisted Smallow.

'Do I indeed!' said Ransome. 'Well, in that case, let us drink to my silence!'

So saying, he reached across Smallow and snatched the bottle he had spied in the painter's bag.

Smallow reacted immediately, trying to grab it back. But the larger man, full of pent-up frustration, pushed him away with ease. Then he brandished the bottle in the air.

'I see you've been keeping this for yourself,' said Ransome. 'Well, I think it is time you shared it around.'

Smallow stared at him, his eyes wide with anger and fear.

'Give it to me!' he said, barely managing not to shout the words.

Not that anyone would have noticed in the general clamour that was now back to its normal raucous level. Ransome held the bottle aloft, while his other hand kept Smallow at bay.

'I think not,' said the baronet. 'I think this should be my reward.'

Smallow looked desperate.

'It's a present,' he breathed. 'A special gift. For a fellow painter. You must let me have it back.'

But Ransome was not to be defeated. He had seen a good deal of Smallow over the last few months, and he did not like the man. Yes, the painter had provided certain questionable favours during that time – but he needed to be constantly put in his place.

'Well, my friend,' said Ransome. 'If it is a special gift, then I can think of no one who deserves it more than I do. Don't you think?'

'But you don't understand,' continued Smallow.

Perhaps he should just admit it. Tell Ransome the truth. That the bottle was poison. Except that doing so would only lead to more explaining. More trouble. More mockery.

'No,' said Ransome. 'It is *you* who do not understand, my dear Smallow. For if you do not show some humility and respect with regard to your betters, then I may just have to say something more about that sad whore's death. Because *now* I find that, without a strong drink to settle my mind, I have the most astonishingly clear memory of what you told me about the matter very soon after it happened.'

Smallow sat back, his eyes ablaze. Would Ransome do that? Dare he? And who would believe him?

And then the horrible reality of the situation dawned on him. Yes, of course, that was *exactly* the sort of thing Ransome would do. And he would do it with a laugh. Just as he was laughing now.

For Ransome was clearly enjoying making the fat, slimy bastard squirm. Yes, he would win this unseemly little squabble because he was better and stronger. And what's more, he had a hold over the other man. The shiny, little shit had no choice but to yield to his superior power.

'Very well,' said Smallow at last, freeing himself

from the other's grip. 'The gift is yours. Drink it with my blessing. Drink off this potion. For you said it yourself. The price is your silence.'

He was now looking intently into Ransome's eyes. They were unfocused, but still twinkling with triumph and the thought that, in his usual bullying way, he had once again put the odious little artist where he belonged.

'Good,' said Ransome. 'I knew you would see it my way. In the end.'

As he said this, he set the bottle before him on the table. He pulled out the stopper and lifted it to his nose.

'It would appear to be very good brandy,' he said, his lips curling with appetite and desire. 'You could not have chosen a better gift for me – your most noble patron.'

With that, he raised the bottle to his lips and, in a purposeful show of reckless bravado, proceeded to drain it to the bottom. Glug by terrible glug.

Smallow looked on in horror, knowing that the baronet would never have drunk an elixir like this before.

Finally it was done, and Ransome slammed the bottle back down on the table. He stared back at Smallow, his cruel, flat face expressing a mixture of contempt and pride.

A few seconds passed.

Just long enough for Smallow to look around and see that no one was taking any notice of them. Then it happened.

Ransome stood up, shakily, his expression turning first to one of confusion and then pain. He staggered back a pace or two, one hand feeling for the wall and support. Then his face contorted into a look of alarm.

His skin turned white, his mouth dropped open, and a terrible belching noise rose up from his gut. His eyes were now wide and looked as if they might erupt from their sockets. His free hand grasped at his throat, ripping the neck-cloth away and throwing it onto the floor. Then he suddenly bent double, groaning, and clutching at his stomach, before jerking upright again, his face looking as if all terrors imaginable were coursing through his brain.

There was another giant spasm. Followed by a sickening sound that seemed to come from deep within him.

And then he fell to the ground. Heavily. Smashing his head against the corner of the table. The impact pitched his body into the middle of the room, where it lay twitching like an animal mortally caught in a trap.

Had the man suffered a fit? What was going on? A group of young rakes turned to look in disgust at the convulsing shape of the baronet, who lay in a crumpled heap, his head in a puddle of puke.

With attention now focused on the foul and putrid figure of Ransome, Smallow reached out to retrieve the bottle and stopper, stuffing them back into his satchel. Then he stood up and crept by the other side of the table, holding the bag close to his chest. Someone was calling for Moll. A peering crowd had formed. No one saw as Smallow slid by, his eye on the door and escape.

As he squeezed past the burgeoning band of gawping drinkers, he wrenched the knife from where it stood stiff in the wall and slipped it into his coat pocket.

§

Mr Flint, the old tailor, was standing at his window with a candlestick in his hand.

He had been looking out into the Piazza. The rain was heavy now and the wind strong. But it was not enough to drown the other sounds. There was no such thing as a quiet time in the square. Whether it was early morning, noon, or late at night, any passing peace was soon fractured by the Piazza's cries, shouts, and numerous noises.

His wife did not know what a blessing it was to be so nearly stone-deaf. He looked across at her and she smiled, nodding. Which made him conscious that it was no real blessing at all. For all that he might complain about the racket, he could not conceive of living in the Piazza without it. It would, he thought, be like living there without the colours or the smells. Hardly a place at all. Hardly a life at all. He looked at his wife again. How does she bear it?

So it was not the noise itself that made him take note, so much as its nature.

To start with, it sounded like an animal howling. But then, some minutes later, he heard it as a call. And this time it was nearer. Outside the house.

'Hello! You there! You up there!'

And, for a reason he could not put his finger on, it was as if the words were directed specifically at him.

§

Smallow stumbled into the centre of the Piazza and bayed up at the sky like some wounded creature.

This latest fit of anger and lunacy had been brewing

for weeks. Months even. Just the previous night he had been shouting out into the open square. Now, just twenty-four hours later, he was back again. And this time it was worse.

His obsessions were getting the better of him. In particular, his plan to humiliate William Hogarth. And to poison him.

Only a short while before it had all seemed so clear.

He would go to the Bedford Arms and show the princely portrait to the assembled company. He would tell them it had been painted as an act of sycophancy – but then rejected by the fawner himself. He would ask them to guess the name of the artist. It would be a direct challenge to Hogarth. A challenge for him to rise to the bait. And if he did not, then he, Smallow, would expose the work as a piece of Hog Art, and invite the pig to deny it. It would cause uproar. And the Bedford's customers would ridicule the great Mr William Hogarth mercilessly.

Then there was the potion. That would be left at the sign of the golden prick. With a note. 'To cheer you up – after your giving *us* such a laugh! – a drop of the best, from your friends at the Bedford.' He would have to disguise his handwriting, of course. There must be nothing that could tie the bottle back to him. But he was a fucking artist, for God's sake! What could be easier?

So the plan had finally come together. Yesterday's outburst in the Piazza had been replaced by a more considered approach. His hot-headed temper had given way to a cold-blooded resolution.

Until Ransome spoiled it all.

The bastard.

The poison was now gone – and could not be easily replaced.

But at least he now had another weapon in his possession. The knife. Could he use that instead? It was less to his taste. But it was at least *some*thing.

Now might I do it pat.

But *how*?

Even as he asked himself the question, he could feel his energy seeping away. He peered up into the squally night and howled once more. It sounded a note of pain and frustration, rather than rage or courage.

He staggered on, stumbling his way across the marketplace to take shelter under the arches at the east end of the Piazza. A brace of harlots latched onto him, offering to warm him up and dry him out. But he gave them short shrift – telling them to get back to their nunneries.

No one else bothered him while he stood there shivering. He was out of the driving rain but the water in his wig still ran down his smooth face. It formed a constant series of drips on the end of his nose. He shook his head and tried to think.

The church bell struck the hour. Ten o'clock. And as it did so, he felt a new and different darkness rising in his heart, as if he were walking in a more shadowy world of spirits. The few lamps he could see appeared spectral through the sheeting rain. He became more aware of where there was light. And where there was not.

He clutched his bag close to his dripping peacock-blue coat and adjusted the sodden wig once more. Then he trudged along the arcade a few yards further, towards one of the lights he could see. It was in the window of a house he knew well. The house where *she* had lived. Where Al Alcazar lived. Where Jeremiah Potts lived.

Then he stopped suddenly.

Potts.

Of course.

That would work. Potts was under his power. He could use Potts to help him execute a *new* plan. A *new* way of humiliating William Hogarth.

Not in the Bedford. No, Smallow was now feeling less confident about that. What if the other artists rallied behind their man? What if they took against *him*?

No, he would lure the Hog out of there. And Potts would be his means for doing it.

It was a good idea, and Smallow's mind was sparked into action again. He put his hand into his coat pocket and felt the bone handle of the knife. A smile formed on his face for the first time since leaving Tom King's. Yes, he would manage it all in Potts's room.

The humiliation.

And the killing too.

In Potts's room.

But first he had to get there.

He tramped damply from the arcade into Tavistock Row and up to the front door.

Damn.

Except it was not so surprising that it should be locked during the hours of darkness.

He stepped back and looked up again at the light he

could see. It was on the first floor. He tried to recall who lived there.

Yes, he remembered now. It was an old couple. He had seen them on the stairs. Could they let him in?

The rain was still drifting across the square in waves. His drenched face started to shout.

'Hello! You there! You up there!'

Nothing at first. A small movement of the light. Then the window opening. And the head of the old man. It looked out suspiciously, curious despite the downpour.

'Down here!' called Smallow, waving his free hand above his head. His other hand still held the bag close to his chest. The old tailor swivelled his head and peered at him.

'It is Mr Jonathan Smallow,' the voice called from out of the storm. 'Jonathan Smallow the painter. You know me. I have been to this house many times. To visit Mr Alcazar. And Potts.'

The old man showed no sign of having seen him before.

'Can you let me in?' Smallow called. 'Please,' he added as an afterthought. 'I am a gentleman painter and I need to visit Jeremiah Potts on a matter of urgent business.'

Gentleman. Matter of business.

The old man looked at him more keenly now but still said nothing. Then as suddenly as his head had appeared, it disappeared again – and the window was closed.

Smallow cursed.

But then he saw the candle moving. Perhaps the old man was coming down.

So he waited. Soaked.

He was just convincing himself that the light had been

moved only to discourage further interruption, when he heard a sound. The door creaked open. The old man stood there, holding the candle above his head.

'You say you're a gentleman,' he said gruffly.

'Indeed I am,' said Smallow.

'Then I can rely on you to act in a gentlemanly way,' said the old man. 'On a matter of business.'

Smallow swallowed the urge to push past him with another curse. Instead he felt in the pocket of his waistcoat before dropping a coin into the outstretched hand. The old man stared at it and then stepped to one side.

'You can't take the candle,' he said. 'You'll have to go up the last part in the dark.'

'So be it,' said Smallow. 'I know my way.'

§

I suppose it is likely I would have adopted Master Fleabane for many good reasons.

It is something I have never regretted, and which gives me a great deal of pleasure every day. Yet, in writing these confessions to myself, I have perhaps been more acutely aware that Flea is also my family, and having decided that I could never be wed or a mother after what happened on that fateful night, he also represents much more than my Christian duty. He has perhaps helped me to lay some ghosts.

Although others remain.

And one has just appeared.

§

The old tailor lighted the way up the first flight of stairs.

This part of the staircase was strong and stable with stout bannisters. Mr Flint stood on the first-floor landing and stared suspiciously as the gentleman-artist continued his way aloft. Then the old man turned and went back into his room. The light went with him. Smallow was left in the dark.

He knew that the stairs from the first to the second floor were a danger to life and limb, with gaps in the handrail and holes in the steps themselves. The damp smell of mould was more pronounced than he remembered. But his eyes were becoming accustomed to the shadows, and he could see his way well enough for other memories to return. Including, in the ghostly air of the musty stairwell, the image of Kitty Smith, dead and tangled. With her ghastly face.

He gritted his teeth and passed grimly on, along the short landing towards the final flight. The narrow and enclosed stairs that led to Jeremiah Potts's garret. Smallow paused and felt the knife in his coat pocket. Then he crept forward, bracing himself against the wall.

Ahead he could see a sliver of light below the attic door. And he could hear voices. A man and a woman.

§

I cannot say that I do not believe in ghosts.

There is too much of this life that lies beyond my comprehension, and I trust that all will be revealed in due course by the goodness of the Almighty's great favour.

Yet I do not readily give credence to the tales and wonders of which so many speak. I would hope that I should keep my mind open on such matters. And so it is that I hesitate to make any firm pronouncement about what I believe I may have seen. Whether it be ghost or not. And only now do I set it down.

The recollection is out of time. But what is time in the matter of ghosts?

I had been walking under the arcade. It was that time of day when the market has mostly ceased and there is an almost unnatural lull in the activity of the place. I was crossing James Street, going towards King Street, and the figure was approaching from that direction. There were not many people about, and so I may have noticed him for that reason alone. But his wooden leg made him more singular. He appeared to be disconcerted by my sight and halted, turning his head away. But then, as I crossed his path, he faced me, and doffed his hat in greeting. Momentarily I decided that he would ask for alms, and I thought myself glad to have some pennies about me.

But he did not. He simply bowed low, and addressed me with these words:

'A good day to you, Miss Prudence.'

Then he replaced his hat and continued on his way, the sound of his wooden leg upon the flagstones diminishing as he went.

I know I had hesitated slightly at his speaking my name – my first name – but I carried on, persuading myself that it was perhaps not so unnatural that someone passing through that part of Covent Garden should have heard something of its residents.

But as I continued into King Street, I knew it was his face that had made such an impression upon me and created a distraction in my soul.

And there was something of a shiver in my spine. For his face spoke to me of former days.

It was a handsome face, with penetrating eyes, high cheekbones, and a sun-tanned skin below a full head of hair that was partly tied back, but which also hung loose. And I felt myself much confused.

So why do I call him ghost rather than man?

Why do I not name him?

For no reason but that he is not of this world and time, but of some other.

This thought I found hard to put out of my mind. And, for some reason, I began to hope.

§

Smallow knocked on the door.

'Potts,' he called. 'It's Smallow. Here on business.'

He could sense ripples of unease inside the room. There were muffled words. Then the door opened a few inches, casting a shard of light across the visitor. Jeremiah's long face appeared in the gap.

'Aren't you going to ask me in?' said Smallow.

Jeremiah glanced over his shoulder, then stood to one side. Smallow walked in and looked around. He noted an easel and a painting to his right. To his left, a thin, pale woman sat on the edge of a narrow bed.

Jeremiah continued to watch nervously, noting how

wet Smallow was. He pointed towards a chair. The visitor sat down, arranging his sodden coat around him. He placed his bag against the leg of the chair.

Jeremiah cracked his fingers and tried to breathe more evenly. But in his heart he wanted to scream. That Mr Smallow should land himself on him again. And now.

'This is Mr Jonathan Smallow, painter,' he said through tight lips to the woman on the bed. 'And this lady, Mr Smallow, is Miss Catherine Pargeter.'

There was a pause while he considered the implications of what he had just said. Then he added, with great deliberation:

'To whom I am affianced.'

Smallow sneered and grunted a greeting in Catherine's direction.

'Potts,' he said, 'I want something.'

'Of course you do,' said Jeremiah, who was still standing.

There was no irony in his voice. It was the simple statement of someone who knew he was trapped. Who felt that everything had caught up with him. That time had run out.

Smallow took a package from his bag, stood up and moved towards the centre of the room. On the easel was a picture of a woman, attended by a boy, making her way across the Piazza. It was not as obviously demented as Potts's other works – but was still piteously poor.

Smallow took hold of the picture and threw it against the wall. Then he began untying the package he was holding. One of the cords had knotted, so he took a knife from his pocket and cut the string. The wet, sacking wrapper fell to the floor, revealing a small, unframed, painted canvas, which he placed on the easel.

If Jeremiah was already discomfited by the sight of Smallow, he was devastated by what he now saw. For it was the very canvas he had stolen. There was no other word to describe what he had done. It had been theft. His heart started to pound and his mind raced. What devilish scheme was playing through Mr Smallow's head? *Now* what?

Catherine, with only the barest idea of what was going on, stayed where she was, numbed by confusion.

'Ah,' said Smallow, seeming to enjoy the moment. 'You clearly remember our princely friend.'

Jeremiah said nothing and simply stared at the image. Smallow addressed Catherine for the first time since his curt greeting.

'Your lover was so good as to acquire this for me,' he said. 'A favour in return for my promising not to tell the authorities. Not to tell them about ... how he killed the strumpet who lived on the floor below.'

Catherine turned white. Jeremiah looked dismayed.

'It's not true,' he said. 'Don't believe him, Catherine. I didn't push her. It was *him*. I *saw* him.'

He pointed a long finger at Smallow, who had resumed his seat.

'Ransome told him to do it,' Jeremiah continued, his voice trembling. 'And I was a witness. Don't listen to him. He's threatened me before with the same thing. To make me steal. But it's all lies.'

Smallow laughed.

'Yes, I can just see the magistrate believing that, can't you?' he said. 'Faced with a choice between a gentleman's testimony made on oath and the desperate hogwash of a cheap thief, which do *you* think he will regard as true?'

He adopted a theatrical voice and began to wave his hand about.

'On one side,' he crowed, 'we have an eminent painter who asserts that a poor, insane felon, in a fit of madness, pushed a harlot to her death. A most definite form of lunacy that can be attested simply by looking at the man's state of mind. And at his abominable attempts to paint.'

He mimed being mad, ending his dumbshow with a wide grin.

'And on the other side,' he went on, 'we have a very sad story concocted by the lunatic himself who would have us believe that it was the eminent gentleman who committed the foul deed! Not only that – but that the eminent gentleman was acting on behalf of a most illustrious member of the English nobility.'

Smallow could barely contain his mirth at the absurdity of such a choice.

'I ask you, my dear,' he said, addressing Catherine once more. 'Which account do you think the magistrate most likely to favour? Eh?'

Jeremiah was wringing his hands.

'But it's the truth, Catherine,' he said, his voice hardly more than a croak. 'I saw him do it – and the memory has plagued me ever since.'

Miss Pargeter found herself appealed to from both sides, as if she were at once judge and jury. But she had not the faintest understanding of what was being contested. She knew that a woman had fallen to her death in the building. Jeremiah and Mr Alcazar had helped to tend the body. But what was all this talk of murder? And who *was* this Ransome? That was Lady Belinda's new name. It could surely not be Belinda's husband that Jeremiah was referring to. Could it? His next words removed all doubt.

'Sir Marmaduke wanted her dead,' he said. 'She was causing trouble. Saying too much. And he was about to be married. To a very large fortune. He promised Mr Smallow commissions. Artistic work. If Kitty met with an accident. I *know*.'

He pointed at Smallow again.

'He *told* me,' Jeremiah almost cried. 'When he swore me to silence. He told me the truth. But then he said the truth was nothing. Nothing compared to *his* truth. And that he would say that *I* had done it.'

Catherine was petrified. Smallow was still laughing, but more quietly and in a considered and menacing way.

'You see what I mean, your honour,' he said, maintaining his courtroom performance. 'This base robber of other men's canvases is mad at so many levels. To paint those abhorrent things. To invent such stories. To defame two prestigious and respectable gentlemen. The deranged rapscallion you see before you can hardly be considered a model of right thinking, your honour. How could you possibly take on trust – or even on oath – the words of such a crazed wretch?'

Jeremiah was distraught.

'But you know it's not true, Mr Smallow,' he said. 'How can you do this to me, sir? How can you do this to me *again*? Have you not already broken me, Mr Smallow? Look at me. Just look. And in all Christian charity, have mercy upon me!'

Smallow stared at the poor man who stood quivering before him.

'Mercy?' he sneered. 'Mercy? Who am *I* to have mercy?'

There was a pause.

'Except,' he went on, 'there is no reason why, once again, the truth – *my* truth – must find its way into the shell-like ear of the magistrate. Not immediately, at least. Perhaps I *could* show some ... consideration. And, yes, it may indeed be mercy. But only *if* ...'

He leaned forward on his chair.

'Only *if*, Potts, you continue to do everything that I tell you.'

Jeremiah's face was drained of colour. He did not know whether he was grateful for any small stay of execution – or even more terrified of what might now be demanded of him.

§

In the Bedford Arms, William had managed to talk and drink himself into a better humour.

Hayman had been describing the latest developments in a project aimed at painting scores of pictures to decorate the supper boxes at Vauxhall Pleasure Gardens. This led to them swapping tales of things they had witnessed at Vauxhall over the years. It occasioned a good deal of merriment and banter. Even Alcazar appeared to enjoy the exchange.

This jolly mood dissipated, however, when Jeremiah Potts approached their table with a worried look on his face. William sat up, stiff-backed. So, there would be no need for a hunt after all. The quarry had come to him.

'Ah, Mr Potts,' said Hayman, as if he were inducting some noble gentleman into the orbit of their conversation. 'We were just discussing the delights of the Spring Gardens at Vauxhall. I'm sure you yourself must have dallied in the Dark Walks on more than one occasion. Do tell us, pray – what is the most salacious act you yourself have witnessed there?'

Scott coughed into his ale. Alcazar looked uncomfortable, guessing that Vauxhall's entrance fee of a shilling was almost certainly beyond his close neighbour's everyday means. William's smile had also faded, and he was looking at Jeremiah with a new intensity. The man's arrival there was surely no coincidence.

Jeremiah ignored the banter, his face a picture of seriousness.

'I have a message for Mr H,' he said.

Hayman, however, was not to be put off his raillery quite so easily.

'Is Mistress Hogarth becoming impatient for her hot toddy perhaps?' he said.

He laughed, but Alcazar and Scott remained quiet and straight-faced.

'Carry on, Jeremiah,' said William, pushing his loose cap back from his forehead with a paint-stained hand. A frown had settled across his brow. Jeremiah cleared his throat, swallowed hard, and delivered his words as if they had been recently committed to memory.

'Mr Jonathan Smallow – sends his compliments – and invites the great Mr William Hogarth – to visit him and the Prince of Wales – at a location close by.'

He paused to consider whether he had relayed the message in full. Then he added:

'You are to come alone.'

William had already risen, his jaw jutting pugnaciously. He stood there for some seconds, staring into space and brushing down the front of his long and dirty russet coat. It might almost be believed that he had been summoned to meet the Prince of Wales in person – and was reflecting on the fact that he was less than well-dressed for the occasion.

Needless to say, the invitation sounded as cryptic and nonsensical to his companions as it was crystal clear to William. The other three painters looked at their friend. Alcazar was quiet but his expression was that of a worried man. He could feel the tension radiating from William's body. Scott sat back with a look of total incomprehension on his face. Only Hayman ventured a comment, for his attention had been caught by the mention of Smallow's name. He knew only too well that his good friend had a deep antipathy towards Smallow – and that the feeling was mutual.

'Don't go, Will,' he said. 'If Smallow's sending his compliments, you can be sure *some*thing's not right. And what's all this about the Prince of Wales? Is that some kind of code? What's the bastard up to now?'

William opened his mouth. For a second it looked as if he might explain. But then he closed it again and turned towards Jeremiah.

'I'm ready,' he said. 'Lead on.'

Hayman stood up as well.

'Don't be a fool, Will,' he said, his face now flushed. 'Smallow's gulling you. I don't pretend to understand what's been going on between you, but he's not worth it. Let it go.'

William again looked as if he might say something, but once more decided against it.

'Let's go,' he said to Jeremiah.

'Then I'm coming with you,' said Hayman.

'No, Frank,' William said, his mouth set hard. 'You'll do no such thing.' He then turned to Scott and Alcazar.

'I appeal to you, gentlemen,' he said. 'Keep our friend here in order. And make sure he stays with you.'

William's face made it plain that he was in earnest. Hayman knew there was nothing to be gained by making a scene. To persist in his argument would simply lead to a hell of a row – and also put his friend in a worse humour than he clearly was already.

'Don't let him play you, Billy,' he said in a softer, more intimate tone, using the name he called his friend when they were in their cups. 'You don't need to rise to it. You're above all that. You know you are.'

William recognised the change and responded to it.

'Thank you, Frank,' he said. 'I know what you're saying.

But Smallow has hold of something. Something that's mine. I need to get it back. And now's as good a time as any.'

He was choosing his words carefully, trying to make it sound as if it were simply a piece of outstanding business rather than anything more serious. Hayman looked doubtful but decided not to push his point.

He sat back down with a thoughtful look on his face, while William, pulling his cap lower, followed Jeremiah out of the Bedford Arms.

§

Jane and Prudence stood at the window, looking out into the Piazza.

But they did not spy the hunched figures of Jeremiah and William as they picked their short way around the pools of water.

Their assumption was that William was still in the Bedford Arms, and they were glad the heavy rain was not such as to tempt him to leave the place. And if he was with Frank Hayman and Samuel Scott, so much the better. They would keep an eye on him.

So the women focused their attention on the foul weather and the effect it was having on the world outside. The central marketplace was now deserted, apart from the odd person running for cover. The arcades at the east end of the square, however, were congested. A mix of theatregoers, harlots and their culls, and other folk seeking shelter. It was presumably the same along the extended stretch of arcaded space that ran past the front of Prudence's house. That walkway was directly below her drawing-room, so was not visible from the window. But the general murmur of voices, and the odd shout, suggested that there too people were competing for space and refuge. It was also a favourite venue for sedan chairs, lining up to await their late-night fares. So it needed little imagination to bring to mind the likely hubbub passing just a few feet below where the two women were standing.

It all made them even more glad they were safe and warm indoors.

§

'He's in my room,' said Jeremiah as he and William left the tavern.

'And so is my lady friend, Miss Pargeter, I'm afraid. We were not expecting him.'

William just nodded. He could understand why the other man appeared so shaken.

Inside the house on Tavistock Row Jeremiah had left a single candle alight, close to the door into the Alcazars' room. He took hold of it and proceeded to lead the way. As they ascended the first flight of stairs, William was aware that he had not been in the house before. Any business with Jeremiah was always conducted at the sign of the golden head. However, he knew the building was no more than a few yards from where he and Jane had lived for a while after they left the Thornhills' house and before they moved to Leicester Fields. The memory was enough to make him feel he was returning to a part of his past.

At the first landing Jeremiah stopped and cautioned William to watch his step. The next flight was unstable, he said. It was important to take care. With this warning ringing in his ears, William was suddenly conscious of the absurdity and danger of the situation. Why on earth was he doing this at all? Why should he put himself at risk by attempting to parley with someone like Smallow? Frank was right. Smallow was not worth it. And perhaps the portrait of the Prince of Wales was not worth it either. He should simply have ignored Jeremiah's message.

Except that his rancorous enmity towards Jonathan Smallow was once again rising in his throat. And it tasted bitter. William knew in his heart that it was not about the painting of the Prince, or even the theft as such. It was about something that had been gnawing at him for much longer than that. It was the fact that there had always been a deep-seated hostility between the two men. And what's more, on the one and only occasion when there had been a physical confrontation – all those years ago – it was Smallow who had prevailed. The rational voice in William's head knew, of course, that none of that mattered. But the overly-sensitive, prickly, vain side of him chafed at it still. It was a running sore, and every time he heard talk of how Smallow had mocked him, it simply stoked the fires of irritation.

So, no, this was not about his property. It was about his pride and his peace of mind. And it was about putting an end to the animus that had been eating away at him for almost longer than he could remember.

All these thoughts cascaded through William's mind as he fumbled his way up the last two flights of stairs towards what he now realised must be the highest point of the house. The place where he needed to reach some kind of resolution.

Once and for all. One way or another.

§

The man with one leg had watched the events in Tom King's closely.

He knew none of the players but had an instinctive sympathy for the young woman with the knife. He also had an equally strong loathing for the tall, arrogant Sir Somebody-or-Other who appeared to be the object of her anger and revenge.

The fact that Sir Somebody had been very drunk was all too clear. His collapse soon afterwards was, in that respect, perhaps no great surprise. Although the attendant confusion suggested that his inebriation was unusual and extreme. A few cries were heard. 'He's had it.' And then 'He's dead. Stone dead!'

But then the clamour itself died down. A more reasonable voice was heard above the rest.

'No. He's not finished. I can feel a pulse. But his head is sorely broke. He should be got to his home. And a physician called. Does anyone know where he lives?'

Snatches of information were then volunteered by several people, all wishing to demonstrate some familiarity with the figure of Sir Marmaduke Ransome, baronet, and resident of St James's. Indeed, a group of three or four men appeared to be fervent about bandaging his head, in spite of the foul spew in which it lay. They then proceeded to carry him – in stately style – out into the night air, which one knowledgeable soul declared would no doubt reinvigorate him. However, finding a veritable tempest howling outside, they quickly retreated back inside again. It would be better to wait for some form of transportation.

All this was no doubt conducted in a spirit of comradeship or even simple humanity. Although there were some unfeeling wits who ascribed the actions to blatant self-interest. There had been, it seems, some rumour of likely recompense. It was even suggested that the fervent individuals had called upon Tom King personally to witness their deeds of selfless charity, with a view to his communicating the facts to the soon-to-be-recovered – and presumably grateful – baronet in the days to come.

With attention focused on the removal of Sir Marmaduke, less notice was taken of the young woman who had been his accuser. Tom had carried her senseless body into the curtained alcove behind the bar and settled it gently on a small couch. Moll called after a man who appeared to be on the point of leaving. A certain Dr Rock.

'I know you're no blessed good with blood and gore,' she said to him. 'But have a look at little miss here, will you? She's got a fit upon her. Mayhap one of your smelly salts will bring her round. If you have any about you.'

Moll did not wait to hear the doctor's reply, as she pushed him towards the alcove. She was more interested in supervising the clearing up. The baronet had left quite a mess.

The man with one leg was curious and concerned. He had heard Dr Rock spoken of by others in the coffee-house that very evening. And the stories did not fill him with confidence about the man's medical skills. He glanced over his shoulder to make sure he was not observed. Then he rounded the end of the bar and drew back the curtain just enough to glimpse inside the alcove.

§

William followed Jeremiah into his garret.

The first thing he saw was the painting of the Prince of Wales, standing proud on an easel to the right. To his left was a woman. She was shaking. There was no sign of Smallow. William took another step forward into the room.

'So here he is at last,' said a voice behind him. 'The great Mr William Hogarth.'

William turned around to face the man who had been hiding behind the door. It was Smallow, his face smooth and pink below an expensive and dripping-wet wig. His shiny but sodden peacock-blue coat looked to have been designed for a grand, royal court occasion rather than a damp night in Covent Garden. Bright silver buckles adorned his shoes, marking him out as a man of fashion and some means. Even more striking than his coat and shoe buckles, however, was the fact that he was holding a knife – and pointing it menacingly at William. The blade winked and twinkled in the candlelight.

With his free hand Smallow closed the door. Then he

chuckled to himself. His eyes flickered from one face to another, appreciating the symmetry of the tableau. He had his back to the door and immediately opposite him, some six feet away, stood William. To Smallow's left Catherine trembled by the bed. She was staring straight ahead at Jeremiah, who was fidgeting a few feet to Smallow's right. In the space behind William and Jeremiah was the Prince of Wales, smiling imperiously from his easel. Behind the royal presence lay that part of the room which constituted Jeremiah's studio. At the far end was the casement that led out onto the roofs, and against which the rain continued to stream.

William was struck dumb, not because he was afraid of Smallow or even the naked blade, as malicious as both appeared. But he was at a complete loss as to what Smallow's intentions might be. And he was also concerned for the safety of the other two people in the room. If it were only he and Smallow together, he could at least make some decision about how he might defend himself. But the presence of Jeremiah and the lady rendered the situation that much more precarious.

So it was that this theatrical tableau remained stock-still for more than a minute, frozen by tension and unease. The taut silence was punctuated only by a few sounds. Small whimpering noises from Catherine and Jeremiah. Deep breathing and throat clearing from William. Plus Smallow's infernal sniggering. William thought he could also hear the pounding of his own heart. Or was it a throbbing in his ears? He began to clench and unclench his fists. Finally Smallow spoke.

'The great Mr William Hogarth,' he said again.

The repetition was partly to underscore the note of derision he wanted to strike. But it also betrayed his indecision about how to proceed. Having now finally ensnared his hated enemy, what should he do next? William watched Smallow intently. He was looking for any sign that might indicate how the scene could be brought to an end. A flicker of tiredness or remorse. Sympathy or despair. Something. *Anything* that William could turn to his and the others' advantage.

But what he *did* see worried him. For the thing he discerned in Smallow's expression was not the emotions of hate, envy, or even just greed. It was a picture of madness. Smallow's face was starting to twitch, and as the spasms became increasingly severe, he began to laugh more wildly. It seemed clear that he was having to make a sustained effort to deny, or disguise, what was happening to him.

Smallow shook his head a few times, as if attempting to rid himself of the persistent flies that buzzed about his eyes and ears. But there were no flies in the room. Only the demons that curled around his neck and flitted across his line of sight, tormenting him at his moment of triumph. Evil spirits. Or at least that was how William interpreted the strange contortions and shudders that now plagued the face below the sodden wig.

The hand holding the knife began to droop. Just slightly. But then Smallow raised it again, pointing the blade at the others in a way that appeared even more menacing than before. He looked to be experiencing some kind of fit or seizure.

'The great ... Mr ... William ... Hogarth,' he said yet again.

Perhaps he was trying to pull himself back into a stronger state of mind by rehearsing the same phrase. But he was slurring his words. William risked taking his eyes off the man for a second or two and glanced quickly at Jeremiah and the woman. They were no longer gazing at each other but were instead staring at the marks of disintegration on their persecutor's face.

Smallow was biting his lip. He seemed all too aware that something was very wrong. That something was wrong with *him*. But perhaps it would pass. If he kept talking.

'So what makes a man great, do you suppose?' he managed at last.

He was blinking as if he were making a gargantuan effort to focus both his eyes and his power of reasoning. But his speech was thick and ever more slurred.

'Some are born great,' he said. 'Some achieve greatness. Some have greatness thrust upon them!'

Then be began to laugh again, but in a way that sounded more like a rasping cough than an expression of mirth.

'No doubt the line means nothing to you, Mr William Hogarth,' he continued. 'For you have never had to play a part. As some of us have. But you will see. You *will* see! It is time for me to take my rightful place on the stage of life. I'll be revenged on the whole pack of you! And you, the great Mr William Hogarth, will be the first!'

He had recovered some of his former spirit. And he brandished the knife more vigorously to emphasise the point.

'Yes, Mr William Hogarth,' he went on. 'We shall see who will rise – and who will fall!'

Just then, however, there was a shout from below stairs. Down in the hallway.

'Will! Will!'

It was Hayman's voice.

'Will! Are you up there?'

Smallow's eyes were suddenly ablaze. They roved restlessly from William's face to Jeremiah's.

'Traitors!' he breathed, backing slightly towards the door. 'Treason and murder ever kept together!'

His face began to twitch again.

'You!' he continued, spitting the word at Jeremiah. 'Tell whoever it is to stay where they are. Otherwise there'll be blood! Go! Now!'

Jeremiah was shaking uncontrollably as he left the room, bestowing one last mournful glance in Catherine's direction. William could hear him nervously descending the stairs in the meagre light that was escaping through the gap where the door had been left ajar.

Then there was another sound. Jeremiah's own strained voice, as he called ahead of him.

'Stay below! Stay down below, I beg you!'

Smallow turned towards the door to catch at the words. And as he did so, William saw his chance.

With great effort, and a grunt he was unable to suppress, he launched himself at Smallow.

§

Hayman was not easy after William left the Bedford Arms.

Yes, his friend had made it clear that he needed to go alone. And he did have Jeremiah with him. But Hayman could not sit idly by while Will was getting himself into … well, goodness knows what.

A short time passed. Together with Alcazar and Scott, he made some attempt to move the conversation onto other matters. But it kept coming back to the same thing. What William might have let himself in for.

'Where have they gone, do you think?' Hayman said, concern writ large on his face.

Scott shook his head dolefully.

'No idea,' he said. 'Jeremiah said it was nearby.'

'So let's start with Jeremiah,' said Hayman, standing up, now clearly determined to follow his friend. 'He lives in the same house as you, doesn't he?'

The words were addressed to Alcazar, who had risen too.

'He does,' he said. 'At the top. Nearest the angels.'

He held his door key in the air to show that he could provide access for such an ascent.

'Then let's go,' said Hayman, pulling on his greatcoat.

The three of them were now convinced that they should not have let William leave without them. They bundled themselves out into the wind and the rain as quickly as they could and crossed the few yards to the house at the end of Tavistock Row. Alcazar opened the front door and they almost fell into the entrance hall.

Hayman was already shouting as loudly as he could.

'Will! Will!'

§

Prudence was thinking of sending Master Fleabane back out again.

She and Jane wanted to know if William was still encamped in the Bedford Arms. Jane, however, felt awkward about subjecting the young man to another wet walk across the marketplace, even though Prudence reassured her of Flea's relish for such an expedition. So the two women moved back to the window to see if the treacherous weather had abated at all.

Prudence's vision was more accustomed to spotting details in the square, and it was she who made the discovery.

'Oh God, preserve us all,' she said.

It was barely more than a whisper, but Jane immediately picked up the urgency in her voice.

'What is it?'

She strained her eyes to try to see what Prudence had spied.

'There's a man on the roof,' said Prudence. 'Over there.'

She pointed directly across the Piazza towards Tavistock Row.

'And I think I know who it might be,' she went on, turning towards Jane.

Jane's face tightened.

'Flea! Flea!' called Prudence.

Only a few seconds elapsed and then the young man stood before them.

'Flea,' said Prudence. 'Fetch our mantles, please. Then

run round to Mr Crust's house and let him know that he and the watch are needed. When you have done that, come and find Mrs Hogarth and myself. We shall be outside.'

Flea needed no further encouragement. He furnished the ladies with their capes and headed out into the storm.

As he left the house, he noticed that a number of people had now ventured into the middle of the square, despite the driving rain.

They were all looking up towards the roof opposite.

§

The man with one leg was appalled.

As he drew back the curtain, the scene that met his eyes brought blood pumping to his head and bile rising in his throat.

The young woman had fainted away and was lying unconscious on a small couch which was against the wall of the alcove. A man – it was Dr Rock – was leaning over her. But he appeared to be administering neither comfort nor medication. Instead, he had lifted her petticoats and was examining her in a way that was highly indecent.

The man with one leg was inflamed with anger at what was so obviously a terrible abuse of the girl's vulnerability. Before Rock had time to react, he had been grabbed by the throat. The other man then lifted the considerable weight of the doctor's body and held it pinned against the wall.

Rock's feet dangled and twitched an inch or two above the floor.

A strangulated choking sound issued from his frothy lips.

§

By the time Prudence and Jane emerged into the square, the crowd was bigger.

The rain had eased slightly but the wind still played havoc with hats and wigs. Some folk had moved from the shelter of the arcades. Others had come out of Tom King's and the Bedford Arms. As word spread, various other Piazza establishments emptied their clientele into the centre of the marketplace. There was a spectacle to be witnessed. Something not to be missed. A man declaiming from the roof-tops. And in this weather too!

Listen!

What's he saying?

'Blow, winds, and crack your cheeks! Rage! Blow! You cataracts and hurricanoes, spout till you have drenched our steeples, drowned the cocks!'

What!

What did he say?

Something about hurricanoes. It sounded like hurricanoes.

No. It was cocks! Cocks! 'Tis always cocks in Covent Garden!

Much laughter. And coughing.

He's one o' them actors.

You're right. Just puffing the latest play at the theatre.

What is it? King Lear?

King Lear, my arse! Old King Cock more like!

More laughter.

All eyes were focused on the very top of the buildings

in Tavistock Row. This was a better show than anything else on offer.

A man was clinging to the ridge of the roof. He must have climbed out of a window and onto the tiles. The wind lashed him with rain while he shouted something at the wild skies above him. But now he had stopped. Or so it seemed.

Jane and Prudence pushed their way through the crowd to the edge of the marketplace where it bordered Tavistock Row. Jane was hailed by a familiar voice.

'Mrs H! Mrs H!'

It was Frank Hayman. He was with Mr Alcazar and Samuel Scott.

'Mrs H,' he repeated, his shock all too evident. 'How is it that you're here?'

It was more an exclamation of disbelief than a question, and Jane made no attempt to answer. She could see the horror in his eyes. And he could see the fear in hers.

'We tried to get in, Mrs H,' he said. 'We tried to help. But we had to withdraw.'

As he mouthed the words, he realised they would probably make no sense to Mrs Hogarth. But he was not sure what else he could say. She was shaking and another, taller, woman had wrapped her arm about her shoulders.

'Is it … William?' Jane said, her voice small in the chaotic night air.

Hayman just looked at her, his lip trembling.

'I fear it is,' he said.

Jane and Prudence looked up again, although it was now more difficult, knowing what they did.

But despite the sheets of blurring rain, it seemed only too clear – no matter that they continued to hope and pray it was not the case.

A small man was edging along the coping, very slowly, a foot or so at a time. It was a characteristic and all too familiar figure. A long russet coat flapped about his legs and was caught up by the wind every few seconds. A loose cap was pulled low over his head. His predicament on the slippery tiles looked perilous. For he was not holding on. In fact, he had something in each of his hands. But what? It was difficult to make out.

In his left hand was something flat. A package of some sort or a book perhaps. Possibly a picture. It was easier to see his right hand, for he was waving it about. And it held something shiny. Even through the cloaking rain, it glistened. Was it …? Yes, it was.

A knife.

There were a few more shouts. But most of those in the crowd were muttering amongst themselves and asking questions of each other.

So *is* he an actor?

I don't think so. Madman more like.

I thought they was the same thing!

Who *is* he then? Does *any*one know?

Why's he up there?

And what's he carrying?

Stupid sod! He should be using his hands to hold on!

Don't 'e know it's dangerous, shinning around on wet tiles wiv no 'ands?

Of course he don't, you twat! 'Tis hardly the act of a

rational yooman bean to go roof-hopping in a tempest, is it now!

He must be drunk. That's what I reckon.

You don't say so! Heaven help us! So what are *you*, then? A bleedin' mystic!

Of course he's fuckin' drunk!!

Jane tried to shut out the burr of comments. She could feel herself shaking. She knew she must be communicating all kinds of terror to Prudence, who still had her arm about her, but she could do nothing else. She was powerless in the face of whatever was going on. And she had no idea what it was, or why. She just knew that she wished it was over – and that William was back on solid ground, standing at her side. Safe.

But then there was a shriek from the crowd, and she could not stop herself from looking up again.

The man on the roof was trying to look back over his shoulder. Back to where he had come from. And he was shouting something again. But she could not hear what it was. There was too much other noise. Yes, it looked like he was shouting to someone else up there.

But if there *was* anyone else, the other person was out of sight – at least from where Jane was standing. There was just a faint glow of light. A window? Perhaps the window through which the man had climbed out? Could he get back there? Is that what he wanted to do? Or was he trying to escape from someone? Oh, what on earth was happening? Why was he there at all?

Prudence had no more idea of what was going on. But she continued to hold her friend's trembling body against her own, trying to keep Jane as warm as she could. She was also praying very hard.

Always thy will, Lord – but please, *please*, ... let this end well.

The crowd was even larger now. What did it matter that they were wet? This was worth getting soaked for. No one could remember the last time they had seen a man on the roofs. Whatever might happen next, it had already been quite a night. Those who had been in Tom King's could hardly believe their luck. First, a baronet who had nearly drunk himself to death and had to be carried out of the place by six men ...

I thought it was eight men.

No, it was ten. At least.

And now *this*! A madman on the roof.

And a madman who looks as like to fall.

§

Rock's eyes had almost popped out of his head.

The grip about his throat was tight. It was cutting off his supply of air. But the other man was not about to let go. Instead he held him firm. The doctor's face began to turn purple while his tongue lolled out of his mouth, saliva dribbling down his chin.

'You bastard,' said the man with one leg. 'You dirty bastard! You're a stain on the human race. A curse on womankind!'

And with that, he spat a huge gob of phlegm into the doctor's face. It landed mainly in one eye. Then, just when it looked as though Rock must surely die from strangulation, the other man let go. The fat body dropped to the floor like a sack of potatoes.

The man with one leg looked down at it with disgust. Monster. But then another thought. What of the young woman? He should make sure that she was unhurt.

He turned back towards the couch. But there was no one there.

She had disappeared.

§

And then the cry that Jane most feared hearing, even though she already knew.

'It's Mr Ogarf!' came the shout from someone in the crowd. 'Mr Ogarf the painter. 'E was in the Bedford tonight. It's 'im, I tell yer!'

A few more mutterings and calls. Several other people also wanted to claim ownership of having seen Mr Hogarth in the Bedford Arms on that very evening.

Then there was a united gasp from the assembled company.

All eyes turned once more to the roof.

The man was trying to stand up. He put his arms out to balance himself, even though he was still clutching something in each hand.

Jane felt a movement around her and saw that Flea had pushed his way through the throng to be alongside his mistress. He was accompanied by the stern figure of Louisa Crust.

'My husband is consulting with the watch,' Louisa said bluntly. 'They'll see how they can get him down. He'll probably have go back the same way he came out.'

Prudence nodded. She was remembering the view from Jeremiah's room across the roofs. Was that how he had got there?

Jane was not listening. Or at least she did not hear. There was a loud buzzing in her head, and she could now not bear to turn her eyes away from what was happening so many feet above her. The rain continued to fall in sheets, gusted every now and again by a buffeting wind.

Yes, there was no doubt about it. The man was standing up – *William* was standing up. Why was he doing that? Was he really so drunk he did not know where he was? And why was he still holding those things? He should be using his hands to cling onto the roof.

But now he's waving them above his head. Oh my God! What's going on? What *are* those things? A painting? A dagger, is it? What's he doing? What is he *saying*?

For he was shouting again. Into the face of the wind and the rain. The words were indistinct and carried away by the sound and fury of the storm. Slurred words. Perhaps drunken words. But some of them could still be made out.

Just.

'Behold! For I have triumphed! He thought to have *me* in his power. But I have escaped from the role he would have me play. He will no more think to mock *me*. For he is finished. Finished! Whereas *I* ... *I* am the great Mr William Hogarth!'

And then everyone's heart stopped.

Watching, mesmerized, as it all played out before them.

The slight toppling over of his body.

Then the terrible swaying as he regained something of his balance.

And a moment of stability.

Hearts in mouths

Before his top half pitched awkwardly once again, tipping him headlong.

And still he clutches those things in his hands.

Let them go, for God's sake! Let them go!

Grab the coping. Grab it!

But no – the falling forward.

The last desperate lunge – but too late, as the hands finally give up their possessions. The painting and the blade.

And then the tumbling down, and the awful screeching noise as the body slices across the tiles, dislodging several as it goes.

With nothing to stop it.

While a hush deepens through the square, as the crowd breaks up, backing off from the area immediately below.

As the man careers down the final feet of the sloping roof before, with one last desperate flailing of arms, the body descends in an instant to the unyielding cobblestones below.

The skull hitting first.

Smashing against the ground with a sickening sound that is heard by all who recoil in horror from the splash of blood and brain.

§

The floor of Tom King's was now in no worse a state than usual.

Betty had done a good job with mop, pail and scrubbing brush. No trace of Sir Marmaduke's vomit remained to trouble those customers of a delicate disposition.

Moll was happy to get on with business. The place would soon be even more crowded, and she needed every square inch available. However, she had better check on the young woman first. With any luck, Dr Rock will have roused her with some smelly salts.

Squeezing past Tom, who was moving a barrel behind the bar, Moll slipped behind the curtain and into the alcove.

'Oh, for gawd sake!' she said.

Her voice combined surprise with the tired acceptance that some things were all too predictable.

'I wish you men would keep your bodily fluids to yourselves!'

The comment was prompted by the fact that Rock was perched on the edge of the small couch, his head between his legs, drooling and dribbling something onto the floor. Whatever it was – and Moll did not wish to interrogate it too closely – it was creating an inauspicious pool that needed clearing up straightaway.

'Betty!' called Moll, sticking her head back through the curtain. 'Mop and bucket again, if you will!'

There were jobs to be done. Moll had neither the interest nor the time to enquire into what was wrong with the drunken doctor.

Or, for that matter, what he had done with the young woman.

For there were now new noises coming from outside. Something was going on.

§

The rain had almost stopped but no one seemed to care.

Some gathered round, keen to inspect the broken body. Others looked away, happy to find less distressing distractions. A few noticed the other things that fell.

A knife clattered to the ground about twenty feet away, close to where Mr Alcazar was standing. He bent down and picked it up. It was oddly familiar, especially its bone handle. Then he reeled back in horror. It was his wife's kitchen knife. The one she was always frightened of cutting her fingers on.

A small canvas, a painting, had snagged momentarily on the guttering before falling to the ground further off. A linkboy rescued it from a puddle and was about to make off, but suddenly found his collar gripped from behind. As he squirmed and turned to view his assailant, he could see only a large, dark shape towering above him. And a wooden leg. The boy surrendered the picture, secured his freedom, and scarpered as fast as he could. The one-legged man – the picture concealed beneath his coat – then stumped across to where the body lay.

The onlookers had formed a ring around the fallen man but there was a gap in the circle where blood trickled into a culvert that ran down the side of Tavistock Row.

Just beyond the group stood Jane, her head buried in the shoulder of Prudence who was holding her tenderly but firmly enough to prevent her collapse. Flea stood close by, waiting to do whatever his mistress might ask of him.

Hayman was there too, staring but not seeing, his vision lost behind the tears that filled his eyes. Scott was sitting on a step, his head in his hands. There was much murmuring amongst the crowd. Someone said more loudly that the watch should be called. It was answered by the sharp voice of a long, gaunt man who called back that they were already there. This was followed by several muttered asides to the effect that the newly arrived spare and bony figure belonged to none other than Mr Crust himself.

Indeed, under his hawkish direction, two burly men in long coats were moving the spectators back, preparatory to assessing how best to proceed without causing further mess or distress. Jane looked up and turned towards them. She knew she had to confront the truth. It would be painful beyond imagining. But she had to look first. And to confirm what everyone had already witnessed. The untimely death of William Hogarth.

Prudence felt it too. She braced her friend against her body as they made small, slow steps together towards the dreadful mass that lay stretched out before them. The gathered company either knew or sensed who it was approaching, and they shuffled aside with muted expressions of pity and shakes of the head. Many of them were used to the sight of death – but that a wife should have to suffer such a gruesome scene was far beyond what most of them had experienced or could imagine.

William's soft, but now blood-soaked, cap had been thoughtfully pulled down by one of the watchmen so that it covered what remained of the crushed head. Jane glanced at it briefly before averting her eyes as she endeavoured to stand up straight without the aid of her good friend. She was staring straight ahead, her lips taut, as she tried to still her trembling heart. But gradually, with deep breaths, she found herself able to bring her gaze slowly back to the shape that lay before her.

She glanced down at the feet that protruded from the bottom of the long and familiar sodden russet coat.

And as she did so, she felt herself go completely rigid.

She turned to Prudence and saw that she had seen them too.

The shoes, scuffed though they were by the violence of the fall, had upon them a pair of bright, silver buckles.

§

It was difficult to suck in enough air, so contracted were their throats.

The two women held each other and stared down, almost unable to take in what was before them. And then they felt a presence at their shoulder. A man who was breathing hard. It was Jeremiah. He too cast a glance at the body on the ground but then quickly looked away again. He seemed desperate to say something. Prudence, perhaps sensing his purpose, gently turned Jane away from the corpse so that she was facing the supplicant.

'Mrs H,' gasped Jeremiah. His face was flushed and

beads of sweat stood out on his forehead. 'It's *Mr* H.'

Jane winced, her face tightening with pain. Prudence gripped her more firmly. Jeremiah saw in her expression only what he had anticipated. Hurt, worry, questions.

'He's insensible, miss,' he said.

He was looking now at Miss Hyssop whose face was also deeply furrowed.

Jane shook her head. She did not understand. What did the man mean? Insensible? *Insensible!*

Jeremiah was confused and despairing. What was he to do, other than repeat what he had already said?

'Please come, Mrs H,' he said. 'To my room. For Mr H is insensible *there*. And I cannot wake him.'

Jane stared at him with wide eyes. Jeremiah, fearing she might accuse him of having abandoned her husband, continued to convey the message and make his case.

'Catherine – that is, Miss Pargeter – is nursing him, Mrs H. But you should come.'

Jane and Prudence looked at each other, amazement lighting up their tired faces. They held each other and turned back towards the body on the ground. The men from the watch were still circling, trying to decide how best to lift it without doing further damage. The two women stared again at the shoes and the silver buckles. Then their gaze moved up the russet coat towards the shattered head. It was now more visible than before, for the watchmen had adjusted the cap once again to cradle the cracked skull and what had been spilled.

It was an awful sight. A very badly disfigured face, one eye still open and seeming to stare up at the louring sky. It was difficult to tell who it was. Or rather who it had been. But one thing was clear.

It was not William.

§

Jeremiah led the way.

Jane came next, leaning on the arm of Francis Hayman. Prudence followed with Mr Alcazar. Flea and Samuel Scott brought up the rear.

Once inside the house, Mr Alcazar lit candles, two of which he gave to Jeremiah and Hayman. He then made Miss Hyssop and Scott as comfortable as he could in his room, while Flea stood guard at the door. It was agreed that, given the situation and state of the stairs, only Jeremiah, Mrs Hogarth and Hayman should ascend to the top.

The noise had roused the house's other tenants. As the party passed the first-floor landing, the old tailor opened his door cautiously.

'It's all right, Mr Flint,' said Jeremiah. 'There's been something of a to-do. But it's all over now. Please don't trouble yourself or your good lady.'

The old man nodded but looked suspicious as he withdrew back into his chamber. There had been more than enough disturbance for one night.

At the next landing a young woman stood alone. The stairway was narrow at this point, and she waited for the group to pass before using the stairs herself. Dressed in a long, dark coat and carrying a bag, she shielded her face from the glare of the candles and nodded at Jeremiah. 'Evening, miss,' he responded as he went by. As the threesome began their final climb to the top, they could hear behind them the young woman descending the stairs at a quicker rate than was advisable in the gloom. Then the sound of the front door slamming shut.

The ascent to the garret was made in single file. Jeremiah went first, then Jane. Hayman hung back until the other two had entered the room. It was partly a precaution, as he feared the confined stairway might not support the weight of all three. But it was also because, whatever state William was in, Mrs H should see him first.

Jane feared the worst. It was a blessed relief to know that it was not her husband who lay dead in the Piazza. But that revelation had given no clue as to what condition she would find him in. Jeremiah had said almost nothing, his mournful face conveying only nervous concern. Within seconds, however, her heart was dancing – even if her body felt only a leaden tiredness after the shock and the challenging climb.

The room was wider than she had imagined and lit by more candles than would usually have graced such a humble dwelling. Her eyes went immediately to the left where, on a low bed, William lay, propped up against a cushion. Next to the bed, sitting very upright, her hands gathered in her lap, was Catherine Pargeter. As soon as she saw Jane, she stood up, embarrassed.

'I'm so sorry,' she said. 'But I'm afraid Mr Hogarth is still a little faint. That is to say, he is much better than he was, if you see what I mean.'

Jane was so happy to see her husband alive that her eyes filled with tears as she sat herself on the side of the bed. William looked at her from under drooping eyelids, his expression bashful.

'Hello, old girl,' he said. 'And how are *you*? I'm a bit knocked about, I'm afraid.'

The words were slightly indistinct, but otherwise the voice sounded like the man Jane knew and loved. His paint-stained right hand rubbed ruefully at the bristles on the top of his head and the stubble of his chin. He took Jane's fingers in his left hand and raised them first to his lips and then to the side of his head. She could feel a large swelling and see, even in the candlelight, how discoloured the skin was.

'What have you been doing to yourself?' she said.

'I hit me head on the damned door,' he said.

Then he sighed and gave Jane's hand a squeeze as he leaned back onto the cushion. Noting his tiredness, Catherine decided that she should add some commentary to relieve Mr Hogarth of the need to weary himself further.

'I'm sorry,' she said. 'But the *other* man – he was threatening Mr Hogarth with a knife. Well, he was threatening *all* of us really, I suppose. After he sent Jeremiah out of the room to tell the others not to come up, ... well, I'm sorry, but it was then that Mr Hogarth did what he did.'

Jane was smiling, tears running down her cheeks. William was looking away.

'He threw himself at the other man,' Catherine went on. 'The knife fell on the floor and I was much afeard as the two of them rolled about trying to hit each other. But as they fought, Mr Hogarth hit his head sorely against the edge of the door. I'm sorry, but is this all right?'

The question seemed to be a request to know whether such a narration was of interest, or merely a distraction.

'It's wonderful, Catherine,' said Jane. 'Please go on.'

Catherine looked pleased that she had finally found a way to be of some use on this most bizarre of evenings.

'Well, I'm sorry, Mrs Hogarth …'

'You must please call me Jane, Catherine. We are, I hope, very much friends.'

Catherine nodded fervently.

'Well, I'm sorry, Jane,' she said. 'That is, thank you. But I have to tell you that I thought Mr Hogarth might have been killed. But, as you can see, he was not. Anyway, …'

She tried to recover her thread.

'As I was saying,' she continued. 'Mr Hogarth looked like he might be dead and gone. But the other man, he was fine. So he stood up and looked around and found the knife. And I thought, oh no, he's going to kill Mr Hogarth for sure. Except that I thought Mr Hogarth was *already* dead. And perhaps the other man did as well. For he didn't do anything with the knife. He just put it on the floor next to the picture of the man that had fallen off the easel. And then he did the thing that surprised me the most, Mrs Hogarth. That is, Jane.'

Catherine paused, waiting for permission to continue.

'What did he do, Catherine?' said Jane, even though she had already worked out what it must be.

'Well, I'm sorry, Jane,' said Catherine, 'but it was the strangest thing. The other man took off his fine blue coat and threw it into a corner where his wig was already lying. For that had come off in the fight. Then he pulled off Mr Hogarth's long coat from his insensible body – and got his cap too – and he put them upon himself. Like he was pretending to be Mr Hogarth.'

Jeremiah positioned himself next to Catherine and put a protective hand on her shoulder.

'I'd come back into the room by then, Mrs H,' he said. 'And I couldn't have been more astonished, I can tell you. For I saw Mr H lying on the floor but could do nothing to help him. Mr Smallow picked up the knife and the painting and told me to open the casement, so he could get out onto the tiles. If you're very careful, Mrs H, you can get across to the corner – where Tavistock Row meets Southampton Street – by going from roof to roof. I once saw a young lad do it for a dare.'

Jane had been quiet during the account, her gaze going between Catherine, Jeremiah and William, who seemed to be half listening and half sleeping. But at this point she decided to speak.

'He could not leave by the stairs,' she said.

'He could not,' confirmed Jeremiah. 'Mr Hayman and Mr Alcazar – and I think Mr Scott too – were below in the hallway. I was ordered to tell them to stay where they were and not approach any closer. Otherwise blood would be shed.'

Jane nodded thoughtfully. It sounded as if it had been a close thing. She looked up and nodded at Jeremiah, inviting him to go on.

'Well, Mrs H,' he said. 'Once Mr Smallow had gone out

by the casement, Catherine and I tended to Mr H and were mightily relieved to find he was still breathing. Between us we heaved him onto the bed and Catherine fetched some water to bathe his sore head.'

Jeremiah cast an admiring glance at the woman he had described to Smallow as his affianced.

'It was only after that,' he went on. 'It was only then that I came down into the Piazza to see what was going on. Which was when, of course, I saw how it ended. For Mr Smallow at least.'

Jane gave Catherine's hand a squeeze, and then reached out to clutch Jeremiah's as well.

'You are both saviours,' she said. 'Truly you are.'

§

What I have witnessed this night can hardly be captured in words. Perhaps one day, soon I hope, I shall be able to recount it, and even perhaps connect it to so many other thoughts that have been burning in my brain.

But that time is in the future and not for tonight.

Tonight I have been blessed by the news, conveyed to me personally and with great warmth by my dear friend Jane Hogarth, that her husband is alive and well. Or at least as well as might be expected after such a vexatious experience.

There is so much that we should all be thankful for. And, in due course, we shall.

But for tonight, I must record that a man has died in a most strange and horrible way. A man for whom I could have nothing but the emptiest of feelings. A man who did me great wrong.

Yet a man for all that.

And so, late as it is on this dark night, I must humbly pray to our Lord God, and petition him to have mercy on the soul of such a sinner as this man was.

For it is not for us to judge, but Him alone.

It is for us to try to show compassion, for the sinners as much as for those sinned against, and to trust in His great mercy.

For we do not know the hour. And our time on this earth is oh so brief.

§

Hayman lost little time in plaguing his friend about 'the death of the great Mr William Hogarth'.

'So, you see,' Hayman told everyone at the Bedford Arms. 'We are stuck as we were before. The *great* Mr William Hogarth is dead. And we are left with the same *jackanapes* and *lobcock* William Hogarth that we've all had to put up with for the last twenty years!'

William screwed up his face and tried to remind himself that Hayman really was his friend. But it was starting to wear thin. He had now heard the quip at least three times.

Fortunately there were other things for people to gossip about.

Within a day or two, news filtered through from St James's Square that Sir Marmaduke Ransome had passed away. He had apparently shown some signs of rallying when first returned to his home – but then lapsed into a stupor from which he did not recover. The cause of death was recorded as a fit of the ague, brought on by an excess of strong drink.

By then, the death of the painter Mr Jonathan Smallow had been declared to be an accident – the result of a boisterous prank gone wrong. Mr Crust issued a notice reminding patrons of Covent Garden Piazza that climbing onto the roofs was a danger to life and limb.

No one made any suggestion that the two deaths might have been linked in any way.

Jeremiah disposed of the bag and empty brandy bottle that had been left in his room and did not give them another thought.

Prudence and Jane sent notes of condolence to Belinda. They agreed they would wait a few days before visiting her in person.

Nothing much changed in the general pattern of life in the Piazza. Flea was encouraged by his mistress to have his ears and eyes open for anything that might be of interest in relation to the events of the dramatic evening – not that he needed much prompting. But there was not a great deal to report. Tom King's coffee-house went on much as before. There was no indication that the baronet's fate had had anything to do with the place itself. The death of a known rake from one excess or another was, after all, a common occurrence. Flea noted that Dr Rock made no expeditions into the Piazza for a week or so after that very stormy night. But following this brief interregnum, the doctor reappeared once again, trafficking tinctures of one kind or another to an enthusiastic public with his usual display of theatrical salesmanship.

Mrs Alcazar returned from her sojourn in the country looking slightly more robust than when she left. Although the colour drained again from her cheeks when her husband told her of the night in question. Very soon there was a new tenant in the building, as the room below Jeremiah's was let to a former prize-fighter who sold firewood during the day and served as a linkman during the night.

Sarah Bell, the young woman glimpsed leaving the house, was never seen or heard of again.

§

Morning – some two weeks after the night of the storm.

Miss Prudence Hyssop, with Master Fleabane in attendance, had been invited to a very special occasion in St Paul's Church at the west end of the Piazza.

It was a wedding.

A wedding in which Miss Hyssop had already been instrumental – a prime mover, indeed. For the ceremony would not have been taking place there and then had it not been for Miss Hyssop's influence with the rector and her generous monetary gift to enable the purchase of a special licence.

The bridegroom stood next to Flea, the two of them looking equally uncomfortable in tight-fitting clothes. Prudence smiled encouragement at them, but both insisted on maintaining faces of intense concentration and seriousness. Every now and again the bridegroom bent his knees, making low, bowing flourishes with his hands. Prudence was not sure whether this constituted the practising of courtesies, or merely the flexing of muscles – a way of warding off numbness or the shakes.

A few minutes later came the bride, wearing a long, dark cape over her dress. It made the pallor of her face appear even more pronounced than usual. Her expression conveyed nothing other than unalloyed astonishment.

She was accompanied by her father, who looked as if he had been dressed by a tailor with a sense of humour. He was also wearing a wig that, in common parlance, had seen better days. As far as the gentleman himself was concerned, however, there could hardly have been a day more thoroughly new-minted than this. The broad smile that contorted his usually saturnine face did not slip once during the whole of the church service and social gathering that followed.

Close behind the bride and her father came a well-built, sun-tanned man who was additionally notable for having a wooden leg. The bride's father had felt it fitting that they should have some escort on their short walk from the print shop. He had therefore closed the business temporarily so that his new assistant could bear witness to the nuptials.

Prudence looked at him, recognising the man she had noticed in the Piazza. And as she did so, she again felt a shiver run down her spine as her mind filled with ghostly and more corporeal thoughts. Through an act of intense concentration, however, she put all such notions out of her head and gave her full attention to the ceremony being played out before her. The marriage service was brief, and the happy couple were soon declared to be man and wife, to the great rejoicing of the small party that had gathered for the occasion.

Mr and Mrs Jeremiah Potts, arm-in-arm, then led the way down Southampton Street towards the Strand and on to Mr Pargeter's shop, which had been provisioned for a modest wedding breakfast. They were followed in turn by Miss Hyssop on the arm of Mr Pargeter, and then Flea, walking beside the gentleman with the wooden leg, who had been introduced as Mr Samson.

During the short perambulation Mr Pargeter proudly expounded to Miss Hyssop on the benefits of the marriage. It was not only a demonstration of the profound personal attachment between the two 'young people' but was also a very positive step forward from a commercial point of view. Jeremiah's knowledge of the trade and his network of contacts made him a very suitable partner for Catherine as she prepared to assume 'wider responsibilities'. Indeed, Jeremiah would move into the family home above the shop with immediate effect. Mr Pargeter would then take on more of an overseeing role, ensuring that the business kept pace with the expanding market, whilst Catherine and Jeremiah looked after 'operations'.

Prudence nodded but said little, not wishing to intrude on Mr Pargeter's obvious delight. She could not help thinking, however, that the division of labour was likely to be less than equitable, and that Catherine and her new husband would do most of the work. Mr Pargeter, in recognition of his seniority, could presumably spend a greater proportion of his time watching the world go round.

The workload would also be shared with Mr Samson, who had already proved himself a very able and conscientious shopkeeper. He was also extremely popular with customers – 'in spite of his wooden leg', as Mr Pargeter was at pains to point out.

'It is fulfilling to have chosen someone who is so strong and can carry so much,' he added in a way that was more a comment on his own business acumen than a compliment to Mr Samson. 'He will also become a very near neighbour of yours, Miss Hyssop,' he went on. 'The spare room he has been using over the shop will be turned into a private parlour for Catherine and Jeremiah. So Mr Samson will likely take over the tenancy of Jeremiah's lodging in the Piazza.'

Whilst Mr Pargeter was expatiating on his own good fortune, Mr Samson was in conversation with Master Fleabane about matters of a different kind. Flea was desperate to know more about the wooden leg – as well as the real leg it had presumably replaced. Mr Samson smiled at the bluntness of his young questioner but was only too willing to expand on the history of the two legs.

'The first one was lost at sea,' he began enigmatically.

Flea could not stop himself from thinking that it had perhaps been misplaced or dropped overboard during a storm.

'I was pressed, you see,' said Mr Samson. 'When I was not that much older than you are now.'

'Pressed?' said Flea, open-mouthed.

He knew what the word meant, of course, but had never met anyone who could lay claim to such a thing.

'Taken off for a navy boy,' continued Mr Samson. 'Made to swallow strong drink so that I was senseless. And then waking up to find the sea toiling below, and me adrift in the middle of the ocean on course for the Bermudas.'

Flea could not get enough of this.

'And that's when the leg went?' he said.

'Well, not straight off,' said Mr Samson, smiling widely and showing a set of pearly teeth that lit up his suntanned face. 'It was a year or two later, when I knew my way around, as it were. We were in a scrap with a privateer and a masthead fell across my leg, smashing it good and proper. The surgeon had to whip it off.'

Flea could not believe his luck. For a day that had begun so unpropitiously, with the donning of a tight tog, had turned into a right old tale of derring-do.

'And you've been a one-legged sailor ever since?' said Flea.

It was more a statement than a question and was said in a flat tone that nevertheless conveyed every atom of Flea's delight and admiration.

'Not exactly,' said Mr Samson. 'I carried on for a year or so – but then it was not so easy for me to be aboard ship. So I got a job as an overseer on a plantation in the Carolinas. The wooden leg didn't matter so much there – specially as I'd been working hard to build up the strength in my arms.'

He playfully encouraged Flea to feel one of his biceps, which the younger man was only too eager to do.

'It was enough for me to keep order,' Mr Samson went on. 'Don't mess with peg-leg, the workers used to say!'

He laughed as if it had all been a jolly jape. But there was a tightness around his eyes that made clear it had not been an easy part of his life. Not that any of that was observed by Flea. He was still astounded by the fact that his companion could walk as well as he did, especially on the rough and cobbled road surface.

Ahead of them all, of course, walked Mr and Mrs Potts. But it is not known what *they* talked about on the way back to the shop.

§

During the wedding breakfast Prudence had her first opportunity to talk to Mr Samson.

Flea was sitting quietly in a corner, his attention focused entirely on a particularly juicy game pie. Mr Pargeter was proudly introducing Mr and Mrs Potts to a few commercial neighbours whom he had invited in to mark the occasion by 'taking a sip'.

Prudence felt anxious at speaking to a man her imagination had already settled on as something of a ghost. But his relaxed and gentlemanly bearing encouraged her to open the conversation, even though she could feel a trembling in her breast.

'Mr Samson,' she said. 'I understand we are to be neighbours. Mr Pargeter tells me that you are moving into what has been Jeremiah's room.'

Mr Samson smiled broadly.

'Mr Pargeter has indeed suggested the move,' he said. 'And I can see there is a certain neatness to such a scheme. But I fear it will not be practical.'

He raised his wooden leg an inch or two off the floor and cast a rueful glance in its direction.

'I'm afraid this fellow,' he continued, 'might be less than pleased to haul up and down all those stairs every day!'

Prudence was not sure whether to mirror his smile or look sympathetic.

'So, yes, Miss Prudence,' he said. 'Or rather Miss Hyssop, I should say. Forgive me.'

He had paused as her name settled on his lips, and it seemed to her that he had a faraway look in his eyes.

'Yes, Miss Hyssop,' he repeated slowly. 'I will be looking to find myself some accommodation in or near the Piazza. But I fear it will not be in that particular place. One way or another, however, I'd be honoured if you would at least regard me as a neighbour and friend in waiting – and so address me by my given name.'

He looked into her eyes and added:

'Sam.'

And with that one small word she recognised everything that she already knew but had not permitted herself to believe.

For at once she could see him both as he had been back then and as he was now. In her soul she had known it from the moment his ghost first greeted her in the Piazza – even though she hardly dared hope it might be possible. That he really could be the same Sam Harris she had known and loved all those years before.

They stared at each other, not saying anything for some seconds, while an abundance of feelings and thoughts tumbled through their hearts and minds. It was a silence brimming with what could not be put into words. And it was perhaps only natural that such a tension should be broken with a question that sidestepped the bigger issues by focusing on a detail.

'But Samson?' Prudence said at last. 'You were Harris then. Sam Harris.'

He chuckled.

'So I was,' he said. 'But when I was pressed and asked my name, in my fear and confusion I said "Sam, sir". They must have written it down as "Samson", for I've been Samson ever since.'

Prudence was finding it difficult to take it all in.

'And so ... Jeremiah's room,' she said. 'The room you are *not* moving into ...'

'Is the same room I lived in when it was Mrs Sparker's house,' he said. 'All that time ago.'

He pulled another thoughtful face.

'Which is, I think,' he continued, 'another reason why it's best I set up home somewhere else, don't you think? Life may be like a circle in so many ways – but there have to be limits. Times when it's right to strike out afresh. Wouldn't you say so?'

Prudence nodded. And then they spent some more seconds simply smiling at each other as tears began to well up behind their eyes.

'But, yes,' he then said, coughing and making some attempt to disguise the emotion that had engulfed them both. 'It's right peculiar, eh?' he said. 'You couldn't make it up!'

This time Prudence gently shook her head – another sign of agreement and amazement. She leaned on a chair to steady herself. He made a small move to support her but drew back when it was clear she was in no danger of falling. They shared another glance. As if to agree. It was still too soon. They should wait.

'You must visit me,' she said, breathing deeply. 'If you would like to,' she added, feeling that perhaps her words had been a little too peremptory. 'That is to say, I would be honoured if you would pay me the first of your neighbourly calls.'

Another smile. The assumed air of formality was now less a failure of will. It was a shared secret, and all the more precious and enjoyable for its happening in the midst of such a public gathering.

Mr Samson bowed to her.

'It will be a pleasure and a privilege, Miss Hyssop,' he said.

'Prudence, please,' she quickly countered.

'An especial pleasure and privilege, … Prudence,' he said, before adding two more words. 'Dearest Pru.'

No one had called her Pru for sixteen years. Only one person, indeed, had ever called her Pru. It was almost enough to tip them both over the edge. Almost. But they hung on. Sam coughed again.

'It will also,' he said, 'be an opportunity for me to give you something I'd like to pass into your care. Something that fell into my hands a couple of weeks ago. I've not been sure what to do with it. But I've been keeping it safe.'

Prudence tried to think what it might be, grateful to have something specific on which to concentrate her thoughts.

'Shall we say tomorrow then?' she said, not wishing to let the moment slip.

§

Two days later Prudence paid another visit to the sign of the golden head.

As usual, she and Jane had a great deal to tell each other. And there was also something to be delivered. A package small and light enough for Prudence to carry herself.

'It's a painting,' said Jane as she began to undo the wrapping. Then suddenly she changed her tone. 'Oh my God! It's *that* painting, isn't it?'

She increased the speed with which she was tearing at the brown paper and saw that she was right. The canvas bore the marks of having been knocked about – in the same way that William still had the bumps and bruises of his ordeal. But overall, like its creator, it was recognisably whole.

'I'd almost forgotten about it,' said Jane. 'Where did you get it?'

Prudence smiled, enjoying the look of delight on her friend's face.

'Someone who lives close by,' said Prudence. 'He picked it up where it fell on the night of the storm. He guessed it might belong to William but was not sure how best to find out. Then he brought it to me.'

'But that's wonderful,' said Jane. 'William will be so pleased. We must reward the person who found it. Is it a man? What's his name?'

Prudence smiled.

'You are very kind, dear Jane,' she said. 'But I know he would wish for nothing in return. Other than knowing the painting is back where it belongs.'

Jane thought for a moment and then started to laugh.

'Oh, I shouldn't really,' she said.

'What is it, dear Jane?'

'I was just thinking of where the painting belongs,' Jane went on. 'And remembering that it once belonged on poor Belinda's wall.'

Prudence smiled.

'Pictures can be very promiscuous things!' she said. 'And, in any case, we should perhaps not think of Belinda as being quite so poor as we might have done.'

'Your meaning, Prudence dear?'

'Well, Jane,' Prudence carried on. 'I just happened to meet her in the Exeter Exchange. She was beautifully dressed in black. But I have to say that she did not, in all honesty, appear to be mourning so very deeply.'

'Indeed!'

Jane was desperate to hear more, for there had been much speculation following the demise of Lady Ransome's husband.

'You know what Belinda is like,' said Prudence. 'She has never been one to forego the opportunity to provide a full and frank assessment of her financial position.'

Jane laughed again. She so enjoyed the humour that

often underpinned her friend's calm demeanour. And for some reason, Prudence seemed more buoyant than usual.

'So,' she continued, 'it may not surprise you that Lady Ransome took me to one side and made it very clear that, much as the passing of Sir Marmaduke had cast something of a pall over her life, she was bearing up well. Especially, she said, as the terms by which her father had gifted her substantial dowry ensured that, in the event of her husband's prior death and in the absence of any offspring, the entire estate reverted to her. Yes, there are Sir Marmaduke's debts to be honoured – and they are, as you can imagine, far more substantial than any wife might reasonably have feared. But in the estimation of Belinda's man of business, it will still leave her with a significant sum once the Herefordshire property has been sold and the mortgages redeemed. Her intention is to rent a smaller house, but to remain close to St James's Square.'

'And presumably set her cap at some other nobleman who has an eye for a merry widow,' said Jane with a twinkle in her eye.

Prudence nodded.

'Belinda did not say it in quite so many words,' she said. 'But she had to rush away to prepare for a dinner engagement at the home of Augustus Horniman, the Earl of Shaft.'

'Oh, but he's a hundred and three, isn't he?' exclaimed Jane. 'And hardly likely to fulfil the duties of a husband, if you know what I mean.'

Prudence's eyes were now twinkling as well, but all she said by way of response was:

'Exactly, my dear Jane. Exactly.'

They looked at each other in a conspiratorial way and giggled. Yes, Prudence was most definitely in a far livelier mood than her friend had seen her for some time. Then Jane returned to the matter of the painting.

'Did Belinda make any mention of *her* portrait?' she said.

'Not a word,' said Prudence who had now assumed a mock serious face.

'Perhaps she'll make a present of it to the Earl,' said Jane. 'Something to keep his spirits up, if nothing else!'

At this they both laughed more loudly, although they knew they were doing it out of relief as much as anything else. It was a sign that they were consciously putting behind them several of the issues that had weighed so heavily over the previous weeks.

After another minute of merriment, however, they assumed a more reserved air.

'Right,' said Jane, rising from the couch. 'Shall we go and see William? I know he's looking forward to seeing you. And he'll be so glad you're returning his lost painting.'

§

William had been busy since Prudence's last visit to his studio.

Two paintings stood side-by-side on easels, and another two had been positioned carefully against the wall. The artist himself was mixing something in a bowl and seemed pleased to welcome the women into his space.

'You'll forgive me if I do not take your hand, Prudence,' he said gruffly, holding out a dirty and paint-covered palm by way of explanation. 'I'm extremely mucky, I fear.'

The comment did not, however, stop him from rubbing the offending hand over his stubbly face and bristly scalp. The action deposited a large smudge of purple pigment across his brow. It complemented perfectly the heavy bruise that could still be seen on the side of his head.

The slight distraction in his manner was exacerbated by the curiosity that blazed only too clearly in his eyes. What was it his wife was holding behind her back?

Could it be …?

The presentation of the portrait of the Prince of Wales was graciously received by William – although his mood was nowhere near as joyous as Jane had expected. He held the canvas tenderly and stared as if he could not quite remember painting it – or why he had done so. Then he pulled a rueful face and put the picture on the floor, with the painted side towards the wall.

'It seemed like a good idea at the time,' he said. 'But *now* …,' he went on in a much lighter tone as he rubbed his hands together in anticipation.

'*Now!*' he said again, 'I want to show you something *much* more interesting. Or at least I *hope* it is!'

He gestured towards the first of the easels.

'You know *this* one only too well,' he said. 'As "Morning", it heralds the rest of my new series – *The Four Times of the Day*.'

He moved to the second easel.

'This is "Noon",' he said.

Prudence and Jane took in the complex arrangement of people pictured somewhere in or near Soho. The spire of the church of St Giles-in-the-Fields could be seen in the background.

William then edged around the easels and pointed to the two canvases that were propped against the wall.

'These have only just been started, but they're coming along well,' he said. '"Evening" and "Night".'

The women looked at the paintings carefully, chuckling in particular at the wit of "Evening". It showed a large woman with her much smaller husband on their way to an entertainment near Sadlers Wells in Islington. There seemed to be just the tiniest hint of Belinda in the depiction of the woman, thought Prudence. Surely just another one of life's little coincidences.

'They are truly wonderful,' she said. 'Each one a masterwork. They will change the way people see modern London. And modern people too.'

Jane was mostly enjoying the fact that her husband seemed so recovered – and so happy with life, work, everything.

'Do you have a favourite?' she asked him. 'Of the four.'

He was rubbing his face again, as if such kneading might make the decision easier.

'It can only be "Morning",' he said. 'It's the one that has most to say, I think. But also the one with the strongest centre, the clearest focus. And that, I have to say, is down to you, Miss Hyssop!'

Prudence smiled broadly at William's theatrical bow.

'You are too kind,' she said. 'And I am deeply honoured. But you must, I beg you, bear in mind what I said when you first invited me to view the picture.'

William looked as if he was trying to remember. Jane could not recall it either.

'And what was that, dear Prudence?' she said.

Prudence took a deep breath. She was conscious that she might be overstepping the mark by once again being so frank.

'The painting is beautiful,' she said. 'The composition enthralling, the colours bewitching against the deep, dark scene. For all its satirical purpose, I find it very moving for any number of reasons. However …'

There was a moment of quiet, broken only by a small snort from William.

'However,' repeated Prudence. 'When, William, you translate the painting into a print, I will depend upon you to use your burin as sharply as your wit – and to make the woman a more obvious vehicle for your exquisitely barbed commentary on Covent Garden. A figure caught, as many of us are, between the pleasures and pains of London life. Between the love and the loathing that coexist in this great metropolis of ours. You will, I trust, make her less a poetic enigma, and more an object of satire herself.'

William's face, far from showing any unease, was now flushed with appreciation and agreement. For her part, Jane was delighted that her husband appeared so engaged by what Prudence had said.

However, she still had one concern.

'But my dear Prudence,' she said. 'You may have said something similar when first you saw the picture – but that was *then*. Time has moved on. Now we *know* you. We know you as a warm and compassionate friend – and certainly not as an object of satire.'

Prudence smiled back, grateful for Jane's affection but concerned that such personal intimacy should not blur the broader theme.

'The woman in the print will not be me,' she said. 'It will not be me, any more than the woman in the painting is me. In years to come, when people admire the work of Mr Hogarth, they will judge the *images* and not the people who may have played a humble role as models in their formulation.'

William was wiping his fingers on his jacket. He took a step towards Prudence and stretched out his two hands – still paint-stained – as a sign of thanks and respect.

But as he drew closer, he seemed to change his mind. Instead of taking her hands in his, he threw his arms around her neck and embraced her warmly, before awkwardly planting a kiss on the side of her face. Then, realising that what he had done might be considered less than gentlemanly, he quickly stepped back again. There was a bashful grimace on his face as he looked from Prudence to Jane.

Neither woman knew quite what to say. They were both standing, open-mouthed, staring at one another. Then Jane rushed forward to embrace Prudence as well, and the two of them burst into a kind of laughter that seemed to involve a good deal of crying.

William was not sure whether to be embarrassed or pleased by what was taking place only a few feet away –

and in his studio, his workplace for goodness sake!

He took the finished "Morning" from the easel and replaced it with the incomplete "Evening". Then, picking up his palette and brush from the table, he sat down on a stool in front of it.

'Right,' he said with great purpose.

The single word signalled that the meeting was now at an end.

'Time moves on,' said Jane.

'As must we,' added Prudence.

And so saying, the two of them made their way out of the studio and back upstairs.

EPILOGUE
Not the Last Word

I am persuaded that my words can never convey what I have learned, and what I have loved, in the weeks that have passed since I began once again to commit more of myself to my journal.

Paintings are so much more eloquent – but I lack the skill to speak their language.

For they are protean and never stay still – no matter that they are constrained by their physical characteristics.

There is a saying that every picture tells a story.

Yet I must believe that every picture tells so much more than just one story.

And that no one of those stories is ever complete.

Historical Note

First a word about dates. Although 1st January was often seen as marking the New Year, England retained the 'old style' Julian Calendar (as opposed to the 'new style' Gregorian Calendar) until 1752. In the Julian Calendar the first day of the New Year was 25th March.

Several characters are based on historical figures: William Hogarth (1697-1764), Jane Hogarth (1709-1789), Dr Rock, Tom and Moll King (plus Black Betty), as well as the artists, Francis Hayman and Samuel Scott.

Richard Rock (1690?-1777) was the most well-known 'quack' doctor of his day. Newspaper advertisements promoted his 'Tincture for the Teeth' and 'Cathartic Antivenereal Electuary'. He was the model for the stouter of the two doctors in Plate 5 of *A Harlot's Progress* (1732). In the painting of 'Morning', the doctor named on the placard in the middle distance is one Dr Miller. Hogarth changed it to Rock for the print.

Tom and Moll King opened their 'coffee-house' around 1720. Moll continued to run it after Tom's death (1737) until 1745. She died two years later. A certain mythology has arisen around the coffee-house and the Kings. The place was a popular nocturnal venue where prostitutes could meet clients – although the Kings made sure no beds were available on the premises. A 1735 print by George Bickham the Younger depicts the space inside. Black Betty was a noted member of the Kings' staff and is referenced in another contemporary print – the satirical 'Monument for Tom K—g' (1737).

Francis Hayman (1708-1776) and Samuel Scott (c. 1702-1772) were close friends of Hogarth and well-known painters in their own right. Scott painted Covent Garden Piazza twice between 1756-58. The more finished version is in the collection of the Duke and Duchess of Bedford at Woburn Abbey. A less finished version is at the Museum of London.

The other characters in the novel are (so far as I know) fictitious – although the figure of Felipe ('Al') Alcazar was inspired by the artist Balthasar Nebot (active between c. 1730 and 1765). Nebot's origins are unclear, although he was probably Spanish. He painted four similar views of Covent Garden Piazza, the first of which (also in the Woburn collection) dates from 1735. The other three (which differ in some details) were probably painted in 1737. One is in Tate Britain, one in the Guildhall Art Gallery (City of London), and the third is privately owned. Nebot was suggested partly because of his family circumstances. He married in London in 1729 or 1730, and the registers of St Paul's Church, Covent Garden, include references to the burials of five of his children between 1731 and 1739, and of his wife Mary in 1742.

The four canvases of *The Four Times of the Day* were split up when they were sold. 'Morning' and 'Night' are now part of the National Trust Bearsted Collection at Upton House, near Banbury, Warwickshire. 'Noon' and 'Evening' are in the collection of the Duke of Ancaster, and part of the Grimsthorpe and Drummond Castle Trust.

The print series based on the paintings was issued in 1738. It is generally accepted that Hogarth did the larger part of all the engravings except 'Evening', which is labelled 'Engraved by B[ernard] Baron' (1696-1762).

There has been no serious suggestion that the woman depicted in 'Morning' is modelled on a specific individual, let alone anyone personally known to Hogarth. In that respect, the greatest fiction of *Mr Hogarth's Morning* is the notion that the picture is underpinned by a personal story. In fact, since the time of the image's creation, commentators have consistently characterised the woman as an anonymous 'ladybird' – someone who espouses moral (specifically Christian) values whilst enjoying (or envying) sexual liaisons. When Henry Fielding – a great friend of Hogarth – created the character of Bridget Allworthy in *The History of Tom Jones, a Foundling* (1749), he explicitly linked her description to the image (Book I, Chapter XI).

Since then, no one has challenged this view of the woman depicted in 'Morning' as a hypocritical voyeur. Even art historians less inclined to pronounce on her moral values have mostly described the figure as a 'prude' and an 'old maid'. Elizabeth Einberg (*William Hogarth: A Complete Catalogue of the Paintings*: Yale University Press, 2016) calls her an 'elderly spinster', pointing out that 'the unkempt appearance of her footboy and the use of pattens (normally a working-class item – the well-off would hire a sedan chair) do not speak of great wealth. Her only entertainment is going in all her finery to church' (p. 171).

In researching the context of other images of Covent Garden created around the same time, I came across a very small, poor quality black and white photocopy of a picture in the Witt Library at the Courtauld Institute in London. The image bears an attribution to 'R. [amended in pencil to 'B.'] Nebot'. I have found no other references to the image, so have to believe that it is most likely a copy of the Hogarth original. It is, however, a 'copy' in the very loosest sense. It was this picture I had in mind in relation to Jeremiah's 'copy' of 'Morning'.

A final word on the painting of Frederick, Prince of Wales (1707–1751). I have seen no suggestion that Hogarth undertook a portrait in order to curry favour with Frederick. However, in the Royal Collection there is a painting of the prince that is attributed to Hogarth (ref. RCIN 400592). It is one of a pair of small scale portraits of the Prince and Princess of Wales thought to have been painted at the time of their marriage (27 April 1736). As the Royal Collection's website points out, there are clear arguments against the Hogarth attribution. Nevertheless, as I was developing the story-line around the creation of a princely portrait, it seemed too good a connection to pass up. The very brief description of the missing portrait in *Mr Hogarth's Morning* is therefore based on that picture.

Thom Braun
London 2024

ALSO BY THOM BRAUN

Hungerford Stairs
An Untold Tale of Charles Dickens

Following Charles Dickens's death, his friend and biographer, John Forster, discovers a 'lost' manuscript that provides a radically different view of the year the young author spent working in a blacking factory. But is the account fact or fiction?

In the 1820s the Dickens family arrive to start a new life in London. Charles ('Charley') is just eleven and looking to continue his education. However, instead of being sent to school – and as his family fall deeply into debt – he is put to work in a boot-blacking factory at Hungerford Stairs.

With his father soon cast into the Marshalsea debtors prison, Charley's eagerness to earn an extra shilling sees him drawn into a criminal network led by the dark figure of Mr Magnus. The combination of demeaning factory work with this new and dangerous criminal activity places a huge burden on Charley, at a time when his mother and siblings are increasingly dependent on him.

Life becomes even more complicated when Charley is approached by the mysterious Mr Hesketh. How can the future novelist balance the demands of family, paid work and the London underworld amidst a situation that moves swiftly from casual abuse to violence, and ultimately the hangman's noose?

For more on Thom Braun and his books, please see
thombraun.co.uk